Chapter 1

Angelique stared fixedly out over the grounds of the convent, her thoughts as bleak as the high gray wall that cut off her view of the street beyond. Though *Les Pauvres Clares* had treated her with nothing but kindness the five years she had been in their care, today she felt more than ever like their prisoner. Why could they not let her go? Especially now that the school had been ordered to close its doors and the nuns to leave at once. Why must they insist that she go with them to the convent in Belgium?

Instantly Angelique was swept with guilt for her uncharitable thoughts. Sister Thérèse and the others were losing more than their beloved convent. They were in danger of having a whole way of life taken from them, for were they not being asked to renounce their vows and leave the cloister as well? *Tiens*, their entire world was tumbling down around them.

Angelique was filled with pity for them, but still it changed nothing.

Why could the gentle sisters not understand that her heart, too, was breaking? They mourned the forsaking of a way of life dedicated to poverty, chastity, and obedience, a vow to exist shut away from the rest of the world behind the great stone walls. But she, Angelique Eugenie Gilbert, was half-Creole and half-American. Her spirit thirsted for the freedom they willingly denied themselves, the freedom that had been hers growing up on her beautiful Saint Dominique!

On the West Indian island on which she had been born, La Cime du Bonheur, the house built by her father, stood on a high promontory overlooking the sea. The walls were of stone, but they were not gray and cold like those of the convent. They were covered over and rendered smooth with the paste made from rice so that they glistened whitely in the sun beneath their roof of red tile; and in their stolid fastness were carved great windows that were always open to the blessed wash of the trade winds off the sea. In her mind's eye she saw the curved avenue that led to the front of the house, the cobblestoned drive bordered by tall, stately cedars, the sweeping lawns embraced by palmettoes and logwood fragrant with golden blossoms, and along one side and the back of the house, the wide piazza where the family gathered. In such a house one could never feel shut in. One had only to open one's eyes to behold vast blue skies and a limitless expanse of sea.

Behind her, Sister Thérèse threw up her hands in exasperation.

"I tell you, Angelique, he is a man of the devil, this Jean Paul Marat. And his friends, Danton and Hebert, too. God grant that it will go no further. But since the march on Versailles, no one is safe. Not even the king and queen. They gave us less than one week to send away our students. And now they have closed the doors of Le Couvent Sainte-Clare and let no one in or out except for old Coquille! *Mon Dieu!* These people will stop at nothing until they have their Republic, I am sure of it."

The harassed nun spoke eloquently and with great passion, but Angelique, unfortunately, was listening with only half her mind, a circumstance which was not lost on the good sister.

"Angelique, you have not heard one word I have said," she declared. "I warn you, the Reverend Mother cannot countenance this foolish plan of yours. If you are caught

8

trying to steal over the walls, you will be thrown into prison and who knows what will happen to you then? Wait, *ma petite*. Have faith. We will be granted permission to leave for Belgium day after tomorrow, you will see. And then, when we are safe in Brussels, you can send word to your father."

"And how can you be so certain?" at last demanded the slender girl standing at the barred window, her back to the room. Turning sharply, she impaled the sister with magnificent flashing eyes, startlingly violet-blue against the pallor of her face. "*La Mère* has not the right to keep me here against my will."

"Against your will? What foolishness is this? You were given into our care, child. Your papa—"

"*Mais non,*" Angelique interrupted with such dignity that the older woman's blood ran suddenly cold with fear for her. "I am not a child. I am a woman of nearly one and twenty. I am of the most competent to decide these things for myself. As for my father, I have already sent word by another that I am coming home to Saint Dominique. Frederick Herman Gilbert is not French, and though he may be of the very rich, he is not like *les grands blancs.*" Angelique's voice was filled with contempt for the wealthy white planters, who would do anything to keep the power they wielded over her beloved island. "He is American. He will know that I cannot hide in a convent. Not now, when the whole world is being torn apart with these cries of '*Liberté! Égalité! Fraternité!*'"

She pronounced these last with a hard bitterness oddly at variance with her youth and fresh innocence. In awe, Sister Thérèse beheld the glorious eyes darken and grow suddenly opaque. Shivering a little, she traced the sign of the cross over her plump bosom before she caught herself. Then, instantly berating herself for a silly old fool, she clasped her hands sternly before her. But, indeed, had she not known the truth of the girl's parentage, in times such as this she might have believed the rumors that Angelique Gilbert carried in her veins

9

the blood of the African *Rodu* priestesses.

Such foolishness, she told herself. Angelique was a lovely girl—generous, quick-witted, bright, and blessed, for the most part, with a vibrancy, a keen *joie de vivre* that gladdened the spirits of those around her. In her heart she knew this, but deep inside she knew as well that this same Angelique was also a bewildering mixture of shadow and mystery, a strange creature of shifting moods and seemingly uncanny insight.

"Angelique!" she murmured, her heart full of pity for this child who had always seemed different from the other girls—almost as if she had been born of some other plane of existence. "What is it that troubles you so?"

Sister Thérèse paled as Angelique's voice whispered through the taut stillness of the room like the murmur of wind that presages the storm.

"In my dreams I see the Goat Girl," answered Angelique, her eyes huge and staring. "She dances to the throb of a thousand drums. *Rada* drums! And the terrible Pethro, which summons the god who thirsts for the blood of the sacrifice. I see him with the swollen belly— Damballa, the Serpent, engorged with the blood of tens of thousands of the dead. And still he is not sated! No, nor will he be. Not until he has drained the very heart of the sugar islands!"

The girl blinked and drew a sharp breath as if recalled from somewhere far removed in time and place.

"Tiens!" she exclaimed, her delicate features pale against the raven tresses that framed her face. "Why do they not see that the cursed cries of the revolution will tear my beloved Saint Dominique into a million pieces? And there is nothing anyone can do to stop it. Dearest Sister, can you not see that I *must* go to L'Arbalète in the Rue Faison? The letter of the American captain said he has taken rooms there until the time of his departure on the twenty-third—tonight! I must speak with him. He is the friend of my father. He will see me safely to Port-au-Prince before the season of the hurricanes begins anew."

Sister Thérèse, torn between pity and fear for the safety of her young charge, sank heavily onto the single, straight-backed chair in the cell. Mother of God grant her wisdom. For weeks—ever since the young man of color had come to speak with the impetuous Angelique—she had watched the child draw more and more into herself. Merciful God! How thin she had grown! And how could it have been otherwise when she picked over her food without appetite and when her sleep was restless and sporadic, troubled by these disturbing dreams? In something like despair she beheld the dark shadows beneath the huge, tormented eyes. Indeed, the finely honed bones of the face protruded beneath the smooth translucence of her skin to create an aura of fragile beauty not unlike that of fine porcelain.

Still, all of this was deceptive, as Sister Thérèse well knew. For beneath that exterior of almost ethereal loveliness there thrived a strength and stubbornness of will which had often proved daunting to the nuns of Ste. Clare. *Per Dieu!* It was as if Angelique Gilbert's ardent spirit consumed her from within, and if she continued so, might not the flesh prove too weak to sustain her? In spite of the present danger, might it not be the wiser course to set Angelique free from her cage—now, before the mobs descended on the convent and dragged them all into the streets?

Seeing the uncertainty in the nun's kindly face, Angelique dropped to her knees before the older woman and clasped one of the worn hands to her cheek.

"Sister Thérèse, try and understand. As *Maman* lay dying of the fever, she made Papa swear he would send me to the good sisters of Ste. Clare. She wished her daughter to acquire the gracious manner of a lady, the accomplishments of a woman of gentle birth, the knowledge of a world beyond the shores of our little island—all that befits the daughter of a family of wealth and position. These things you have taught me, and more. For, even as my father reared me to believe that

11

one should not be judged by what one has, but by what one does in this life, so, too, have you instilled in me the knowledge that wealth should be married to generosity and position to humility. I have learned well, and now I beg you will help me, dearest Sister." Pressing a hand over her breast, she turned the full force of her gaze upon the other woman. "Papa has need of me. I feel it—here, in my heart. It is time I returned to take my place at his side before it is too late."

For a long moment the sister stared with a feeling of helplessness into the lovely face turned compellingly up to hers. Then at last she shook her head as though to break the spell wrought by the marvellous eyes.

"Oh, very well, Angelique!" she said, rising from her seat. "Enough. I shall speak with the Reverend Mother. *S'il plaît à Dieu*, perhaps she may be persuaded to arrange a meeting between you and this American sea captain. More than that, *enfant*, I cannot do, *ça se comprend?*"

With an effort Angelique restrained her bitter disappointment. She had hoped for much more than this from her old friend and mentor, but she knew when it was pointless to argue any further. Sister Thérèse could become as stubborn as the donkeys of Saint Dominique if pushed too hard.

"Yes, of course," she said, concealing her eyes beneath the thick veil of her eyelashes. "I understand." Then forgetting everything but the thing gnawing at her within, she rose abruptly to her feet. "Oh, *la vache!*" she cried harshly. "Who are we trying to fool? It will all be for nothing!"

"For shame! Such language, Angelique!"

"I care not. It is what I feel, what I know is the truth." Fitfully, she began to pace about the room. "*La Mère* will not change her mind, and I shall not see *le capitaine* before he has gone."

"Have we taught you nothing of faith?" demanded the sister, her look censorious on the girl. "Pray to God for guidance, my child. And have patience. If it is meant to be, you will have what your heart desires."

And if she waited for such a miracle, thought Angelique bitterly, she doubted not that she would be an old woman—or gone from this world—before any such thing should come to pass. *Tiens!* The minutes were flying on swift wings, and already the afternoon was waning. In less than three hours the day would be spent, and, with it, her only chance to seek out the Capitaine Locke. But, *non,* she *would* not wait. She would follow the plan that had come to her as she read the captain's letter, the letter, which had seemed like the answer to a prayer. She had already the gown and the other things she would need, and it should not be too difficult, surely, to find her own way to the inn. *Per Dieu!* She would do it! She would escape from the convent in the guise of a peasant!

All at once her eyes sparkled with excitement. *Mais oui.* It would be the grand adventure, would it not, to find her own way through Paris to the officer who in the American Revolution had been Papa's savior?

Unexpectedly her pulse quickened at the thought that soon she might actually meet the man about whom her father had woven such stories as to make one marvel. She had been fourteen when Herman Gilbert returned home from the war, full of the tales of the young naval officer who single-handedly had captured an English man-of-war, routed an admiral's fleet, and won for himself the sobriquet of the Yankee Sea Wolf. From that time on, she recalled with a faint, reminiscent smile, Wesley Locke had loomed in her girlhood both as a dashing hero and as something of a devil with the marvellous laughing blue eyes—eyes, had said her papa, that could charm the heart of a woman or laugh in the face of danger. This was what a man should be, she had told herself and wove fantasies of the day that she would be a woman—beautiful like her *maman*—a woman to tame the rogue in a man and make of him her love.

But, alas, that was many years ago—*before* the *mamaloi* Mozambe had told her the terrible thing about herself,

13

the thing which made her a creature unfit for any man's love. *Pour l'amour de Dieu!* Why could she not have died at birth rather than ever to learn the truth about herself? she thought, but almost immediately, she suppressed her anguish with a recklessness born of despair. If she was unfit to be any man's wife, what did it matter? She could still be *une femme de ménage*—a mistress to any man who might suit her. She was both wealthy and fair to look upon. She could make her own choice and still retain her freedom.

Besides, none of this was really to the point. Wesley Locke had been the romantic dream of a young girl—a child. By now he must be of the very old. No doubt he was grown bald and had the great paunch like her beloved Papa, she told herself, unaware that a small sigh escaped her lips.

It didn't matter. Even though she found him old and ugly, she could not but revere the man who had given the gift beyond measure—the return of her papa to his home and to his family—to her mother, who even then had lain dying. For had he not paid the terrible price of captivity in the English prison-ship for his generosity? Indeed, had he not suffered torture and near death at the hands of his cruel jailers, a fate which, but for him, would have befallen her dearest Papa? Even had she not sworn to make her way back to Saint Dominique, she would still have gone to L'Arbalète to see Wesley Locke. She owed him the debt beyond paying.

Having made her decision, Angelique looked up to find the other woman watching her closely. *Voyons!* She was the fool, she told herself. Already she had permitted those keen old eyes to see too much of her thoughts. If the nun had even the smallest idea of what Angelique intended, she would set herself to guard her charge like *un gendarme* over a desperate criminal. Without a doubt, this was true, for no one knew her heart better than did her dearest Sister Thérèse—she, who from her arrival at the convent had been like a mother to her. *Alors!* She

14

must be of the most careful if she were to retrieve her error.

Summoning what was meant to be a repentant smile, she spread wide her hands.

"Forgive me, Sister," she murmured, unaware that, in spite of her demure posture, the roguish dimple peeping forth at the corner of her mouth gave her more the appearance of a naughty but beguiling child than that of a woman ready to decide her own affairs for herself. "You are right, of course. I will try to do as you have advised. Only, go now, I beg you, that I may pray that God will be with you when you speak with the Reverend Mother."

Sister Thérèse's glance narrowed sharply. It was not at all like Angelique to give in so easily when her heart was set on a thing.

"You are up to some mischief, Angelique Gilbert," she said, waving an index finger in that face so full of innocence. "It will be better for you if you tell me what it is—now, before it is too late to save you from your folly."

Instantly the regal head lifted proudly. The violet eyes flashed dangerous sparks, and suddenly Sister Thérèse was reminded of the girl's mother. Eugenie DuFour, too, had been proud, unpredictable and headstrong, all of which had led her finally to elope with an American adventurer against the wishes of her family. *Dieu merci!* Surely such a thing could not be carried in the blood!

"Of what would you accuse me?" demanded Angelique haughtily. "Have I not said I would do as you have asked? Bah. You are like all the others who shake their heads and say, 'Angelique is impossible. Angelique is abandoned by God.' They think I am mad and not to be trusted. Is that what you think of me, too, Sister Thérèse? Is my word worth nothing?"

"You have not given me your word, my child," the nun observed shrewdly. "But only a great deal of foolish shouting."

"It is this talk which is foolish. With every second we stand here arguing with one another, the time grows

15

shorter. But then, perhaps it is that you, too, do not believe *la Mère* will be moved to grant me this favor. Is it because you know my prayers will be for nothing that you tarry here when you might already be in her presence? If this is so, tell me, and I will ask no more of your time."

"Angelique, I have never lied to you. You know this. I have told you I would speak with the Reverend Mother, and I will. I want only your assurance that you will wait patiently for my return before doing something foolish on your own."

As if she could not contain herself any longer, Angelique flung up her hands.

"Do not ask what I cannot give!" she exclaimed, turning to pace two steps away. But immediately she came back again. "This man has been sent here by God, and you cannot see it. Providence has granted this blessing, and you would throw it away in the name of prudence. *Mon Dieu*, I begin to think you *want* to see me cast homeless into the streets of Paris!"

At last the nun's stoic calm was pierced.

"Angelique! You *know* I could not want such a thing!" she uttered in accents of shocked disbelief.

Angelique winced, feeling the wound she had inflicted like a knife thrust into her own heart. Instinctively her hand went out as though to snatch back her impetuous words. But Sister Thérèse did not notice. Indeed, she had forgotten the girl's presence. "Mother of God," she whispered, her face suddenly very old indeed. "The whole world turns upside down. Never did I think to behold the day when the girls of Ste. Clare would not be safe within these walls."

Angelique bit her lip to keep from crying out for forgiveness. Never had she meant to hurt her dear friend, and yet what else could she have done when every fiber of her being, every instinct pulsating within her, told her to flee the convent before it was too late? Somehow she knew in her heart that to retreat now from her chosen course would be never again to see Papa or her Saint Dominique.

"Well, then?" she heard herself say, though inside she wept for Sister Thérèse and *Les Pauvres Clares*. "It is better that you go now, *oui?* Then, perhaps, one of the girls of Ste. Clare, at least, will no longer be a worry to you."

The nun blinked and for an instant gazed blankly at Angelique. Then with a sigh she seemed to come back to herself.

"Yes, perhaps," she answered slowly.

Still, she hesitated. Indeed, it was only with the greatest reluctance that she allowed herself to be maneuvered toward the door; and once there, she paused gazing searchingly at the girl.

"Very well, Angelique, but I, too, shall pray," she said meaningfully. "I shall pray that God in my absence will guard you from the consequences of your own impetuous nature."

"*Ainsi soit-il!*" retorted Angelique, stone-faced. "So be it!"

At last the nun turned with a sigh and, shaking her head ponderously, retreated down the empty corridor.

Her heart was pounding wildly when Angelique pushed the door closed and leaned for a moment with her back against it. *Tiens!* She was certain the keen-witted nun had perceived the truth of what she meant to do, and for the split second, she had believed she meant to ruin everything. She was a knowing one, the Sister Thérèse, but her heart was as generous as it was wise. When Angelique left the convent, she knew she would go with the nun's blessing.

Hastily Angelique brushed the back of her hand across her eyes. How greatly she would miss her! And how fervently she prayed that the dearest sister would make her own way to safety very soon, for never could she be

17

compelled to forswear her vows made to God. Rather would she die first!

Making the sign of the cross over her breast, Angelique pushed away from the door and with a delicious feeling of rebellion, flung off her white cap. At last it was *finis*. She had kept her promise to Papa. For five years she had worked hard at her studies and tried always to do as the sisters wished of her. And if she had not always succeeded, so what? The roguish dimple popped out as fatalistically she shrugged. Only God was perfect.

With a heart that had not felt so light since before she had boarded the ship sailing from Port-au-Prince for this land of her mother's, she set about gathering the things she would need for her journey. This, she soon discovered, was not the simple matter she had envisioned it to be. In five years she had accumulated many things, not a few of which had the power to bring a twisted smile to her lips or a mist to her eyes with the memories they evoked. Choosing what to take and what to leave behind would soon drive her mad, she thought, discarding for the fourth time the exquisite red pagoda sunshade, which on her twentieth birthday had been presented to her by le comte du Vallenoir, her so very charming cousin. In the end, save for the rosary beads given her by Sister Thérèse and some fine pieces of jewelry left her by her mother, she decided to burden herself with nothing which was not of a practical nature.

Then at last the task was done and she had stored everything away in a battered straw valise and a large bandbox. Anxiously she glanced at the watch pinned to the bib of her apron.

"Oh, *la vache!*" she exclaimed to the empty room. "Angelique, you are the fool, for you have let more than one hour go by while you could not make up your stupid mind."

Wondering what she had been about to take so long, she flung off the white bibbed apron and plain blue gown, which all of Paris knew were worn by the girls at the

18

Convent of the Poor Sisters of Sainte Clare. Then hastily she retrieved a homely bedgown from the back of her wardrobe and slipped it over her head.

A frown wrinkled her small nose as, moments later, she stared at the reflection in the looking glass of a slight figure draped in brown flannel shot through with vertical red stripes. Critically she studied the plain white cap that concealed the mass of raven curls, the red scarf draped around the slim shoulders and tucked in front beneath the black apron tied about the tiny waist, and, finally, the unattractive black boots peeping out from beneath the hem of the unlovely skirt.

All at once a small gurgle of laughter escaped the pursed lips.

"How wonderful!" she giggled, clapping a hand over her mouth in glee. "No longer are you Angelique Gilbert, the heiress, but Angelique, the Nobody. *Bien joué!* You have done well!"

"Still—," she mused. A roguish gleam leaped to her eyes as she glanced across the room at the stone fireplace, its fireless grate cold and black with soot and ashes. "There is yet one thing lacking."

With a small moue of distaste, she dug her fingers into the ashes and smudged her smooth cheeks and ivory-white forehead with soot. Still not satisfied, she soiled the back of her neck as well, then scrubbed her lily-soft hands with it until they were covered with filth, the nails rimed with black. When at last she had added a few similarly artistic touches to her clothing, she stood back, pleased with the effect.

"Yes, that's just right," she nodded, deciding it would not be necessary after all to add the odor of garlic and onions to her disguise. "Bah! *C'est plus qu'il n'en faut!* It is more than enough already without that. Besides, there is not the time. Coquille and his wagon will be ready to leave by now, I think."

Pausing only long enough to leave Sister Thérèse a generous purse accompanied by a hastily scribbled note

that begged her forgiveness, Angelique hurriedly swathed
her figure in a long black cloak and pulled the hood well
over her head so that her face was hidden in shadow.
Then gathering up her valise and the bandbox, she
opened the door and peered up and down the shadowy
corridor.

Discovering the hall deserted, she realized the girls
who remained must be at their prayers. *Voyons!* It was
very late indeed. Still, it was perhaps better so, she told
herself, for all the inhabitants of the convent, students
and nuns alike, would be cloistered in their individual
cells. There would be no danger of encountering a soul
until the bells in the tower announced vespers, and by
then, *s'il plaît à Dieu,* she would be long gone.

Deciding that never until this moment had she had a
true appreciation of the hour of meditation, she made her
way on tiptoes past the seemingly endless parade of
closed doors and slipped undetected from the dormitory
into the open-air cloister. From there it was only a few
steps to a short passage, which ended at a carved oak
door. Her blood sang in her veins as she let herself
through into the outer courtyard and swiftly shoved the
door shut behind her.

"Dieu merci!" she whispered thrillingly. "It is not so
difficult, this business of running away. And now if only
I may find Coquille has not left without me!"

On swift feet, she fled past the ancient mill and the
great kiln made of brown brick, then finally through the
clutter of old storehouses, until she came to the tumble-
down cottage inhabited by Coquille. Pressing her back
to the wall of the house, she paused just long enough to
catch her breath before peering around the corner into
the small yard at the rear.

A long sigh escaped her lips at sight of the wagon in its
usual place beneath the sagging branches of a weathered
elm, and, standing slack-hipped, its head down, the sway-
backed gray gelding waiting in the traces for Coquille.
Already the wagon was loaded with the baskets contain-

ing the loaves of bread the Poor Sisters baked for the needy, and soon the old man would be leaving the convent to deliver them. *Tiens!* Just a few minutes more and she undoubtedly would have been too late. Even as she thanked God for her continuing good fortune, Coquille himself emerged from the house—tall, stoop-shouldered, and gaunt as ever.

"P-s-s-s-t! *Ici,* Coquille. Over here!"

The old man jerked to a halt, his head canting at a bony angle.

"Eh? *Qu'est-ce qu'il y a?* Who whispers the name, Coquille? Speak up! I haven't all day."

"*Sacriste,*" muttered Angelique, rolling her eyes skyward. The old fool would tell the whole world she was there. Tossing caution to the wind, she took up her valise and bandbox and stepped boldly around the corner of the house. "It is I, Uncle—Angelique Gilbert. I have come as we agreed. And now you will take me up in the back of your wagon and hide me in one of the baskets. Even so will you carry me with you when you go through the gates of the convent!"

Chapter 2

Dusk, wrapped in a thick fog rising from the Seine, fell over the city like a shroud. Shivering in the chill air and cursing the old man for abandoning her after she refused to pay the additional, outrageous sum he had demanded, Angelique clutched numb fingers more tightly about the handle of her valise and thought longingly of a hot meal before a warm fire if ever she should reach the accursed inn on the Rue Faisan. *Per Dieu!* How she longed for her beloved island of sun-drenched beaches and thickly wooded slopes rising steeply to embrace the dazzling sky. She was Creole, and this land of her mother's people was enough to freeze her very soul!

A heavy sadness filled her at this thought, for it had conjured up the memory of Etienne Joliet, the young man from Port-au-Prince whom she had encountered weeks earlier at the opera. Even after five years she had recognized him at once—tall and slender with the black eyes and easy supple grace, he had been one of her playmates in the old days. Foolishly calling out his name, she had hurried over to him, though he had been in the company of two other men and a woman with black, glittery eyes. To her dismay she had found him distant and polite, suspicious of her motives in coming over to him. The others had moved away, leaving her alone with him.

"Am I *un grand blanc* to be shunned by Etienne Joliet?" she had demanded, gazing up at him with the hurt plain in her eyes. "Or is this now how you greet all your old friends?"

He had answered her coldly, his voice wooden.

"You are white and your father is a wealthy plantation owner," he said. "Is that not enough to make you *un grand blanc?*" Then, at her startled gasp, he had looked sharply away. "It is a time of great change, mademoiselle, of grand hopes and grave danger for a man of color. It is difficult to know who one's friends are in such times. If I have offended, I most humbly beg your pardon." But his bow had been neither humble nor relenting.

"Then I am sorry for it—*and* for you," she had retorted, and granting him a cool nod of the head, had hurried to catch up with the rest of her party. But she had not been able to dismiss him so easily from her thoughts as she returned to her seat. Nor had she ceased to be uneasy at all that she had sensed behind the thinly veiled hostility. All was not well on Saint Domnique.

It was that very night that the dreams had started. The distorted visions of hatred and violence—the horrifying nightmares of her father, lying bloodied and dead. And more terrifying still—the images, like glimpses into hell—images of herself, savage and half-naked, dancing to the beat of the Pethro drum.

Not surprisingly, she must have appeared hollow-eyed and even fey when Etienne called on her at the convent two days later. He had seemed troubled at the change in her, even sincerely apologetic, and at last he had in measure opened up to her.

"You have been gone for a very long time, Angelique," he said, standing with his back to her, his eyes fixed on the statue of the Holy Mother at the far end of the garden. "Saint Dominique is not the same as when you left it." Suddenly he turned to face her. "*I* am not the same. Perhaps you will understand when I tell you that one of those men I was with at the opera was Vincent Ogé."

24

Angelique stared at him, her heart suddenly pounding. For what Creole had not heard of Vincent Ogé?

The son of *une femme de ménage* and a French general, he had been educated in France and now led the vanguard of the free men of color in their struggle to achieve political equality with the whites. To *"les affranchis,"* he was a bold leader. To the whites he was a dangerous radical. That, to Etienne, he was a hero was made obvious to Angelique as she listened to him talk of the young revolutionary.

"Thanks to the efforts of Vincent Ogé," he said, his black eyes fierce with triumph, "the Assemblée Nationale has at last decreed in favor of the free men of color. Anyone, twenty-five and older, who owns land or has paid taxes for two years, will be allowed the right to vote. Angelique, do you not see? It is everything we have been waiting for. And now Vincent must return home to make sure those rights are realized in Saint Dominique. He will go in secret, under an assumed name, and I, Etienne Joliet, shall go with him."

"But, Etienne," Angelique cried, suddenly very much frightened for her old friend, "are you sure this is the wise thing? The white planters will not be easily persuaded. There is no telling what they might do to you."

"Vincent Ogé is not afraid. We are emissaries of the Revolution. *Liberté! Égalité! Fraternité!* Nothing can stop us—not even *les grands blancs*—with such ideals to guide us. They will give us what we demand, or we shall drive them from Saint Dominique. This, I swear to you."

Angelique's heart sank at the impassioned avowal. *Sacriste!* For a man of color, these were dangerous sentiments, sentiments which could only breed discontent among the African slaves and make worse the fear and suspicion that already separated the whites from the free men of color. Sentiments, indeed, that could only threaten the safety of everyone on the island.

Such things she had tried to tell him, but Etienne

would not listen. The inflammatory writings of Jean Paul Marat had made him both deaf and blind to anything which did not extol the Revolution.

Then suddenly he had turned on her.

"You tell me to be patient, Angelique Gilbert. That in time things will get better without the need for violence. But I tell you my people have run out of patience. What can you possibly know what it is to be free and colored in Saint Dominique?" he flung at her with the accusing eyes that yet haunted her in her dreams. "The daughter of Herman Gilbert is denied nothing."

Never could he know how his words had pierced her heart! For it was true—all that he had said. Never had she been made to suffer the injustices Etienne had known all his young life—not she, who had been reared the daughter of a wealthy white planter! And what if it had been otherwise, she wondered, how would she feel then about this revolution that was shaking the foundations of her world? *Tiens!* What price would she be made to pay for the changes taking place in Saint Dominique—she who all her life had lived the great lie?

Etienne, seeming to sense the change in her, had soon taken his leave after that. Graciously he had offered to relay to her father any message she might wish to have sent. His had been a generous gesture, one which might place him in great peril. Thanking him, she had told him to tell her father to look for her, for she was coming home on the first ship on which she could book passage.

Angelique had not been able to sleep that night for worrying about Etienne, who was to sail home bearing with him the seeds of revolution. But she worried for the safety of her papa even more. In spite of her meager twenty years, she felt very old, for in her heart she knew that in a land where the slave far outnumbered the free, whether white or of color, only trouble and great suffering could come from such brashness. Indeed, to try to erase overnight all that had grown out of nearly three centuries of slavery must surely be to bring utter destruction down upon Saint Dominique!

Suddenly she shuddered, as if an icy hand had reached out of the darkness to touch her heart.

"*Sacre bleue!*" she muttered, clutching her cloak more tightly about her. "You are the silly fool to come out on such a night as this, Angelique Gilbert." Still, she knew in her heart she would have dared a great deal more if it meant she would find herself at last on a ship bound for home.

Resolutely shaking off her somber mood, she quickened her pace. It was becoming very late, and the streets of Paris were no place for a woman alone at night. They were the haunts of *les citoyens* who had yet to benefit from the storming of the Bastille. Had not the hungry peasants marched on Versailles less than a year ago and laid siege to the royal palace? Were not the king and queen even now virtual prisoners in Paris? And thanks to the growing popularity of *les Cordeliers* thoughout the city, was there not much suspicion and resentment among the poor for anyone remotely resembling the aristocracy?

Oui, all of this was true. So much so that she could not feel safe even in her borrowed peasant garb. But even worse, her feet were of the most painful from the wretched boots she wore, her hands were half-frozen from the miserable cold, and her arms felt ready to drop off from the cursed burdens that they bore. In truth, she was very much afraid she could not go another step, when she caught sight of a street sign through the drifting veils of fog.

"*Dieu merci!*" she breathed gratefully. "It is the Rue Faisan!"

Following the directions she had wheedled out of Coquille, she turned right along the narrow alley dwarfed by the tall houses. Like great toy blocks stacked precariously one atop the other, the upper stories of the buildings jutted out over the street so that it seemed Angelique traversed a dark and airless tunnel. Light-

27

headed from having missed too many meals that day and made ill from the stench rising from the refuse in the street, she was nearly reeling on her feet when at last she found herself beneath the weathered sign bearing a crossbow and arrow.

"At last! L'Arbalète," she exclaimed, feeling the blood pounding in her head. "And it is a very good thing, too, I think." All at once a frown creased her brow. *Plut à Dieu* that I have come to the right inn. This is not at all the sort of place in which one would expect to find the owner of great wealth and many ships. *Tiens!* It has the look of the pig pens!"

And, in truth, in spite of the fact that the clamor of many voices issued from within, there seemed little to recommend the Crossbow to anyone of even modest means. Its sole pretensions to refinement consisted of a brick front, which someone at one time or another had caused to be painted a garish yellow, and bow windows, encrusted with grime, which embraced a battered door.

It didn't matter. Even had she not been too weary to consider the hazards she ran if indeed the captain were not to be found within, she had come too far to turn back now. Resolutely, Angelique squared her slim shoulders and entered the inn.

Inside, she was inundated by boisterous shouts and raucous laughter, which made her head ache even more than before. But worse was the stench of stale beer mingled unfelicitously with the rank odor of sweat from a seeming multitude of unwashed bodies. Nearly gagging, she tried to shove and elbow her way past the outer fringes of the crowd, but the sheer press of numbers formed an impregnable barrier.

"Tiens! The whole world is here!" she muttered beneath her breath. So many people, and all of them shouting at once. For a sinking moment it came to her to wonder if she had stumbled into an angry mob intent on working themselves into a fit of violence. She had heard such tales from the sisters of the convent. Almost she

turned and fled the way she had come, when suddenly a taut silence fell over the crowd as if the whole world had drawn a single, suspended breath all at once.

"*Qu'est-ce qu'il y a?*" Angelique whispered thrillingly to two women standing next to her. "What is it?"

A slow heat suffused her cheeks as the one nearest turned to sweep her from head to toe with a bold, insolent stare. Unconsciously, Angelique's head came up, her eyes defiant as they met the other woman's, look for look. To her surprise, a glimmer of grudging approval softened the hard features.

"Some fool has dared to take up with the woman of Pierre Labete," answered the woman, shrugging fatalistically. "They will goad him into a fight and then take what they want from him. I have seen it happen before." Suddenly she laughed. "He is a handsome rogue with a purse full of gold, which he cannot take with him to the devil. What a pity. He could have left La Coquette to Labete and taken me instead!"

"Quiet!" hissed her companion with an uncouth gesture. "The stranger speaks to Labete."

Her curiosity piqued, Angelique strained to see over the shoulder of a burly peasant, when someone jostling her from behind slammed her hard into the man's broad back.

"Ouf! Clumsy oaf. What do you think you are doing?"

In dismay, Angelique found herself gazing up into a grisly face, whose least daunting aspect was a jagged scar etched across a jowled cheek from jaundiced eye to bulging jaw.

Hungry and nearly exhausted, Angelique felt something snap inside.

"Pig-face! Foul-breathed toad! Who are you calling a clumsy oaf? It was the fault of the buffoon who shoved me into you. I was only trying to see what is going on."

For a split second the brutish eyes narrowed to pinpoints on the slight figure standing hands on hips and bristling with angry resentment. Angelique hardly had

29

time to regret her hasty temper when suddenly the surly mouth opened wide in a great, booming guffaw.

"So, the angry little mouse wishes to see, eh?" he chortled in huge amusement. "Hey, Armand." Angelique let out a stifled gasp as two gargantuan hands encircled her waist and swung her high off her feet. *"La Petite* is in need of a place in the front. She wishes to miss nothing of the bloodletting."

"Eh? Then give her to me. You! Gaston! Pass the little bloodthirsty one where she can see."

"No! Put me down, you son of an ape," cried Angelique, striking ineffectually at the grinning oaf with her fists. "Wait, you fool! My things!"

Her struggles were to no avail, and Angelique was passed over the heads of the crowd from one burly set of arms to another, till at last she found herself thrust ignominiously to the fore. Hopelessly entangled in the folds of her long cloak, she stumbled and fell headlong at the center of the cheering spectators. Her sole consolation was to discover her bandbox and valise had followed immediately after, landing still intact at her feet. Her cap, however, had been lost in the struggle and her luxurious mass of raven hair tumbled wildly about her back and shoulders as she picked herself up and faced the jeering crowd with gloriously flashing eyes.

"Swine!" she flung back in the face of the catcalls. "Sons of goatherds! The devil take all of you!"

"Ouïee!" an old hag cackled. "The little hen has a feisty tongue."

"Hey, Pierre," shouted someone else. *"La petite poulette* would see how a man can be whittled down to her size with the great knife of Labete."

"Not the knife, buffoon," jeered the old woman. "It's the *blade* she would wish to see. The blade of Labete for the little pullet!"

Angelique blushed furiously as the crowd took up the crudity in the form of a chant.

"C'est la lame de Labete *pour La Poulette!"*

"*En voilà assez!* That is enough!" roared a hairy giant of a man. Shoving Angelique roughly aside, he drove the crowd back with a deadly looking twelve-inch butcher knife. "This is a matter between Labete and this man who has dared to put his hands on my woman."

Only then, as the center of the room magically cleared, did Angelique behold the apparent cause of all the furor. At a table, not ten feet from where she stood, sat a gentleman in the company of a full-blown beauty with black, glittering eyes.

The woman she gave little more than a cursory glance, noting in passing a shapely expanse of bosom bulging precariously above an extreme décolletage and a striking, somewhat exotic beauty, which was yet marred by a certain hardness about the full mouth and intriguingly slanted eyes. For a moment Angelique had the peculiar feeling that she knew her from someplace, then mentally she shrugged. No doubt it was only that she had seen her kind before in Saint Dominique. She was *une cocotte*, seductively beautiful on the outside and on the inside, a heart as cold as the ice. With a shrug, she dismissed her, but not so the man. One look at him and she found her attention fairly caught.

Long and lean, he sprawled negligently in the chair, his booted legs, crossed at the ankles, stretched carelessly out before him. One elbow was propped on the armrest, two slender fingers supporting a high-boned cheek, as with infuriating indifference he ran his gaze over Angelique and apparently found her wanting.

The devil! she thought and, giving a toss of her curls, coolly returned the compliment, sweeping his length with a disparaging glance.

Tiens! The man's clothing, like everything else about him, showed that he cared nothing what anyone might think of him. Even so, the plain white shirt, worn open at the throat, suited him very well, she conceded with the greatest of reluctance. And, indeed, to her discomposure, she found her glance lingering over the strong, masculine

31

column of the neck where it emerged from the open collar, the golden mat of hair curling just above the V, and the muscular hardness of the chest tapering to a long torso. Nor could she help but notice the manner in which the fabric hugged broad, powerful shoulders. Even more disturbing, however, were the wide leather belt, which embraced a most pleasingly lean, narrow waist, and brown cord breeches, tucked into the tops of high leather boots—breeches that seemed flawlessly designed for particularly well-molded, muscular thighs.

Voyons! Here was a man to draw the glance of a woman! she thought, and looking up, beheld a glint of laughter in eyes she suddenly discovered were of a spellbinding blue. Like the clear depths of the sea over the coral reefs of Saint Dominique, she mused distractedly, noting as well that his hair, a golden brown shot through with sun-streaks, showed an intriguing tendency to curl over a high, handsome forehead, tanned, like the rest of his face, to a deep golden bronze. Dark eyebrows and eyelashes, a long, straight nose, and a firm chin with a cleft gave the impression of a strong-willed, stubborn nature. His wide mouth, quirked in a half-smile of ironic amusement, suggested a recklessness, a devil-be-damned attitude. This appealed strongly to the unruly streak within herself—the "wildness," as the nuns had used to call it, which they could neither comprehend nor tame. He was in his late thirties, she decided, and if she knew anything, *un mauvais sujet*—an adventurer and a ne'er-do-well.

Still all of this could be deceiving, she sensed, for there were lines etched at the corners of the eyes and mouth, which hinted at an inner hardness. Like steel, tempered to an unbreakable toughness, she thought, and wondered at it with a strange stricture of the heart.

She had not long to contemplate the curious effect the stranger's appearance had on her, however, as Labete chose just then once more to make his presence felt.

"*You*, pretty cock!" he growled, turning his back on

32

the spectators and stalking toward the object of his rancor. "Get up from that chair. I will teach you what it means to try and take what belongs to Pierre Labete."

For a moment longer, the blue eyes held Angelique's, until she was aware of a hot blush of resentment and something more flooding her cheeks. Instinctively her head came up in a gesture of proud disdain. Then, laughter flickering in their depths, those compelling orbs released her at last and turned lazily to appraise the towering giant.

"I beg your pardon," murmured the stranger in soft, drawling French, having a trace of a foreign accent. "Was there something you wanted?"

Angelique choked back an unwitting bubble of laughter. *Voyons!* He was the cool one, was he not. Almost she expected to see him yawn in the face of Labete, so utterly unconcerned did he appear, when a slender fellow, with the darkly handsome if somewhat dissipated features of a good-natured rogue, leaned a trifle unsteadily over the seated man's shoulder.

"I think he means to cut you up in little pieces, my lad," he observed rather thickly in English as he struggled to focus bleary eyes on the glowering giant. Apparently, little liking what he saw, he gave a comical grimace of distaste and swung his head in a ponderous arc toward his friend. "Why don't we just leave the wench to the big gapeseed, Captain, and call it a night? You did mention something about an early start in the morning for Rouen and the ship, as I recall. With any luck we might even catch the evening tide and be quit of this dreary land of the Gauls. I've a yearning for warm seas, tropical islands, and friendly, warm-blooded women."

"Ah, but, my dear Gideon," the captain cynically observed, "surely you must have discovered by now that one place is as good as another. And one woman much the same as every other. Some fairer, perhaps. Some livelier between the sheets. But in the end, there is little to distinguish them."

33

"Then why put yourself to so much trouble over this one?" demanded the rogue with a contemplative belch. Obviously more than a little drunk, he reeled, then steadied himself with a heavy hand on his friend's broad shoulder.

"Perhaps it merely amuses me," shrugged the captain, an enigmatic smile hovering about his lips. Deliberately he raised his glass in a salute to the coquette observing him with a doubtful frown on her lovely brow. Uncertainly she smiled back at him, though it never reached her eyes.

"Damn me, if I don't think you are up to your old tricks again," complained the man called Gideon, shaking an accusing finger in the lean, handsome face. "Just when I was beginning to think there was some hope for you. Try not to kill the poor bastard, will you? I've little hankering to be the first to test the blade of Monsieur Guillotin's bloody machine."

The captain's faint grin was anything but reassuring.

"I shall try my best to oblige you, Mr. Fisk," he promised, with mock gravity. "However, there would be a certain ironic humor in such an end for the Yankee Sea Wolf, would you not agree? The final jest as it were."

Oh, *la vache!* groaned Angelique to herself as, reeling with the sudden shock of enlightenment, she struggled with the enormity of her discovery. *Tiens!* She had found him—Captain Wesley Locke! And the fool meant to get himself killed over a harlot! *Sacre bleue*, it did not bear thinking on. If he fell to Labete, everything she had done would be wasted. And what's more, she would be marooned in this terrible pig-place until morning. The other alternative, that of wandering the streets of Paris alone all night, was one that she refused to contemplate, even for a single moment. As Labete intervened with an impatient growl, Angelique uttered a hasty prayer that the reckless captain would choose caution over foolish pride.

"I am waiting, m'sieu," Labete prodded, towering

34

menacingly over the small table.

"Perhaps, my friend, you should think again before you bite off more than you can chew," came the answer couched in bored accents. Gideon Fisk groaned and rolled his eyes ceilingward. Angelique's heart sank.

Labete, apparently amused, flung back his unkempt head and laughed disagreeably.

"Ah, but *you*, little cockerel," he promised with the grin of the wolf, "I will swallow whole. Babette! Move away from this *gobeur*. You will not want to see me teach this miserable gull the sad lessons of this world."

Babette, however, was apparently not the least put off by such an eventuality. *Au contraire*. It was obvious to Angelique that the brazen-faced hussy was enthralled at the prospect.

"Bah! You are a big clown, Pierre Labete," she spat contemptuously. "Do you see a band of gold on this hand? *Non!* I am not your wife to be ordered about by an ugly ox with cow-dung for brains. Go away, Pierre, before you make of yourself the big fool."

Angelique glimpsed the captain's friend retreat casually to a nearby table and his hand close surreptitiously around the neck of a wine bottle. Then Labete let out a ferocious growl.

"Eh? You dare speak like that to Pierre Labete?" he roared, his great paw of a hand going up as though to strike Babette across her painted face. "*Putain!* I will teach you to whore around with every man who dangles a fat purse in front of your face."

Angelique blanched, expecting to see the woman knocked brutally to the floor, when Locke's tall figure stepped coolly between them.

"The mam'selle and I were about to enjoy a little wine and some quiet conversation, and our plans, I'm afraid, do not include an ill-mannered oaf," he said, his pleasant tone oddly at variance with something that Angelique sensed in him, a dangerous quality too subtle for the hulking brute to recognize. "However, I see no need for

35

any unpleasantness. Why do you not simply take yourself off and find another woman. The little tart, perhaps. *J'en ai vu bien d'autres.*"

The strangled cry of outrage that came in the wake of that speech issued not from the glowering giant, but from the "tart" whom the gentleman had singled out with an indifferent nod of the head.

"*Goujat misérable!*" exclaimed Angelique, confronting him with her glorious eyes flashing. Never had she been so insulted! It was bad enough the arrogant rogue had had the gall to assume she was a whore, but to add as well that he "had seen worse" was to invite her wrath down upon his head. "Wretched cad! Who do you think you are to offer me up like some second-best prize?—Peut! I spit on you, you—you pimp, you *maquereau des femmes!* It will serve you right if this *cocotte* and her big friend succeed in their plot to kill you and steal from you your gold, *vous-savez?*"

Her tirade spoken in a mixture of French and English had seemed to amuse him, but her final words, meant as a warning, brought a sudden, steely glint to his eyes. Then just as quickly it vanished, leaving them vaguely sleepy and just a little bored.

"You would seem to place a high value on yourself," he drawled, and with cool effrontery ran his eyes over her from the top of her raven head to the tip of her booted toes. "Dollar for pound, I wouldn't judge a tumble with a scrawny, hot-tempered tadpole worth even a single silver-piece, American. But then some might like a wench covered with dirt, and feisty."

The swine! fumed Angelique, her fingers itching for something to throw at the arrogant captain. Instead she impaled him with a look of haughty disdain.

"From one such as you, a purse full of gold would not be enough to purchase even the least of my favors," she retorted contemptuously. "Bah! You are no man for a real woman of passion."

A distinct tremor of laughter trembled on his lips, but before he could make a reply to her boast, Labete obtruded himself once more on the scene. Evidently the big man was through playing games. Shoving Angelique aside, he towered menacingly over the captain.

"Enough talk! You will fight Labete like a man, or you will die like the miserable coward. Draw your knife, Gascon! I would see if you are as good with a blade as you are with your tongue."

"Then by all means try me," invited the captain. A mocking grin on his lips, he swept the giant an ironic bow. "I shall do my humble best to satisfy your curiosity."

Voyons! cursed Angelique, realizing in a blinding flash of insight that the captain cared not a damn that he was allowing himself to fall into the trap against which she had taken pains to warn him. *Au contraire.* The madman was vastly enjoying himself!

Then Labete, livid with rage, lunged at his intended victim. In a move too swift for Angelique to follow, the captain stepped lightly aside, a knife flashing out of nowhere into his hand. Deftly he caught Labete by the arm and spun him hard around, while with the light touch of a master, he slashed out and down. Instantly the giant's baggy trousers dropped, and Labete stood revealed in all his dubious glory.

"With my blade, you dimwitted buffoon," grinned the captain, the blue eyes lit with a reckless devilment of laughter, "I have no equal. As your lovely Babette was soon to have discovered." He shrugged. "With a knife, I fear I am only passing fair."

"You son of the devil!" roared Labete as, white-faced, he pulled up his pants and held the slashed waist bunched in one huge fist. "You tried to cut off my balls!"

"On the contrary, I thought merely to ventilate them. It seemed you were in need of a cooling-off, my friend."

The onlookers' loud guffaws at this sally did little to

37

soothe Labete's offended dignity. The heavily jowled face twisted in a savage snarl. Brandishing the knife in his fist, he lumbered at the foremost of the leering spectators.

Negligently the captain stuck out one booted foot. In an instant Pierre Labete was, by the force of his own momentum, sent hurtling headlong into a great wooden cask, which shattered on impact. In awed fascination, Angelique watched the felled giant struggle to shove himself up from the shambles of splintered wood and metal hoops. But in the end, a shudder shook the massive body and with a groan Labete collapsed and lay still.

"It would seem the raging bull has had enough for one evening," observed Gideon Fisk, coming forward to prod the prone figure experimentally with his boot. Apparently satisfied with the outcome, he raised the bottle in salute of the vanquished giant before upending it to polish off the wine.

In the wake of the uneven skirmish, the captain shrugged.

"I confess, I, too, grow weary of the whole affair. And since it seems an answer from Miss Gilbert is not to be forthcoming, I see no purpose in waiting any longer."

Fisk's dissipated features noticeably brightened.

"Now you've come to your senses, Captain," he applauded, clapping a hand to the other man's shoulder. "The sooner we shake the dust of this place the better I'll like it."

"I, too, would shake the dust, m'sieu," murmured a husky voice at the captain's shoulder. "Please. You will take me with you, *non?*"

Together, the two men turned to look at her, one, incredulous, the other, faintly amused, but Angelique had eyes only for the captain.

"I could not help but overhear, m'sieu. You have a boat, it is true?"

"Not a boat, doxy," corrected the dark-haired rogue with a wounded air. "A ship. The *Yankee Sea Wolf*, to be precise. The finest little lady to be found anywhere, bar none."

"*Oui*, I understand," Angelique replied, though she had hardly taken in a word. She seemed to have been swallowed up in a vacuum in which there existed nothing and no one but herself and the tall man with the dangerous, laughing eyes. She felt the breath shallow in her throat and the blood warm in her veins, and suddenly she realized she wanted more from him than could be hers as Herman Gilbert's daughter, a delicate creature to be protected and kept at arm's length until she could be safely delivered to her papa. *Non*, before she gave herself to the revolution and the nightmare she had been given to see in her vision—the nightmare waiting for her in Saint Dominique—she wanted to know what it was to lie with a man—*this* man, who had loomed in her childhood as a hero. She would teach him she was no "tadpole," but a woman, and if he already thought her a whore, all the better. The fiction would make it easier to seduce him to her bed. And, after all, it was not a husband she wanted, or even a beloved, but a man to be to her *un amant*, her lover.

Then all at once it came to her that she would tell him nothing of herself. Angelique Gilbert she had left behind at the convent, and until she reached her papa, Angelique the Nobody she would remain.

Her gaze had never wavered from the captain's, and now she lifted her chin in an unconscious gesture of pride.

"I am willing to work for my passage," she declared. Her thick eyelashes fluttered briefly downward with a sense of what she did. But almost immediately they lifted again. "If you take me with you, *M'sieu le Capitaine*," she said steadily, "I promise you will not be sorry."

She had to force herself to breathe normally as a single dark eyebrow shot up in the handsome brow. Then the devil smiled, and all at once she felt the blood rush to her

39

cheeks as his hand reached out to touch her bare arm near her breast in the way that a man touches a woman.

"How are you called, little one?" he murmured, stroking her lightly with fingers that made her flesh quiver deliciously.

"A-Angel—" she began, then bit her lip, mortified and angry at herself for what she had almost revealed.

Still, he seemed satisfied, repeating the name "Angele" in the manner of one savoring the sound of it. "Yes," he mused, "it might even suit you if you were cleaned up a bit." Inexplicably, she held her breath as his fingers wove themselves through her raven tresses. A frown flickered briefly across his brow. Then his gaze found hers again and for a seemingly endless moment he held her with eyes that seemed able to see into her soul.

At last he broke the spell with a reluctant bark of laughter.

"You make an intriguing offer, *ma petite poulette*," he remarked in his easy, drawling French. "And it is a long voyage back to the West Indies. Still, I'm afraid it is not my practice to feather my bed with fledglings." His hand dropped to his side. "Go home to your *maman, enfant*, and give yourself time to grow up. The day for bartering yourself for a man's favors will come soon enough."

Angelique suffered a single swift thrust of mortification at his rejection. Then a dangerous spark leaped in her eyes.

"Wait!" she cried as he started to turn away. One small hand caught his sleeve, while the other slid provocatively up over the hard chest to the back of his neck. She felt him stiffen, saw his lips thin to an impatient hardness. Then she impaled him with the blue-violet blaze of her eyes.

"I am no infant, m'sieu," she whispered huskily, pulling his head down to her. "And I have no mother."

Had she taken time to think before she acted on impulse, her courage most certainly would have failed her. But she was French and Creole, and her instincts

40

were those of a woman. Reaching up on tiptoe, she kissed him, lingeringly and with all the sweet fire of her youthful innocence. Arching against him, she molded her soft, supple body to his and with a heady sense of triumph felt his lips at last respond to hers with the first leap of desire. So, she thought, savoring the sweet awakening within her of a woman's power, which could ignite the fires of a man's lusty passion. He thought she was a child, but she would show him she was much more than that.

Then all at once she felt his arm close ruthlessly about her waist, and she gasped as inexorably he crushed her to him.

Never had she kissed or been kissed by a man before, and certainly never by a man such as this. The masculine leanness of his body against hers, the muscles like flexed steel, sinewy and hard, aroused in her a multitude of bewildering emotions, first and foremost of which was fear—primitive and instinctive—the fear of a strength far greater than her own, strength which gave the power of mastery over another, the power to enslave.

She tensed, tried to pull away. His fingers entangled in her hair held her mercilessly, even as his mouth moving sensuously over hers overpowered and subdued her fear. His tongue thrust itself between her teeth and ravaged her innocence. In wonder she felt a melting pang awaken somewhere deep within her and build to a trembling thrill of pleasure. Like a sultry wave engulfing her, saturating her with moist, feverish warmth, it spread outward from her vitals throughout her whole body, until her limbs felt rubbery and weak and her lungs labored to breathe.

Then, for the first time it was given to her to glimpse what it was to be a woman with a man. It was a yearning to lie naked in the clasp of powerful arms, to touch and be touched, to glory in the suppleness of her woman's body molded to the lean hardness of the man's, to arouse and unleash the controlled power she sensed in him, and at last to possess and be possessed.

41

Still she resisted, knowing instinctively that to succumb was to be forever changed, until at last she felt inundated by the liquid flood of sensations welling up within her. With a low groan, she gave in to them, gave in to his kiss, which robbed her of her will and made of her his slave to do with as he wished.

Chapter 3

A gusty sigh broke from Angelique's lips as Captain Locke released her. Her head lolled back against the lean hand still clasped in her hair, as with wide, uncomprehending eyes, she stared up into his face.

"*Tiens!* Are you the son of the devil to kiss like that?" she murmured, having forgotten for the moment that she played the part of a Parisian tart.

An amused smile twitched at the corners of the captain's mouth. Then, realizing what she had said, Angelique flushed in swift consternation.

"If it was something other than what you expected, *ma petite coquine*," drawled Locke—with the insufferable condescension of a kindly uncle to a naughty child, Angelique fumed; his "little rogue" indeed!—"I'm afraid you have only yourself to blame. As for myself, I have found that it is true what they say about fire. Those who choose to play with it are very likely to find themselves burned."

At those final words, Angelique came to herself with a jolt. How dare he lecture her as if he were somehow above what had just passed between them! Even yet the blue eyes smoldered with the desire that *she* had aroused in *him*. In this she could not be mistaken. Captain Wesley Locke had wanted her as much as she had wanted him. Or, nearly as much, at least, she amended with a faint, roguish grin. Well, she would show him that she was neither a fool nor a child.

"*C'est vrai?* And you do not like these flames which burn?" she queried, deliberately misconstruing his meaning. "Then I am sorry for you, for one should rejoice in these passions of the heart. As for the kiss— never mind." She shrugged, gazing up at him out of the most limpid of blue-violet eyes. "With me to instruct you, there is yet hope your lovemaking may be improved. Though," she added, with a faint puckering of her lovely brow as if struck by a sudden afterthought, "with a man of your advanced years, one cannot be at all of the most certain. What is it they say?—the thing about teaching the old dogs the new trick?"

In the background Fisk let out a snort, and Angelique had the satisfaction of seeing Locke's dark eyebrows narrow sharply, followed almost immediately by the wry leap of appreciative laughter in the compelling orbs. Then, without warning, a hand gripped her by the arm and jerked her hard around to meet the icy stare of an infuriated Babette.

"You sneaking little bitch!" hissed the seething beauty, not quite so lovely in a cold rage. "Do you think you can come in and take over what is Babette's? He is mine, do you understand? I saw him first!"

"Bah," Angelique retorted. "You are not so stupid, I think. Even you must see that this one belongs to nobody but himself. He is the rogue. And he knows now what *you* are—*and* what you and your Labete intended for him. Now take your filthy hands off me!"

A look of terrible malice distorted the China-doll features.

"*Touche-à-tout!*" she shrieked. "Meddlesome busy-body!"

"*Intrigante!*" Angelique instantly countered.

Without warning, Babette struck her viciously across the face. Angelique staggered back a step. Then anger, sudden and overwhelming, surged through her like a

44

white-hot flame. Hardly knowing what she intended, she drew back a balled fist and belted the sneering French woman in the mouth. The crowd let out a jubilant roar as Babette spun halfway around and went down on one knee. Slowly she lifted her head, the back of a hand to her cut lip, the other out of sight in the folds of her dress near the ankle.

Never had Angelique seen such hatred in a woman's eyes as greeted her then. She felt the hairs at the nape of her neck prickle with warning. Too late. The *cocotte* came to her feet, Labete's long-bladed knife, which had lain discarded on the floor, clasped in her hand. Angelique drew up short, the blood draining from her cheeks as Babette deliberately advanced toward her, a murderous gleam in the coal-black eyes.

"Come on. What is the matter? Why do you not fight?" she taunted, holding the knife menacingly before her. "Can you be afraid? But then you should be. Because I am going to cut up that face of yours. When I am through with you, no man will ever look at you again."

Warily Angelique retreated, her eyes fixed with a sort of horrified fascination on the glittering point of steel. *Voyons!* What had she got herself into now?

"Mesdemoiselles! Messieurs!" exhorted a harassed-looking man, the inn-keeper no doubt, wringing his hands in the folds of a filthy brown apron. "Enough, I beg you! Take your trouble somewhere else," he pleaded.

No one paid him any heed, least of all the stalking hellcat. Nervously, Angelique flicked her tongue over dry lips. Then, with the quickness of the cat, Babette swiped at her with the knife. Just as swiftly the captain's arm shot out, his fingers closing about the slender wrist in a grip of steel.

"I think, *ma petite belle,*" he observed with a mocking smile, "we will keep this a fair fight." Babette gasped as he wrenched the weapon from her hand. "You should have informed me, *cherie,* that you had already entertained plans for the evening. The addition of Labete to our party would tend to put a damper on things. In fact, it would seem I owe it to Angel, here, that you and Labete will not be dining off me after all." Releasing her, he surveyed her with singularly cold eyes. "A pity, really. With you, I was prepared to deal generously. Instead, in the circumstances, I fear I really must cry off."

"I do not know of what you are accusing me. She has told you the lies! All lies!" fumed Babette, white-faced and shaking with fury. "You said you wanted the company of a woman. You said you would pay handsomely, and now you refuse. You play Babette for the fool, *non?* For *this* I wish Labete had killed you!"

Gideon Fisk clucked his tongue reprovingly. "Ah, ah. You should not let your fangs show," he crooned in heavily slurred French as he waved an admonitory finger at the seething beauty. "It is very unattractive and not, I think, the way to a man's heart, let alone to his purse."

Babette let out an explosive, *"Oh!"* and, snatching a wooden bowl out from under the nose of an erstwhile diner, let fly at the drunken rogue.

"Look out!" cried Angelique and gasped as Fisk, in the process of belching, tottered back on his heels in time to avoid the projectile meant for him. Incredibly it sailed past within inches of his face and made unerringly for a less fortunate victim some three feet behind him. A blistering oath rent the air. Fisk, reeling drunkenly to follow the path of the object in flight, took one look at the hapless fellow in the process of slinging greasy gobs of mutton from his person and did the unpardonable. Throwing back his head, he gave forth a resounding belly-laugh.

"Eh? You laugh at François Baptiste?" demanded the wretch, a hefty 185 pounds of solid muscle. Without waiting for an apology, he charged Fisk with the force of a battering ram. Fortunately, Locke was there before him, shoving the weaving Fisk to one side as he shattered a chair over Baptiste's beefy shoulders. The big Frenchman dropped like a lead weight and never moved a muscle.

"Let that be a lesson to you," Fisk hiccupped and, leaning precariously over the luckless fellow, nearly toppled forward on top of him.

"Steady, Fisk." Locke grinned and hastily pulled his friend upright, only to come face to face with an older replica of the man he had just felled.

"Hey, *you!* That is my brother, you swine!"

"No doubt I am sorry, then—for your mother," pronounced Locke as, ducking beneath the other's roundhouse swing, he delivered a bone-crunching right to the jaw.

Hardly before the dust settled from the jarring impact of the body striking the floor, a war whoop rang out above the din of the crowd. "*Vive la Révolution!*" The innkeeper groaned and dodged a chair that came hurtling through the air. Then utter chaos broke loose as the room erupted into an unbridled free-for-all.

Angelique, swallowed up in the turmoil, lost sight of Babette and the two Americans. Retrieving her bandbox and valise from almost certain trampling, she sidestepped flailing arms and gouging elbows and started to work her way in the direction in which she had last seen the captain. Since this was the scene of the heaviest fighting, she had, perforce, to resort to extremely unladylike tactics to make any headway at all. Wielding with telling efficiency a four-inch hairpin carved from ivory, she cleared a path through the heaving bodies. Then finally she spotted Locke and Gideon Fisk, and all at once she felt her heart skip a beat.

"*Sacriste!* The fools mean to get themselves killed!" she swore upon beholding them, poised back to back, in the midst of a melee that seemed destined momentarily to overwhelm them. Even as she watched, she saw an angry brute clutch Fisk by the throat and force him down across a serving bench, obviously intent on throttling the life out of him. It soon became evident, however, that Fisk bore a charmed life as his groping hand found and

47

closed about a corked wine bottle. The man at his throat never knew what hit him.

A low whistle escaped Angelique's lips. *Voyons*, this was a man blessed. Not only did he discover the means to save himself, but he had done so without breaking the flask. A reluctant giggle burst from her lips as she saw him lift a booted foot to shove the inert body to the floor, then, perching on the bench, draw the cork from the bottle with his teeth and indulge himself in a long, and apparently satisfying, drink.

Her mirth quickly changed to consternation, however, at sight of Locke about to be borne down by overwhelming odds. She saw a wiry figure at the forefront of perhaps half a dozen men leap at the captain, caught the flash of a knife in an uplifted hand. A scream rose to her throat then died as she beheld Locke drop beneath the thrusting blade and clasp the villain by the collar and the belt. Using his would-be assassin's own momentum, the captain hefted the startled Frenchman above his head and heaved him bodily into the midst of the others. They went down like ninepins, bowled over beneath the weight of the human projectile.

Angelique saw the flash of strong white teeth against the captain's tanned face as he turned then to meet the onslaught of a club-wielding peasant, and all at once it came to her that the stories that were told of him were all true. In a fight he was fearless, a madman who laughed in the very teeth of danger, just as her papa had said.

Yet there was one thing her papa had failed to mention, something which she had sensed almost from the first moment she saw the long figure sprawled carelessly in his chair, something she sensed now in the reckless abandon with which he threw himself into the thick of the fighting. Captain Wesley Locke lived on the hard edge of danger by choice. In truth he seemed to revel in it, placing himself at risk with the insouciance of a man who cared naught what became of it—or himself. And it was this which made him so daunting, indeed, so invincible, a warrior.

And yet, how very strange, flashed briefly through her mind. In truth, she could not comprehend why a man blessed by fortune should flirt with death. *Alors!* To be so foolhardy, the brave captain must be greatly disenchanted with life.

She was not to be given time to contemplate this intriguing possibility, however, as it was at that very moment that she caught sight of glittery coal-black eyes in a face distorted with malice. *Voyons!* It was Babette. And, there, too, was Pierre Labete, stealing toward the captain's unguarded back. All at once her blood ran cold.

Intent only on warning the man who had saved her father, Angelique bounded forward.

"Capitaine, behind you!"

The sound of an explosion nearly deafened her, and a blow like a fist in her side slammed her hard into a table. Dizzy and strangely weak, she shoved herself up. Then, as in a dream, she felt herself endlessly falling, till at last the floor rushed up to meet her. There was a dazzle of pain as the back of her head struck, and for a stunned moment she lay struggling to ward off the darkness that threatened to engulf her. Sensing someone draw near to stand over her, she forced open her eyes and in dazed disbelief stared up into the gloating features of the triumphant Babette. For an instant it came to her again, that vague feeling of recognition. Then her breath caught in her throat at sight of the small pistol, trailing smoke from the barrel. As awful realization dawned on her, she saw Babette smile coldly and, turning, vanish into the crowd. At last she shut her eyes against the sudden wash of pain, like a red-hot ember spreading fire through her flesh.

She must have swooned for a short time, for the next thing she knew, she had come to, her lungs laboring for each painful breath and her senses reeling drunkenly. It was all very strange, she thought, feeling curiously detached from herself and yet acutely aware of everything going on around her. For in truth she could almost feel the sudden silence, like a pall hanging over the inn, and she knew though her eyes were closed that the whole world must be looking down at her. The thought came to her that she did not care very much to have everyone staring at her, but somehow she could not find the strength to do anything about it. Then someone knelt beside her, and she felt the cool touch of fingers against her throat.

"She's alive, Mr. Fisk. Summon that fool, LeBon. We'll need a room and clean bandages—if there are any to be had in this miserable excuse for an inn. Do what you can, Gideon."

"Aye, Captain. Though somehow I don't think our fat landlord is going to be any too happy about this."

The captain made no reply, and Angelique was carried on a swell of pain to the edge of oblivion as strong hands eased her over on to her side. Vaguely she was aware of those same hands working to stanch the flow of blood from her wound. Then for awhile she knew nothing, till the sound of voices raised in argument teased her back to the surface of awareness.

"I am of the most sorry that such a thing should befall a guest in my house, m'sieu," importuned a voice of long-suffering. "But I beg of you, try to understand. If the little one were to die under this roof, it would be very bad for business. It would mean an investigation. You are a man of intelligence. You must see the presence of *les gendarmes* would drive away my customers."

"I see that you leave me with very little choice, M'sieu LeBon," responded the captain's steely accents. "Fisk, summon a cab. It seems we won't be staying after all."

"And what of the damages, m'sieu? Who is to pay?"

"Pay, m'sieu? *Someone* will pay for what has happened here tonight. But I think it will not be me. And if this wench dies, there *will* be an investigation. You may be sure of it. Well, Mr. Fisk? Why are you still standing there? Was there something you wanted to add?"

"Only that M'sieu LeBon is in a very big hurry to get rid of us, and I cannot but find that just a little suspicious. Perhaps, Captain, he is not the innocent bystander he pretends to be."

"Curious that we should be thinking along the same lines. Perhaps, Fisk, as soon as we've seen to the girl, you should go in search of a policeman. The sooner *les gendarmes* are made aware of events, after all, the sooner we can expect an accounting."

"No, *messieurs!*" shrieked the extremely hard-pressed LeBon in tones of near-panic. "I assure you that will not be at all necessary. I have just remembered the chamber adjoining your own is at present unoccupied. No doubt it will suit La Petite most admirably."

"Funny how mention of the law tends to jog a man's memory," Fisk observed philosphically in an undertone as the harried innkeeper hurried away to fetch the key to the aforementioned room. "'Specially if he's got something on his conscience."

Angelique became aware of someone kneeling beside her.

"Never mind LeBon, Mr. Fisk. Fetch the box and valise, and be quick about it. The chit is bleeding again."

Then a pair of strong arms eased beneath her shoulders and knees and lifted her. A frown creased her brow as the pain came, swift and merciless, and, determined not to cry out, she caught her lip hard between her teeth. Then at last she came to rest against a pleasingly firm, masculine chest. Finding the steady beat of the captain's heart beneath her cheek somehow soothing, she relaxed with a small, nearly imperceptible sigh.

There was the sound of hurried footsteps approaching.

"I have it, Capitaine. You see, I am of the most cooperative."

"I see that you would not hesitate to knock me in the head if you thought you could get away with it," replied the captain coldly. "Which is why you will lead the way. Get going, LeBon, and I suggest you try nothing you

51

might be made to regret later."

He was already moving as he finished, carrying her as effortlessly in his arms as if she were no more than a child. Still, even through the daze of pain, she could sense the quiet urgency in his quick, purposeful stride. *Alors!* It must be very bad, this wound in her side, she thought with a sharp twinge of regret, regret which was quickly supplanted by fear as it came to her that once he had seen to her present needs there would be nothing to keep him from leaving her. He would sail back to America without her, and she would never see him again—or her dearest Papa. *Mon Dieu!* She would be left to the mercies of this pig-man, LeBon! She must find the strength to tell him who she was before it was too late!

She was vaguely aware that she had been borne up a long flight of stairs, which they had left some moments before, and now she felt him pause, heard the sound of a door being opened. His curt orders to LeBon to fetch brandy, a roll of flint, and hot water was flung over his shoulder as he crossed the room and leaned down to lay her carefully on a lumpy cot. She felt his hands moving over her, undoing the fastenings of her cloak as he began to disrobe her. Fretfully, her head moved against the coarse pillow. Her fingers clasped at the fabric of his shirt and desperately clung.

"Do not leave me," she groaned, trying to hold back the fog that was closing in around her. With an effort she forced open her eyes. "Do not leave me here alone, I beg you."

The captain's face, oddly grim, swam into focus. His low voice cut through her panic.

"No, I won't leave you. Not until you're better. Lie still now. Let me tend your wound."

"No! First I must . . . tell you . . . !"

She started up, then cried out as the pain clawed mercilessly at her body.

"There, now see? You'll only hurt yourself if you

52

thrash about." Strong hands clasped her shoulders and firmly pressed her toward the bed. She fought them, hurting herself in her struggle to make him understand, until at last her strength gave out. In a daze of pain, she collapsed, sobbing weakly, against the pillow.

La vache! You . . . don't . . . understand. I am not . . . what you think."

"Then you will tell me when you have rested. For now, you must trust me, Angel, if you are going to get better."

A frown creased her brow as, feeling herself sinking into the depths of an abyss, she tried hard to remember what it was she had wished so desperately to tell him. But at last she felt too weary even for that. One last time she made herself open her eyes. Her lips curved weakly in a smile that was whimsical, as the handsome face, strangely blurred, swam into view above her.

"It is the very bad luck, I think," she murmured, her voice curiously thick, and felt herself adrift on the fringes of a dream. As she watched the dark eyebrows draw together in puzzlement, her eyelids began slowly to drift down over her eyes. "I could have shown you what it was to make love to a woman of Creole blood," she managed on a long, weary sigh, "but now I think maybe I will die in this cold land of my mother."

She had succumbed to the welcoming arms of oblivion even as the final syllable breathed through her lips. And so she did not see the unwitting leap of rueful amusement in his eyes at the first half of her speech harden at the last to an exceedingly grim resolve. Only Gideon Fisk, lurching unsteadily into the room with Angelique's bandbox and valise clutched awkwardly beneath his arms, was witness to that unexpected phenomenon.

"Christ, she didn't make it, eh?" he muttered hoarsely, as he dropped the baggage unceremoniously to the floor. "That's too bad. She seemed a game little piece."

"Game? Aye," answered Locke without lifting his eyes

from the still face pale as death against the pillow. "Little piece? I wonder." Suddenly he seemed to shake himself. "Whatever she is, she deserves better than to die in a place like this. See what is keeping LeBon, Gideon, while I get these clothes off her. There's no time to waste if we're going to save her."

Fisk, grappling with the enormity of the captain's words, visibly brightened.

"You mean she's *not* dead? Well, why didn't you *say* so. Could've sworn from the look on your face that she'd already cut anchor." Then as the captain gave him a piercing glance over his shoulder, Fisk grinned. "Take it easy. I'm going, I'm going. I may be drunk as a skunk, but you can't count me out. Not by a long shot."

"That's good, Gideon," crooned the captain, all the more compelling, somehow, for the softness of his tone. "Because if you fail me now, I'll have your hide. Do we understand one another?"

Fisk favored the other man with a suddenly arrested look, his grin slowly fading. At last he shrugged.

"Sure, Wes, sure. What's not to understand?"

As if it took actual physical effort, he tore his eyes away from his friend's damnably unnerving stare and walked to the door. There he stopped.

"You and me, Wes," he said, without looking around. "We've been closer than most brothers. Seen more than most men live to tell about." Deliberately he opened the door. "If you think I've forgotten how you kept me alive when everyone else, including myself, had already given up, then, old friend, you're way off the mark."

Meeting Locke's eyes briefly over his shoulder, Fisk stepped into the hallway and left the captain staring after him.

Only then did Locke let his weariness show. Christ, he must be getting old, he reflected, thrusting the fingers of one hand angrily through his hair. He understood Fisk all right, understood him as well as he understood himself.

54

Hell, who was Wesley Locke to call anyone to account, and especially a man like Gideon? They had been through the bloody gates of hell together. Disgusted with himself for having vented his ill-humor on Fisk, he deliberately closed his mind to everything except the puzzling wisp of a girl who had seemed so determined to get herself killed for a stranger.

Working swiftly, he rid the inert form of shoulder scarf and apron. "Bloody hell!" he muttered to himself, becoming acutely aware of the crimson stain spreading slowly beneath the slight figure. It took only a second or two for him to discard the notion of struggling with the numerous, absurdly small fastenings down the back of a dress that was not only homely in the extreme, but filthy as well. He'd buy the chit a new one. It might even amuse him to see her becomingly gowned. Cleaned up a bit and with a little more flesh on her bones, she could be a comely enough wench.

Without further ado, he grasped the front of the bodice in both hands and ripped it open to the waist.

For an instant he reeled under the exceedingly uncomfortable feeling that he had just violated something fine and exquisitely lovely. He had hardly been prepared, after all, to be met by the sight of small, perfect breasts and milk-white skin that looked to be satiny smooth to the touch. Silently he cursed. Christ, but he should have been.

Downstairs in the common room when she had come near enough for him to catch the subtle scent of olive oil and rosemary in her hair, he had realized there was something about the chit that did not ring true. He had even made sure of it, for when he had crushed a raven curl in his hand, he had not been surprised to discover it felt as soft and silken as it had looked to be. Unfortunately, subsequent events had taken precedence over the intriguing paradox his discovery had uncovered —an apparently low-born female, as filthy and poorly clad as the rest of her kind, who yet apparently made it a practice to cleanse and anoint her hair with expensive soap and hair tonics? Obviously and quite naturally she must have assumed, when adding the finishing touches to what could only have been meant as a disguise, that no one would be given to glimpse beyond the soiled face and extremities to what lay beneath her peasant gown.

All at once he was extremely curious to hear what exactly the chit *had* been about to tell him before she lost consciousness. Concerned at the present time, however, with saving her from the consequences of her foolhardy venture, whatever it was, he made short work of stripping her down to the buff. Only then did he gain a clear picture of the difficulties that lay before him.

The handsome lips thinned to a grim line at sight of the small hole oozing blood. The wound in itself was not mortally serious, having failed, from the looks of it, either to penetrate very deeply or to hit anything vital. The real difficulty lay in the fact that the pistol ball, after having entered at an angle between two ribs, had apparently lodged somewhere inside, which meant that, to find it and get it bloody well out, the wound would have to be probed before it could be cleansed and properly bound.

Christ! He had removed lead from living flesh before, but the flesh had never been that of a girl hardly older than a schoolroom miss, one, moreover, with so damnably little flesh to spare! From the looks of her, there was not one chance in hell that she would survive his crude attempt at surgery.

He was to discover, however, that he had failed to take into account the variables of an apparently indomitable spirit and an exceedingly strong will to live. No little time later she had indeed survived the anguish of seemingly endless probing. Locke, sprawled in a chair at her bedside, his gaze speculative on the delicate contours of the face reposed in sleep, could only marvel at so much tenacity in such a tiny slip of a girl.

Still, the worst might be yet to come, he reflected dourly, observing the unnatural flush in the formerly pale cheeks. With a wry grimace, he reached for the bottle of brandy on the floor beside him and, tipping his head back, took a long pull. It promised to be a very long night, he decided, propping the bottle on top of a muscular thigh as he leaned wearily back in the chair to watch and wait. A very long night indeed.

Chapter 4

Locke sprawled on the padded bench beneath the stern windows, his shoulders propped against the frame, and stared at the shadowy figure in the bed. He was weary and heartily tired of his unlooked-for adventure, which had placed the mysterious Angel in his charge. But, most of all, he was worried.

Suddenly he cursed. It was nearly a week since the girl had been wounded, and still the fever showed no signs of lessening. With a sense of helplessness he wondered how much longer she could possibly hold on or how much longer he could bear to be cooped up in the cabin with her, watching her tormented by the cursed dreams. Besides, it was past the time when he should have been quit of Rouen. Only the surgeon's insistence that she might grow worse at sea had kept him bound to the shores of France this long.

In sudden impatience with the stifling confines of the cabin, he came to his feet and stared out the window. He could feel the ship pulling against her anchors. The tide was changing. If they weighed anchor now, they could be well on their way from France within the hour. But if they waited . . .

Hellsfire! Maybe the surgeon was right. Maybe she would do better on land. But not here, not in the turmoil of revolutionary France. If it was land she bloody well needed, he would take her across the channel to England.

It was almost midnight when Locke made his appearance on the quarterdeck. Without preamble he ordered his first mate to muster all hands and prepare to weigh anchor. They were leaving France as soon as the ship could be made ready.

Fisk, who knew his captain's moods better than anyone, realized at a single glance now was not the time to question his orders. If the captain wanted to make sail in the dead of night and in the middle of a rainstorm, that was his business, he declared to the disgruntled crew, freshly rousted from their hammocks. "Aye," growled a burly seaman. "An' it's the French tart who lays ill in the captain's cabin, I expect, that's driven him to it. There ain't no place on a ship for a female. Turns the luck bad, it does."

The rumble of agreement was cut short by the captain's steely voice from the quarterdeck.

"If you are quite through exchanging pleasantries, Mr. Fisk," he commented acerbically, "I would be pleased if we could get under way before the tide turns."

Flushing beneath the captain's heavy sarcasm, Fisk fairly thundered the order to rig and clear sheets. In an instant the decks were swarming with activity as the ship made ready to unloose her moorings.

In the midst of running out sails and securing the anchor, neither Locke, who was issuing orders from the helm, nor Fisk, who was busy relaying them, was aware when one of the men ducked furtively through the cabin hatch and stole along the dark companionway to the captain's private quarters. Cautiously he opened the door and slipped inside.

For a moment Salvador Chantal waited with his back to the door while his eyes adjusted to the lantern light. A soft rustle of movement and a low groan from the bed brought his head around. Noiselessly he glided across the cabin.

At sight of the pale face against the pillow, a shudder shook his frame. "Eugenie," he murmured, his eyes suddenly haunted. "How like you she has become. *Merci Dieu!* It rends my heart to look upon her. And yet how beautiful she is. Petite and delicate like her *maman.* You would be proud of her, *bien-aimée.*"

Angelique, as if sensing his presence, moved her head restlessly against the pillow, and instantly Chantal was returned to an awareness of what had brought him there. His hand, going out to touch the pale brow, drew back as if burned.

"Mozambe taught her student well," he muttered grimly. "The poison does its work."

Dropping to one knee beside the bed, he took a vial from a leather pouch slung at his waist. Quickly he removed the stopper. Then leaning over the girl, he clasped either side of her face with his hand and gently forced her lips open.

Angelique, her mind caught up in a tangled web of the dream of Damballa and the Pethro, groaned and tried to turn her head away.

"*Non,*" she panted. Chantal held her. Quickly he poured three drops of the liquid between her lips and then released her.

"*C'est bien,* Petite," he murmured, stroking her cheek lightly with the back of his hand. "You will begin to get better now."

At his touch, Angelique's eyes flew open. She stared wildly into his face. "The flames," she muttered fretfully. Deliriously she tugged at the neck of the garment she wore. "The flames of the *loa.* I cannot bear them. Make them go away."

As her restive movements bared the slender column of her neck, Chantal's gaze narrowed sharply. Slowly his hand went out to touch the blemish, like a brand in the

61

shape of a crescent moon.

"The mark of the curse of Mawu," he whispered. The lean hand clenched in a fist. This, like the dreams, was also the work of Mozambe. But was he not Chantal, a sorcerer of the faith, and was he not sworn to protect the daughter of Eugenie? For once in his life, he would use the power of sorcery with a fierce gladness. Leaning over the girl, he began to speak softly in her ear.

It was the whispery, sing-song chant of a *tonton macoute*, the sorcerer who steals the souls of children. With a groan, Angelique struggled to break free of its spell.

"*Non!*" she cried out. "It is madness. Mozambe lies. Mozambe lies!"

Chantal, holding her as she tried to leave the bed, stiffened as Locke burst through the doorway.

"What the bloody hell!"

Hastily Chantal sprang to his feet and backed before the cold anger in his captain's eyes.

"It not be what you think," he said, his hands raised before him as he watched to see what the other man intended.

Ignoring him, Locke shoved past Chantal and went to the girl, writhing in the bed.

"*Easy*, Angel," he muttered, as with strong hands he lifted her against his shoulder and reached for the medicine waiting on the table by the bed. Grimly he placed the cup to her lips and ordered her to drink. Frantically she turned her head away.

Again Locke spoke to her, his voice sharp with impatience.

"Angel, *listen* to me. You have nothing to fear. I won't let anyone hurt you. Do you hear me? You are safe here with me." Something in his tone caught her reeling mind and held it. For a moment she grew quiet, listening. "Yes, that's better. You are ill. And if you want to be well again, you must take your medicine now and lie still."

The cup placed once more to her lips shattered the

moment. With a strangled cry, she knocked aside the hand that held it.

"No. It is a trick! Blood . . . of the . . . sacrifice," she panted. "Oh, God, I cannot bear it! Why will no one listen? *Je ne suis pas de* Fon. *Mon Dieu, je ne suis pas de* Fon."

It was a litany that Locke had heard more than once in the past week, one that wore his patience thin. In no mood to tolerate her in her present state, he pinned his troublesome patient against a powerful shoulder and, grasping the cup, tipped its contents ruthlessly down her throat.

He held her until the sedative at last began to take effect and with a groan she gradually went lax against him. Carefully he eased her down against the pillow. For a long moment he stared at the pale, weary face and marvelled that even heavily dosed with laudanum, the slight figure in the bed yet twitched and groaned softly, struggling against whatever nightmarish demons sought to possess her.

Unaccountably, he found his hands clenched in fists as he watched her wear herself out with her torment. Then his face hardened with a slow-mounting rage at the man who had brought on this latest setback. Turning, he coldly surveyed the shadowy figure, standing impassively beyond the fringes of the lamplight.

Salvador Chantal's slanted eyes, a nearly colorless pale blue, stared expressionlessly back at him. Clad only in calf-length white trousers, he stood with bare feet spread slightly apart, his arms folded across the lean, brown chest and waited. He was probably in his late thirties or early forties, old for a slave, and had the look of the mulatto with possibly a strain of Arawak in the high, flat cheeks and almond-shaped eyes. The captain's lips thinned to a grim line as he glimpsed the telltale marks of old scars, crisscrossing the chest and the tops of the shoulders. Apparently someone had gone to extreme lengths to break the man—and obviously had failed, he thought, noting the arrogance in the proud cast of the chin and slim back, the contempt in the almost imperceptible curl of the lip.

"What are you doing here? Speak up, damn you!"

The maroon stared impassively before him. Twice before he had tried to reach the girl, and both times *ce capitaine* had ordered him away before he could give her the healing potion. And if he were foolish enough to try to make Locke understand, it would surely be no different. The world of the *Rodu* was beyond the grasp of the white man. And yet only he, Chantal, stood between Angelique and the curse of Mawu. Somehow he must warn Locke of the dangers surrounding the daughter of Eugenie. Somehow he must make sure *le capitaine* delivered her to Saint Dominique.

The scarred shoulders lifted in a shrug. For the sake of Angelique, he would do what he could to reach *le capitaine.*

"The black man Jubal say I come see Capitaine. I knock. I wait. Then I hear the woman she is weeping. Chantal think maybe she needing someone help. But that one, she run from the Pethro *loa*, Capitaine. And now she have die she want come back reborn. There no be nothing you can do for her until the curse she is broken."

The captain appeared anything but amused at the man's cryptic utterances.

"Is that what you told her—that she has been put under a witch's spell?" he demanded coldly.

"I tell her only what she needing to know if she want to be free of the evil ones."

"The only evil here, Chantal, is what you have worked in this girl's mind. Or maybe you're going to tell me you didn't know she'd taken a pistol ball in the side?"

There was no mistaking the faint, mocking light behind the maroon's careful mask. *Le capitaine* was no different from all the rest, he thought contemptuously.

"I no can say how this curse been done," he lied. "The ball, maybe she dipped in the powder that come from the cemetery earth and the bones of the dead. Chantal never see this woman before, but he know she belong to Mawu-Lisa. See," he said, pointing to the blemish where the slender column of Angelique's neck met the soft curve of a milk-white shoulder—the small scar in the shape of a crescent moon. "She have on her the moon-sign of Mawu, she, who rule the night. That woman, she been branded with the mark of one chosen for the sacrifice. I think she have powerful enemy want her dead. Make powerful magic bring her back to them."

Locke silently cursed. He had already expended seven nearly sleepless nights on his unasked-for charge, who thus far had resisted his every effort as well as the more recent ones of his ship's surgeon to pull her out of the blasted fever. And now, if Chantal were to be believed, he could chalk the whole thing up to a bloody *Rodu* curse.

Suddenly the humor of the situation struck him. No doubt, he mused wryly, it had been at the inspiration of the gods, too, that Chantal should suddenly show up at the docks in Jamaica to replace the seaman washed overboard in a wholly unseasonal hurricane. Add to that the fact that he had been found skulking outside the door to the girl's cabin on not one, but two separate occasions, however, and one began to question not only the gods' motives, but Chantal's. And now this. Bloody hell, he thought. The last thing he needed was to have it leak to the crew that the woman on board—the woman who was already considered bad luck—was cursed as well.

Still, Locke, who was neither credulous nor a fool, could not dismiss out of hand the possibility, however remote, that there might be something to all this nonsense about curses and spells. The mind was a strange thing. If the girl herself believed she was in the power of the *Rodu*, might not that be enough to put her in a fever? A glint of irony darkened his brow. After all, he had seen for himself what superstition could do to the minds of sailors if the luck turned bad.

One thing was sure, he mused, observing the other

man's impassive features from beneath hooded eyelids. He was developing a hearty dislike for the runaway slave, if, indeed, that's what he was. Chantal had all the earmarks of trouble about him. And unless he missed his guess, there was a deal more to the man than appeared on the surface. Not that the maroon didn't play the ignorant savage to perfection, reflected Locke cynically, but he'd wager a shipload of goods that in spite of that blank face, the man was no bloody fool.

A pale glint came to the captain's eyes. He had seen that look too many times before not to know it for what it was—a mask to hide the inner thoughts of the man. He had beheld it in the vacant expressions of prisoners, slaves, even disaffected sailors with mutiny on their minds. The handsome lips thinned to a hard line. He had seen it in himself after his release from the *Jersey*—the first time he had had the mischance to come face to face with himself in a looking glass. A man stripped of everything but his cursed will to survive was quick to learn his only defense was to appear as mindless as an idiot.

Impatiently Locke swept such thoughts aside. The past was past, and he had more pressing matters, like finding answers to the questions surrounding the mysterious Angel and what the bloody hell Chantal was doing in his cabin with her.

Curse the man! Angel had been quiet enough when he left her to see to matters topside. He'd give a pretty penny to know what the maroon had said or done to set her off again.

"Tell me about these Pethro *loa*," he drawled carelessly, turning back to the other man. "If it is a curse, why should the 'unseeable ones' be after Angel? This enemy, whoever it is, must have had something to rouse them up against her."

The maroon's expression did not show his surprise. *Le capitaine* knew something of the *Rodu*. But could he be brought to believe? he wondered.

"They gods be wanting punish those who no honor the unseeable ones, Capitaine," he answered, continuing to stare straight ahead. Then suddenly he seemed to hesitate. "She say she not of the blood. Many who want pass for white say the same. Maybe that why the gods of the Fon very angry, you think?"

Locke turned away to conceal the jolt of surprise that had just shot through him like a lightning bolt. Unwittingly the image of blue-violet eyes flashed into his mind, and silken skin the color of ivory. That African blood might run in Angel's veins could not have been further from his mind. Still, it could explain a great deal that was puzzling about the girl. Her insistence that she was not what she seemed, for instance. Or the fever, which hung on in spite of the fact that the wound itself was already well on the way to being healed. And then there were the dreams that surfaced even when she lay under the influence of a sleeping draught. Both might very well owe their source to something eating at her deep inside. Obviously Angel was hiding *something*. It was that, after all, that had intrigued him about her from the very first.

His gaze fell somberly on the restless figure on the bed.

"And how may the bloody gods be appeased, I wonder," he muttered cynically to himself.

A faint gleam flickered in the maroon's pale blue eyes.

"You want leave her to me," he dared to suggest, apparently bolder now that it seemed the captain had come to believe in the reality of a curse. "That woman, she have be made to accept loa. She have die to come back reborn. The spell, I turn back on the witch who did this. Then this woman, she free of the evil."

Locke could almost feel the man's eagerness. A grim smile touched his lips. Curse or not, it would be a cold day in hell before he let the bloody savage work his vile spells over the girl. The very thought of Chantal alone with the

67

exquisitely beautiful Angel, lying helpless and naked before him, was enough to make the bile rise to Locke's throat.

"Yes, you'd like that, wouldn't you, Chantal?" he murmured, his eyes singularly cold beneath drooping eyelids. Deliberately turning his back on the other man, he reached for a decanter of port and casually poured himself a drink. "I doubt there'd be a man jack on board this ship who wouldn't envy you such a job." Only then did he glance over his shoulder at the taut figure, partially obscured in the shadows. "However, so long as I'm captain of this ship, you and everyone else will confine themselves to whatever duties have been assigned them. And unless you want to find yourself in irons, I suggest you see to yours at once."

The slim, sinister figure appeared to leap with anger, quickly doused.

"Oh, and, Chantal, in the future," Locke added, his voice dangerously soft, "it will be a lot healthier for you if you make no attempt to come anywhere near these quarters—or the girl. Do I make myself clear?"

At last Chantal shrugged, his expression as sullenly inscrutable as it had previously been fierce with expectancy.

"Chantal only want help, Capitaine. By and by you see you no can change nothing. One day you will come look for Chantal. Then you know without him help, that woman, she going to die."

It was an ill-omen that would seem to hang in the air long after the maroon was gone.

Hell, Locke swore softly to himself as, a glass in one hand and the decanter of port in the other, he sank ill-humoredly onto the padded bench before the stern windows. Maybe there was a curse. In fact, the whole bloody voyage had seemed dogged by bad luck since his old friend and partner in the West Indies trade had decided to send him on a wild goose chase to fetch his daughter home from France.

Blast Herman Gilbert and his elusive offspring! On his hurried visit to the convent four days after events at the Crossbow, Locke had discovered the place deserted. Deserted, that is, except for a demented old caretaker named Coquille, who had kept babbling some nonsense about bread baskets and ungrateful aristocrats. He had been able to learn nothing from him other than the fact that the nuns had been turned out and the convent closed down. Questioning the local police officials, a priest, an archbishop, and the girl's cousin, le Comte du Vallenoir, had proven equally fruitless. Apparently Miss Gilbert had simply vanished off the face of the earth. With the result that he not only was faced with the unpleasant prospect of confessing his failure to Herman Gilbert, but he found himself saddled as well with a breathtakingly desirable young female who seemed destined utterly to disrupt the uncomplicated drift of his life.

Emptying the glass and promptly refilling it, he bitterly cursed the luck that had landed the chit in his lap. He was excessively weary of the entire affair and heartily wished he had taken Gideon's advice to leave the mysterious Angel in the charge of a Paris physician. Curiosity more than anything else had prompted him to take her with him when three days ago he determined he could no longer put off returning to the ship. Curiosity and a deucedly uncomfortable feeling of responsibility for the chit, which, in spite of his best efforts, he could not quite shake.

Blast Angel and her stupid meddling! he thought savagely. He had not asked her to place herself in danger for his sake. Handling Labete had been child's play. Had the girl stayed out of it, the outcome would have been no less the same. Pierre Labete would still have ended up wondering what hit him.

As if drawn, his glance went to the girl. Who the deuce was she? he wondered, as he had done almost continuously since fate had been so unkind as to place her in his keeping. And why the blue blazes had she to appear so cursedly small and vulnerable? He was acutely conscious of mounting frustration as he studied the pale oval of the face, delicately hewn and bewitchingly lovely against the tangled blue-black mass of hair that tumbled in wild profusion over the pillow. Thoughtfully his gaze lingered over the fine sweep of eyebrows in the sensitive brow and the sculpted arch of high cheekbones, pronounced beneath smooth, flawless skin. Her nose, small and short, displayed an intriguing tendency to turn up at the end, while her delightfully pointed chin hinted at the stubborn, unruly streak he had already been given to see at its most maddening. If there were indeed African blood in her veins, he could see no sign of it in her, and her sylph-like beauty and dainty proportions put him more in mind of a pampered young beauty than a Parisian tart—as did the contents of her luggage, which he had not scrupled to search in the hopes of finding some clue to her identity.

Somehow he had not been surprised to discover the battered valise and bandbox contained articles of clothing that must have cost someone a pretty penny. He had already seen the exquisite creature that lay beneath the disguise, after all. And after that, the gowns and other expensive items had not seemed all that out of keeping with everything he had already surmised about her. Those soft and shapely hands, for example, had obviously never known hard labor. Nor, having beheld the proud flash of those magnificent eyes, could he conceive that she had ever served in the capacity of lady's maid or someone's hired drudge. He had seen the type of females employed as paid companions to querulous old spinsters and shrewish widows, and he was very certain his Angel would not have lasted in such a position longer than it took for her to lose that gloriously hasty temper of hers. A matter of perhaps five minutes, certainly no more than that.

No, in spite of the dirt, whose welcome absence revealed the lovely perfection of face and limbs, and the

70

humble raiment, which had met an equally inglorious end, Angel was neither common nor shabby genteel, but a young woman who had been used in her own right to the finer things in life. He'd stake his life on it, which was why, upon having also discovered a small fortune in jewelry concealed in the folds of one of the gowns, he had not been immediately moved to brand her a thief. A locket containing a miniature of a woman so close to Angel in looks that he could only suppose it to have been a portrait of her mother, that and the outmoded settings that comprised most of the pieces, seemed evidence enough; after all, that these were family heirlooms from which she would not willingly be parted—not even to purchase passage aboard a ship bound for the West Indies, if that was what she had truly been after. Of course, there was one other explanation for all these seeming inconsistencies about the mysterious Angel, one that, thus far he had refused seriously to contemplate. A hard glint came to his eyes. If she truly *was* a whore, she was obviously a very successful one.

In sudden disgust, he drained his glass and poured himself another. Somehow he found himself most damned reluctant to admit he could possibly have been mistaken in judging her an innocent. Setting aside for the moment that cursed unnerving kiss, which, untutored though it had seemed, had yet heated his blood to the boiling point—a reaction, he admitted wryly to himself, that was as wholly unsettling as it had been unexpected—he could still have sworn she was as untouched as new, driven snow. There was something in her bearing, or maybe it was something he had glimpsed in those blue-violet eyes, so cursed deep a man could damned well lose himself in them. An undefinable something, a quality, that somehow had put him in mind of his kid sister as a young girl, full of the devil but fine, and as innocent as a kitten.

Suddenly he thrust savage fingers through his hair. Hellsfire! He must be bloody well crazy if he thought he

71

had seen anything in this chit to remind him of his incomparable sister Sabra, a woman whose beauty was rivaled only by her courage and nobleness of heart. Such a comparison was as absurd as it was far-fetched, he told himself.

Even so, a curiously baffled smile twisted at his lips. No matter how hard he tried, he could not deny what he had felt as, gazing down into that lovely face, so beguilingly young and innocent-seeming, he had listened to the little baggage offer herself shamelessly to him in exchange for passage aboard his ship. It had come to him then, and again later, when she had rested so trustingly in his arms as he carried her upstairs at the inn, that his mysterious Angel, far from being the whore she pretended to be and that he himself had publicly branded her, was in reality a delicately bred female in desperate need of a man's protection. It had, in fact, come to him to suspect that she might be the girl that he had been sent to find—Angelique Gilbert, Herman Gilbert's daughter.

The names fit all right, but then, why the bloody disguise? he wondered. And why offer to sell herself for passage to Saint Dominique when if she were Angelique Gilbert, she must have known he was there expressly to take her home to her father? No, it just didn't add up, and he was precisely back where he had started from. Who the hell was she and what was she so afraid of that she had been willing to go to such lengths to get him to take her to the West Indies and to Saint Dominique in particular? Unless—! All at once a singularly grim look came to his eyes. Unless Chantal was telling the truth and someone really did want the chit dead. The powerful white plantation owners perhaps? Or maybe it was the other side, the free mulattoes, who wanted the same rights and privileges under the law as were accorded the whites. Not that it mattered, he thought. If Angel had gotten herself mixed up with either faction, she would have incurred some very dangerous and ruthless enemies. If they had tried to kill her once, it was a foregone conclusion that they would try again. And if he knew anything, Chantal knew a lot more about it than he let on.

Locke felt a tingling of nerve-endings at the thought. All his instincts warned him there was more at risk here than the girl. He had not needed Herman Gilbert's suggestion that he keep a sharp eye peeled for anyone or anything suspicious on this voyage. Any fool could see all hell was about to break loose on bloody Saint Dominique, and with people's survival depending on the regular arrival of ships bearing cargoes of food, any treachery was possible. After their stopover in France, the *Sea Wolf* carried enough in her holds to provision a rebel force for several months, or, denied a town under siege, to hasten its surrender by weeks. The safety of his ship and his crew might depend on his finding out just exactly who Chantal was and what devilry he was up to.

Having gone full round with his reasoning, he chided himself for a bloody fool. If there was any truth to what Chantal had hinted at, the chit was very probably the discarded by-blow of some wealthy West Indian plantation owner. That would explain any gentility he might have sensed in her, *and* that dazzling display of pride. It was hardly uncommon for the issue of a favored mistress to be granted all the advantages of the legitimate half-siblings, so long as the proprieties were observed and the father's mantle of protection remained intact.

But what if Angel's father had met an untimely end? he reasoned, suddenly grim. She must soon have found France, and especially Paris at the present time, an extremely inhospitable place in which to be stranded. Shunned by her blood-kin and their kind for her mixed blood and illegitimacy and by the vulgar for her unmistakable air of quality, she would have had a deuced hard time just surviving. What woman, especially one that was both young and exceptionally beautiful, would not choose to sell herself if the alternative was to wind up dead in some miserable alley?

She could hardly be blamed if she had taken the easy

way out. Even as young as she was, one look into those angel eyes would be enough to make most men willing to do anything, fight to the death for her if need be, kill for her—hell, even marry her if they had to—just to possess her. Hellsfire, who was he trying to fool? He could hardly deny that his thoughts had been anything other than prurient from the moment he saw her, furious and full of fight, flinging her defiance at the jeering crowd, and, subsequently, at himself. Even with dirt on her face, she had outshone every other female there. Obviously she had had all the fire that made a man's loins ache to take such a magnificent creature and make her his. And it was only that she had seemed so absurdly young and he, by comparison, so far much older, old enough, in fact, to know better, that he had not dragged her upstairs to his room at the inn and taken her then, before the disastrous brawl had broken out.

If she could arouse that kind of desire in a man without even trying, only a fool could expect her to resist using it to her advantage, he told himself—or hold it against her when she failed to resist the temptation. His lips curled in a singularly chilling smile. After all, his own mother had not been proof against woman's inescapable frailty. Indeed, if she had not already, he did not doubt for a moment that the wholly enchanting Angel eventually *would* succumb to the weakness inherent in all of her sex. And then would end whatever momentary fascination she had aroused in him, he mused, cynically aware that no matter what reason might tell him, *he* was the kind of fool who *would* hold it against her, hold it against her that she had turned out to be no different from any of the other women he had known, save one.

That thought, far from clarifying the curiously ambivalent feelings Angel had aroused in him, served only to exacerbate them and his own dissatisfaction with himself for having indulged in them. Nor did it help one bit that he could not forget her disturbing presence in his bed. If there had been any alternative to keeping her in his own quarters, he would not have hesitated to have her removed and placed under the sole supervision of his ship's surgeon. As it was, in a ship full of men, only here could he insure both her safety and her privacy.

Shivering, he became aware that he had been soaked to the skin while he was on deck overseeing the ship and the crew as they weighed anchor in a pelting rain—could it have been a scant thirty minutes ago? he marveled wryly. It seemed like hours since he had returned to discover Chantal bent over the writhing figure of the girl.

Bloody hell! he swore softly to himself, as irritably he stripped, then buffed himself dry with a towel. What did it really matter who or what she was? In a few hours they would anchor off Christchurch, and then he would be rid of her, along with any lingering sense of responsibility he might have felt for her welfare. She would be safe enough in England from the growing unrest across the channel, and any riddles posed by her possible involvement with Chantal could doubtlessly be resolved with or without her continued presence on board his ship.

His mind firmly made up on that score, Locke propped weary shoulders against the heavy frame embracing the stern and, ignoring the fact that he was naked, stretched his legs out before him on the padded bench. Broodingly he stared out the window at the gray bulge of the sea. In the morning he would have the girl settled in an inn somewhere, and by evening, he would find himself being ushered into the presence of the Duke and Duchess of Waincourt for the first time in over seven years. A curiously whimsical smile hovered about the handsome lips. He supposed he would have to primp for the occasion. As little as he cared for the bloody English aristocracy in general, this was one lord and lady whom he would not willingly dishonor.

Feeling the tension ease out of his long frame, the captain let his thoughts drift where they would, and it was not long before he began to succumb to the soporific effects of seven nearly sleepless nights and the ship's steady roll to the swells.

His last conscious thought before sleep finally claimed him was of pleading blue-violet eyes and small hands that clung to him as the girl called Angel begged him not to leave her. Frowning, he resolutely banished the memory, only to lapse, finally, into uneasy slumber, disturbed by dreams of the provocatively beautiful Angel, who had sworn she could have shown him what it was to make love to a Creole woman.

At the stroke of three bells, Locke stirred, instantly awake to the feel and the sounds of his ship. For a moment he lay still, trying to pinpoint what had disturbed his slumber. However, not only had the rainstorm, confined to the coast, given way to clear skies dazzled by a three-quarters moon, but the constant creak of the wooden beams reassured him that all was well, the ship holding steady to the course. Slowly he relaxed. Thus far, it was promising to be a swift and uneventful passage, with nothing to require his presence topside again before dawn.

Sometime in the night the flame in the lantern had gone out, leaving the cabin drenched in moonlight and shadows. All at once he went still as, out of the corner of his eye, he caught a flash of movement. Carefully, he turned his head and for a moment stared in mute surprise at the pale figure that stole noiselessly toward him.

Had he been of a superstitious bent, he should have been taken aback at sight of the girl, swathed in one of his shirts, which was far too big for her, and staring down at him out of eyes that appeared enormous in a face white as death. As it was, he was a great deal more intrigued by what he sensed in her fixed expression—a resoluteness of purpose that held him spellbound as with tantalizing deliberation she untied the drawstring at the neck and let the garment slide off her shoulders and down her slender length.

A pale glint came to his eyes as he beheld her, clean-limbed and beautiful, her hair a tangled mass of curls falling about her back and shoulders to the tiny waist. Unwittingly his breath caught at sight of the small, perfect breasts, the upthrust promise of the nipples.

So, he thought coldly, she was a whore after all.

Then almost immediately the handsome lips curled in cynical amusement. Apparently the gods had decided to be generous. And who was he to question fate? Not that he would actually go so far as to dishonor himself or the girl—whore or not, she was, after all, under his protection, which meant he was bound by his own peculiar code of ethics to do nothing that might encourage her—but before he sent her packing to her bed, he might as well have a small sampling of her wares. If nothing else, he was most damned curious to discover what had made her worth a king's bloody ransom in jewels to her previous lovers. No doubt she must be a blessed angel between the sheets.

Chapter 5

Angelique bolted into wakefulness, her heart pounding, the vision that had come to her as she dreamed the dream of *la prise des yeux* yet vivid in her mind. Her eyes had remained open as the *loa* descended the Path of the Great Tree. She had felt the weight of the god on her shoulders, had heard the whisper of his voice in her ear. Incredibly, the consuming flames had ceased, leaving her wondrously cool and suffused with an odd sense of buoyancy, a curious feeling of peace. And then the vision had come, clearer and more terrifying than any she had known before.

Mon Dieu, she moaned softly, covering her face with her hands as though to shut out the dreadful image of her papa, lying horribly wounded amid the smoldering ruins of La Cime du Bonheur. *Tiens!* She would go mad with the visions of the Pethro gods that tormented and possessed, of Mozambe and that other one, the *tonton macoute,* who had been a stranger to her and who had seemed somehow separate from the dream and yet a part of it still. She shuddered with that memory of the sorcerer, the nearly colorless eyes, his body marked all over with the scars of the most hideous—*Voyons!*—the sound of his voice, chanting frightening things in her ear. But then, *Dieu merci,* the other one had come to save her from him. *Tiens!* How real it had all seemed!

Suddenly her brow knit in a small, puzzled frown as she tried to separate threads of reality from the confused fabric of illusion. She had been so frightened in the dream until the vision had come, the vision of the tall man with the sea-blue eyes that laughed in the face of the sorcerer and banished his evil whisperings from her mind. Yet the powerful arms that had held her with the great gentleness had seemed real, as had the voice telling her not to fear. It had come to her then that so long as she remained in those arms, nothing—no one—could ever harm or frighten her again.

A cry had seemed torn from her heart when they left her, and even now she longed with her whole being to feel them around her again. But it must all have been a dream, like the distant fantasies of a young girl listening to her papa tell the stories of a fearless hero, and the confused threads of memories of an inn and a handsome captain from America. *La vache!* He was of the most *stupide,* she thought, the reckless fool who risked his life for *une cocotte.* Then suddenly she went very still as the reality came flooding back to her.

L'Arbalète had not been a dream. Nor had Babette or the sound of a pistol shot and the blow like a fist in her side that knocked her to the floor. Her hand found the square of lint held in place over her ribs with strips of court plaster. The wound! *Oui,* and it must be very much better, for there was not the great pain that had made her feel sick and weak before, but only a sharp tenderness when she touched it or moved. Then suddenly she blushed hotly, realizing that she was clothed in naught but a man's linen shirt.

Voyons! If it was true, then, all that she remembered, she very much suspected it was Locke's shirt that she wore and Locke who had disrobed her. For had he not borne her in strong arms to a small room in the inn? And when she had been terrified that he would leave her, had he not promised he would stay with her until she was better? She had tried to tell him the truth about who she

80

was, but he would not let her speak. And now she was here on his boat. *Mais oui*, it had to be.

An impish grin tugged at her lips. *Sacriste*, what would Papa say could he see her now? He would roar like the great bull. His face would turn purplish and his neck would bulge. *Hein!* She did not think Captain Locke would laugh at such a sight. And what, she wondered suddenly, had *le capitaine* felt when he beheld her as she had been fashioned by God? An uncomfortable flush spread through her body and limbs at the thought. Then almost immediately the roguish dimple flared. This, she would know soon enough for herself, *non?*

The susurrus of slow, measured breathing whispered through the silvery darkness, the breath of a man submerged in sleep. Her heart suddenly pounding, Angelique threw off the bedcovers and slipped noiselessly from the bed. The captain was there, on the padded bench before the great stern windows. Her breath came hard in her throat as she beheld the lean, masculine body gloriously bathed in moonlight.

Mon Dieu! How beautiful he was, she thought, marveling that she had ever imagined she would find him old and fat, with the big belly like her papa. Sight of the bare chest, with its golden mat of hair, and the long, supple torso, rippled with muscle, aroused strange and unexpected sensations in the pit of her stomach. *Ouïe!* It was true he was no longer a boy. He was all man, this one! She felt her face grow warm with the impure thoughts that crept unbidden into her mind, the desire, like a slow-mounting heat sweeping the length of her body. Then her breath caught at the distant clang of the ship's bell.

As she sensed the man come awake, she could almost hear her heart beat, could almost feel the blood course through her veins. Her mouth went dry as she glimpsed the pale glimmer of his eyes in the moonlight and felt the night charged with an unexpected sense of inevitability.

Hein! she thought, running her tongue over suddenly parched lips. What was it about this man that made her

81

stupid and weak? The things he had said to his friend at the inn—*voyons*, the things he had said to herself—should have been enough to warn her away from him. What did it matter that he had treated her wound and in a dream had even saved her? She did not fool herself into thinking she could be anything more to him than a woman no different from any other wmoan, a thing—a *whore*—to be used and instantly forgotten. He had the heart of stone, and still would she go to him.

She knew it as well as she knew that no good could come from it. With him there would be no turning back, no going halfway. He would take everything she had to give and leave her with nothing if ever she were fool enough to love him. *Et ce fut là le diable*, she mused ruefully: there was the rub. The Capitaine Locke was a man whom women could not stop themselves from loving, for though his heart might be cold, in his hands there was both gentleness and strength, and in his eyes, the laughter that hid pain. What woman would not sense these things and know, too, that one of her sex must have made him as he was? From the beginning it must have been this which had drawn her to him, the danger in him, and the recklessness—and *oui*, the sense of aloneness in him not unlike her own. It drew her now. She was in truth like the stupid moth who did not know enough to stay away from the flame.

Then all at once a reckless gleam came to her eyes. Very well, she told herself, if that was the way it must be, then it would be so. She would have the moment of passion and it would be enough. She would show him that to be made love to by a Creole woman was a thing never to be forgotten. Willing her limbs to cease their trembling, Angelique stole toward the unsuspecting Locke.

It was very odd. She had the sensation of one dreaming of being awake, and yet as she drew near to him and came to a halt, she was perfectly aware that the long, lithe form on the bench was no mere figment of her imagination. Suddenly her heart nearly failed her as she realized that he had turned and was looking at her with eyes obscured in shadow. Somewhere within the recesses of her brain, a small voice clamored a warning. But that thing inside herself, the wildness, perhaps, or the bleak sense of aloneness that she had carried with her for so long, firmly banished it. She knew only that her whole being cried out to have him touch her, to feel the comforting strength of his arms around her, and that it was for this that she had not told him the truth about herself. *Alors!* It was surely for this that she had had the vision. Something inside of her had been trying to tell her that it was meant that she should lie with him, if only for this once.

Unashamedly, she slipped the shirt off her shoulders and let it slide slowly down her arms.

The sound of Locke's sharply indrawn breath went to Angelique's head like wine. Perhaps the captain did not think she was a child after all, she thought, experiencing a momentary sense of triumph. Which was a very good thing, because otherwise it was doubtful she could have found the courage to go on in the face of his unnerving silence. In fact, it was painfully obvious the captain meant to do nothing to make things any easier for her, she realized, noting the ironic expression on his lean features. It came to her then that he was waiting to see what she would do. *Hein!* Maybe the wretch did not think she would go through with it or maybe he thought she was not enough the woman for him!

Such a thought lent sudden sparks to her eyes. Very well, *M'sieu le Capitaine*, she firmly told herself. Was she not French Creole? She would find the way to make his blood burn with the desire.

Her heart was nevertheless in her throat as with sensuous deliberation she lowered herself to the bench beside Locke, one leg folded beneath her, and slowly ran her fingers through the mat of hair on his chest. At the involuntary leap of muscle beneath her touch, the roguish dimple peeped out at the corner of her mouth. So, he was not so much the man of steel as he would wish

83

to appear, she thought, taking perverse delight in exploring the fascinating length of his torso with hands that teased and tormented.

Tiens! He was magnificent! Not big and bulging like the peasant she had once seen lift the great boulder single-handedly from the road, but supple and lean, with the sinewy strength of a warrior who would move with the great quickness and agility.

Thrillingly, she was aware that she was in truth playing with fire, but the knowledge, rather than intimidating her, only made her all the more daring. Lowering her head, she pressed her lips to the pulse that throbbed at the base of his throat. A soft thrill went through her as she felt the powerful frame tense. Then, losing herself in the heady game, she began a slow, titillating journey, tasting and savoring with her tongue and the moist softness of her lips the delicious maleness of him—the powerful chest, the nipple, masculine and intriguingly rigid, *voyons*, the muscled ridges of the abdomen! When, finally, she came to the lean, narrow waist, her breath had quickened and she felt feverish with the unfamiliar flood of sensations sweeping her body. Her blood pulsed with flame as she beheld his member, swollen and erect, seeming to sprout from the curling mass of hair on his groin. Forgetting herself, forgetting everything but the overpowering yearnings that drove her, she bent to him.

"Enough!"

It was as if the harsh expulsion of the captain's breath unleashed all the savage fury of a storm. A cry was torn from her as ruthless fingers clamped brutally in her hair and dragged her, unresisting, up against an unrelenting chest. For an instant she thought she must swoon as she stared entranced into his eyes, like piercing points of flame between slitted eyelids. Then, "Witch!" he growled, and, clasping steely fingers in her hair, he drew her mercilessly to him.

His mouth closed cruelly over hers, punishing and arousing her with a ruthlessness that ravaged her

84

innocence, even as it set her body aflame with desire. Terrified at what she had unloosed, she silently fought him. To no avail. She was not proof against his strength or the swelling tide of sensations welling up inside her.

His kiss tormented and abused the soft tenderness of her lips, until at last they parted. Instantly his tongue entered her mouth, probed in hard, quick thrusts the moist, sensitive depths. Feeling the shuddering response of her supple strength melding to his, he subtly altered his caress to a slow, sensuous searching that melted the last of her defiance. A groan welled upwards from her belly as she pressed against him with terrible desire, mindless and unbridled, a sweltering heat that seared the length of her body. As of their own accord her arms entwined about his neck and feverishly clung.

A sigh burst from her lips when at last his mouth released hers to explore the tantalizing sweetness of her breasts. She thought she must die as with his tongue he teased and caressed and then, molding his lips to the pink thrust of her nipple, he sucked, first one and then the other. And all the while, his hands wove delirious trails of rapture over her hips and thighs, drove her mad with some as yet unrealized yearning as they searched out and discovered the secret places of arousal along the exquisitely sensitive curve of her back. Then at last he sought the swelling bud of her greatest desire. Uttering sigh after sigh, she writhed as a sensuous thrill of pleasure ripped through her belly. In anguish she arched above him, her breath coming in ragged gusts, as, feverish with desire, she willed him to enter her.

Locke's own breath came harsh and uneven in his throat as he beheld her, supple and beautiful, her head flung back as she responded to his practiced lovemaking with a wild, sweet abandon. She was an angel, pure fire and passion, a sensuous creature of sinuous grace and subtle power molded into delectably soft feminine curves and valleys. And she was a demon, tantalizingly lovely, arousing him to a feverish pitch of desire in a manner that made all other women pale in comparison.

He had had perhaps more than his share of women, but not since his very first had he known one who so thoroughly excited his senses or filled him with mindless, uncontrollable lust, and never one who aroused such savage want that all else was driven from his mind but the desire to conquer and possess. The pleading in her eyes, the unbearable need in the fingers that clutched at his shoulders, fed his own sweet ecstasy of desire. He could feel the muscles of his neck and back corded with the effort to prolong the moment till at last he should release them both from their exquisite torment. Summoning every ounce of an iron will, he fought to control his need, the fiery ache in his loins to plunge deep into woman's warm, living flesh. But at last he could bear it no longer. Spanning her waist between strong hands, he lifted the wondrously lithe body on top of him.

Needing him now with a seemingly insatiable ache that filled her whole body, Angelique eagerly parted her thighs to him. Her breath caught in her throat as unerringly he guided her to the pinnacle of his desire. Her hands braced against the powerful shoulders, she waited, willed him to end her anguish, and still he held her off, savoring the musky scent of her arousal, the soft suppleness of her, poised, quivering with anticipation, above him. A low groan left her lips as his hard manhood pressed tantalizingly upwards against her swollen orifice. In agony, she writhed within the merciless clasp of those hands that kept her from him, in bitter torment dug her fingernails into the muscular shoulders. A strangled plea broke from her depths.

"Capitaine, I beg you!"

Then at last did he force her down upon him. Brutal with his own insupportable need, he thrust deep within her.

Her agonized cry as he plunged through the virginal membrane sliced like a knife through his heart. Savagely he cursed, made suddenly bitter with realization. Then

86

instinctively she was moving, carrying them both on a swelling tide of passion which he was powerless to stop. Pitilessly he moved with her, punishing her with every thrust of his hardened member, until the greater ecstasy of their combined striving for completion blotted out everything but the cresting pinnacle of desire. With an explosive groan he spilled his seed into her, felt the shuddering burst of her own rapturous release, followed by sigh after sigh as succeeding waves of pleasure rippled through her body. At last, trembling and weak, she sank down on top of him, her face hidden in the curve of his neck.

Grimly he waited for his own heart to cease its fierce pounding, while his mind grappled with the terrible reality of what he had done. What a fool he had been not to trust in his own instincts! Unwittingly, he had ravished an innocent and one, moreover, whom he himself had placed under his protection. It didn't matter that *she* had come to *him,* an angel of seduction, and had woven her sensuous spell over him. He was neither inexperienced nor naive. He should have been able to control both his body and his emotions. That he had not was mute evidence of the tempest she had unloosed in him with her cursed silken touch. Good God! She had even fought him, silently with her fists and her body, but her defiance had only whetted his lust, and, believing her a whore, he had ignored the tumult in her eyes, had thought the resistance in the supple frame only a Cyprian's ploy to excite him. And, Christ, how it had, incensing him beyond rationality as nothing else ever had before.

But not even that could compare with the exquisite madness her capitulation had aroused. She had given in to him with a sweet, wild abandon that even yet was like intoxicating wine to his senses. Who in God's name was she? She was no whore, he had irrevocably proven that. Nor, in spite of the seductive aura that enveloped her every movement and expression, the promise that seemed to lurk in those cursed beautiful eyes, could he believe her either low-born or wanton. He had yet to discover why she had done what she did—perhaps, motivated by a misguided sense of gratitude, she had thought to repay him for taking her in and caring for her wound, or maybe she foolishly thought she was adhering to the terms of the bargain she had offered at the inn—or perhaps, and suddenly his eyes gleamed with a dangerous glint, she had *meant* from the very first to entrap him.

Whatever her rationale had been, the fact remained that everything that had come—after she had so foolishly presented herself to him like some prize package he had neither asked for nor wanted—had been born of instinct rather than knowledge. And therein lay the true marvel of what she had wrought and perhaps the real secret of her allure. Not since his extreme youth had he consorted with a female of untaught innocence; one, moreover, who responded as nature had intended, without the inhibitions that were to be expected of a proper young miss.

That thought brought a wry grimace to Locke's grim face. Whoever or whatever she was, he was honor bound to make it right with her. On the morrow when he disembarked at Poole, leaving Fisk in charge of the ship during his brief sojourn in Hampstead, the girl would go with them. No doubt Waincourt carried enough influence to make possible a hurried ceremony. And, if nothing else, his dearest Sabra would be delighted to lend a hand in his legshackling, he reflected sardonically. She had, after all, been bedeviling him for years to marry. Christ, he had forgotten about Gilbert and his blasted offspring! Obviously, that was one promise he would be unable to keep, he thought with a wry grimace. He was now irrevocably committed to an Angel of seduction, one whom he meant to punish with great relish for her duplicity.

Angelique, unaware that her future had thus been firmly settled, in Locke's mind at any rate, lay dreamily listening to the strong beat of his heart beneath her cheek. He was very marvellous, her capitaine. As was this lovemaking, which left her feeling sated and wondrously languid. Like the great lizard made torpid from drinking in too much of the sun, she mused with a smile that was half-whimsical and a trifle off-center.

Often she had wondered how it was between a woman and a man. Never had she thought it would be like this! The capitaine had made her to burn all over with the fever that inflames the brain and fills the body and soul with *la grande angoisse*. It was the great anguish, that yearning of the most terrible for something, some final, magnificent end which only he could grant and which maddeningly he had kept from her until at last she had been made to beg for his mercy. And then, when it seemed the swelling ache could not be borne even one second more, to feel the man plunge into her swollen flesh!

Ouïe, such pain as she had suffered as he had ripped through her maidenhead with the so savage fury! And stilll the pain had been nothing to the fire that had yet burned, the flame that his touch had aroused and that his flesh within hers had only kindled to an ever greater need. It was as if the capitaine had unleashed something she had never known existed within her, a fierce storm of desire, like the hurricane that sweeps over the sea, and gloriously she had given herself to its fury, to the man thrusting deep inside, again and again. *Per Dieu!* She thought she must swoon as she had felt him spill forth his seed inside of her, and then suddenly to burst within and feel one's self melting in blissful shudders of release. It was like dying the great death, *cette grande passion!*

She was filled with the wonder of it all, and with a poignant grief that it had had ever to come to an end. *Voyons!* What a child she had been to think that she could be satisfied to lie with this man only once. Never would there be another who could make her burn with such passion, or make her ache for a man with such tenderness. In her heart, she knew this, just as she knew that she would always carry the memory of this night with her. Never would she be free of the terrible yearning to feel his arms around her, to know the savage flames of desire, the fierce burning that only he could arouse, and the glorious peak of rapture that he alone could give her. With his touch he had inflamed her and from this night on had forever enslaved her to the passion that was theirs alone.

A wave of tenderness swept over her as she listened to his slow, regular breathing and realized he must have fallen asleep. *Hélas!* It was very cruel, this fate which would bind her to him. Even now, she ached with the thought that inevitably they must be parted. How would she bear ever to go on without him? But even more, she did not know how she would face him on the morrow, perhaps to see the coldness in his eyes when he looked at her, the indifference of a man to whom one woman was the same as every other.

Suddenly she shivered, touched by the chill in the air. *Voyons*, it would be better if she slipped away now before he awakened, better to cover her nakedness from his eyes, lest he see too much that was in her heart.

Holding her breath, she pushed herself up and experienced a sharp pang of regret as she felt his now flaccid member slip free of her body. Carefully she eased her weight off him and turned to look for her discarded garment, which lay in a heap on the floor. Kneeling, she gathered it to her breast, then rose and turned once more to look on the face of the one who had taught her what it was to be made love to by a man.

Her breath caught suddenly hard in her throat as she discovered him watching her with the eyes that turned her heart cold.

Unwittingly she drew back.

"What is it, Angel?" he queried softly. "Has it only now occurred to you that we've yet to agree on the terms for your services? Just out of curiosity, how much do you intend to demand for tonight's dubious pleasures?"

Hurt by his sarcasm, Angelique bit her tongue to keep from lashing out at him in anger. *Sacriste,* what had she expected—that he should melt with tenderness for her? He believed her a whore. She must be of the most careful not to disappoint him.

Never in a thousand years would he guess what it cost her to summon the coquette's small, tantalizing smile.

"I do not understand, *mon Capitaine,*" she replied, with magnificently feigned innocence. "You wish to pay for what I would give freely?"

His sardonic bark of laughter shattered the last of her illusions.

"You laugh. Why?" she demanded, impaling him with huge flashing eyes. "You think it is amusing, what I have said?" Bitterly she lowered her hands, which still clutched the man's shirt, and flung back her hair so that nothing should be concealed from the steely glint of his gaze. "You have found me satisfactory, *oui?*" Radiating youthful pride in every delectable inch of her body, she dared him to deny it.

Locke smiled coldly, cynically amused. Hell, "satisfactory" did not begin to describe what she had been.

"If it's flattery you want," he said instead, the searing intensity of his gaze curiously at odds with the chiseled hardness of his face, "then I'm afraid you have a great deal to learn about your chosen profession. A man expects to have to woo a respectable woman. But a whore, he pays *not* to have to waste time in small talk. For my money, I prefer the latter."

Angelique stifled a gasp of outrage.

"And me, I would have a man of passion," she flung contemptuously back at him. *Tiens!* He was of the most disagreeable, *ce capitaine,* she fumed, but the odious Locke was to prove more disagreeable still.

"Brava, Angel," he applauded. "Your performance is nearly flawless. You almost make me believe I've misjudged you yet again. Unfortunately, now there

91

would seem to be incontrovertible proof to the contrary, wouldn't there."

The mocking eyes raked over her with deliberate insolence. Angelique, suddenly and excruciatingly aware of her nakedness, hastily averted her face to hide the hot rush of blood to her cheeks. *Sacriste!* She must have been mad to let a foolish dream rule her head. In truth, she would rather feel the cold touch of the serpent on her body than the loathsome eyes of this captain who had no heart!

Obviously she had been delirious with fever to think Locke was anything but cruel and unfeeling. He was playing with her, the way the cat plays with the mouse. But never would she give him the satisfaction of knowing he had shamed her! Proudly, her head came up to reveal magnificent flashing eyes. Angelique Eugenie Gilbert would crawl before no man, least of all this one. Rather would she die first!

"Very well, m'sieu," she rejoined coldly. "You want the business arrangement, the pleasure for money, without complications. *C'est bien.* We make the deal now, *oui?* You tell me what you think it is worth, the pleasures I have given you."

Something flickered in his face, like surprise or a vague sense of disgust, but whether with her or himself, she could not be sure. Then just as quickly it was gone, leaving Angelique uncertain as to what she had seen or if, indeed, she had seen anything. There was, however, no mistaking the mockery in his reply, couched in accents heavy with irony.

"I've been known to be generous on occasion, but for what you have given me this night not even a shipload of gold bullion will suffice, will it, my love?"

"You think I would ask so much?" she retorted, eyeing him uncertainly. *Hein,* he talked in the riddles she could not understand. "I am not so greedy, I think, m'sieu."

A look of boredom passed over the lean countenance. "Greed is what the world turns on, isn't it? What are you

92

waiting for? Ask anything you want. You may be sure I'll grant it if it lies within my power to. But then, you already knew that when you placed yourself at my convenience, didn't you, my sweet, conniving Angel?"

Le diable! Le goujat misérable! La vache! She could not think of a name bad enough to call him. How could a man of his years know so little about the heart of a woman?

"You think you know so much," she flashed back at him, no longer caring what he thought of her, "but you are of the most *stupide*. It was not for gold that I have lain with you."

"No, not for gold," he agreed in a voice of velvet-edged steel. "Still, no one, least of all a woman, gives anything away without expecting something back in return. Let's see, what could you possibly consider just compensation? Not jewels. You already have a small fortune in those. And somehow I don't think it's this shipload of goods."

"But no, I want none of these things! I tell you I wish nothing from you except that you will leave me alone!"

"Leave you alone?" His abrupt laugh was like salt to her already raw nerves.

"It is enough!" she cried, driven nearly to distraction. "What is it you want from me?"

"The truth, my deceiving little Angel."

"Oh, *la vache!* I wish you will stop saying that! Why do you insist on calling me your angel?"

She did not see the sudden gleam of interest in the look he gave her then. She was trembling all over with cold and the terrible pain in her head. She hardly knew when he abruptly rose from the bench and crossed to her in a single swift stride. A strangled cry burst from her lips as without warning he swept her up in his arms.

"I call you that because you told me it was your name," he said, his eyes boring holes through her as he carried her to bed. Laying her down, he covered her nakedness with a blanket, then provocatively he leaned over her. "Or was that a lie, too, my love?" he queried in tones that made the blood rush, hot, to her cheeks.

Hastily, she glanced away.

"Of course not," she stammered, wishing he would stop looking at her in such a way as to freeze her soul. "I *am* called Angel. It is only that you confuse me. I do not understand always the English, you see."

"No, but you understand well enough what happens when a woman—a *virgin*—tricks a man into making love to her." At these words, Angelique went white as death with sudden terrible comprehension. *Hein!* The fool thought she had lain with him to trick him into marrying her! "Yes," murmured Locke, apparently satisfied, "I can see by the look in your eyes that you do. And I've got to hand it to you, Angel—or whatever your name is—I've been hunted by the best, but you topped them all."

At the utter contempt in his voice and manner, something snapped inside. In fury, her hand shot out to slap the hateful face. Locke was the quicker. Angelique gasped as he caught her wrist in a merciless grip. In truth this was no dream, she thought. Then she forgot everything but the need to lash out at him to assuage her humiliation and anger.

"Bah!" she exploded. "You think you are the big man. Peu! You are less than nothing, a coward. In your heart you are afraid to let yourself feel anything, and so you think everyone else must be like you. But for myself, I am of the most sorry for you because I know you hide behind the laughing eyes nothing but a very great emptiness." The terrible flash of those very same eyes made her quail inside, but pride made her go on in the face of his withering anger. "You, *M'sieu le Capitaine*," she said scornfully, "are afraid of *me* because in truth I want nothing!"

"Nothing?" he queried in a voice that sent shivers down her spine. She could not keep herself from wincing at the touch of his hand to her cheek. Provocatively he ran his fingers down the side of her neck to the shoulder, until coming at last to the crescent-shaped scar, he stopped and looked at her with eyes that somehow hurt

94

her. "Not even a name to make an honest woman of you? Or, to be more precise, *my* name, perhaps to take the place of the one that was never really yours?"

Angelique's eyes widened in horrified disbelief. *Hein!* He *could* not know the secret that tormented her! And yet her heart cried out for her to deny it, to shout that it was all a lie.

"You are mad," she whispered hoarsely.

"Mad? I must have been to let myself be drawn into your cunning net of lies. But I think I begin to see things very clearly now." A strange glint came to his eyes, and for a moment he seemed to be looking through her rather than at her. "Believe me, there are worse things than being a bastard," he said, more to himself than to her, she thought. Then suddenly he appeared to shake off whatever mood had momentarily laid hold of him as the old mocking smile curled his lips. "But then, it would naturally be harder on an unprotected female, especially one who was both young and beautiful. At any rate, it hardly matters now, one way or the other, does it."

In stunned disbelief she watched him turn away and brusquely pull on his breeches and boots. Then flinging on his shirt, he strode swiftly toward the exit as if he could not get away from her soon enough. But unexpectedly he paused, his hand on the door.

"We disembark at first light," he said, glancing briefly over his shoulder at her, "and as soon as the arrangements can be made, we will be married. I suggest you get what sleep you can—now, before the day is upon us."

In a single swift movement, he turned and left her, and only then did her tongue find release.

"I will never marry you!" she cried after him. "Do you hear, Capitaine?"

With a strangled sob, she collapsed against the pillow, the back of a knotted fist pressed convulsively to her mouth.

"Que Dieu me juge! I can never marry *anyone!"*

Chapter 6

Angelique did not know how long she lay staring
listlessly at the beams overhead before at last she dragged
herself from the bed and, wrapped in the bedsheet, began
to prowl fitfully about the small cabin. Her thoughts were
far from cheerful as she contemplated her immediate
future. *Le capitaine* had said they would disembark at
first light and as soon as he could arrange it, they would
be married. *Hein!* He had not even made it a proposal, but
an order, as if she were one of his sailors who must obey
him without question.

Angelique's eyes flashed blue-violet sparks at the
memory of his arrogance. But almost immediately a bleak
look replaced their angry sparkle. It was her fault she was
in this terrible mess, for in truth she had been a child not
to realize he would discover the moment he entered her
that she had never before lain with a man. But then, *had*
she realized it, it was doubtful that she would have
thought it all that important. How was she to know he
would consider himself honor bound to marry her? He
had believed her a bastard, and in Saint Dominique such
girls became mistresses, not wives.

Alas, there was so very much that she did not know!
After all, these matters concerning lovers were hardly
things one would choose to discuss with *Les Pauvres
Clares*. A naughty dimple flashed briefly at the thought of

Sister Thérèse trying to explain any such thing. It was absurd, such a notion. But what had come of this night's folly was not. She very much feared she had landed herself in the big kettle of fish. *Voyons!* How she wished her *maman* had not been taken from her before she was old enough to understand what it was to be a woman. Never had she dreamed such things could become so complicated.

Oh, *why* had she not told Captain Locke the truth about herself from the very beginning? she groaned and knew instantly that she was only trying to fool herself. In truth, if she had it all to do over again, she would have done everything the same. Whatever else came of it, she could not regret having experienced *la grande passion*. Instinctively she knew it was a gift, this thing that had flared like the great fire between them, a precious thing of the body and the soul, which was given to very few to know.

Then why, whispered a small, insidious voice, do you not accept what fate has offered, Angelique Gilbert? Would it be so very wrong to marry this capitaine who with a look could hold her spellbound, with a touch could arouse the fiery passion of her soul? Had he not come to her in a vision, this man with the laughing blue eyes, and in her dream saved her from the *tonton macoute* who had thought to enslave her spirit with the sorcery of the most evil? Perhaps it was meant that he should take her far away from Mozambe and all the doubts to which the priestess's hushed words at Port-au-Prince had given birth. After all, if they never reached the ears of *le capitaine*, what did Mozambe's malevolent whisperings matter? They might be nothing more than the ravings of a mind that had been twisted by bitterness and hate. And if there was some grain of truth in them—so what? Who would know? Soon there might be no one left on Saint Dominique who would even remember the daughter of Herman and Eugenie Gilbert, let alone care what had happened to her.

Feeling the subtle coils of temptation slowly tightening their hold on her, Angelique writhed on the bench. How clearly she seemed to envision the happiness that might be hers if only she were to give in to it. To escape the terrible throes of revolution that threatened to shake the very foundations of Saint Dominique! To be free of the dread secret that weighed upon her soul! To be free of the curse of Mozambe! These alone were enough to weaken her resolve and seduce her will. But to be wife to this man who already had enslaved her heart, this was asking too much of the beneficence of God.

No sooner was that thought formulated, than Angelique suddenly froze. *Mon Dieu,* what foolishness was this? She could not *wish* to be wed to Wesley Locke! *Voyons!* They did not even like one another, she told herself, and knew at once that it was a lie. If circumstances had been different, if her past were not tainted with the terrible uncertainty, if she had not told him the great untruth about herself, the lie that could never be taken back and must consequently stand between them like an invisible stone barrier, she could have liked *le capitaine* very well. In truth, he was everything she had dreamed of in a man—strong, handsome, and virile, and yet intelligent as well, a man to whom others would look to lead them, a man to make a woman *feel* like a woman.

From the first she had sensed these things in him. And also those other things that set her back up and made her temper flare—the arrogance in him, and the irony, the cutting edge of his humor—*Sacriste!*—the hardness beneath the laughter, which encased his heart like armor and kept everyone away. If she forced such a one to wed her, it would not be happiness that she could expect, but only the bitterness and endless strife. No, only a fool could believe a man like this one would ever forgive a woman for having trapped him. And only a coward would choose to flee from discovering the truth about her past. Because Angelique was neither of these, she knew she could not wed Captain Locke—not like this, in shame and dishonor. In truth, how would she ever face her beloved papa again if she repaid the debt to *ce capitaine* in such a manner?

What a pity! In her heart she knew that, if Angelique Eugenie Gilbert had met him first, she might have tamed this difficult man and in time perhaps even brought him to love her. But, alas! Angele the Nobody could only in the end drive him irrevocably away.

So be it! she thought, lifting her head in bitter defiance. It was better this way. She must make the capitaine understand that she could never be brought of her own accord to marry him. *Sacriste!* It would not be easy. He was a man used to having his own way. In truth, she could not see how it was to be done unless somehow she convinced him that she alone was to blame for what had happened between them. And to do that she must make him believe she was one who was unworthy of his sacrifice.

How slowly the hours seemed to creep by as she went over and over in her mind what she would say and do when the capitaine returned for her. She would present to him the cool facade of a woman who could not care less what he thought of her, a woman to whom the moment of passion was but a small diversion that meant nothing. She would laugh and flutter her eyelashes at him in the shameless manner of *les jeunesses,* the girls who lived only for the good time, and she would tell him she had no wish to be tied to any man, least of all to one for whom she could never feel anything but the very great indifference. And only she would know it was all a lie! she thought. That is, if her unruly heart did not betray her!

Weary of her thoughts and determined to make herself up to look the part she had chosen, Angelique carried her battered valise to the bed and threw it open. A wry gleam came to her eyes as it came to her that *le capitaine* had taken the very great pains to put everything back as he found it. Never would she have known he had searched her things had he not pointedly mentioned her small fortune in jewels. Then all at once the roguish dimple peeped out at the corner of her mouth. What must he have thought when he discovered the gowns made up by some of the finest *couturières* in Paris? And, then, to find the jewels that had belonged to her *maman!* These were hardly the possessions of a girl forced to offer herself in trade for passage to the West Indies. He must have been greatly perplexed to explain these inconsistencies.

Still smiling to herself, Angelique pulled one of the gowns from the valise and shook out the delicate folds of pale blue sarcenet. Calling for neither hoops nor panniers, it was a daringly simple creation of the kind worn only by the most avant-garde of Paris. *Mais oui,* she mused, clasping the lovely thing to her breast. This should do nicely.

Sometime later, Angelique twisted and turned, trying to see herself in the capitaine's small looking glass. It would do, she thought to herself. The gown, draped in the lastest Parisian fashion from a high, belted waist to a short train at the back, served to emphasize her slender build. This, along with her hair caught up high on top of her head and allowed to cascade down her back in a riot of loose curls, made her appear taller. A frown creased her forehead as it came to her that the locket of unadorned gold, which graced her neck, might be better suited to an innocent young girl than to a woman of the world. But immediately she discarded the notion of exchanging it for one of the more ornate pieces. She had chosen it in the hopes that the likeness of her *maman* next to her heart would give her courage, and not for all the world would she change it now.

A hand fluttered to the soft swell of her breasts above the daring décolletage. *Per Dieu!* With little more than the single thin petticoat and silk stockings beneath the feathery light fabric, she felt almost naked, and in truth, the clinging skirt did little to conceal the supple curves of her body. But this was only as it should be for a woman of the easy virtue, she bitterly reminded herself, and let her hand drop to her side. With a sigh, she sank onto the padded seat and stared blindly out the stern window, her thoughts turning again to the dreaded interview with the captain.

How easy it was, alone within the gloomy confines of her small prison, to think of the manner in which she would refuse him. But when at last the ship rounded a jutting arm of land to enter a wide, pleasant harbor, rising slowly to gentle hills, she experienced a swift surge of panic. Soon now he would come! she told herself and felt her whole body taut with the waiting for the sound of footsteps beyond the door. But there was only the shouting and the great bustle of activity from the decks above as the ship made anchor. After a time, Angelique rested her chin wearily on her knees folded to her chest and looked out on the small village fronted by fishing boats and graced by the sweeping towers of an old Norman castle.

Vaguely she wondered what place they had come to as she stared at the thatch-roofed houses with their walls of stone shimmering whitely in the morning sun. How very English were the clipped hedges and neat gardens, she mused whimsically, and the strands of ivy embracing the mullioned windows. An odd little pang invaded her breastbone as she found herself imagining herself in such a house filled with the prattle of children, imagining herself enveloped by the love of a strong man with the laughing blue eyes. But immediately she caught herself.

Voyons! she swore. Coming abruptly to her feet, she turned her back on the scene from the window. She was the fool to let herself think such thoughts. Those things were not meant for her. Oh, if only she would not feel this terrible queasiness in the pit of her stomach, like a hand clenched about her vitals as she waited for Locke to come!

The brisk rap on the door caught her unawares. Sharply she turned, her pulse leaping madly.

"Yes?" she called breathlessly. "Who is it? What do

you want?"

"It's Gideon Fisk," came the reply, couched in a pleasing Yankee drawl. "Wes sent me, Angel. To fetch you."

Initial disappointment, mingled with relief, gave way irrationally to a sudden spark of anger. So, *le capitaine* was too much the coward to come himself, she fumed. He must send someone to do his dirty work. Very well. Maybe she could make of this Fisk an ally. If all else failed, she would have no choice but to simply slip away, hopefully to find passage on an English ship bound for the West Indies, and in this she might have need of help.

"One moment," she answered, her mind made up to feel out this friend of the captain. Reaching for a kerseymere shawl slung carelessly across the foot of the bed, she draped it hastily about her shoulders before taking a deep breath to steady the flutter of her nerves. "Very well, m'sieu. You may come in now," she said, careful to school her features to reveal nothing of the tumult within.

Gideon Fisk, more than half-sober for the first time in longer than he cared to remember, stopped short at sight of the slender girl regarding him watchfully from the far side of the cabin. A low whistle breathed through his lips. Limned against the stern windows, the sunlight forming a halo about her, she appeared a veritable angel of loveliness.

"Egads," he declared, observing her with frank admiration, "who'd have thought fancy clothes and a little scrubbing would make such a difference! Angel, you fair take a man's breath away."

Startled imps of amusement leaped in the beautiful eyes at such praise. Deciding she liked this unaffected rogue very well, Angelique dropped, laughing, into a curtsey.

"*Merci beaucoup, m'sieu,*" she gurgled, bedazzling him with her smile. "You are of the most kind, I think."

An answering grin tugged at the rogue's lips.

"And you, I think, are not what you've made yourself out to be," he shrewdly countered. "No wonder Wes has been so damned keen to keep you under wraps. If the lads got a peek at you in that get-up, he'd not get a lick of work out of 'em. Who in thunderation are you, Angel? And what the devil were you doing in that cursed inn decked out like a rag-vendor's daughter?"

Little liking the turn the conversation had taken, Angelique favored him with a vague flutter of the hand.

"But I do not understand you, m'sieu," she murmured. Lowering the thick veil of her eyelashes, she gazed provocatively up at him out of the corners of her eyes. "You make the mountain out of the molehill, *non?* I am Angele, the Nobody. Can we not leave it that way?"

A reluctant bark of laughter greeted that sally.

"Hell, Angel, it don't matter to me what game you're playing. I reckon it's Wes's headache. And somehow I begin to think that when he met up with you, he may have taken on more than even he can handle. It might be you'll even be the making of him."

Angelique gazed doubtfully at the grinning rogue.

"'The making of him'?" she queried, suspecting he was poking fun at her. "You will explain this to me, please."

Enjoying himself hugely, Fisk crossed in a leisurely manner to a carved wine chest and availed himself of the captain's private stock of brandy.

"It's simple enough," he said as he poured them each a generous libation. Turning, he handed a crystal goblet to Angelique, who, afraid he might think her a mere child if she refused, hesitantly accepted it. Fisk smiled his approval before sprawling on the stern bench with the air of a man who owned the place. "I think you'll agree that our Captain Locke is no ordinary man. In fact, I expect he'd just naturally stand out pretty much in any crowd. It's not just his looks, either, though I'm not denying he's been uncommonly blessed in that respect. It's more like he's got an air about him."

"An 'air,' m'sieu?" queried Angelique, noting with

interest the subtle alteration in Fisk's mood from one of levity to a seriousness not at all in keeping with his usual insouciance. "I am afraid I do not understand you."

As if made uncomfortably aware all at once that he had allowed himself to drift out of character, Fisk let out a rueful bark of laughter.

"No, I don't suppose you do," he answered, seeming to derive some sort of ironic amusement from her puzzlement, "you being a woman and all. Let me put it this way: A man looks at Locke and knows a real man when he sees one. Generally he doesn't look any farther because that's all he needs to know. But a woman, on the other hand. She looks at Locke and suddenly she doesn't know which end is up. She's got to find out what makes him tick. It's the 'air' he's got about him, like a puzzle that can't be solved, but she's got to try. The funny thing is he don't even realize he's got it. If you tried to tell him what it was that draws women to him like bees to honey, he'd likely laugh in your face."

"*Mais oui,*" agreed Angelique with a brittle smile. "He would say it was the gold that draws them."

Fisk laughed and toasted her with his glass.

"I see you have already learned a great deal about our man."

"I am neither the fool nor the idiot," Angelique retorted, giving a small toss of her raven curls. "I am well able to see these things for myself. So. What *is* it that gives your capitaine this 'air' of which you speak? Something from his past, perhaps? A woman who breaks his heart? The love which proves false?"

She must have sounded a little *too* casual. Fisk's grin made her blush in anger at herself.

"Neither and both." He shrugged. "But that's beside the point. The thing is that you're the first female who shows some sign of being able to give friend Wes a run for his money. Not that I don't see you giving in to him in the end, but it would seem to me you've already managed to do something no other woman has before."

105

"Truly? And what is this great thing which I have accomplished?"

"You made him mad as hell! Egad, you should've seen his face when he came on deck! He's got everyone on board shivering in their boots. Not a man among them'd dare so much as look crossways at him."

Seeing little cause for rejoicing in this description of Locke's present mood, Angelique's heart sank. Fisk, however, had obviously derived immense enjoyment from it. In truth, he wore the distinct expression of a man inordinately pleased with both her and himself.

"Bah! What do I care if he is angry?" she demanded heatedly, apparently having forgotten that she had spent the past several hours plotting how to evoke just such a reaction from the troublesome captain. "He is overbearing and mean, a man who knows only to bully and give orders. He has no heart, *ce capitaine!* And you think it should matter to me that he goes raging like the bull from this cabin? I am sorry, m'sieu, if you have been made to suffer because he is in the ill-humor, but for myself, I am glad of it!"

"Hell, you'd be a fool if you weren't," chortled the rogue, grinning from ear to ear. "Good God, Angel. Don't you have the least inkling of what you've done? You've managed to jolt Captain Wesley Locke, the man noted for his cool head and iron nerve, out of his bloody indifference. That's no mean feat, let me tell you."

Angelique gazed doubtfully at the beaming Fisk.

"You are making of me the fun, *non?*" she queried, frowning.

"Hell no, Angel. I wouldn't hoax you about a thing like this. I'm trying to tell you you might just be the one to save Captain Wesley Locke!"

In spite of herself, Angelique's heart skipped a beat, but immediately she caught herself. Have a care, Angelique! she chided herself. There was no way of knowing if this Fisk was a man to be trusted. It would be better to pretend the very great indifference.

"Save him?" she demanded haughtily. "By all means. But you will pardon me if I do not see how I can be of any help. *Le Capitaine* Locke is a man who needs no one. Perhaps you forget I saw him in L'Arbalète. If ever there is some kind of danger, he can take care of himself, I think."

"Well, and who said he couldn't? He's yet to meet his match in a fight," declared Fisk expansively. "The thing is, it's himself he needs saving from."

At her look of incredulity, Fisk grinned and polished off his brandy. Then rising, he sauntered to the wine cabinet and reached once more for the decanter. "You haven't touched your drink, Angel," he observed sapiently, sloshing two fingers in his glass. "It'd be a shame to waste good liquor. 'Course, if you're not used to it, it can pack a powerful jolt. Might be, you'd like something more suited to a lady."

Angelique, who had never imbibed anything stronger than the diluted wines served with a meal, tossed her head in fine disdain.

"You do not need to concern yourself," she flung defiantly back at him. "You who guzzle like the big fish. I will drink when I am ready."

"Sure." Fisk shrugged dismissingly. "Suit yourself. I don't mean to rush you." Then, taking the decanter with him, he returned to his seat before the stern windows. Thoughtfully, he stared into his glass before remarking, "Y'see, Wes wasn't always so damned keen for trouble. Oh, he never ran from a good fight, but it wasn't till after the war that he seemed always to be looking for it. It's like he's got a devil in him that won't leave him alone and the only way he can deal with it is to go out and get rip-roaring drunk, then smash a few heads together. Maybe that was all right when we were younger, but let's face it. I'll never see twenty-eight again, and near as I can figure, West must be close to ten years older than me. There comes a time when a man ought to think about settling down."

"And you have someone with whom you would wish to do this settling down?" queried Angélique softly, strangely touched by Fisk's obvious devotion to his friend. To her surprise, a faint dusky hue invaded the dissipated cheeks.

Fisk gave her a somewhat crooked smile.

"As a matter of fact, a letter tracked me down in Jamaica not too long ago. From a girl I was kind of sweet on once. It put me in mind of things the way they were before the war. Seems she hasn't never married. Been waiting for me to come back home to Charleston."

"And you will go, *oui?*" prodded Angélique.

"Well, I'm not denying I'd be tempted, if things were different."

"You mean if you had not your friend to worry about," Angélique interpolated.

"You've just about guessed it," Fisk admitted wryly. "I owe Wes more than my life, and I don't reckon it'd be right for me to leave him in the lurch. If he had someone to look after him, a good woman maybe, who'd give him something to think about besides whatever it is that's driving him, I expect I could go to Charleston and that girl with a clear conscience. The trouble is, Wes is pure poison where women are concerned. I'd begun to think there would never be a female who could break through that reserve of his, but you begin to give me some hope, Angel. Honest to God, before today I'd never seen him so het up over a woman."

This time it was Angélique's turn to blush, but Fisk, warming to his subject, failed to notice.

"Y'see," he said, gazing off the stern as if it were a window on the past, "Wes and I go back a long way. We served together for awhile during the war. Then, later, long after we'd gone our separate ways, we ended up by chance in the same stinking British prison. If it hadn't been for the captain, I expect I'd 've breathed my last on that miserable hulk of a prison-ship."

"You were with him on the *Jersey?*" exclaimed

Angelique without thinking, her eyes enormous in a face gone pearly white.

Fisk, who had been about to take a drink, suddenly stopped with the glass halfway to his lips.

"What'd you say?" he uttered, eyeing her strangely.

Angelique shook her head in mute consternation. *Voyons!* She was the stupid fool to let loose her tongue.

"Oh, no, Angel," Fisk warned her. "I heard you. You said, 'the *Jersey*.' Now how'n hell would you know that? Just *who* the devil *are* you?" he demanded. "And don't try to tell me *Wes* confided that little tidbit to you, because I'm not likely to swallow it. That's one subject West Locke won't talk to anyone about, least of all to a female."

Made thus aware of the enormity of her error, Angelique abruptly turned her back on Fisk and in a single gulp emptied her glass. The fiery liquid seared her throat and brought tears to her eyes, and it was only by a supreme effort of will that she did not disgrace herself by choking. Weaving slightly from the effects of the potent spirits exploring her deplorably empty belly, she carefully set the glass on the captain's table while she sought to gather her wits about her.

"It is of no importance how I know this thing," she said, in a muffled voice. Then, flinging caution to the wind, she came back around again to impale Fisk with an eloquently pleading look. "I beg of you, m'sieu. Do not ask me the questions I cannot answer. It is enough for you to know that I mean your capitaine no harm, is it not?"

But already Fisk had straightened on the seat, his eyes wide in sudden comprehension on her face.

"Damn me if I haven't guessed it!" he exclaimed, slapping an emphatic hand against his thigh. "You're Herman Gilbert's daughter, or my name isn't Gideon Aloysius Fisk! Angele—short for Angelique, is it? But of course it is. I never forget a name. Angelique Eugenie Gilbert. Good God, lass! Why didn't you tell us who you

109

were back there at the inn? Wes has been half mad trying to find out where you'd disappeared to."

"And he must go on wondering!" cried Angelique, furious at having given herself away. "If you are truly his friend, you will swear to this, m'sieu."

Fisk stared at her for a stunned moment, apparently rendered mute by the desperation in her voice and manner. Taking advantage of his uncertainty, Angelique sank with unconscious grace to her knees before him.

"He must never know the woman he took in and cared for was the daughter of his very old friend," she murmured, clasping his hand between her own small ones. "For his sake, and for mine, you must promise you will tell him nothing."

A sudden glimmer of understanding shone briefly in Fisk's eyes at sight of her silent pleading. As if drawn, his glance strayed to the rumpled bed then back to the lovely face again. In spite of herself, Angelique blushed.

"Ye-es. Maybe it would be best at that," Fisk muttered feebly.

"Your word, m'sieu. You will give me your word?"

Fisk's gaze never left hers as, with the air of a man who foresees dark days before him, he deliberately drained his glass and refilled it before giving her an answer.

"I expect Wes'll have my gizzard if he ever finds out about this. But, hell yes. I give you my word on it."

Angelique, feeling suddenly weak with relief and perhaps more than a little giddy from the brandy, let her cheek come to rest against Fisk's knee.

"I thank you, m'sieu," whispered softly between her lips, along with a silent prayer that he would see fit to keep his promise. "You will keep my secret. And you will help me, *non*? To get free of this ship and *ce capitaine* before it is too late?"

A strangled oath erupted from Fisk. "Now wait just a bloody damn minute!"

"I know it is a very great deal to ask, M'sieu Fisk," Angelique hastened to add, "but you see, I have no one

110

else to turn to. You must help me—for the sake of your capitaine."

His gaze fixed with something of horror on the beautiful face turned eloquently up to his, and Angelique intent solely on winning him over, neither one of them was aware that the door had swung open or that a tall figure loomed ominously on the threshold.

The captain's soft drawl fell on their ears like a thunderbolt.

"Well, Fisk? We're waiting."

Fisk shot to his feet as if stung, nearly knocking Angelique sprawling in his haste. His face went from a sickly white to a dusky red as he met the look in his captain's eyes.

"Aw, Wes, what'd you want to go sneaking up on a fellow for?" he complained, apparently hoping to breeze his way through. "You came close to scaring me out of half a year's growth."

"Did I?" Locke queried with a steely grin. "Then I suppose I should apologize. Perhaps in the future I might even arrange to have myself announced before entering my quarters."

"But of course, m'sieu," interposed Angelique, having taken advantage of the brief exchange to rise majestically to her feet. Unfortunately the effect was marred somewhat by her brief stagger at the end, which elicited a steadying hand from a none-too-steady Fisk. "It is only what one would expect of a gentleman, is it not?" she finished, and punctuated the thought with an involuntary hiccup.

Had her purpose been to draw the captain's wrath down upon her own head, it would seem she had succeeded admirably. Almost her heart failed her as those piercing blue eyes swung from the unfortunate Fisk to rest with icy intensity upon herself. Instinctively her back stiffened at the contempt she saw mirrored there.

"And what I stumbled upon was exactly what I should

111

have expected from one who is obviously *not* a 'lady,'" he uttered cuttingly. "Congratulations, Angel. It would seem you have made another conquest for yourself—in my second-in-command. Unfortunately, it will do you little good. From now on I'll not let you out of my sight until our business is done, and then you may do as you will for all I care. My part in the farce will be finished."

Never had she known such fury as shook her then.

"Bah!" she exclaimed, flinging up her head in regal defiance. "You think because I am the big nobody that you can do whatever you want with me, but in this you are wrong."

Determined more than ever to give the odious captain the proof of the pudding and made rather more daring by the alcohol at work on her brain, she sidled suggestively up to Fisk, who would have been more than happy to remain naught but an unobtrusive observer had he been given any choice in the matter.

"I am not your slave, *M'sieu le Capitaine*," she declared with magnificent scorn. "And never will I be the wife of a man like you. M'sieu Gideon, he understands the heart of a woman. But you, you know only to bully and shout." Espying the glass held by the unhappy first mate, she snatched it from his hand. "I would do anything—even throw myself into the sea—to be free of you," she proclaimed grandiloquently, and throwing back her head, tilted the fiery liquid down her throat.

The brandy went down more smoothly this time, and with an air of triumph, Angelique blithely flipped the empty glass in a soaring arc over her shoulder.

"Would you, indeed," murmured Locke, his eyes narrowing to glittering blue points of steel as he watched Fisk exert himself mightily to save the goblet of exquisite cut crystal from plummeting to an untimely end.

Angelique's chin shot up in proud defiance.

"On my oath, I swear it!"

An ironic gleam of humor twitched at the captain's lips as it came to him that the chit was clearly three sheets to the wind. It took no more than a fraction of a second more for him to decide to call the brazen little hussy's bluff.

In a single, long stride he reached her side and, clasping merciless fingers about her arm, dragged her toward the stern window. Before she had fully grasped the significance of her new dilemma, the window was flung open and Angelique found herself staring into the gray swell of the sea. Behind her, she heard Fisk's horrified protest, summarily cut short by the captain.

"Well, Angel?" queried Locke, thrusting her forward on the bench. "It's your move now. Or is your boast as false as everything else about you?"

Sacriste! groaned Angelique, one hand pressed to her forehead. If only her head were not spinning so, maybe she could think what to do. Feeling close to hysteria, she made the error of glancing up into the eyes of the captain. *Hein!* He had the look of the pirate who waited for her to walk the plank, she thought, and choked on a helpless gurgle of laughter. It was absurd, this hopeless muddle she had got herself into. Then, suddenly, it came to her that it would serve him right if in truth she did fling herself from the window. After all, would not anything be better than to back down now before the odious Locke?

Carried on the crest of an irresistible impulse, she climbed unsteadily to her feet on the padded bench. Then swaying, she faced the capitaine with an ebullient sparkle of defiance.

"Very well, *M'sieu le Capitaine,*" she stated simply. "You wish to see me jump?" She shrugged. "Then I will jump."

"Hellsfire!" cursed the captain, lunging toward the slender figure, poised on the brink of destruction. Too late. With a lilting cry, she turned and dove headfirst from the window.

To Angelique, who, from earliest childhood had entertained a decided passion for the sea, this was no different from a hundred other dives she had made.

113

Until, that was, she hit the water.

The icy plunge into the sea took her breath away. Then, to her dismay, she found her limbs hopelessly tangled in her skirts, and suddenly she panicked. As she frantically struggled to claw her way to the surface, pinpoints of light danced before her eyes, until at last she experienced an odd sort of peace steal over her. So, this is what it was to die, flitted tranquilly through her mind, just before steely fingers clamped ruthlessly in her hair and dragged her, choking and sputtering, to the surface.

"You stupid, insane little fool!" rasped savagely in her ear as she found herself clutched mercilessly to Locke's unrelenting chest. Irrationally hurt by her rescuer's scathing utterance, she began furiously to struggle.

"Let me . . . go!" she gasped, shoving with all her strength against the offending chest. "You said I could go free."

"And so you would," growled Locke, tightening his grip, "if I had even an ounce of sense."

Exhausted by her efforts, Angelique abruptly gave up the pointless struggle.

"Oh, *why* do you p-pers-sist in h-holding me against m-my will?" She gasped through teeth that had begun to chatter with the cold. "C-Can you n-not s-see that I l-loathe you?"

Cursing, Locke dragged her roughly to him.

"Don't think for a moment that I haven't been asking myself that very same question," he admitted harshly, acutely aware of the slender body pressed, trembling, against his lean length. Nor had the unbearable pressure beneath his breastbone, occasioned by the sight of the slight figure plummeting toward the water, lessened in the least. Almost he could have throttled the cursed girl for having put him through such a moment.

It would have been difficult to say which of the two was more relieved to hear Fisk's ringing shout to "hold on," as he, along with two other seamen, made toward them in one of the ship's boats. Angelique, having been

114

rendered considerably more sober by her plunge into the bay, was more than ready to be hauled out of it. Trembling in every limb, she huddled gratefully in the woollen blanket Fisk thrust unceremoniously around her before turning to help Locke into the boat.

"Christ, Wes," he muttered, performing a like service for his captain, "you took an awful chance goading the girl like that. Any fool can see Angel's as pluck as they come. You might bloody well have known she would jump."

The captain's chilling look was anything but encouraging.

"Thank you, Mr. Fisk, for those words of wisdom," he murmured in a voice designed to flay a man to the quick. "Now, if it is not too much to ask, perhaps you could see your way clear to getting us aboard the bloody ship!"

No fool, Fisk immediately ordered the boat around, but a close observer could not have failed to note the faint gleam of a smile on his lips as he took his place foward.

Angelique, sitting rigidly in the sternsheets of the boat, her eyes fixed straight ahead, did not notice it. Nor did the captain, whose brooding stare never once left the profile of her face as the small craft came about and made with all haste for the entry port.

Chapter 7

More miserable than she could ever recall having been in her life before, it was all Angelique could do to drag herself up the side of the ship to the entry port. Nevertheless, when Locke, who was waiting to assist her, reached down a strong hand to haul her the rest of the way up, she pointedly ignored it.

"Me, I do not need your help," she flung up at him and, amidst the hoots and calls of the sailors gathered to catch a glimpse of the captain's latest peccadillo, she stepped haughtily onto the deck.

Instantly a cheer went up, and for a moment Angelique stood, torn between embarrassment and her own strong proclivity for the mischievous. Finally, not averse to giving the captain back some of his own, the latter won out. Holding out her sodden skirts, she gave them a grand curtsey. The din that that aroused brought the color to her cheeks and a wholly impish grin to her lips as, straightening, she cast a glance sidelong at the captain.

He stood at ease amidst the clamor of his men, his wet clothes clinging to the long, lithe form and his brown locks falling, disheveled, over his forehead. Still, she thought she had never seen a man more striking in appearance. Or one more obviously held in esteem by the men he commanded, she thought as she listened to them rib their captain.

117

"Hoowee! Looks like the captain's gone and caught himself a real live one this time, lads."

"She'll be like to trim 'is sails for 'im, *she* will."

"Aye. Best fetch up now, Captain. She'll have you backin' yer tops'ls and dancin' a jig 'fore she's done wi' ya."

Locke cocked a sardonic eyebrow at his grinning first mate.

"It would seem," he observed drily, "that the men's spirits are high."

He waited until the laughter at that bit of acerbic humor died down. Then casually he turned to address his next observation to his third-in-command, a towering black man of Herculean proportions who was standing a few paces to his side. "It makes me think, Mr. Henry, that perhaps I've been too easy on them of late. In fact, I begin to wonder if they would not learn more respect for their captain if all shore leaves were cancelled for the next few days."

"Aw, Captain," groaned one of the sailors. "You wouldn't do that, now would you?"

"Ah, Jedediah, my lad, but I very much fear that I would," returned the captain with a lazy gleam of a smile. "Of course, it would mean Fisk here, as first mate, would have to remain aboard in order to instruct the men in their deportment." Ignoring the general rumble of dismay that ensued in the wake of that telling speech, Locke continued with a slight shrug. "Unfortunate, I admit," he said, "but what would you have me do? It's a captain's duty to maintain the proper discipline of his crew. Well, what do you say, Mr. Henry? How does a journey to see an old friend strike you?"

"It strike me jes' fine, Cap'n," Jubal Henry admitted with a huge grin over Locke's shoulder at a dumbfounded Fisk.

"Well, then, I guess it's all settled." Having thus dealt with his refractory crew, Locke next turned his attention to the girl, who was eyeing him with outraged disbelief.

"And now, Angel," he murmured, extending his crooked arm to her with insufferable arrogance, "if you have quite finished making a spectacle of yourself—?"

Speechless with the injustice of what he had done, Angelique stared impotently into the blue, mocking eyes. *Hein*, he was an ogre, this captain who took his anger at her out on his poor men! Even worse, however, was the certainty that he had done it solely to make a point. If she tried to use his men against him, it would be they who paid for it, not her. Oh, it was too low!

Knowing that she would only make matters worse if she did anything further to arouse his displeasure, she clamped her mouth shut and, disdaining to take his arm, stepped haughtily through the cabin hatch into the murky companionway beyond.

Behind her she heard Fisk call out to the captain and glanced back to see the two men engaged in a low-voiced debate. Then she turned and walked on till she neared the captain's quarters. Unwittingly, her breath caught as a sinister figure loomed suddenly out of the shadows directly in her path. Blinking, she gazed up into a face she had thought to see only in her tormented dreams. Her hand rose to her mouth as though to stifle a scream at sight of the hideously scarred chest and shoulders.

"You!" she breathed, her voice a hoarse whisper of sound.

"You know me, *c'est bien*," he whispered back.

"No! You came to me in the dream of Mozambe. I heard you chant the words of the sorcerer. This much I remember, but you I do not know."

She saw the gleam of white teeth, then winced as a callused hand caught her hard by the wrist.

"You know me," he repeated in a voice that sent chills down her back. "Now, woman, hear me. A man say his name Poissac come to Cap Français. That not his name, and that fella come with him no be Jean Paul Moreau. You know that fella him call Moreau. And you know him steal up the mountain alone at night to Cime du Bonheur.

119

Him bring word to the white man Gilbert. You know, woman. And them that track that fella down, *they* know."

Angelique's face went white as death.

"Poissac was the name Vincent Ogé was to use. Etienne!" she gasped. "It was Etienne Joliet who went to see my father. *Mon Dieu!* Tell me! What have they done with him?"

"That fella Etienne no live to see the head of Vincent Ogé be sitting on a pole," he pronounced in a soft voice belied by the hard glitter in his eyes.

Angelique reeled, then caught herself.

"No, you lie!" she breathed, her heart like a dead thing in her breast. "Why should I believe you? Who *are* you?"

"I be your friend. When you burning with the evil, the spell I turn back on the woman who did this. That woman belonga Etienne Joliet."

"Etienne? Babette was Etienne's woman?" Instantly she knew it was true, knew where she had seen her before—at the opera, waiting with his friends for Etienne to join them. "But how . . . ?"

The sorcerer's hand shot up in warning.

"H-s-s-t! *Le capitaine,* him come."

Instinctively Angelique froze as a light step sounded somewhere behind her. Then a hand thrust a necklace of beads in her palm and curled her fingers tight around it.

"You want see Herman Gilbert again, Missy," warned the sorcerer, releasing her, "you go home. You go now, Missy," he said and, stepping back, was swallowed up in the shadows.

"No, wait," called Angelique, reaching out a hand as if to snatch him back again. "At least tell me your name. Tell me why I should trust you."

"Chantal watch over you," he whispered back at her from out of the darkness. "You no see him, but always Chantal there, you be needing him."

The voice faded and died, and suddenly she could sense that in truth the man was gone. Lifting the necklace

120

to the dim light, she felt her mouth go suddenly dry.

"Jumbi beads," she muttered aloud. The blacks wore the little red and black seeds to ward off evil spirits. Feeling a *frisson* of warning, she thrust the thing deep into the pocket of her petticoat. Then Locke came up behind her and grasped her by the arm.

"What're you doing here?" he demanded, pulling her around to face him. "Who were you talking to just now?"

"Wha-at?" she stammered, staring blankly up into the fierce glitter of his eyes. "N-No one. I was talking to no one."

She was lying. He knew it without having to see it in her face. He didn't need her to tell him who it was either, he thought grimly, letting go of her arm. It was Chantal. There would hardly be anyone else she'd be willing to lie to protect, not with Fisk topside.

Feeling her tremble, he grimly shoved her through the door into his quarters. Quickly he hung a blanket across one corner of the room and gruffly ordered her to get out of her wet things and into something dry.

Some little time later, Angelique, becomingly gowned in a blue velvet caraco and matching skirt, emerged from behind the blanket. Defiantly she stood at attention as the odious Locke turned from completing his own toilette to run his gaze over her. From her hair, caught up on top of her head and falling in damp curls down her back, to her dainty feet shod in blue leather half-boots, she presented a breathtaking vision of defiant young womanhood.

An appreciative gleam ignited briefly in the steely eyes. Hellsfire! he thought. Even after a dunking that would have put most females he knew into bed, smelling salts to hand, his mettlesome Angel had come out looking more beautiful than any woman had a right to be, and just as undaunted. Who the devil was she? he thought, his lips thinning to a grim line. Damn her lovely eyes! He'd

121

give a great deal to know what it was that she would risk drowning to keep him from knowing. And maybe even more to know what she had been doing with Chantal.

Suddenly angry at both her and himself for the untenable position in which he found himself, he suffered an immediate relapse into his earlier ill-humor.

"Sit down, Angel," he said coldly. Deliberately he turned his back on her and returned to the tiresome business of tying his neckcloth before the small looking glass. "I'll be through here in a minute. If you've any sense at all, which I very much doubt, you'll fortify yourself while you can with hot coffee and a bite or two to eat. I think you'll discover the turbot is tasty enough. But if you can't find the stomach for it, I suggest you at least try some bread and cheese. The ride before us promises to be tedious enough without having a swooning female on hand to make matters worse. Do I make myself clear?" he finished, reaching for his coat and shrugging it on over broad shoulders before turning at last to look at her again.

A singularly grim expression came to his eyes. Angelique had not moved, but stood with hands folded at her waist, her expression uncompromising.

"Of course, m'sieu," she answered in a hard little voice. "You make yourself very clear. You would fatten me like the lamb for the sacrifice to your stupid sense of duty. But I tell you I am not hungry. I wish only a ship to take me as far away from you as possible."

The muscle leaped along the lean line of his jaw as he studied the determined cast of the young face. Damn the chit, and her pride! What did she expect from him? That he should simply dump her on the pier, alone and unprotected, then blithely go his way as if nothing had ever happened? Had she been born in a bloody convent to be so blasted naive? His blood ran cold at thought of the spirited Angele left to her own devices in an unfamiliar land. Even if she did not fall to the first beggar intent on knocking her alongside the head for her valuables, her treatment at the hands of the gentry would hardly be more merciful. Without even a female companion to give her respectability, she would soon find there were any number of gentlemen who would consider her fair game for their lusty pleasures. Hellsfire! he cursed softly to himself. Even if she had not the air of a gently born female, he could not have abandoned her to so uncertain a fate. And besides, there were still questions he needed answers to—questions concerning her relationship with Chantal.

"I see," he murmured, flicking an imaginary fleck of lint from his sleeve. "You are quite determined then?"

"*Oui, m'sieu,*" she stated simply, though a shadow of something flickered in her eyes. Surprise, was it, at what seemed a leavening of his mood? he wondered cynically. Or fear that he might take her at her word? Suddenly weary of the whole affair, he abruptly dropped all pretense.

"Ah, but you see, I am even more determined," he uttered chillingly. "Like it or not, you placed yourself in my protection as soon as you flung yourself into the path of that cursed pistol ball. Until you can convince me you would be better served to go your own way, I'm afraid I have no choice but to insist on this marriage."

"Oh! But you are of the most impossible!" exclaimed Angelique, flinging up her hands in exasperation. "How am I to convince you of such a thing? I have already talked myself blue in the face. You tell *me* what I must do to get through to you."

A startled gasp burst from her lips as suddenly he loomed over her, his eyes like piercing points of flame.

"Tell me who you are and what the devil you were doing in the Crossbow dressed in rags," he said, his fingers clamping like a vise about her wrist. "You tell me that, Angel, and then maybe I'll see fit to leave you alone."

Her heart hammering beneath her breast, Angelique ran her tongue over suddenly dry lips. *Voyons!* That you must never know, *M'sieu le Capitaine*, she thought with a sinking heart, for then you would certainly see no way out of this trap I have gotten us in.

But, even worse, it suddenly came to her, he would become a part of that other thing, the peril that threatened Saint Dominique and La Cime du Bonheur. For Locke's own safety, she must get as far away from him as possible, and soon, if ever she wished to see her papa again.

"Well, Angel?" he prodded, in no mood to be generous.

The contemptuous curl of his lip set her back up, and all at once she was shaking with anger.

"Very well, m'sieu," she answered bitterly. "You want to know who I am, then I will tell you." Scathing in her contempt, she yanked her hand away. "It is just as you have already guessed. My mother was a Frenchwoman who ran away with an adventurer. An American with the fat purse. He took her to Saint Dominique, and one night a black man . . . he-he broke into her house and he raped her. Is this what you wished to hear, m'sieu? It is even as you thought. I am Angele, the bastard, and I carry in my veins the blood of the *Rodu*. A man does not need to wed such a woman. It is better that he make of her the mistress."

For a long moment Locke stared at her, his eyes seeming to bore holes through her, until with a brittle laugh, she turned away to hide from him the anguish in her heart. How very like the truth it sounded when these things were spoken aloud! she thought. Her heart like lead in her breast, she relived the dreadful moment when Mozambe had whispered this very same story to her long ago on the docks of Port-au-Prince.

Behind her, she heard the captain cross deliberately to the wine cabinet, and with a sense of déjà vu, heard brandy slosh in a glass.

"If what you say is true," he said in measured tones after a moment, "then what were you doing in France?"

124

She shrugged, knowing she trod a slender line. "What does it matter?"

"It matters to me. There was another girl, who was to send word to me at L'Arbalète. A girl living in the Convent of Ste. Clare. She never showed up, but you did, didn't you, Angel. Quite a coincidence, don't you think?"

Angelique paled and plucked nervously at a fold in her gown.

"'Coincidence'?" she echoed, lifting her eyebrows in sublime innocence. "I-I fear I do not understand you."

Locke, watching her closely, smiled ever so faintly.

"You still have not told me your name or how you came to be in that wretched inn," he prodded.

Voyons! she cursed to herself. He was putting two and two together: Angele the Nobody and Angelique Eugenie Gilbert; the girl at the inn and the girl to whom he had sent the letter at the Convent of Ste. Clare. Very quickly she thought.

"That other one," she said, deliberately meeting his gaze. "She was Angelique Gilbert, was she not? I know, because I, too, was at this very same convent."

"Really?" murmured Locke, never taking his eyes off her. "But how very convenient for you."

"Mais oui," she flung back at him. "When one is an embarrassment, it becomes of the most convenient to be sent to the convent. There, no one needs to know the secrets of shame, you see. But alas, the revolution comes, and the convent, she closes." All at once she turned the full force of her eyes upon the cold-faced captain. "You must understand. It seemed like a miracle sent from God when Angelique Gilbert read to me the letter you write to her. You see, m'sieu, the daughter of your friend Herman Gilbert had no wish to return to Saint Dominique. She has decided to become a nun, she tells me. For this, she will go to Belgique with *Les Pauvres Clares.* But me, I have nowhere else to go. And so I think to myself: *Ce capitaine,* he has not seen Angelique perhaps for a very long time,

and so maybe he will not know her. *Ainsi*, I think maybe I take her place. Only, when you ask me my name, I cannot make my stupid tongue say Angelique Gilbert. Instead I decide to offer myself in exchange for the passage home. After all, you are not so very bad-looking, and me, I am a woman." She shrugged indifferently. "It is all very simple, *non?*"

Locke was watching her with the eyes that seemed to strip her bare, but somehow she found the strength to face him without flinching.

"Yes," he said, "simple. Maybe too damned simple."

"You do not believe me?" Angelique demanded haughtily. "But I am not this daughter of your friend, I promise you. I am Angele DuFour," she declared, taking her mother's maiden name out of desperation. "What reason could I have to lie? If in truth I wished to entrap you, I would be of the most *stupide* not to tell you I was this Angelique. But me, I have no wish to marry anyone, and so I tell you the truth about myself."

It was a telling argument. As a matter of fact, he hadn't the least idea why she would lie about it. And yet it was too blasted neat. One thing only was certain. Whoever or whatever she was, she had deserved better from him than to be branded a harlot and then ravaged. And if in truth she had no one, that was all the more reason to go through with his plans for her. Right or wrong, he fully intended to make her his, and then the devil help them both!

"Put on your cloak, Angel," he said with an air of cold finality. "We've a long road before us."

With a sense of stunned disbelief Angelique watched the handsome head go back as the captain finished off his brandy. Then once again he was looking at her, the arrogant eyebrow lifted mockingly.

"Was there something in what I just said that you failed to comprehend?" he queried insufferably.

"Bah! I understand *nothing* of what you say, m'sieu. But what does it matter? You are obviously the madman,

126

and me, I am the fool."

Turning on her heel, she snatched up the cloak, lying in readiness across the bed, and, flinging it around her shoulders strode without a backward glance out the door.

The short boat ride from the ship to the docks lining the harbor was accomplished in taut silence. Once ashore, Locke wasted little time in hiring a coach to take them north, and it was not long before they found themselves traversing a narrow road that wound through a gentle land of low-lying hills. The sky, overcast and gray, and the air, chill and damp with a lightly falling mist, perfectly suited Angelique's less than sunny mood. Beside her, Locke dozed in the corner, his curly-brimmed beaver pulled low over his eyes and his long legs propped carelessly on the seat facing him.

They had spoken hardly a word since leaving Christchurch, which meant that Angelique had been granted more than enough time alone, with only her cheerless thoughts to occupy her. In the throes of a merciless headache and nearly ravenous with hunger, she was not sorry when the coach, arriving at an inn set on a crossroads, turned into the arched portal and came to a halt. As Locke stirred, aroused at last, a stablelad bounded forward.

"Will 'ee be standin' down, gov'nor?" he shouted up at the occupants of the coach.

Locke, stifling a yawn behind a languid hand, glanced incuriously out at the two-storey walls of stone embracing a rectangular courtyard.

"Perhaps," he drawled indifferently, "if the fare warrants it. How much farther to Briarcroft?"

"No more than two hours, does the weather hold. An' if'n it doesn't, a long night's walk. Beggin' your pardon, sir, but I'd fortify myself with a bite, was I you. The fare be plain, but it goes down well with a pint or two."

"I'll trust your word for it, lad," replied the captain,

flipping the youth a coin. "There'll be another like that one for you if you see that the coachman and my man are well taken care of."

Testing the coin between his teeth, the youth grinned hugely. "You can count on me, gov'nor," he said, and, flinging the door open, he waited for the gentleman and his lady to descend.

Locke, apparently in no great hurry to test the truth of the boy's claims for the inn, shifted his glance speculatively to the slim figure sitting stock-still beside him. A wry frown creased his brow. In spite of the defiant tilt of the chin, he could not mistake the weariness in the faint droop of the shoulders. Furthermore, the girl was as white as a sheet. He'd wager a purse full of silver that her wound was causing her discomfort, and if she wasn't more than a little ill from her recent dissipation, he'd bloody well eat his hat. Damn the cursed pride of the chit! Not only had she not uttered a single word of complaint in the three hours they had been on the road, but she had remained obstinately upright in her corner, refusing to give in to her obvious fatigue with a stubbornness that would have done credit to the saltiest of his sailors. It would be a miracle if her stubborn pride did not land her flat on her back again.

"Well, Angel?" he murmured, cocking a sardonic eyebrow at his troublesome charge. "Perhaps now you are ready to swallow a mouthful or two along with your pride?"

Angelique, who was indeed feeling battered and more than a little ill-used, was in no mood to be conciliatory. "I have not the hunger," she replied haughtily, keeping her eyes rigidly to the fore. And in truth she would rather have perished from want than be forced to accept even a morsel from *ce capitaine,* who had made of her the unwilling prisoner.

The captain's mouth hardened to a dangerously thin line. Then suddenly he shrugged.

"Very well, then," he drawled. "Personally, I could

eat a horse, but you suit yourself. You will, of course, be pleased to keep me company.''

Angelique, not deigning to answer, stared sulkily out on the courtyard bustling with activity as Locke stepped down amidst the clamor of barking dogs and the shouts of 'ostlers hurrying to remove the cattle from their traces in order that a fresh team could be brought. Informing the driver in a few curt words that they would be taking the noonday meal at the inn before going on, he turned to hand Angelique down. After only the briefest glance into the uncompromising blue of his eyes, she obediently took his arm and allowed him to lead her into a common room boisterous with guests—an entourage of young bloods assembled for a hunt, they were informed by the harried innkeeper, his bald pate shiny with perspiration.

Locke pulled a purse from his greatcoat. Money exchanged hands, and moments later Angelique found herself being ushered up narrow stairs to a private sitting room adjoining a small bedchamber. Wordlessly she crossed to the curtained window; gazing out on the encroaching boundaries of trees, which marked the beginnings of New Forest, she waited for the innkeeper to light a fire laid ready in the fireplace.

"I'll send Ned up as soon ever as I can with hot water and towels. I expect your missus'll be wantin' to freshen up a bit. And perhaps a bottle of something for yourself, gov'nor?''

"Brandy, if you have it. And hot coffee for my—wife, if you please. I'm afraid she may have taken a chill on the road.''

The innkeeper, noting the frosty glance the young beauty bestowed on the gentleman, could not doubt it for a moment. Indeed, from the looks of her, the lad would need more than a whole pot of coffee to warm that one. Deciding they would do better without his presence, he hastily made his departure.

Angelique, suffering the aftereffects of too much brandy, was indeed in no mood to be charming. So much so, in fact, that she had had to bite her tongue to keep from blurting out that, not only was she not the wife of this capitaine with the eyes that mocked, but that she was the victim of a vile abduction. Alas, her head hurt, and she very much feared that in all the shouting that would have come in the wake of such a declaration, she would inevitably have become most dreadfully ill. *La vache!* It would have been better had the capitaine left her to drown, she thought, pressing her fingers to throbbing temples. It was of the most obvious that he was enjoying himself very much at her expense.

It was thus with mixed feelings of relief and dread that she heard the door close at last behind the innkeeper and knew she was alone with the captain. Ignoring the mocking curl of handsome lips, she sank gratefully onto a stool before the fire and stretched cold hands out to the blaze. *Voyons!* Was it not bad enough that she felt ill and nearly frozen to the bone without having to suffer the capitaine's eyes boring holes between her shoulder blades? She frowned darkly, thinking of the journey, which thus far had been anything but pleasant.

While Locke slept, Angelique had stared moodily out the coach window without really seeing the green, rolling hills, the occasional spinney of oak and beech, or the neatly tilled fields bordered by hedgerows. Had it not been for the second-mate's watchful presence on top of the coach, she might have slipped away any number of times. As it was, she had worn herself out contemplating her immediate future and berating herself for having made a muddle of things. Had she not acted so stupidly, it might have been Fisk riding guard and she might have been well on her way back to the coast.

Poor Fisk, she mused sardonically. Because of her, he had been assigned the onerous task of remaining behind with the ship. In his stead had come Jubal Henry, a black man who dwarfed even the captain in pure physical stature. Yet in a way Angelique could not but feel relief at the substitution. Fisk, far from proving a safe ally, after all, had only managed to complicate matters further with the captain, who, true to his word, had not let her out of his sight since the morning's fiasco. Except, of course, she judiciously amended, for the time it took her to change into the modest caraco and skirt Locke himself had chosen from her meager wardrobe.

An angry blush stained her cheeks at the memory. *La vache!* He treated her like the disapproving papa with the child who could not be trusted!

Then immediately her anger faded before the stark reality of her plight. *Sacriste!* Things were turning out for the very bad, she thought, uncomfortably aware of Locke's stony presence at her back. It had been bad enough before, when the lie she had told him and her own pride had seemed the only obstacles to giving in to him. But now there was Chantal to consider, and all that his cryptic utterances had seemed to imply.

Babette was the woman she had seen with Etienne at the opera! Even now she found it of the most difficult to believe she had not known her. True, she had given the woman at the theater only a cursory glance, and yet not to have recognized at once the hate in those glittering eyes! Even harder to grasp was how Babette could have known that she, Angelique Gilbert, would be coming to L'Arbalète in search of the American captain. And yet in her heart Angelique knew that Babette had been waiting for her, waiting to put the pistol ball in her because she blamed Angelique that Etienne was dead. It had to be. And because of her, *le capitaine* had been in danger!

How had Chantal known? she wondered, shivering. He said he had used his magic, the magic wielded by the *tonton macoute,* to save her from a witch's curse. Why? Who was he? What did he want from her? Then it came to her that he, like the dreams, had been sent by Mozambe to call her home. It was the power of the *Rodu,* the magic that the old *houngan* had told her no one could escape. No matter how far one ran, one could never hide from the unseeable ones, or from a curse of the *Rodu.*

If she did not return to Saint Dominique, the ones who wanted her dead would come for her again. This she knew in her heart. Just as she knew that, if the capitaine got in their way a second time, they would not hesitate to kill him.

Mon Dieu! she groaned to herself. Not even a necklace of jumbi beads would save them if she did not soon find a way to escape and return to the island, to Cime du Bonheur and her papa, who she very much feared had something to do with everything that had happened. She had in truth behaved very foolishly; and, as a result, the capitaine to whom they both owed the debt beyond paying might be made to pay for it with his life!

Her unrewarding thoughts were interrupted by a rap at the door, followed almost immediately by the entrance of two servants bearing trays laden with food. Angelique thought she must swoon as the tantalizing aroma of pork pie, stewed peas, and freshly baked bread assaulted her nostrils. On shipboard and later on in the coach, she had not been in any state to think overly much of her stomach except to wish it would cease to churn in a most nauseating manner. But she was young and basically healthy, and not even the dread that weighed upon her could wholly depress her spirits. Now it came to her that never before in her life had food smelled quite so wonderful.

Voyons! she thought regretfully. What a fool she had been to let pride rule her head, for though in truth she did not see how she could go on without eating something, the thought that it must be crow was totally unthinkable.

It was at that moment that a tall shadow loomed ominously over her.

"In case you hadn't noticed," announced the captain, detestably cool, "the table is laid, mademoiselle."

Instinctively Angelique's back stiffened.

"That, m'sieu," she retorted, "is nothing of my concern."

The hand that shot out and dragged her to her feet by

the arm gave her no time to regret her ill-considered answer. All at once she found herself staring into eyes flecked with steel.

"Perhaps not," Locke murmured softly, "but unfortunately you have made it mine. You will eat, Angel, if I have to force every morsel down your lovely throat."

For an instant their glances locked, Angelique's ablaze with resentment and the captain's grim with anticipation. Then unexpectedly, a roguish dimple peeped disarmingly out at the corner of Angelique's mouth.

"Are you very certain that you would go so far, m'sieu?" she queried.

Locke's eyebrows swept upward in his forehead.

"You may be sure of it," he replied in no uncertain terms.

"In that case," shrugged Angelique, "there would seem little point in resisting you any further, *oui?*"

"Pointless in the extreme, I quite agree."

"Bien!" said Angelique, suddenly grinning. "For in truth I think I cannot wait another moment."

Locke's gaze narrowed speculatively on the girl, as with a toss of her raven curls, she jerked her arm free and flounced away from him to the table. Christ, the chit was as unpredictable as the sea. A wry smile twisted at the handsome lips. And fully twice as maddening. Now what the devil, he wondered, was the brazen little hussy up to? His musings were interrupted by Angelique's artless query.

"Pardon, m'sieu, but do you not intend to join me?"

A reluctant grin twitched at his lips at sight of her beguiling innocence. Why not? he shrugged to himself. At least his future wife promised to be anything but boring.

Taking the chair across from her, Locke proceeded to do justice to the meal set before him.

Chapter 8

Angelique, intent on dulling the sharp edge of her hunger, for once ate as if her life depended on it. She dined heartily, savoring each delicious bite, and, emptying her plate, even asked for a second helping of pork pie. But at last, heaving a little sigh of contentment, she laid down her fork and settled back to sip the last of her coffee. *Alors!* She had never known plain food to taste so good. Already her head had ceased to ache and she felt much more herself than she had since coming awake in the captain's quarters the night before.

No sooner had that thought crossed her mind than she was made acutely aware of the man leaning back in his chair across from her. Locke, having finished sating his own appetite some time before, had been watching her make up for the breakfast and lunch she had missed. But now he stood and without a word crossed to the stone fireplace. Lighting up a cigar, he leaned one arm on the mantelpiece and stared broodingly into the flames.

For a moment Angelique hesitated, torn between unconscious pique at his abruptness and a strange tumult of emotions, chief of which was the yearning to be done with the ill feelings between them. At last, giving in to an impulse that she did not fully understand, she, too, pushed away from the table and went to stretch her hands out to the cheerful blaze.

For a long while they remained thus, neither making any attempt at speech, and Angelique, feeling immensely better after a hot meal, felt herself slipping gradually into a rather more generous mood. Lowering the thick veil of her eyelashes, she sneaked a peek at Locke out of the corners of her eyes. Involuntarily, her lips quivered at the sight of the stern mouth and ominously set line of the jaw. *Voyons*, he had the look of a man on his way to his execution! she observed, and in spite of the gravity of the situation in which she found herself, felt an insane urge to giggle.

Locke's acerbic drawl caught her unawares.

"And just what the devil have you found now to amuse you at my expense, I wonder. I'm sure you can understand if I seem just a little uneasy. So far, you've not only managed to embroil me in a barroom brawl, rendered me the ravisher of innocence, and landed me in the drink, but you have at the same time put yourself within a hairsbreadth of being carved up by a butcher knife, flung yourself at the receiving end of a pistol ball, and embraced haphazardly an ignominious death by drowning. Really, Angel, you tax my powers of amazement."

Oh! It really was too much. The captain's penetrating assessment of her recent indiscretions set her off into a helpless peal of laughter.

When her convulsions had subsided enough to allow for speech, she replied, "I think I must beg your pardon, m'sieu. For truly I never meant for any of these things to happen. What is it that you would have me say? One day I will look back on this time as a great adventure, and it is you whom I must thank for it. Three times have you saved my life, and for that, at least, I must be grateful."

She had spoken unaffectedly the thoughts that came from the heart, and so she was not prepared for his reaction. As she looked up, she beheld a warm light of humor spring to his eyes, and for a moment their glances locked in sudden understanding. In the next instant,

136

they had both burst into laughter.

"N-Never will I . . . forget th-the look on your face," she gurgled, her lovely face alight with the memory, "j-just b-before I j-jumped. 'Hellsfire!' " she mimicked in a deep voice.

"Ah," Locke said, taking in the wholesome glow laughter had brought to her cheeks, "but even that could not possibly compare to the expression of horror poor Fisk wore, when I burst in on the two of you in what could only be described as compromising circumstances. That in itself was priceless."

"Oh, *mais oui*. That, I had almost forgotten," she squealed and went into renewed paroxysms of merriment.

In her abandonment, she brushed against the captain, one hand pressed to a heaving breast as she struggled to fill her aching lungs with air. How natural it seemed that the captain's arm should slide down around her shoulders and pull her snugly to his side. Only then did she realize that he was no longer laughing. Lifting her head, she gazed quizzically up into eyes of a spellbinding hue. Suddenly she went still, her mirth quite forgotten.

"You know, you really are a remarkable woman, Angel," Locke murmured, a curiously arrested look in the gaze he bent upon her. "It might even be that we could make this thing work, if we gave it half a chance. In spite of what you might think, I'm not a difficult man to get along with. Just don't expect too much of me, and in return I won't ask more than you're willing to give. As for the rest of it—as my wife, you'll have the freedom, and the means, to do pretty much as you please. So long as you don't abuse the privilege, I won't be likely to interfere. Actually, I see no reason why we shouldn't do very well together."

Not proof against him in this softened mood, Angelique let her eyelids flutter downward.

"Y-You make it all sound very pleasant," she replied haltingly. *Voyons!* Why must he make it so very difficult? "And yet I think I must refuse your offer of the most

137

generous. I am not at all suitable, m'sieu. Please, you must believe me when I tell you there is no reason for you to sacrifice yourself in this way."

Her heart nearly failed her as she felt the hard leap of muscle in his arm.

In an instant it was as if their brief moment of shared camaraderie had never been.

"I suggest that you let me be the judge of that," he uttered coldly. "Whoever, or whatever you or anyone else thinks you are, has no bearing here. You will marry me. In that, you *have* no choice."

"Then you are the fool!" she flung back at him, her head coming up to reveal eyes gloriously ablaze. "What makes you think you can tell me what I will or will not do? Me, I am not your slave."

The twin points of steel in his glance seemed to lance right through her.

"No, not a slave," he agreed. "Or a whore. And obviously pleasant garb ill-becomes you. Tell me the truth, Angel. What, exactly, *are* you?"

Well aware that she was skating on dangerously thin ice, Angelique nevertheless plunged recklessly ahead.

"I have already told you," she said. "I am the nobody! A creature of no account. And still you have not the right to order me about. I gave myself to you, wishing nothing else in return. It meant nothing to me. *You* mean nothing to me. Why can we not leave it at that?"

She had made a mistake. This, she knew as soon as she saw the sudden hard gleam of purpose in his eyes.

"Because," he said, "I think you're a bloody liar!"

He moved too quickly for her to evade the brutal clasp of his hands upon her shoulders. And before she could scream for help, he had already rendered her silent with his mouth pressed cruelly over hers. *Voyons!* It was not fair, this power he had to set her blood aflame with desire. In truth, she had neither the strength nor the will to fight him.

As of their own accord, her lips parted beneath his,

138

and, uttering a low groan, she strained against him, any power she might have had to resist melted away before the sweeping tide of passion that engulfed her, mind and body. With all her sweet young strength she responded to him, returned his embrace with a fire that was not of the body alone, but, had she only known it, of the heart as well.

They were both breathing heavily when at last Locke released her mouth and gazed for a seeming eternity into her eyes, sultry with the storm of passion he had aroused. A satisfied smile curved his lips. Then, bending down, he caught her behind her knees and shoulders and swept her high up into his arms.

"I'm afraid you're going to have to give me some sort of proof that this means nothing to you," he murmured huskily. "Proof that you're really as indifferent as you claim. Tell me honestly that you want me to stop. Say it, and you'll have your freedom. You have my word on it."

She stared back at him, desperately willing herself to deny him, but the look in his eyes held her mesmerized as he carried her to the bed and, laying her upon it, leaned over her.

"Well, Angel?" he queried, sending delicious shivers down her spine as he nibbled tantalizingly at her neck below the ear. "It's now or never. Say it—a simple 'no,' and after today you won't ever see me again."

Suddenly she felt the terrible significance of what he offered like a physical wrench to her heart. One word to set them both free. One word to end the fantasy forever. One word only.

"No," she uttered in a hoarse whisper of sound. "I do not want this to go any further."

She felt him grow ominously still above her and opened her eyes to find his gaze on her like glittering points of steel.

Somewhere deep inside a voice cried out for her to take it back, and in truth she felt her heart withering before that awful, searching glance. But pride would not let her, and desperately she clung to the bitter knowledge that only thus could she pay back the debts beyond paying. For what her father owed him, she would set him free. And for what she owed him, she would make him utterly despise her.

"You see, m'sieu," she said, managing the semblance of a mocking smile. "It is just as I have said. My heart is cold like the heart of the courtesan for whom these things can mean nothing."

"That was not the impression you gave just a moment ago," Locke sapiently observed. "Or last night, for that matter."

"Last night was . . . last night," declared Angelique, giving a small shrug of the shoulder. "After all, I am a woman, and you, you must know, have a body to entice a woman with even the most cold of hearts. I-It was not that I was—how you say—disap*pointed*. It is only that today, m'sieu . . . today, I am afraid I feel only the great indifference toward you. Oh, it is true, maybe for one moment I think it might be amusing to make sport with you, but then I remember—" Her hands flew up in a gesture, purely Gaelic. "So many difficulties already from the one moment of abandonment. And suddenly— just like that—I feel nothing."

"Really," Locke murmured with uplifted eyebrows. "Just like that?"

"*Mais oui,* 'just like that,'" Angelique agreed.

A curious gleam flickered in the captain's eyes, and, knowing that while her lips said one thing, her heart was crying out quite another, she judiciously averted her face.

Consequently, she did not see the faint quiver of the handsome lips.

"I-I am of the most sorry," she went on, "if this wounds your pride. But you have asked me for the truth, you see."

"You're right, I did, Angel," he drawled in a voice that sent an involuntary shiver down her back. "And I'm glad you've decided to play straight with me."

She started as if stung as he drew away. Then, compelled, she turned back to peek at him from beneath the thick veil of her eyelashes. Unbelievably she saw his fingers at his neckcloth loosening the knot.

"You don't need to worry about my 'pride,'" he continued, pulling the yard-long length of silk from around his neck with the unconcerned air of a man intent on nothing more innocuous than preparing for bed. Angelique's eyebrows snapped together. "On the contrary, I like a woman who views these things the way a man does," he pronounced and, shrugging off his coat, slung it carelessly across the back of a straight-backed chair placed conveniently near at hand.

Next, the long, slender fingers started on the fastenings of his shirt and Angelique's mouth went dry as seconds later, the shirt went the way of the coat. With a feeling of impending doom she watched him bend over to tackle the chore of removing his boots.

"No expectations beyond the pleasure afforded by a little romp between the sheets," he was saying in that same odiously conversational tone—as if he were performing the most natural of acts, removing his clothes before her. "Both participants enjoy the exchange, and there's nothing to mar the moment—no sense of obligation, no danger of misunderstandings or hurt feelings; each of them is free to go his or her own way when the thing is over." Her eyes widened and the palms of her hands felt suddenly clammy as at last he stood up, presumably to remove the final article of clothing. "Maybe one female in a thousand would look at it that way," he observed, turning his gaze on her at last. "But you, Angel, you're a pearl beyond price. Oh, I admit, you put quite a scare into me when I discovered I had stumbled unwittingly into virginal territory, but now that we've already crossed that barrier, I don't see why we can't indulge in a little—"

Here Angelique decided it was time to intervene,

and tellingly.

"Enough!" she cried. Bolting upright she scrambled backwards till her shoulders were pressed firmly against the headboard. "You promised, m'sieu, that I had only to say one word, and that would be the end of it."

"I said that you would have your freedom, and so you will," he replied. A single eyebrow shot upward in apparent puzzlement. "Pardon me if I fail to see what that has to do with this."

"But-but it has everything to do with it!" exclaimed Angelique, who was not only quite certain that, once started, she could not find the strength to stop him or herself a second time, but that once the love-act was accomplished, she very likely would not have the will left to live without him.

"I'm sorry, but I'm afraid you'll have to be more explicit, Angel, if you want me to understand. Let me see if I've got this straight. You did say, didn't you, that you had the heart of a courtesan?"

"Yes, but—!"

"Yes, I thought that's what you said. And, you also admitted, if I remember correctly, that you weren't exactly disappointed in our little romp last night. That means that you didn't find the experience repulsive or disagreeable, doesn't it? But of course it does," he said, answering his own question before Angelique had even time to draw a breath to speak. "You know it's amazing what two people can accomplish if they just settle down to a little plain speaking. I think we're progressing very nicely, don't you?"

Locke's single, assessing look into fulminating blue-violet eyes might have put some doubt upon his latter assertion. Politically, perhaps, he let his glance slide away as he pursued his line of thought to its no doubt logical conclusion. "And now, granting that everything else you've admitted is true and we perfectly understand one another, then it stands to reason that, without all those 'difficulties' you previously mentioned and for which I freely take the blame, operating as I was under certain misconceptions, there should be nothing standing in the way of our having one last quick fling before the final parting of the ways. Isn't that right?"

"No! I mean, yes," stammered Angelique. The devil! she fumed, realizing how cleverly he had duped her. If she refused him now, it would be the same as admitting everything else was a lie. "I mean, it is not that I would not wish to . . . to . . ." Unable to find a delicate way of putting it, she filled in the blank with suitably suggestive gestures of her head and the hands. "But surely you are in a hurry to reach this place to which you are going? At least that was the impression you gave to me."

"And you were quite right," agreed the captain with a suspicious twitch at the corners of his lips, "but fortunately—or unfortunately, depending on your point of view—it is raining cats and dogs outside. With the roads being what they are, I'm afraid we shall just simply have to put up here for the night."

"Oh!" Angelique exclaimed, turning her head to see that in truth while they had been otherwise involved, the clouds had burst forth with a veritable deluge.

"Quite so," observed the captain, drily. "And now, unless you have some further objection, a headache perhaps, or some female complaint . . . ?" He left the statement incomplete as, insufferably cool, he undid the buttons at the top of his breeches.

"Well, I-I—," she tried, but unable to come up with a thing that would not sound wholly preposterous and contrived, she bitterly clamped her mouth shut. Then, totally naked, he had stretched out on the bed. Angelique hastily averted her eyes from the sight of that magnificent male body propped on one elbow beside her. *Sacriste!* she fumed. He did not play fair, *ce capitaine!*

That was all the time she was to be given to contemplate her dilemma, however, as the devious captain was already looming over her, his hand lifting to fondle a shiny raven lock falling enticingly over

143

one breast.

"It was this, you know, that really gave you away," he observed irrelevantly.

"Gave me a-away?" Angelique faltered, finding it suddenly difficult to think at all coherently. "What are you t-talking about?"

"As soft as silk to the touch and scented with rosemary," he expanded, crushing the curl in his hand. "You'd have been the first peasant wench I'd ever met who squandered money on hair tonics and lotions."

Only then did it come to her that he was referring to the one flaw in the disguise she had worn to flee the convent.

"Bah! I could not bring myself to rub the onion and garlic on my hair and my skin," she blurted, then instantly caught her lip between her teeth as she realized how foolish that must have sounded. Her brow darkened at sight of the glimmer of amusement in Locke's eyes. But by then she had new thoughts to occupy her as those incorrigible fingers moved to tug delicately at the satin ends of the topmost of the bows holding her bodice together in front.

"And who could blame you," he said. Having finished with the top bow, he shifted his attention to the next and the next. "Disgusting things, garlic and onions."

Angelique caught her breath as the caraco fell open to reveal the enchanting swell of her bosom above her silk chemise. Desperately she searched her mind for something to add to the less than scintillating topic of conversation as Locke firmly but gently slipped the jacket down off her shoulders, leaving her no choice but to pull her arms free.

A rather feeble "indeed" was all she could manage, which was not remarkable, considering the fact that the odious captain had lowered his head to explore the intriguing valley between her breasts. As little shocks of pleasure shuddered through her entire length at the featherlight caress of his lips and tongue, she was hardly

144

aware that he had surreptitiously released the drawstring at the back of her skirt. She knew only that his hands were driving her deliciously mad as they worked the velvet fabric down over her hips and thighs. Finally, impatient to be near him, she arched, helped him to free her of the stupid clothes that kept him from her.

When at last she had been relieved, not only of the skirt, but of her chemise, half-boots, and silk stockings as well, she uttered a small groan and pulled him down to her, her mouth seeking his with an eagerness that surprised even him.

Locke returned her embrace with the sublime feeling of a man who has stumbled by accident upon a delectable feast. Calling into play his not inconsiderable experience, he made love to her, teasing and arousing her, seeking out the sensitive areas of her body until she writhed in mounting ecstasy and long sighs of rapture shuddered deliriously through her entire length.

Never had Locke known such a woman. Once aroused, she was generous and uninhibited in her lovemaking, giving of herself freely, responding to his touch with innocent abandon. She was all sweet suppleness and fire, was his Angel. Her wondrously lithe body roused him to a feverish pitch of desire. She wrapped her legs about him and embraced him in the warm, moist cradle of her thighs. She molded herself to his lean, muscular length and moved sensuously beneath him. She caressed him with her lips and tongue. Her hands ran feverishly over the rippling muscles of his back until they shaped themselves to the firm masculine buttocks and pressed him hungrily to her. It was all he could do to maintain control over his swelling desire to take her, and at last he drew back, biding his time until her need should become equal to his own.

Angelique, feeling him withdraw, uttered a small cry and arched toward him. Her fingers clutched at the muscular shoulders, but mercilessly he held her away as he stroked her quivering body with hands and lips that deliberately learned her flesh. Helpless shivers coursed down her spine as he ran his tongue lightly over the exquisitely sensitive column of her neck and, coming to the base of the throat, molded his lips to the throbbing pulse. She groaned and lifted toward him, her blood on fire, as he traced the swelling contours of her breasts, the nipples peaking with desire, her waist, so small he might have spanned it with his hands alone, and finally the intimate place between her thighs. Sigh after sigh burst from her lips as he teased and caressed her.

She was his slave, and eagerly she gave of herself to him, to the mastery of his hands upon her body, to lips that sent shudders of delight radiating upward from her belly. Her head moved aimlessly against the pillow. She tangled her fingers in his hair and murmured his name over and over in a delirious litany of rising ecstasy, until at last she thought she must die with the unbearable anguish of desire.

With a groan seemingly wrenched from her depths, she braced her hands against the headboard and arched toward him. Quickly Locke came to her. Spreading wide her thighs, he pressed his hard manhood against the swollen orifice of her body. The muscles along his back and shoulders stood out as he poised above her, his own need an aching torment. Calling upon every ounce of an iron will, he held himself away from her as she strained upwards, wanting him, needing him to come into her.

"Tell me *now*, Angel," he whispered hoarsely, his body glistening with beads of sweat. "Tell me that you cannot feel anything for me."

A shuddering gasp broke from her as she stared wildly up into the steel flames of his eyes.

"Tell me . . . you didn't . . . lie," he said, making a shallow foray into her warm, moist depths, then pulling back again.

"Damn you!" she groaned, hating him for using her so, hating him for making her want him until she thought she must die from it, hating him for making her love him.

146

"I-I *cannot*!" she gasped.

A fierce light of triumph leaped to his eyes. Then lifting himself up and back, he drove deeply into the moist, molten depths of her. An anguished cry seemed torn from her as she opened to his thrust. Her fingernails sank into the muscular hardness of his shoulders. Then her slender legs wrapped about him, and she moved with him, everything forgotten but the swelling flood that carried her toward the cresting heights of passion.

She heard him utter her name like a groan as his seed burst forth inside of her. Then her flesh was constricting about his with wave upon wave of glorious release, and she clung to him, shuddering with sighs. Finally they collapsed together into a tangled heap on the bed. His face nuzzled into the warm curve of her neck, he murmured words of endearment.

"Angele. My sweet torment. So soft, so delectably wild. You drive me mad with your beautiful body."

Angelique felt tears of bitterness and anger sting her eyes. He had used her, she thought, like a whore. Worse, like a slave with no thoughts or feelings of her own. His words meant nothing. In truth, they were like barbs stinging her, for he had forced her to confess that she lied when she said he meant nothing to her. Deliberately he had tricked her, while she had felt only the very great tenderness for him, the passion that to her had been something of the most beautiful until he had ruined it for her. It was not fair that she should ache inside for him, when she meant nothing to him. Nothing! The devil! He deserved to be horsewhipped for such trickery!

Thus it was that Locke, lifting his head to look into her face, was met with a stormy shimmer of blue-violet eyes. In spite of himself, he felt his loins leap anew at sight of her breathtaking beauty.

"*Gouape,*" she spat at him. "*Goujat!*"

The odious captain grinned.

"A blackguard and a cad?" he murmured, as though considering the possibilities. "Yes, I suppose you're

147

right. Unfortunately, I couldn't see any other way of getting the truth out of you. And you have to admit it worked like a bloody charm."

"*La vache!*" she ground out between clenched teeth. Her fingers curled like claws, she raked at the hatefully grinning face.

Locke ducked and, clasping her in a bear hug rolled over on his back, carrying her with him. Angelique came up on top, her legs astraddle the muscular thighs. In a fury, she struggled to break free of the arms clamped like steel bands about her back.

"Let . . . me . . . go!" she panted, on the verge of frustrated tears. "I hate you! You are vile and—and mean. I will never forgive you for this. Never!"

"Never is a long time, my love," observed the captain, apparently not in the least remorseful. "Once you're my wife, you may hate me at your leisure. Till then, I propose we agree to a truce. You give me your word you won't try to escape me, and I'll give you mine I won't bind and gag you while we both get some sleep. That seems fair, don't you think?"

"Bah! You would not dare tie me up!" Angelique passionately declared. "And, me, I have already sworn I would do anything to be free of you, *M'sieu le Capitaine.* If you do not let me go, I will scream until somebody comes. And then I will tell them how you have abducted me against my will, do you understand?"

"Yes, as a matter of fact, I'd say you'd made yourself perfectly clear."

The ensuing struggle was of rather short duration, Locke being by far the stronger of the two. In a matter of a few minutes only, Angelique found herself trussed neatly by the wrists to the bedpost. Straining against the strips of bedsheet that comprised her bonds, she stared in impotent fury at Locke over the gag stuffed in her mouth.

"Yes, that should do nicely," remarked the captain, observing the leap of sparks in the beautiful eyes.

"Maybe I should have warned you that while I've

148

never fancied myself much of a gentleman, I am known for keeping my promises. You may believe me when I say I'm sorry it has to be this way, but I did give you your choice, after all."

Bitter tears of anger and humiliation in her eyes, Angelique deliberately averted her face. *Voyons*, what a fool she had been to let pride get in the way of cunning. In truth, she should have known he would do just as he said. Had not her *maman* always told her the wise woman never lost either her temper or her head with a man like this one? Always she had said it was better to employ the smile that beguiles and the few well-shed tears to get what one wanted. Well, obviously she had been right. And, she, Angelique, who had been too naive, too proud, to sink to such tactics, would never be so foolish again!

Exhausted, she at last fell into a deep sleep, aided, had she only known it, by a mild sleeping draught, which Locke had introduced into her coffee. Consequently, she did not know when the odious captain gently eased the gag from her mouth. Nor did she stir when he unloosed her hands and, tying one end of the makeshift rope about her wrist and the other end about his, stretched out beside her.

For a long time he lay watching her, a faint crease in his brow, as she slept with an aura of such innocence about her that he experienced a decidedly unpleasant twinge of conscience at the manner in which he had used her. She looked like a bloody angel, he thought cynically. And there was no denying that she was a glorious creature—hopelessly naive, infuriatingly proud, and appallingly fearless. She was a complete and utter hoyden, wholly unpredictable—a rogue. But glorious nonetheless. As a matter of fact, he was ruefully aware that his finely honed instincts for self-preservation were crying out to him to flee from her just as far and as fast as he could. He told himself that it was some perversity in his character, the stubborn streak, perhaps, or the recklessness that had gotten him into dangerous waters more than a few times in his past, that kept him there. Or maybe it was just his cursed sense of honor. Whatever the hell it was, it was like to drive him bloody well mad before everything was said and done.

At last, cursing himself for a bloody fool, he yanked the blankets up over his shoulders and, determinedly turning his back on the delectable creature beside him, went resolutely to sleep.

Chapter 9

Tantalized to wakefulness by the aroma of freshly made coffee, Angelique stirred, only to snuggle down deeper into the cozy nest of blankets. She lay for awhile, dreamily contented, her thoughts aimless and unfocused. A smile touched her lips as snatches of memory drifted through her mind—warm hands stroking her body, lips that sent fire coursing through her veins, and then, finally, Locke forcing the truth from her. All at once she came wholly awake.

"*Sacriste!*" she exclaimed, recalling all too vividly the humiliation of having been bound to the bedpost and gagged. Her eyes flashing dangerously, she bolted upright. "*Le goujat!*"

"Ah, awake at last, are we?" drawled an insufferably amused voice. "You slept well, I trust?"

Her glance flashed to the tall, handsome figure, lounging carelessly before the fire. She blushed at the look in his eyes, and, made acutely aware that she was indecently exposed from the neck to the waist, snatched the bedcovers to her breast. Rigidly she stared straight before her, the blood singing in her ears.

"Why yes, *M'sieu le Capitaine*. Thank you," she answered coldly, wondering when he had had the decency to untie her.

"Good," he said. The corners of his lips twitched. "I'm

151

sure you'll be glad to hear we'll be going on this morning. The storm broke sometime in the night, and from the looks of it we shouldn't have too much trouble. With any luck we could reach the duke's hunting lodge just about the time they're sitting down to tea. The perfect time to announce our wedding plans, don't you think?"

His ironic bark of laughter made her wince and grit her teeth.

The devil! How arrogant was this capitaine, she fumed, forced to bite her tongue to keep from delivering him a sharp retort. She had learned her lesson all too well the night before. To give in now to her hasty temper would avail her nothing. In truth, with this man it were far better to keep her wits about her. Unconsciously her shoulders drooped as it came to her how very hopeless was her situation. This hunting lodge of the duke, no doubt it was isolated, and once there, she did not see how she would ever get away.

"Perhaps, my love," drawled Locke, interrupting her unrewarding thoughts, "you would care to rise and dress for breakfast?"

"As you wish, m'sieu," she answered with a shrug of indifference. "Perhaps it would not be too much to ask you to turn your back . . . ?"

She could feel his eyes on her and with an effort forced herself not to fidget. Not wishing him to read the despair in her heart, she kept her gaze lowered to the counterpane across her feet. Thus she did not see the flicker of doubt, like a fleeting shadow, cross his face.

Cursing to himself, Locke searched in vain for the spark of defiance that he had come to expect from her. Christ, she had the look of a woman beaten into submission, a pale ghost of the spirited young female who had caused him nothing but trouble from the first moment he had laid eyes on her. His lips thinned to a grim line as he grappled with the possibility that he had gone too far. Good God, if he had broken her spirit! The sudden sharp wrench in the vicinity of his heart took him by surprise, and instantly his mouth hardened.

Hellsfire! What alternative had she left him? He could hardly have gone to sleep trusting that the foolhardy little spitfire would do nothing so rash as to flee, alone and at night, in the fury of a storm. Good God, one might as well expect to fly as expect anything so unlikely of the impetuous Angel. As long as there was the least possibility that her life was in danger, he could see no other course before him save the one he had already determined on.

Catching her taking a peep at him from beneath the luxurious veil of her eyelashes, a sudden gleam came to his eye. On the other hand, he thought, maybe it was time he gave her the benefit of a doubt. Once at Briarcroft, after all, he could hardly expect to keep the little spitfire under lock and key, which meant he had to find some other means of persuasion.

His answer, when it came, was couched in the old, cool drawling accents, which thus far had never failed to arouse her ire.

"But of course, my love. As a matter of fact, I was just going down to speak to the driver, so you'll have all the privacy you need." He paused significantly, a faint, mocking light in his eyes. "I *can* trust you, Angel, not to take advantage of my generosity?"

Startled, Angelique at last turned to look at him.

"Your generosity, m'sieu?" she queried bitterly, her gaze wide-eyed in amazement on the lean figure handsomely arrayed in the French style, complete with flowered waistcoat, dark brown unmentionables and a matching coat, which, despite the careless manner in which it was worn, seemed perfectly fitted to the broad masculine shoulders. "But, Capitaine, you may believe *that* is the very *last* thing I mean to take advantage of."

For the barest instant their glances clashed and held. Then deliberately Locke turned away.

"Excellent," he replied. "I'm gratified to see that you've apparently come to your senses. By the way," he added, slinging on his greatcoat and moving with supple grace to the door, "I've had hot water and towels sent up. And feel free to help yourself to breakfast. I highly recommend the beefsteak and eggs. If there's anything else you need, just ring for the maid. I shouldn't be gone much more than thirty minutes or so. Unless, of course, you require more time than that for your needs?"

"No. It should be more than enough time," she answered falteringly, unsettled by this unforeseen turn of events. Never had she thought following her mother's advice could produce such immediate results!

She was even more astounded, however, that when leaving the room, he made not the least attempt to lock her in. He must be very sure of himself, she thought, frowning. Then instantly she suffered a surge of humiliation as it came to her that he undoubtedly believed he had tamed her into submission.

A spark of resentment kindled in her eyes. She would show him she was not so easily broken. In truth she would rather die than let him know how close she had come to giving in to him.

No sooner had the door closed behind him, than Angelique was out of the bed, searching the room for her caraco and skirt. She found them, laid neatly out on the settee before the fire. A frown knit her brow as she noted that they had been freshly brushed, the travel stains removed. What was more, Locke had obviously ordered her things brought up, for there they were, the battered valise and bandbox, set conveniently out on a bench awaiting her pleasure.

In the wake of the abominable manner in which he had treated her up till then, such condescension, far from gladdening her heart, only made her all the more suspicious. *Voyons!* If she did not know better, she might think the capitaine had decided to woo her. Unexpectedly, she suffered a soft thrill at such a farfetched notion. In truth, her heart gave a little lurch beneath her breast. Then immediately she caught herself. But no, she

154

thought, deliberately conjuring up the memory of the ruthlessness with which he had used her only a few hours earlier. Rather than try to win her heart, it was far more likely he was afraid she would disgrace him before his grand friends, the duke and duchess, she told herself.

But of course, that must be it. It would not be at all convenient, after all, to keep his bride-to-be bound and gagged, and how else could he make certain of her compliance except to buy it with these little acts of kindness? Maybe he even thought to have her melt into his arms upon his return. He would soon learn that he was very much mistaken.

Hastily she washed and dressed. Then, gathering up her valise and bandbox, she started across the room to the door that opened on the gallery overlooking the courtyard. Unfortunately, however, as she came abreast of the table laden with covered dishes, delectable aromas wafted to her and teased her nostrils. To her chagrin, her stomach gave an unladylike rumble. In spite of herself, she hesitated and, chiding herself for a fool, experimentally removed the covers to discover not only the eggs and the beefsteak that the captain had recommended, but also toast and jams, thin slices of ham, apple tarts, and a small pot of hot chocolate.

"*Voyons,* such a feast!" she murmured wistfully. A little voice whispered in her ear that perhaps there might be time enough for just the one or two bites. *Le capitaine* had said the half of an hour, after all, and it could be a very long time before another opportunity to break the fast presented itself. Feeling the old recklessness surge through her like the intoxicating effects of a potent wine, she seated herself and reached for the napkin beside her plate. A small gasp of surprise escaped her lips as a single, exquisite red rose dropped out of the square of linen onto the table.

Sacriste, she cursed softly as with fingers that trembled slightly she lifted the lovely thing to inhale its fragrance. He was a man of the most bewildering, *ce capitaine,* she

155

thought. Never before had she met anyone like him, one moment to send her into a fury and the next to so totally disarm her. With such a one, her life would not be of the stifling dreariness that it had been at the convent.

In spite of herself, her lips curved in a small, whimsical smile as it came to her to wonder what it would be like to be courted and wooed by the detestable captain. *Ouïe*, to dance only once with him at a grand ball or to stroll with him through a moonlit garden, perhaps a pause among the roses that he might steal a kiss!

Realizing all at once where her thoughts had taken her, she came to her senses with a jerk.

"*La vache!* He is the devil, I think," she muttered, "*ce capitaine*, who thinks to win my heart with the rose."

Angry with herself, she rose abruptly from the table and gathering up her things, started once more for the door. But again she stopped and slowly turned, her glance going as of its own volition to the blossom lying on the table where she had flung it down. For a moment she wavered. Then, in something like pique, she set down the valise and bandbox and hastily went back to snatch the lovely thing up. Chiding herself for giving in to sentiment, she pinned the flower to her bodice beneath her cloak, then, opening the door enough to poke her head out, she peered cautiously out onto the gallery.

Her heart gave a little leap as she saw that not only was the gallery deserted, but in the courtyard below, the hostlers were busy hitching a fresh team to a mail coach, preparing to depart. In an instant she was through the door and, running along the gallery, found a wooden stairway that descended into the courtyard. Casting a hasty glance about the cobblestone enclosure for a tall, arrogant figure and seeing no one of that description, she crossed quickly to the waiting coach.

"*Pardon*, m'sieu," she called up to the coachman swathed in a many-caped driving coat. "Do you have the room inside for a passenger?" Having already seen that the interior was empty, she thought this a somewhat

156

foolish question, but the man at the reins appeared to take it all in stride.

"It'll cost you two shillings, miss," he grunted, his voice muffled in a scarf that covered most of his face below eyes, which, in turn, were obscured by a wide-brimmed hat. "Due when we reach the end of the line. Toss your things inside and climb aboard, if you're coming. We've a schedule to meet, and I ain't exactly in the mood for waiting, if you gets my meanin'."

"I understand," she shouted back. It was on her lips to ask at what place she would find herself upon reaching the end of the line, but, afraid to jeopardize her seat in the coach and not wishing to be spotted by a pair of gimlet blue eyes, she obediently struggled to get the door open and, afterwards, to heave her bags inside.

Hardly had she managed the thing and climbed in after them, than the sound of a whiplash cracked through the air. Frantically she clutched at the strap as the coach lurched forward at a madcap pace.

"*Sacriste!*" she gasped. "He is crazy, this imbecile of a driver."

At any moment she feared the coach would turn over on its side as it made a mad dash about the interior of the courtyard and, careering on two wheels, swept out the gate onto the thoroughfare. Nor did the pace let up on the treacherous road fraught with sharp curves and hedged in on both sides by the trees of New Forest.

Angelique, fighting desperately to keep from being thrown from the seat, was battered and bruised before they had covered a quarter of a mile. A string of invectives uttered in a mixture of English and French burst from her lips.

La vache! The fool was either mad or drunk, she thought and uttered a blistering oath as the back wheel, bouncing over an exposed rock, hurtled the coach into the air. They came down with a jar that yanked the strap from Angelique's hand. The next moment found her floundering on the floor. Encumbered by her cloak and tangled in her skirts, she managed to claw her way back onto the seat, only to be knocked immediately down again as the coach maneuvered a hairpin curve. To her further dismay, her valise and bandbox came toppling down on top of her, the latter bursting open upon impact and spilling out its contents.

It was too much! Angelique's temper snapped.

"Stop, you fool!" she shrieked at the top of her lungs. "Stop it—at once!"

It seemed an eternity passed before at last the coach slowed and lumbered to a halt. Bitter tears stung her eyes as she struggled to right herself. Then the door was flung open, and, a blistering set-down all ready on the tip of her tongue, she forced up her head to look at this fool who had done his best to kill her.

Whatever she had been about to say was never fated to go beyond her lips. It was frozen there by the sight of hatefully blue laughing eyes observing her coolly from the opening.

"*You!*" was the only utterance she managed to get out.

"Is it your usual practice to ride on the floor amidst all your baggage, Mad'moiselle DuFour?" Locke queried blandly, taking in at a glance his bride-to-be's less-than-dignified position. Her cloak askew and her skirts hitched up nearly to her waist, she presented a delectable picture of womanhood indecently dishabille.

Angelique gave him a look of venomous dislike.

"But of course, *M'sieu le Capitaine,*" she retorted witheringly. "Just as it would seem to be your practice to steal mail coaches, which you then drive like the devil. What have you done with the driver and the passengers? Bound and gagged them? And left them to die the lingering death? I pray to God that you will be apprehended and hanged for your crimes, m'sieu."

"I'm sorry to disappoint you, Angel, but I'm afraid I haven't broken any laws. Unless buying up all the seats and bribing the driver to let me take the reins to the next post house is a crime. And if it is, I haven't heard of it."

Angelique's eyes flashed blue-violet sparks.

"Oh, how cunningly you laid your plans. Everything —my clothes most carefully cleaned and laid out, the oh, so delightful breakfast, the coach which conveniently waits. Bah! In my heart I *knew* you were setting the trap for me. But why go to all this trouble? I ask myself, when it would be so much simpler to stand guard over me, like the gendarme with the prisoner."

"Simpler, perhaps," agreed Locke, apparently not in the least repentant of his iniquities, "but hardly conducive to teaching you a much deserved lesson, I'm afraid. One of these days maybe you'll learn you can't lie to me and expect to get away with it."

Angelique uttered an explosive *"Oh!"* and, grabbing for the first thing that came to hand, in this instance a tortoise shell hairbrush, flung it at the captain's head.

Laughing, Locke ducked.

"I did not lie to you, Capitaine," she declared, reaching for a brocade shoe and sending it flying in the wake of the first projectile. Locke dodged and lunged for the infuriated Angel in self-defense.

"Where . . . I . . . come from—" he grunted as he pinned the young beauty to the floor in time to save himself from having a gold-filigreed jewel box bounced off his skull, "—that's what *we* call it when someone doesn't tell the truth."

Nearly choking with rage, Angelique rained ineffectual blows with her fists on his back.

"Where you . . . come from," she bitterly declared, "you are all . . . bullies and-and . . . poppinapes of the most arrogant."

An unholy gleam of amusement leaped in his eyes.

"Something of a cross between poppinjays and jackanapes, is that it?"

"Yes, exactly!" snapped Angelique. A blush stained her cheeks at being caught in the *faux-pas*. "All of those things." All at once she ceased to struggle. "I cannot help it, m'sieu, if you mistook my meaning," she said, recognizing the futility of matching her meager strength against his superior one. "I said the last thing I meant to take advantage of was your generosity, but I was referring to your generosity in wishing to marry me. That I cannot and will not do, Capitaine, no matter what terrible things you do to me."

Locke, who had been watching the swift play of emotions cross the lovely face, stifled an exasperated sigh. It came to him that he wished she could bring herself to trust him.

"You," he pronounced in no uncertain terms, "are undoubtedly the most obstinate female I've ever had the misfortune to come across. However, I think you'll find I can be an extremely patient man." Angelique could not keep herself from wincing as he lifted an oddly gentle hand to brush a tear from her cheek. "And reasonably understanding, if given half a chance. Are you afraid of me, Angel?" he added, after the barest pause.

Angelique's belly gave a little lurch. *Sacriste!* He was doing it again—melting her resistance down, battering her defenses with the unexpected gentleness that tore at her heart. How could she tell him it was for him that she felt the very great fear? She shuddered, haunted by the memory of her encounter with Chantal, still vivid in her mind, and by the dreams sent by the *houngan* Mozambe to call her home—and haunted by the memory of Etienne Joliet and the unfinished vengeance of those who believed she had betrayed him!

"Me, I am afraid of nothing, m'sieu," she retorted. In spite of the defiant tilt of the delightfully pointed chin, she could not keep her voice from sounding just the tiniest bit gruff.

A wry smile twisted at the captain's lip.

"No," he acerbically agreed. "You are utterly fearless, which is one of the things I find most appalling about you. Come now, don't you think it's time you came clean with me? What really bothers you so much about this wedding? Nothing you've told me yet gives me any

160

reason to suppose you'd be better off on your own than married to me. Who knows, in time you might even come to entertain a certain fondness for the idea."

"Bah," she flung back at him, "I have heard these words before—from the slavers who trade in human flesh. Can you truly think I should love you for robbing me of my freedom?"

It was a telling blow, one for which he was not in the least prepared. Silently, he cursed himself for a bloody fool. Had he in truth become so insensitive that he could not have seen it for himself—her fierce pride, her passionate refusal to bend or give in to what she saw as his coercion of her will to his. If Angel did indeed carry the blood of African slaves in her veins, she would naturally resist any treatment that hinted of coercion with just such a fierceness. Such a reaction must have been inevitable. But the fact of the matter was that it had never occurred to him to think of it in precisely such terms, probably because it had never made a whit of difference to him what blood ran in her veins. She was Angel, as lovely and spirited a woman as one could ever hope to meet—tempestuous, maddening, argumentative, beguiling, impossibly proud, and utterly desirable—a female, in short, who was desperately in need of a man's protection, whether she liked it or not. It had been that simple. But all at once a great deal about his rebellious love had been made to seem abundantly clear, and suddenly nothing was quite so simple as previously it had appeared. How greatly she must loathe him for having misjudged her and her motives!

For a moment longer Locke studied the averted profile of her face, the smile gone from his lips to be replaced by a singularly hard expression. At last, he moved as if to leave her, when something caught his eyes. The dark eyebrows lifted a bare fraction of an inch in the handsome brow. Then to Angelique's chagrin, instead of going away, he settled more comfortably astraddle her body pinned helplessly beneath his.

161

"You know, it never once occurred to me that you might look at it that way. Funny, isn't it. But then I've never met a woman like you before. One who wouldn't jump at the chance to be my wife. The fact is, I guess I've come to be more than a little cynical—knowing it was my fortune women found so irresistible."

He paused, his hand moving apparently absently to retrieve something that lay on the floor by her head.

"Are you sure you won't change your mind?" he queried, twirling the stem of a somewhat battered red rose between his thumb and forefinger. "About marrying me, I mean."

Blushing furiously, Angelique gave him a withering look.

"No doubt I feel very sorry for you, m'sieu," she retorted. "But, me, I have no interest in your money."

"I begin to believe you don't at that," he commented drily. "It would appear that I may have entirely misjudged you. I might even go so far as to say that quite possibly I owe you an apology."

"An apology, but no, how can you think so? You have only called me the whore, the opportunist who would crawl into your bed to trap you into the marriage against your will. But that was not enough. *Non,* you abduct me and bring me into this country where I am the stranger. You, m'sieu, dared to bind my hands and stuff the filthy rag in my mouth. And now that you have nearly killed me in this runaway coach, you think you owe me the apology? If I did not hurt so very bad from the bruises, I would laugh in your face for such an apology. And now you will let me go free, *non?*"

"No."

At Angelique's gasp of furious dismay, Locke odiously grinned.

"Come now, you must see that I can't turn you loose, unprotected, in a strange land. What I propose is that you give me time to prove to you that I'm not such a despicable fellow as you've made me out to be. A fortnight is all I ask. Two weeks at Briarcroft under the pretense that you have agreed to become my wife. In return, I promise to act the perfect gentleman, and if, by the end of the fortnight, you still feel you cannot go through with this marriage, I agree to take you wherever you wish to go. All the way to the West Indies, if you like. What do you say, Angel?"

Angelique stared at him doubtfully, a frown on her face.

"*Non,*" she said, with a shake of the head. "I do not trust you. You are up to something, I think."

"But I promise you I'm not," he insisted. "It would ease my conscience if I knew you were securely settled somewhere," he went on, when she appeared to be wavering. "And what could it possibly hurt? On your own, it might take you as long as a week, maybe more, to make your way back to the coast, find a ship bound for the West Indies, and manage to book passage. This way, you can settle back and let me take care of everything. Who knows, you might even enjoy yourself a little, and without the worry of wondering how you're going to make it on your own."

"And you, Capitaine. What do you get from this arrangement?"

"I, mad'moiselle, am saved from the matchmaking proclivities of the duchess of Waincourt. I might even have the chance to do a little fishing with the duke, who swears he has the best trout stream in the world right in his own backyard. Otherwise," he shrugged philosophically, "I'll no doubt find all my time taken up at impromptu balls and routs. My dearest Sabra would never overlook an opportunity to show me off to every marriageable female of her acquaintance, I promise you."

Angelique gazed doubtfully at the handsome face. Who was this duchess of Waincourt that he should speak of her with the very great affection? she wondered. The former love, perhaps, who had turned him against all other women? Unwittingly she experienced a sharp stab of jealousy.

"This you would not like, m'sieu?" she queried, her eyes, probing, on his. Somehow she, too, was not overly fond of the idea.

"*Oui*, Angele," mimicked Locke, the laughter dancing in his eyes. "This I would not like at all. In fact, you'd be doing me a very great favor if you chose to save me from it."

The look he gave her made her feel funny inside, and in spite of all the despicable things he had done, she felt herself weakening.

"For only the one fortnight?" she prompted, wanting to make sure of the terms of the agreement. "And then, no matter what, you will let me go free?"

Sensing her capitulation, Locke flashed the smile that had devastated more than one feminine heart.

"Two weeks," he affirmed, shoving himself up and stepping backward onto the step. He held out a strong, supple hand. "And then, if you still want to go, I will either take you where you choose, or make the arrangements to have you taken. Do we have a deal?"

Angelique hesitated, the small voice in her head telling her not to trust this charming side of the captain. And yet, what other choice did she have? At least this way, she thought wryly, she bought herself the time.

"Very well, m'sieu," she agreed at last, albeit reluctantly, and grudgingly took the hand he offered. "It is the deal. For two weeks I will try to be the oh-so-charming fiancée for you. And then it will be *finis* between us."

Locke, helping her up, suppressed a smile. Finished, my love? he thought to himself. I'm afraid not. Not if *I* have anything to say to the matter.

Aloud he said nothing, however, as he applied himself to restoring the spilled contents of Angel's bandbox to their proper place. Then, turning to the girl, who was pretending not to watch him from out of the corners of her lovely eyes, he offered to help her mount once more to her seat in the coach.

A look of distaste crossed her face.

"*Sacriste!* Rather would I walk than set one foot in that torture chamber," she declared with obvious feeling. "*Non.* This time, I ride on the top with you, *M'sieu le Capitaine,* or, me, I do not go to this hunting lodge of the duke."

Locke, observing the determined jut of her chin, wisely forbore from arguing. After all, though the air was brisk, the sun was out, and bundled in a fur rug, she should do well enough, he thought. Besides, it might be to his advantage to have her beside him for an afternoon ride. From all that he had heard described of New Forest, it could make for an extremely pleasant outing.

In short order, Angelique found herself perched on the high seat beside the captain, who took great care to see that she was snugly wrapped in a lap rug before he took up the reins. Releasing the brake, he set the team at a brisk, ground-eating trot.

Grateful to be free of the hateful coach, Angelique contented herself for a time with observing the sun-dappled forest of oak and beech, interspersed with sunny little glens and open meadows, dotted with sheep.

"How very different it is from the jungles of Saint Dominique," she exclaimed presently, hardly aware that she had spoken out loud.

Locke, who had been watching her unawares for some time, grinned appreciatively.

"There is a decided lack of the exotic, I imagine. No incessant chatter of 'woman's tongue.' No silk-cotton tree to stalk the forest at night. Mere gorse, when on the islands passion flowers and orchids grow wild. I'm afraid you must find all this pretty dull by comparison."

Startled at his knowledge of the flora of her beloved island, Angelique glanced obliquely at Locke.

"You know the jungles of Saint Dominique, Capitaine?" she asked, wondering that her papa had never mentioned this before. Always Locke had been the man of mystery, sailing to distant places Angelique had only read or dreamed about. It had even once been rumored that he had perished somewhere in the China Sea. *Hein!* How her heart had grieved to think of the heroic *capitaine*, forever lost to her, slain, perhaps, by cannibals or dying the lingering death of the fever. She was in her second year at the convent in Paris before she heard he had returned, bringing with him copra and pearls from the South Sea Islands, and fine silks and jade from China, a fortune to swell the already rich coffers of the partnership of Locke and Gilbert. The following spring he was gone again, the Orient drawing him like a moth to the enduring flame of the East.

Locke shrugged.

"Most of my youth was spent roaming the Caribbean," he said. "St. Vincent, the Virgins, Antigua, Barbuda—there weren't many ports of call closed to the ships of Tyree and Locke in those days."

"And now you go instead to the far places. The Orient! How I envy you. You must have many stories to tell."

She had spoken wistfully, her eyes shining at the thought of the adventures he must have had while she had been growing up in the convent with only her books and her dreams to nurture her restless spirit. Only then, when it was already too late to call back the words, did she realize the slip that she had made.

"A few," he admitted, after the barest pause, and just a little too casually. It appeared that he would say something more, and Angelique steeled herself for the inevitable, when mercifully a sudden movement off to the side of the road caught her eye.

"Oh, look, Capitaine!" she cried. "There. Do you see them?"

Locke, turning his glance in the direction in which she was pointing, eased back on the reins.

"Whoa! Easy, lads," he called and pulled the team up as a band of wild ponies broke out of the trees.

166

Sleek and fleet-footed, their manes and tails flying, they swept across the road in front of the coach and vanished in a flash of color. Angelique's sweet peal of laughter rang out in the silence left by their passing.

"How beautiful it is!" she exclaimed. "The horse that runs free. And, there, there are so many. Never did I think to see such a thing in England."

A twisted smile played across the captain's lips as he gazed at something no less lovely—Angelique, her eyes sparkling and her eyes aglow with excitement as she strained to catch a final glimpse of the wild ponies of New Forest. Everything else forgotten in the thrill of the moment, she looked anything but the fallen Angel she had tried to make him believe she was. In fact, if anything, she appeared little more than a child—absurdly young and vulnerable, and as unspoiled as the marvellous wild ponies, the sight of which had chased the shadows from her eyes.

Picking up the reins, he set the team in motion again. Whatever questions he had for his infuriatingly elusive Angel could wait for a later time, he decided. It would hardly have been to his advantage, after all, to squander a perfectly lovely day quarreling, especially when he was to be allowed only fourteen to attain the goal he had every intention of gaining for himself.

On the hunt in earnest now, Locke turned on the charm for which he was well known among the ladies of his acquaintance.

Chapter 10

Angelique was sorry when the post chaise, bearing the driver for the mail coach, caught up with them on the outskirts of a small village nestled in the woods. *Le capitaine* could be of the very charming when he chose to be, she had discovered. And in truth, he had exerted himself to engage her interest, describing with a keen wit and vivid detail the distant places he had seen. It was not until much later that she realized how skillfully he was managing to draw her out as well, leading her to relate a great deal more about herself than she had ever intended. Still, she did not think she had given anything away that was too revealing, she reflected, glancing sidelong at Locke's strong profile as he eased the cattle to a walk and finally a halt before a small country inn. She watched him drop with easy, supple grace from the driving seat to the ground and could not deny that she had enjoyed herself immensely in his company.

That thought, unfortunately, spoiled the moment for her, accompanied, as it was, by the realization that she dared not allow herself to become too enamored of *ce capitaine. Voyons*, it was bad enough, this power he had to make her blood burn with the flames of desire. How much worse would it be to wake up one morning and find she had been so foolish as to fall in love with him!

All at once she began to question the wisdom of the

bargain she had struck. Two weeks in the company of this new, oh-so-charming capitaine would fly on the wings of the very swift, and when they had all gone by, she would have nothing but the memories. In her heart she knew that for her it would not be an easy parting.

When Locke reached up to help her dismount, he was met with the sight of a subdued Angelique. He was granted a brief glimpse of huge, troubled eyes, before the thick lashes lowered. A frown flickered across his face. Then his strong hands closed about the tiny waist, and he lifted her down. When next she looked up, his unpredictable Angel had apparently recovered herself. The roguish dimple peeped forth at the corner of her mouth.

"It has been very charming, this ride in the country," she said. Tilting her head to one side, she awarded him a deliberately measuring glance. "But you, I think, have not been entirely fair with me. You have played this game many times before, *non?* In truth, I begin to think you are something of a rake, m'sieu."

Twin glints of laughter leaped to the compelling blue eyes.

"And you, mad'moiselle," he countered, "are perhaps not quite the fallen angel you've presented yourself to be, *vraiment?*"

Angelique's stomach gave a little lurch at the unwonted warmth in his gaze. Tilting her chin at him, she flashed him a haughty look, which, rather than the world-weary woman of experience she had hoped to achieve, gave her more the aura of a roguish young imp.

"An angel, m'sieu?" she retorted with only a tinge of bitterness beneath the flippant tone. "But that I have never been. A devil, perhaps. Or so I was often called at the convent."

Locke stared after her as she turned with a small flounce of her skirts and crossed to the waiting chaise. She was an enigma. One moment an adorable imp who

170

charmed without trying and the next a woman of unplumbed depths who tantalized and piqued his curiosity. One thing was certain, he decided. Miss Angele DuFour was a mystery that was not likely to pall on him in the unraveling.

It seemed to the two, having taken up the journey once more in the luxuriously appointed chaise, that a curtain of silence immediately fell over them. They rode without speaking, Angelique staring moodily out the window while the captain—sprawled comfortably in his corner, his booted feet propped carelessly on the seat opposite him—observed her from beneath the shadowy brim of his hat.

In such a manner they traveled several more miles over narrow, twisty roads, which carried them past scattered farmhouses and through quaint little hamlets boasting little more than a few thatch-roofed cottages clustered about the small parish church. In the shadowed depths of the forest, Angelique glimpsed the flash of birds' wings and, once, the graceful form of a deer, but of the wild ponies, she saw nothing. It was as if they, like the carefree hours engrossed in animated conversation with the man at her side, had been figments of a dream, nothing more, she thought with an odd little pang.

A few moments later, the coach lurched and, slowing, left the main road. At last Locke bestirred himself.

"It would seem we are nearing our destination," he remarked, cocking his head to see out the window. "I fancy this is the drive and that the house lies at the top of the hill."

Angelique, sensing an eagerness in him despite his habitually cool exterior, made no answer. No doubt he was of the very excited to see once more his former inamorata, she thought more than a little irritably, and turned her face to the window.

171

As the post chaise rumbled up the tree-lined drive, she caught glimpses of neat lawns, bordered in hedges, a summer house, gleaming palely amidst a stand of oaks, and in the distance, a silvery ribbon of water curling lazily between two hills. How beautiful it was, this gentle land of the English, and yet how strange that it would fill her heart with a sudden foreboding.

No sooner had that thought crossed her mind than the trees gave way and a noble house seemed to rear up before them.

Angelique, beholding Briarcroft crouched on the brow of a sloping hill, experienced a sudden sinking feeling in the pit of her stomach. The stately old manor of weathered stone dressed in ivy was hardly the simple hunting lodge she had expected it to be. With its twin towers and sculptured bay windows glinting in the sunlight, the great house presented an aspect of Elizabethan grandeur that was daunting to her.

"*Voyons*, who is this duke whose hunting lodge resembles a palace?" she breathed. Then with suddenly fulminating eyes, she turned on the captain. "You tricked me! You, with your words that would charm the snake. How could you have brought me here where I will be like the sore thumb sticking out?"

Locke's eyebrows swept quizzically up.

"I'm sorry, Angel," he observed mildly, "but I can't see what you're upset about. If anything, I'd expect you to feel right at home among the quality."

Angelique flung up her hands in exasperation. "At home, m'sieu? You think I will feel at home in this house fit for kings, when I have only the five gowns to wear and none of them suitable even for sitting down at the table? I am not so ignorant or naive that I do not know how it is with these people of the nobility. I have been to such houses before."

"Not to this house, mad'moiselle," Locke pointed out, insufferably amused at what he must obviously have considered a mere feminine foible. "And not with these people."

"You are a man. What can you possibly know what it is to be a woman among women? It is not bad enough that I am the foreigner—a French Creole among the British—but I must also appear of the very *gauche*. It is for this that you have brought me, I think. To teach me the humility." At last the raven head came up. "Very well, Capitaine," said Angelique bitterly. "You have your little joke at my expense. It is fair, is it not? I, who have wounded your pride, will pay for it."

A steely glint flashed in the captain's eyes, then vanished.

"I think, Angel," he drawled, "that you'll find you are creating a tempest in a teacup. The duke and duchess are not about to snub you. Of that you may be certain. As for my pride . . ." Angelique felt a small shiver travel up her spine at sign of the faint curl of the handsome lips. "I assure you it is quite intact. Furthermore, I mean to do everything in my power to keep it that way. Now, if there is nothing else bothering you, I heartily suggest you relax and simply enjoy the days that lie before us."

For a moment longer Angelique met the infuriating coolness of his stare. Then realizing there was nothing more to be said, she tightened her lips and looked away. As the coach swept up before the imposing portico and stopped, she fought to still the angry throb of her pulse. *Voyons*, was not the blood in her veins as good as theirs? She would show the capitaine and his duchesse that she, Angelique Gilbert, was not ashamed.

A footman dressed in the duke's blue and silver livery emerged from the house and approached the coach, but Locke, without waiting for his assistance, opened the door and stepped lithely down. Turning, he held out his hand to the pale-faced girl inside.

"Come, Angel," he said in his compellingly lazy drawl. "It is time for the duke of Waincourt and his duchess to

173

meet my bride-to-be."

Angelique's fingers tightened in her lap. Then lifting her eyes to meet his, she gave him a look which was deliberately searching.

"Of course, m'sieu," she answered, soberly. "It is only for the one fortnight, after all. And then I will be free of you. This you have promised."

As if accepting the challenge, Locke inclined his head. "Two weeks, mad'moiselle," he murmured, as he handed her down, "can be time enough to topple an empire."

Angelique, ushered by a stone-faced butler into the main hall of the great house, was met by Old World elegance steeped in time. Sunlight streaming through the leaded panes of bay windows at either end of the room brought out the rich grains of old wood paneling and shimmered off polished brass chandeliers suspended by long chains from the high-vaulted ceiling. A huge log crackled and blazed in a magnificent carved stone fireplace that took up nearly one end of the hall. In spite of the obvious wealth evidenced in the oriental rugs and various objets d'art ranged tastefully about the room, however, tapestry-covered sofas, high-backed wing chairs, a ponderous mahogany coffee table, and numerous occasional tables bearing cut-glass lamps lent it a homey quality. It was, she decided wistfully, a house that exuded warmth—a home that bore the loving touch of a woman with a caring heart. Instantly she suffered a small pang at the thought.

Her reflections were interrupted by a light, thrilling step, followed almost immediatley by a throaty cry.

"Wes? Oh, God, Wes, is it truly you?"

Angelique turned in time to see a tall, slender woman fling herself into the arms of the capitaine. Laughing and weeping at the same time, she clung tightly to his neck.

174

"Wes, you've come at last," she whispered brokenly. "I-I had come to believe you never would."

"Now you *are* being foolish." The captain laughed, and, catching her beneath the arms, lifted her, like a child, high into the air. "Didn't I tell you once that no matter where I was or what happened, I'd always find my way back to you?" he demanded, letting her lightly down again.

"You did," she answered, gazing fondly up at him. "You did, but in the end, if I remember correctly, it was I who had to find *you*. And even then, had it not been for a certain odiously conniving British captain, I doubt that I should ever have held you in my arms again. Oh, Wes, it *is* good to see you."

"And you, my darling Sabra, are no less a sight for sore eyes," confessed the captain, smiling—a trifle crookedly, thought Angelique, who felt decidedly *de trop* in the circumstances. "Now, let me have a look at you."

Dimpling naughtily, the woman gave him a deep curtsey, no less graceful for its playfulness.

"As you wish, Captain Locke," she said with beguiling coyness and obediently pirouetted before him. "And what think you? Am I greatly changed after presenting His Grace, not one, but two, lusty heirs and a third on the way?" she queried, cocking her head at him as she came gaily to a halt.

The look in the captain's eyes twisted at Angelique's heart. Never could she hope to see him gaze with such affection upon herself. And who could blame him? she thought, suffering a sharp stab of envy as she took in the exquisite loveliness of *la duchesse*. She was tall and fair to look upon, with the eyes, green like the sea, and hair, the color of burnished red-gold. A man would have to be blind not to be dazzled by such beauty.

"Motherhood obviously agrees with you," he answered her. "You are more stunning than even I remembered you."

"And you, my glib sea captain, are even more provoking than when you sailed away and left me to the tender mercies of my beloved Myles. *Why* did you not write to me? Not one word in the last seven years, Wes! Had it not been for the annual accounting sent to me by your financial overseer, I should never have known that you were still alive, let alone what you were about. Can you imagine what I felt when your message came a scant four days ago that you were on your way here to pay us a visit?"

"I had imagined you might be glad to hear it," remarked the captain, exasperatingly cool.

"Of course, I was glad . . ."

"Ecstatic is more like," observed an amused voice from behind them. "I suggest you don't allow her to pull the wool over your eyes, Captain."

All eyes turned to the tall figure lounging in the doorway. Dressed in buff unmentionables and a bottle-green riding coat, he was perhaps the most striking man Angelique had ever seen. His hair, worn in a queue at the nape of the neck, was black, with a touch of silver over the temples, and his eyes were of a singularly piercing steel-gray. A long, straight nose gave the countenance an arrogant cast, an impression which was further abetted by a stern-lipped, rather cynical mouth—until he smiled, and then suddenly the saturnine features were transformed by the appearance in either masculine cheek of devastatingly sensuous dimples. He was, Angelique judged, in his middle to late thirties.

To her surprise, she beheld a steely glint spring to the captain's eyes.

"You must forgive me, Your Grace," drawled Locke, amusement lurking about the handsome mouth. Deliberately he put the duchess from him. "But I could never get it straight concerning you bloody aristocrats. Do I bow and kiss your hand in greeting, or will an old-fashioned handshake do the trick?"

176

"The years haven't changed you in the least, it would seem. You are obviously the same impudent rogue who earned for himself the sobriquet of the Yankee Sea Wolf. Actually, I should think a sound drubbing is in order, if you persist in playing the impertinent American," remarked the nobleman with the air of one seriously considering the matter.

Angelique blanched, expecting the two strong-willed men to come to blows at any moment. Then, striding forward into the room, His Grace extended a slender hand.

"Hang it all, Wes. It is bloody well time you showed yourself!"

The two men met in a crushing handshake, while the young duchess looked on with a tremulous smile. Only then did those in the room with her seem to become aware of the slender girl watching this apparently joyous reunion with no little astonishment.

"And now," observed the duke, "unless I am greatly mistaken, there is someone here who must think us the very poorest of hosts. Perhaps, old man, you should introduce us to your companion?"

The duke's sympathetic glance in her direction brought a blush to Angelique's cheeks, even as the duchess's chagrined outburst filled her suddenly with confusion.

"But, Wes, how could you have been so remiss!" demanded her grace, awarding the lackadaisical captain a darkling glance. Instantly she crossed the room to the girl and warmly grasped her hands in both of hers. "You must forgive us, my dear. But you see, it has been an age since my wayward half-brother saw fit to make himself known to us. In the norm we are not so rude to guests beneath our roof, I promise you."

For an instant, Angelique felt the blood rushing in her ears as the enormity of the duchess's words bore in on her. Her half-brother! she thought. She had called *le*

177

capitaine her half-brother!

The unexpected warmth of a strong, masculine arm about her shoulders only added to her confusion.

"If you will allow me to get a word in edgewise, Your Grace," came the slow, drawling voice, which had ever the power to thrill her, "I'd be more than happy to make known to you Mad'moiselle Angele DuFour—my future wife."

"Your wife!" exclaimed the duchess, clasping Angelique's cold little hands even more warmly than before. "Oh, Wes, she is lovely. Indeed, I could not be happier for you both."

Angelique, feeling suddenly ridiculously shy, lifted enormous eyes to the radiant face of her hostess.

"*Merci,* Your Grace," she managed in a husky voice. "You are of the very kind, I think. Me, you did not expect, *vraiment?*"

The duchess's delightful trill of laughter charmed and put the girl at her ease.

"*C'est vrai, mad'moiselle,*" she admitted. "You, I did not expect. But never were such tidings more joyously welcome. For if you must know, I had come to despair that Wes would ever find the happiness he so richly deserves. You cannot imagine how I have prayed that one day he would settle down to a home and a family, and now you have come in answer to that prayer. What is more, I shall have the sister that I've always wanted. Now please do cease to call me 'Your Grace.' I am Sabra, and you will be Angel. As for the duke, you may have your choice of a host of names, but I think Waincourt or Myles will come the easiest to your lips. For so they do to mine. And now you must see we are bound to get on famously."

The truth of those final words was evident from the moment Angelique looked up into the warm light of the other woman's eyes. In an instant, her heart was captivated. The lively young duchess was everything she herself would have liked to be—vivacious, charming, warm-hearted, and generous, and with a keen wit and ready laughter that brought joy to the soul. *Hein*, no wonder *le capitaine* gazed upon her with the very great tenderness. And also the duke. At the mere sound of his wife's voice, the stern face of the nobleman would soften with the warm light of love for his incomparable Sabra.

As for the duchess herself, she took the love-starved Angelique to her bosom without a single reservation. At first it was enough that she try to love the girl for Wes's sake, but soon it became evident that she had grown very fond of her for the child's own sake. And yet something about her brother's bride-to-be both troubled and perplexed Sabra.

Perhaps it was her swiftly changing moods—one moment ebullient with laughter as only the very young can be and the next serious and sober-eyed, with a strange sort of haunting melancholia about her. Or maybe it was her eyes, like enormous blue-violet pools, in whose depths one might catch fascinating glimpses of the vital, but seemingly troubled soul of the woman within. She was a mysterious, captivating creature, was Wesley's Angel.

It soon became the goal of the singularly resolute Sabra to uncover the secrets that lurked in those wholly disturbing orbs. Wes, to her disgust, quickly dispelled any faint hope she might have entertained that he would prove a ready source of information. When it came to his bride-to-be, he was evasive as only he knew how to be, and fully as obstinate. She was Angele DuFour, the daughter of a Frenchwoman of aristocratic birth and a wealthy American, who had settled on Saint Dominique. Her girlhood had been spent in a Paris convent, where, it seemed, Wes had come upon her while in search of the daughter of his business partner, one Herman Gilbert. That was all he would tell her, other than a great deal of nonsense about having succumbed to love at first sight, a passion that had proven as overwhelming as it was unexpected, and which he could not find it in his heart to resist. A single glance into the inscrutable laughing blue eyes, and she had unhesitatingly dismissed the entirety of his story as nothing but humdrum.

Not that she could not credit the part about Angel's having captivated her brother at very short notice. With such a bewitching, lovely girl, such a thing was far from inconceivable. The thing was, there was something about Angel that made Sabra afraid for her brother. In fact, she very much feared that while Wes's heart was more deeply committed than even he realized, Angel's was not, and, as a consequence, he was heading for some sort of devastating disappointment—something which she was determined, at all costs, to avert.

One morning soon after her arrival, Angelique found herself being ushered into the nursery by the duchess to meet her two young sons. She had soon made herself a great favorite with Trevor, the aspiring heir, and Ferdy, his scapegrace younger brother, and a boisterous half-hour was passed in a rousing game of Beggar-Your-Neighbor, with Angelique coming up the loser.

"Pooh," she exclaimed, "we will try this again one time soon. Maybe next time you will not beat me so easily, *oui?*"

"It's really only a matter of luck," consoled Trevor in the way of encouragement. "Maybe if you turned your jacket inside out, your luck would change. That's what Cousin James does when he comes the loser."

"Bacon brain," scoffed Ferdy. "Cousin James's always the loser. Papa says he'll lose his bloody shirt one o' these days."

That remark earned a scandalized reproach from his mama.

"Ferdy, where in heaven's name do you pick up such language? I'm sure your papa never said any such thing."

"Oh, yes he did," asserted the young scapegrace, unwilling to budge an inch from the truth. "I heard him.

180

It was just after Aunt Caroline came for a visit, and you asked him to do something about Cousin James's 'un-unfortunate pro-pen-s'ty' for gambling."

"You, my young thatchgallows, were eavesdropping," Sabra accused with a look that should have assured his lips would be sealed for eternity. It soon became obvious she was mistaken in her man.

"I was not. Only a deaf man couldn't have heard it. Papa was awful mad."

"Ferdy!"

"I think, m'sieu Ferdy, it would be best if you beg the pardon of your *maman*," observed Angelique, her beautiful eyes shimmering with hardly suppressed mirth. "It is perhaps the wise man who knows when he has put the wrong foot in the mouth, *vous-savez?*"

A look passed between them, which said a great deal more than mere words.

"Oh, very well," he muttered at last, scuffing the toe of his shoe against the floor. "I do beg pardon, Mama. Though I don't see what all the fuss is about."

"You, young man, have behaved in less than the manner of a gentleman, and while I accept your apology for the moment, I intend to speak to your father about your—er—'unfortunate propensity' to use language better suited to the stables. And now make your bows to Mad'moiselle Angele, if you please. It is time for your lessons."

In the clamor that resulted from that pronouncement, Angelique was induced to give her word to accompany the boys to the stables that afternoon to meet Toby and Percival, their ponies, which had once run wild in the forest. These sons of the duke were of the very charming, she decided as they left the six-year-old heir to the dukedom and his younger brother in the care of Phoebe, their nanny, a redoubtable black woman, who, Angelique had been surprised to learn, was the mother of Locke's second mate, Jubal Henry.

181

A whimsical smile came to her lips as she recalled the reunion of the stalwart black man with his former mistress, the Duchess of Waincourt. It had seemed to the young French girl that he had been received into the household with no less warmth than had been afforded the wayward brother. In fact, she was sure she had glimpsed tears in the lovely sea-green eyes as the duchess had bombarded him with questions concerning the welfare of numerous mutual acquaintances—old Will Skyler, who was still sailing coasters along the New England coast for Tyree and Locke, the shipping partnership that had been formed between Wes's father and hers long before the war. Then, too, there had been Rab Wilkins, for whose cellar the duke and duchess apparently entertained some peculiarly sentimental attachment, John Tully, a saddler who evidently had once been instrumental in sparing the duke's life, and, most peculiar of all, irascible Jedediah Hawkes, who, it seemed, had found *one* Englishman who did not deserve to be hung, drawn and quartered.

It had all been very confusing to Angelique, listening with rapt interest. Still, it had become gradually clear to her that somehow the young duchess had once commanded an American privateer in the late war of rebellion. She had been both intrigued at such a notion and just a little bit daunted at the thought of the willowy Sabra in so perilous a role. But more importantly, it had reminded her of all that awaited her in her own Saint Dominique—the promise of rebellion and bloodshed on a far greater scale than even *la duchesse* could have imagined.

The thought was most troubling to her, for though she had ever a sympathy for the African slaves and the black people, she could not find it in her heart to believe in this revolution. Perhaps she was only the coward, she mused with a troubled frown. And yet what good could come out of so much violence? Very many would die, and very

182

much would be destroyed, these things she knew—in her heart and the dreams, which came to torment her in her sleep.

"Angele?"

Sabra's voice, the touch of an anxious hand on her arm, brought Angelique out of her reverie.

"*Comment?*" She started, realizing the duchess had been speaking to her and that she had not caught a single word of it. "*Pardon,* I am afraid my thoughts were far away. What was it you asked of me?"

Sabra's lips parted and then resolutely closed, as if she suddenly had thought better of what she had been about to say.

"It was nothing, really," replied the older woman, eyeing her strangely. "I was only wondering where you had learned how to deal so well with children. It occurred to me that perhaps you had younger brothers and sisters. But it's not important. Angele, are you in some sort of trouble? Pardon me for asking, but you had such a look in your eyes." Impetuously she laid her hand on the girl's arm. "Is there anything I can do?"

A sudden lump rose in Angelique's throat. How very kind was this duchesse, this sister of the Capitaine Locke. If only she dared unburden her soul to her.

"*Non,* at home there are no brothers and sisters," she answered instead. "When I was a young girl, there was a woman. She was a priestess of the *Rodu*—a *houngan.* When the Africans on my father's plantation fell ill, they would come to her to take the evil away. They believed it was the magic that made them better, but it was instead the herbs, I think. And many times nothing she did was of any use. So many died, especially the children."

A shadow, like pain, darted across the piquant face, then vanished, to be replaced by a wry twist of the lovely lips.

"Mozambe used to let me go with her. Many times I helped her with the infants. Before my thirteenth year, I

183

had aided with the birthing of a child. Just now, when I was playing with your sons, so many things came back to me. I have not forgotten what it was like, being with those other children."

All at once she drew a long, tremulous breath.

"You are very kind, I think," she said, smiling sadly at the older woman. "But there is nothing you can do. Maybe it is only that I am of the little bit homesick, you think?"

"Yes, no doubt that is it," answered Sabra, who did not believe for a moment that that was what was bothering her. "In which case, it is a very good thing that a certain captain appears to have come in search of us. Surely if anyone can erase the sadness from your eyes, it is Wes."

To Sabra's surprise, the girl went suddenly pearly white, so that the remarkable eyes appeared shadowed and huge in the delicate oval of her face. But perhaps even more intriguing was the swiftness with which she recovered herself.

"So," the girl chided with a petulance only partly feigned, "you have decided to leave your fishing long enough to remember Angele and your sister. It must be of the very diverting, this business of tramping about in the mud just to trick the fish into taking the bite."

"If I didn't know better," he mused, provokingly, "I'd almost believe you were angling for an invitation to try it for yourself."

Instantly, Angelique could have kicked him, for no sooner were the words out, than Sabra had taken the line and was flying.

"But that is an excellent idea!" she applauded, eyeing the suspiciously straight-faced captain with approval. "It is a lovely day for an outing! And, oh, you must have a picnic by the pond in the little glade. It is so beautiful there, and sometimes the ponies come in to water. I shall have Cook pack you a big lunch, for I promise there is nothing like fresh air and a little exercise to give one an appetite."

"Oh, but I couldn't!" exclaimed Angelique in instant dismay. The notion of being alone in the wilds with the captain made her heart lurch and her stomach go queasy. "I-I mean, I promised to spend the afternoon with young Trevor and Ferdy. And—and besides, I have nothing which would be suitable to wear. I fear it is quite impossible," she stated with finality, "this crazy notion to go fishing."

Sabra, however, was not to be so easily daunted.

"Nonsense," she declared in no uncertain terms. "The boys will understand, and I'm sure we can scrounge up something suitable for tramping through the woods. There must be trunkloads of old clothes up in the attic from which to choose."

Unable to come up with a single new argument against the proposed outing, Angelique glanced eloquently at the odiously conniving captain. *He* apparently could do nothing more helpful than philosophically shrug.

"I'm afraid you might as well give in gracefully, my girl," he advised as they both turned to look at the duchess, who, calling over her shoulder that she would just have Phoebe help her find a few things, was already headed back to the nursery. "I think you'll find nothing will deter Sabra Tyree Myles, once she's made her mind up about something. Besides, what harm can it do? If you're well bundled up, I hardly think you risk catching a cold. And I promise to take good care you don't end up taking a dunking. What other peril could there possibly be—unless, of course, it's me you're afraid of?"

Instantly Angelique's head came up, her eyes flashing sparks of resentment.

"Oh, how well you do that! It is meant as the challenge, *non?* You see how well I am coming to know you." All at once a dangerous light leaped in the glorious orbs. "Very well, m'sieu. I will go with you—but only if your nephews go also. After all, I did make them the promise."

"And so you did," he chuckled. "And though I

promise I had no intention of eating you, the boys are more than welcome to tag along."

Little more than half an hour later, Angelique found herself wending a rustic path beside the purling stream, the captain's tall figure at her side and the duke's two young sons chasing one another through the trees. The sun glancing through the branches overhead felt warm on her face, so that she did not notice the slight chill in the air. Birdsong charmed her ear, and the unaccustomed exercise invigorated and quickened her blood. It was in truth a glorious day, she thought, unconsciously giving in to the natural propensity of youth to live only for the joy of the moment.

They had gone perhaps half a mile when suddenly the woods parted before a sunlit glade in the middle of which shimmered a still, green pool behind a small rock dam. Bushes still bearing red berries hugged the shoreline, while bracken and furze gave way to thick green grass.

Angelique, only a little disappointed at the marked absence of the marvellous ponies, uttered an exclamation of delight.

"Oh, but how charming! It is all right if we stay here for the little while?" she queried then, grateful, after her recent exertions, to sink down on a fallen log. Immediately the two boys clambered to her side, and instinctively she pulled them to her. "Perhaps it is a good place to begin the lessons for stalking the fish, you think?" she said, addressing the question to them.

"One does not 'stalk' fish, Mad'moiselle Angele," observed the young heir to his father's title. "A deer must be stalked, because he lives on land. But one 'lures' a fish. There is a very great difference, you see."

"Pooh!" cried the younger boy, sticking his tongue out at his brother. "Just 'cause he's going t'be a duke, he thinks he knows everything."

"Ferdy, you little ape. You hold your tongue. I do

186

know a deal more than you, and it's got nothing to do with being a duke. You're just jealous, that's all."

"Unh-unh, not me. I don't wanta be a duke. I'm going to be the captain of a ship and hunt down all the bloody pirates in the world. You just see if I don't."

"But of course you will, Ferdy," interjected Angelique. "You will be a very brave captain and have many wonderful adventures. And Trevor will be a very good duke—generous and wise, like his papa, *oui?*"

"No doubt," observed the captain drily. "And now the two of you see if you can amuse yourselves until lunch is laid out. We'll try our luck with the fish as soon as we've sampled Mrs. Quigly's pigeon pie. How does that sound to you?"

The future duke, a youthful replica of his aristocratic father, gazed up at Angelique with worshipful gray eyes. "That sounds very well indeed, Uncle," he answered. Then smiling shyly, he dashed after his blond-haired imp of a younger brother, who was already off in pursuit of an imaginary pirate.

Only then did Angelique become aware of another pair of gimlet eyes regarding her with disturbing intensity.

"It would seem you win hearts wherever you go," remarked the captain, smiling oddly.

"Pooh!" she exclaimed, feeling the blood warm in her cheeks. "One cannot help loving such boys as these. They are of the very fine, *oui?*"

"Yes," he agreed, "but then you would seem to have the gift for bringing out the best in them." Her breath caught in her throat as he settled on the log next to her. "How unfortunate that the same cannot be said for me. Thus far, I'm afraid you've only sparked the devil in me." Angelique's heart nearly skipped a beat as he reached up to curl a raven lock about his finger. "For that I apologize, but don't expect me to regret what came out of it. Because, my intriguing Angel, I am discovering more and more that I don't. Not in the least."

Angelique, taken aback at this strange new mood of the

187

captain's, nervously twisted her head away.

"You need regret nothing, m'sieu," she uttered in a strangled voice. "Why should you, when it is I who am to blame for everything?"

"Angele . . ."

"No, Capitaine." At last she turned to look at him, something of desperation in her eyes. "I beg you will say no more. You owe me nothing, do you understand? No regrets, or explanations. And least of all the apology. Oh, why can you not see that it would be better if I went away? Now, before it is too late?"

At the end her voice broke, and gripping her hands tightly in her lap, she turned away. Thus she did not see the leap of muscle along the lean line of his jaw or the glint of steel in the look he bent upon her. Slowly he let his arm drop to his side. Then he was himself again— cool, controlled, unreadable.

"Very well," he drawled, "I won't trouble you—for now. But don't think this changes anything. I fully intend to make you mine, Angel. That is the one thing you may be sure of."

Angelique was saved from having to tender him an answer by the return of the boys clamoring to be fed. Taking herself firmly in hand, she rose with a smile for each of them and went about the tasks of setting out their picnic lunch.

The alfresco meal, in spite of everything, was a merry affair, thanks to the antics of the duke's sons and to Locke, who, well aware that he had rushed his fences, was exerting himself to mend them again. Imperceptibly Angelique fell victim to his relaxed and easy manner. She could not resist him, any more than she could resist the ready affection of the children or that something deep within her that craved for love and home and family—all the things that had been denied her in the long years at the convent.

Like a blossom exposed for the first time to sunlight, she expanded beneath the influence of their unquestioning acceptance. For a time, she became a child again, delighting in the new experience of learning how to bait a hook and lure the elusive trout from their hiding places beneath the moss. And always she was aware of the man, a lock of sun-streaked hair falling boyishly over his forehead as he showed her how to cast the line, or the laughter in his eyes as he caught her hastily about the waist to save her from a nasty tumble into the pond.

For the first time she was beginning to get a glimpse of him as he must have been in those happier times before the war, before the months of imprisonment and torture in the British prison-ship *Jersey*. It seemed that the hard lines about his mouth and eyes vanished even as she watched him wrestle in the grass with Ferdy or tackle the job of soothing young Trevor's ruffled feathers when the only fish to strike all afternoon wriggled off the hook.

At last, tired, somewhat dirty and more than a little disheveled, but very happy, they packed up their things in preparation for the homeward trek.

The sun was well down on the horizon, and there was a nip in the air as they paused for one last look at the little glade steeped in deepening shadows. Angelique, shivering a little from the cold, neither stiffened nor pulled away when Locke wrapped a long arm about her shoulders and pulled her snugly to his side. She was too filled with contentment and the lingering magic of the day to be wary.

"I wonder what *Maman* would think if she could see me now," she remarked, gazing with a mock grimace of dismay at her soiled garments and her fingernails rimed with dirt. "When I was a little girl in the big house Papa had built for her, she used to dress me in pink satin gowns with panniers and lace. Then I would sit with her on the verandah, and she would teach me my lessons. Someday I would be the great lady. A rich man would offer for my hand in marriage, and Papa would give to him the handsome dowry. Bah! For this I had to sit for hours, always with my back straight, and learn the things that a lady must know. How I grew to hate those lessons! When *Maman* fell ill with the fever, I was almost glad because it meant I could steal away into the forest, to the grotto high in the mountains where the river makes the azure pool. It was my place, only mine. There I could escape from the heat of the most unbearable, and from the pink satin dresses. I used to swim naked in the pool or lie on the rock ledge and pretend I was all alone in the world." All at once she sighed and smiled crookedly. "Poor *Maman*, she loved me very much, and I did want very much to please her. But alas, I have not turned out at all as she would have wished. I am of the very wicked, *non?*"

"No," Locke answered, a grimness about his mouth. "Willful, stubborn, impetuous to a fault perhaps, and impossibly proud. But hardly wicked. It occurs to me that you might possibly be *exactly* what your mother had hoped you would be."

"Does it," she grinned and, tilting her head back, looked up at him. Slowly her smile faded as his eyes, glittery in the half-light of dusk, caught and held her. "Does it truly?" she whispered.

For a moment longer he held her. Then deliberately he lowered his head.

"Yes," he murmured thickly against her lips. "Truly."

Never before had Angelique known anything like the gentle probing of this kiss. Unlike the other times, when her blood had burned with the great fire, she felt instead the deep stirrings of something far more profound. It was like coming awake without knowing one has been asleep all along, and then to discover an ache of the most tender where one's heart had been. It was all very confusing, she thought distractedly when at last he pulled away and, smiling strangely, gazed for a long time into her eyes, shadowed, had she known it, and vulnerable with the feelings he had aroused in her.

"Come," he murmured at last. "It's late. The duchess is likely to have the troops out searching for us if we don't get the boys home before dark."

"Of-of course," she answered unsteadily, without moving. Then realizing what he had said, she abruptly straightened, her hand going in a purely feminine gesture to her tousled hair. "Of course, we mustn't keep your sister waiting. She will be of the very worried."

But it was not the lateness of the hour or thoughts of the duchess that troubled her as she turned her steps homeward, but something far more disquieting. She very much feared she had done something very foolish when she agreed to go fishing with the captain. And she did not think she would ever be the same because of it.

recognising the futility of matching her meager strength
against his superior one. "I said the last thing I meant to

Chapter 11

Nothing, in truth, was the same for Angelique after that fateful afternoon in the glade. As if a temporary truce had been tacitly agreed upon, the captain no longer baited her. No longer did they indulge in verbal fencing. When they met, Locke was attentive and unfailingly solicitous of her comfort, but he made no further demands on her of an intimate nature. As a result, Angelique perceptibly relaxed. The shadows vanished from her eyes, and a bloom replaced the unhealthy pallor of her cheeks. Never had she known so much of happiness as she did now in the company of these strangers who had taken her to their bosom, and visibly she blossomed in such pleasant surrounds.

As for the duke and duchess, they had from the first accepted her. Save for a short exchange between Locke and Waincourt in regards to the girl's youth, they kept to themselves whatever inner misgivings they might have had concerning the uncertain outcome of the match between Angel and the captain. The duke, occupied with matters concerning the running of his several holdings and with affairs of government, spent much of his time closeted with his secretary so that Angelique did not find herself much in his company. But when he did appear, invariably at the evening meal and occasionally for impromptu gatherings of the family, he never failed to treat her with a graciousness of manner that put her immediately at her ease. Meantime, the friendship between Angelique and Sabra grew steadily stronger.

How it fascinated Angelique to observe Waincourt and his duchess together. Never had she seen two people more in love or more uniquely suited to one another. And yet on the surface, how impossible that so indelible a marriage should ever have evolved between such a pair—Waincourt, strong-willed, self-contained, and cynical, every inch of him the duke, with the unmistakable air of command that went with so lofty a title, and Sabra, impetuous, self-determined, and proud; the unruly American, who could no more keep from speaking her mind than she could stop herself from breathing. And yet somehow Angelique could not imagine the one without the other.

In spite of the fact that Sabra was already into the fifth month of her pregnancy, she had hardly begun to show that she was increasing. She seemed tireless and ever full of energy, and it was only at the duke's insistence that she made it a practice to lie down for an hour in the afternoons. Even then, very often, declaring that she would only be bored to distraction if forced to rely on her own company, she would insist that Angelique come and sit with her.

It was during one of these comfortable cozes that Angelique learned how it was that an English duke should have come to marry an American rebel, one, moreover, who had been both a spy and a devastatingly successful privateer in the war against the British. Not that Trevor Myles had been a duke in those days, for indeed he had not. He had been the British naval captain summoned to American waters to hunt down and destroy Sabra Tyree's very own ship, *Nemesis!*

Angelique listened spellbound as Sabra described in thrilling detail the captain's pursuit of her down the length of the New England coast to Long Island Sound, until, at last, she had managed to elude capture by staging a daring escape over the shoals off Fire Island. That they should eventually be thrown together on land, one the hunter and the other the hunted, only to fall irrevocably in love with one another, seemed all the more fantastic.

"And still you left him after all you had been through together—and even knowing that he loved you?" queried Angelique, who had little difficulty in reading between the lines as Sabra described being separated from her beloved Myles for two long years until the end of the war could bring them together again.

"We were on different sides," Sabra answered with simple candor. "Marriage then would have meant disgrace, scandal, the forfeiture of Myles's command— the end of his career. I could not accept such a sacrifice from him. Nor could either of us have compromised our own beliefs, our separate loyalties, what each of us conceived as our duty. Until our two countries were at peace, it seemed that I had no choice but to leave him. In the end, to have stayed could only have destroyed us both."

"But how could you stay away for so long?" marveled Angelique. "I used to watch *Maman* in those days when Papa was gone to fight in the war. It was the worry that made her sick, I think. The fear that never would she see Papa again. It must have been very difficult for you."

"It was—very difficult," breathed Sabra. "When I learned that Myles had been dreadfully wounded in the Battle of the Saintes, you cannot know the torment I suffered. The thought that I might have lost him forever. I could not bear to stay away any longer. Wes went with me—to Saint Vincent's in the Caribbean. Myles had gone there, seeking some sort of solace for all that he had suffered." A strange, haunted sort of look came to her eyes. "I thought my heart must fail me when I saw him, standing on the verandah overlooking his father's sugar fields. So pale and drawn, the havoc wrought by his wound and all the weeks of torment etched upon his dear, beloved face. Dear God, how bitterly he accused me! I, who had declared my undying love for him, had fled. I was as false as all the promises I had made. He was hard, unforgiving, terrible in his condemnation of me. I shall never forget it, nor the hunger with which he held me when his pain and anger had spent themselves."

Angelique, who had been listening with rapt attention, nearly jumped when suddenly the duchess leaned forward to clasp her tightly by the hands.

"Even now I cannot think I was wrong in what I did," she said. "It was *how* I went about it. I know now I could have faced Myles with the truth. I could have trusted him to understand. How much easier might he have borne the waiting had he only known what was in my heart! And that is why I feel I must speak out now. Angele, whatever it is that is troubling you, I beg you to tell Wes about it. I know my brother. He loves you. I promise you can trust him to help you."

"B-But I do not understand," stammered Angelique, hard-pressed to keep her wits about her. "*Le Capitaine* and I are pledged to be married. This makes you happy, *non?* It is what you wanted? Why do you persist in thinking there is something for which I need the help from him, or anyone?"

"Because I am a woman, and you, my dear, are a very poor liar. Your eyes give you away whenever you think no one is watching you. You love him, Angele, but you do not intend to go through with this marriage—do you."

Angelique blanched and pulled hastily away, her face averted to hide her consternation.

"I'm afraid there is little point in denying it," Sabra gently prodded. "Trevor overheard what you said to his uncle the other day at the pond. You must not be angry with him for coming to me with it. He loves you both dearly, and he could not bear to think of your ever leaving his Uncle Wes. You wanted to leave then, did you not—'before it was too late'? Forgive me for prying, my dear, but I cannot but wonder. 'Too late' for what?"

At last Angelique looked at her, her eyes fierce with

the anguish that comes from a breaking heart.

"Too late to stop myself from falling in love with him! Too late to find the courage to set him free. But I must! I must! I owe him the debt that can never be paid, and in return I have told him nothing but lies. It is of the most ironic, is it not? I, who thought to revere him as the savior of my father, have trapped him into a marriage he cannot want, a marriage that can only bring with it a terrible price."

She had spoken wildly, the words spilling from her as if they could no longer be contained within. But suddenly she stopped. A deathly calm appeared to envelop her as deliberately she faced *la duchesse*.

"You say you know your brother. Well, I, too, have come to know him. If I chose to do as you have said, if I 'trusted' him with this thing I fear, then there would be no stopping him. For the precious honor, he would place himself in the very great danger. Is this what you want for him? Would you have him dead because of me?"

Appalled at what such words would seem to portend, Sabra stared at the girl, white-faced with passion.

"Angele, I-I don't understand. What danger? Who *are* you?"

"One who has already taken more from him than anyone has the right to ask." Turning, she walked to the door, then stopped, her hand on the knob. *"Merci,"* she said, "for how you have tried to help, but you must believe me. I know what I must do. *S'il plaît a Dieu,* I will have the courage to go through with it."

"Angele, no," called Sabra. "Wait!" But Angelique was already gone, the door closed firmly behind her.

For Angelique, the final days at Briarcroft took on a dreamlike quality, which was marred only occasionally by the uneasy awareness that she was falling more and more under the spell of *le capitaine*. He was in truth a devil, she thought more than once as the days passed, irrevocably one after the other. In fact, he had become so attuned to her every nuance of mood, she was beginning to believe he could read her mind. *Voyons!* He appeared to know exactly when to woo her with the sweet words and the careless grin that seemed always meant for her alone. Or when to tantalize and tease her with the marvellous laughing eyes and the easy humor that never failed to bring the mirth bubbling to her lips. He even knew when it was best to leave her to herself—to her thoughts, which inevitably turned to him, as if, even needing to be by herself, she yet could not bear to be without him.

And, dear God, it was true, she thought, staring with a frown out her sitting room window overlooking the neat, sweeping lawn. In her heart she knew it. No longer could she conceive of living a life without him, without the warmth of his gaze upon her, which, like a flame to tinder, ever set a fire glowing within her. When he was by her side, as he was more often than not, her every sense seemed to quicken, so that she experienced everything more keenly than before—the wind against her cheek or the scent of rain before a storm, the sun casting golden beams through rifts in the clouds. His very nearness seemed to fill her entire being with awareness.

It was as if she were a child again, experiencing things anew through his eyes, feeling things she had almost forgotten in the long years spent in the convent. With Locke, she came alive again.

When the weather permitted, they might spend hours roaming aimlessly through the woods, just the two of them, or accompanied at times by the children. Or when the clouds gathered, as they were wont to do in the afternoon or evening, they entertained themselves inside by the fire. There were festive occasions, with all the family gathered, even the duke, who took time from his many pressing concerns to join them in a boisterous game of charades, jackstraws, or "fore-and-aft." Or there were quiet times, stimulating hours spent in conversation.

One afternoon, *le capitaine* took her out and taught her

how to sail a kite on a string. And another, he presented her with two small kittens, then amused himself watching her delight in them. Never had she known such a man or such feelings as he aroused in her with naught but a smile or a glance. She was giving in to him, little by little, even as she had sworn she would. She could not stop herself, and already the fortnight was nearly gone!

"Oh, Papa," she whispered, sinking her forehead against the leaded windowpane, "what am I going to do? I have been *très stupide*. I have let myself fall in love with him!"

As if in answer, a brisk rap on the door interrupted her reverie, and Angelique, expecting the maid with her morning cup of hot chocolate, gave permission to enter.

"Leave it near the sofa by the fire, *s'il vous plaît*," she said without turning around. "I will serve myself. Oh, and, if it will not be too much trouble to have hot water sent up later for the bath, I would be of the most grateful."

"I daresay," drawled an unmistakably masculine voice, "and you may be sure I would feel moved to exact a very particular payment for the service. Say—er—permission to scrub your back, for instance? That, I might find well worth the effort of lugging five or six two-gallon cans of water up three flights of stairs."

Angelique, stifling a gasp of surprise, whirled round to observe Locke, standing just inside the doorway, a picnic basket dangling negligently from one elbow.

"Your breakfast, Mad'moiselle DuFour," he announced, bowing low at the waist. "Where would you like me to serve it?"

"But I do not wish to have you serve it anywhere, m'sieu," she exclaimed, her eyes wide with disbelief at his audacity in coming to her here in her bedroom. "Please, you will leave at once. I have already the headache. Do not make it worse, I beg you."

Locke, observing the pinched look around her eyes, could not deny that she appeared less than her usual self, but somehow he doubted it was a headache that was bothering her. Today was the thirteenth day of the fortnight they had agreed upon. Tomorrow she had to give him his answer. At least, he thought sardonically to himself, she was not finding it easy to come to the point of actually serving notice. It looked as if she had not slept a wink the night before.

Ignoring the protest in her eyes, he stepped firmly into the room and closed the door behind him.

"A headache, is it?" he drawled sardonically cool. "Then, my love, you are in luck. I know just the thing for making a headache go away."

"It would be better if you made yourself go away, I think," Angelique retorted ungraciously, a slender hand rising unconsciously to clutch the front of her dressing gown. Frowning, she watched him set the basket down and, whistling, walk calmly past her to the bed.

"What are you doing here, Capitaine?" she demanded, feeling irritable and close to hysteria. "It is acceptable, the fiancé in the bedchamber before the wedding it has taken place?"

Locke shrugged a broad shoulder.

"Probably not. But as it happens, the mayor's daughter is getting married today," he informed her as he stripped her bed of its eiderdown comforter, spread, and pillows. "Everyone, it seems, has the day off to attend the festivities in town. By the way, I took the liberty of informing Waincourt and Sabra that we'd join them later." Having arranged the bedclothes in a cozy little nest on the floor before the fire, he straightened. "Which means there's not a soul here, but you and I."

"And you have come to make sure I do not starve, is that it?" queried Angelique with an exaggerated arch of the eyebrow. "But how very kind."

"I thought so," agreed the captain, insufferably bland. Coolly he placed a log on the fire, then turned to look at her with a significance that was not lost on Angelique. "Well? What are you waiting for? Breakfast, my love, is served."

With a feeling of impending doom, Angelique stared at him, her mouth dry and her heart pounding. How handsome he looked, *ce capitaine*, with the sun-bleached lock of hair falling carelessly over the forehead. He wore neither a coat nor waistcoat, and his white linen shirt with the full, flowing sleeves was tantalizingly open at the throat. As of their own volition, her eyes were drawn to the sensuous pulse of the vein in the strong column of his neck, to the mat of hair curling above the open V of his collar.

His slow, lazy drawl, vibrant with a wry sort of humor, brought her back to awareness.

"If you continue to look at me like that," he said, "I'm afraid it won't be breakfast we'll be having. Not that I object, mind you. I just thought I should give you fair warning. *You* look positively good enough to eat right now, and I, my love, am famished."

It was on her tongue to tell him to go to the devil. But somehow the words would not pass her lips.

"Are you," she said instead, an odd sort of catch in her voice. All at once his smile faded as he looked into her eyes. They were huge with shadows, vulnerable like a child's, and suddenly he was impatient to have the game over.

"Angele . . . ," he began, the drawl ominously gone from his voice.

"*Non!*" The word, like a cry, seemed torn from her throat, and for the space of a heartbeat, their glances clashed and held. Then hugging her arms in front of her, Angelique wheeled sharply away.

Cursing himself for a bloody fool, Locke forced himself to relax. Easy, man, he thought, his mouth grim as he studied the averted profile of her face. Rush things now, and he might ruin everything. A wry grimace twisted at the handsome lips as it came to him that he was behaving like the veriest lovesick puppy. Christ, he was too old for such games. Maybe Waincourt was right and he *was*

201

robbing the bloody cradle. Maybe he should even give the whole thing up, chalk it up as an entertaining interlude and get back to living his life the way it was before the troublesome Angel dropped, uninvited, into it.

Curiously, the thought gave him no comfort. In fact, he was ruefully aware that the past two weeks had irrevocably changed a lot of things, not the least of which was the burgeoning suspicion that without this hopelessly young and undeniably maddeningly elusive female, his life would not be worth the living. All at once he was supremely conscious of exasperation, like a storm, building in his chest.

"All right," he conceded, willing for the moment to play by her rules, "maybe this wasn't such a good idea. Obviously you're in no mood for company. If you want me to leave, I will."

"*Non!* I mean, yes," she said distractedly, then flung up her hands in hopeless indecision. "*Sacriste,* it must be the headache. It makes of me the idiot."

Locke's sigh sounded loud in the strained silence. Slowly he came to his feet, and, crossing to her, clasped her purposefully by the shoulders. His lips thinned to a grim line as he felt her wince beneath his hands and start to pull away.

"I think, my love," he drawled, tightening his hold on her, "that thus far I've been more than patient, but it just doesn't seem to be getting us anywhere. Why the bloody hell don't you tell me what it is that's eating at you and be done with it?"

When, still, she did not answer, he felt his patience snap.

"*Dammit,* Angel, *look* at me!"

As if to emphasize each word, he shook her, until at last her head came up with a jerk.

"Very well, m'sieu, I am looking," she uttered, white-faced with anguish. He uttered a low curse at sight of her, the eyes huge and wild, like those of a trapped animal. "And now what will you do? Kiss me? Make love to me

202

until, like the slave with the master, I tell you whatever it is that you want to hear from me? I am French and Creole, and the blood of the *Rodu* runs in my veins, but I have no strength to fight the power of your magic, the madness that comes over me at the touch of your hands on my body. I have no pride, m'sieu. Tell me what it is that you want from me."

Angelique quailed before the terrible flash of his eyes. Almost she thought he would strike her. Then a shutter seemed to drop, shutting her out. Nearly flinging her from him, he stalked to the window to stand with his back to her.

Thus he did not see her hand go out to him as though to call him back again, or the anguish in her look as she slowly let it drop. He addressed her without turning, as if he could not bear the sight of her. Angelique saw the strong hands clench on the window sill.

"I have to hand it to you, Angel, you played your part convincingly. For awhile, you even had me believing it wasn't all an act."

Angelique winced at the irony in his harsh bark of laughter. She had to bite her lip to keep from crying out that it was not an act, and only the bitter certainty that she loved him gave her the courage to remain silent.

"I'm returning to the *Sea Wolf* tomorrow. I've already spoken to Waincourt. He'll see to it that you're placed on a ship for wherever you want to go."

Helplessly she watched the powerful muscles ripple across his shoulders beneath the shirt. Then suddenly he turned.

"We still have one day of the charade to go. It had occurred to me you might enjoy spending it in my company." He gave a wry twist of the lips. "Sabra said something about pony races and perhaps an impromptu gathering of some sort here for supper. As for me, I'm through playing games. I'll go now, if that's what you want, or I'll stay. But either way, it's final. There's no turning back, Angel. Either you want me and will marry me, or we end it now. You decide."

Angelique tried to summon the words that would send him away, but he was watching her with the eyes that seemed to see right through her to her very soul, and suddenly she felt bitterness, like bile, welling up inside her. For whatever reasons, he still wanted her. Indeed, for the first time it came to her that in time she could even make him love her. And why should she not? Papa would understand. It was what he had wanted for her, a husband who would look after her and give her the children. Would it be so wrong to snatch the happiness when it was offered? Would not this love in her heart be enough to keep her safe from Mozambe and the evil of the *houngan*'s magic?

But already it was too late. Having misunderstood her silence, Locke had turned and was moving with long, purposeful strides toward the door. A rending pain lanced through her like a dagger thrust to the heart.

"No, wait!" she cried and took a step after him, her hand stretched out as if by that she might stop him.

Her breath caught as he halted. Then slowly he turned.

With her heart in her eyes, she looked into the strong, lean face of this man who had won her, and all at once she felt the recklessness like a flame leaping within, sweeping before it caution, doubts, and the last lingering voice of conscience. For this one chance at happiness, she would forget everything—Papa, Etienne, Chantal—Mozambe, and the red and black jumbi beads tucked away in her jewelry case—everything, but this man in whose arms alone she could know the sweet ecstasy of love.

"Stay," she murmured. Her eyes returning his look with a steadiness that set his heart to pounding, she reached up to undo the front fastening of her dressing gown. With provocative deliberation, she slipped the silken thing off her shoulders and let it fall with a soft susurrus to the floor. "Please," she whispered huskily, "I want you to."

"No," he drawled, his gaze never leaving hers. "I'm afraid that's not good enough. If you want me, Angel, *this* time *you* come to *me*."

A heady thrill went through her, and instinctively she flung her head up in answer to his challenge.

"As you wish, m'sieu," she said, conscious of her own daring, and crossed to him. A flame leaped in his eyes at sight of her, but he held back, punishing her, unwilling yet to trust in her surrender. "Well, *M'sieu le Capitaine?*" she murmured, her shoulders back and her eyes, unafraid, as she gazed up at him. "I have come to you."

She gasped but did not flinch as he touched her. His fingertips traced the supple curve of her breast, teased the tender thrust of the nipple, until at last it grew rigid. And, still, the piercing flames of his eyes held her, seeming to probe her very depths. Then at last a sigh shuddered through her, and, letting her head fall back, she closed her eyes.

"Capitaine," she whispered, her voice husky. Slowly she unveiled her eyes. "Please. Do not make me beg for you."

The sudden flash of steel between the slitted eyelids took her breath away. Then she was in his arms, her heart beating wildly as he bore her to the place he had prepared for her before the fire. There he laid her gently down and, stretching out beside her on the comforter, leaned over her.

Angelique's breath caught in her throat as his gaze moved slowly over her face, a searching caress that came to rest at last, lingeringly, on the soft curve of her mouth. As if compelled, her lips trembled and parted. A faint smile flickered briefly across the captain's lean features, then vanished as, deliberately, he bent his head toward her.

At first he kissed her slowly, sensuously, savoring the sweet sensitivity of her lips parting on a tremulous sigh beneath his. But at last, his mouth hardened, his caress became more passionately demanding. Angelique groaned and clasped her arms about his neck, thrilling to his touch, to his lean masculine body pressed against her softness. He was breathing heavily when he pulled away. His eyes smoldered with the fire she had aroused in him. Quickly he flung off his boots and rolled to his knees, his fingers going to the belt at his waist.

Then Angelique was kneeling before him. With her eyes she stopped then held him spellbound as deliberately she pulled open his shirt. Her hands savoring the muscular hardness of him, she slipped the garment off the powerful shoulders and trailed it down over his arms. His flesh quivered beneath her touch.

"How beautiful you are," she whispered. The enormous eyes lifted to his shimmered in the firelight. She was magnificent, was his Angel. Her fingertips wove a trail of fire over the muscled chest, teasing and tantalizing, until they came at last to the lean waist and lingered. Undoing the fastenings of his breeches, she released his glorious manhood, turgid with need. Her name, like a groan, breathed through his lips as she knelt to him, caressed him with her mouth. Then his strong hands closed powerfully on her shoulders and pulled her down to him on the bed of comforters.

Quickly he aroused her. His hands, seeking out the learned intimacies of her flesh, kindled a raging fire within her. She writhed beneath his touch, arched her supple body against his lean length. She clung to him, running her hands feverishly over the muscled smoothness of his back. And all the while, he devoured her with his mouth—her eyes, her cheeks, the slender column of her throat. With all her young strength, she responded, giving him back what he gave to her. Her generosity was boundless, as was the love pulsing through her with every beat of her heart.

She felt herself rising on a liquid wave of arousal. In anguish, she arched her back, willing him to come into her, wanting him as she had never wanted anything before. Quickly he spread wide her thighs and drawing up and back, plunged deeply within her.

A sharp, keening sigh burst from her depths, then she was moving with him, her hands clutching at the powerful shoulders, as together they rode the cresting wave of passion.

As his seed burst forth within her, she shuddered with the pulsating rhythm of her own release. Locke groaned as her flesh constricted in blissful ripples about his, intensifying his own exquisite pleasure. At last they collapsed together in a tangle of arms and legs to the bed.

As Locke, covering them both with the comforter, pulled her into the cradle of his arm, Angelique heaved a tremulous sigh. *Voyons*, her heart was filled with aching tenderness for this man in whose arms she lay and for the visions of happiness that he had given her to see. How greatly she loved him! More than she had loved anyone or anything before him. More than her poor *maman*, or Papa, or Saint Dominique!

It could not be wrong, she thought, this thing that she had done. Of a certainty she knew now that she would rather die than live without *ce capitaine*. Then, like a spectre come to haunt her, an image of Mozambe rose up in her mind. Unwittingly she shuddered. Surely the fates could not be so unkind as to punish her for it!

Instantly Locke's arm tightened about her.

"Angel, what is it?"

"N-Nothing, *bien-aimé*," she answered, assaying a smile as the captain lifted himself on one elbow to peer into her face. "It was only the little chill, I think."

Locke, his face grim, did not immediately answer. He had seen fear too many times not to recognize it now in the enormous orbs. Silently he cursed, then throwing back the bedcover, made as if to rise.

"Non, don't leave me!" cried Angelique, clinging to his arm.

"It's all right, Angel," he said, startled by the note of panic in her voice. "I'm just going to put a log on the fire. I'll be right back."

207

"No, please. I do not care about the fire. I want only for you to hold me a little while."

A frown darkened the stern brow, and for the barest moment he hesitated, torn between the unfamiliar urge to hold her and soothe away her fear and the fierce desire to shake the bloody truth out of her. She looked so small and frightened that at last he relented.

Sinking back onto the bed beside her, he drew the girl's slight body close to his side and wrapped her securely in his arms. The muscle leaped along his jawline as he felt her tremble against him. But gradually she relaxed, and at length he realized she had fallen into exhausted slumber.

What the bloody hell? he wondered, experiencing an unfamiliar sensation of helplessness. Unaccountably, he felt a sudden premonition like a black cloud of warning steal over him. It was fortunate that Waincourt had made all the necessary arrangements, he thought. The ceremony could be held first thing in the morning. Still, why wait? He wouldn't rest easy till he had made sure of the maddeningly elusive Angel, and the sooner the better.

Lifting his hand to smooth the tangled mane of hair from her face, he smiled grimly.

"Tonight, my love," he murmured softly. "Tonight you will in truth become my wife."

Chapter 12

Angelique groaned and turned her head feverishly against the pillow. It was a dream, she told herself. It was not happening, and, still, she could not stop it.

It had started pleasantly enough. There was a green meadow filled with spring flowers, and overhead, the sun shone in an azure sky. She was humming a tune her *maman* had used to sing to her, and she was conscious of feeling a very great happiness. And no wonder, for out of the depths of a forest the wild ponies had come.

First one, and then another and another, until the meadow rang to their clarion calls and they cavorted and played all around her with their long manes and tails flying. How beautiful they were, the wild ponies. Their great eyes and curved necks, small prancing hooves. Like creatures of sunlight and air. Her heart breaking for love of them, she tried to coax them to come to her. How they pawed the earth and tossed their heads—shy of her and yet unafraid. They sidled nearer and nearer, until she had had only to stretch out her hand to touch them.

And then, out of nowhere—the wind and roiling black clouds. Like ravenous beasts they had come, and swallowed up the sun and the sky. The screams of horses filled her ears, and the thunder of many hooves as the wild ponies fled. Then laughter, malicious and evil, and a hand reaching out of the darkness to grasp her.

209

"No!" she screamed and bolted upright, her hands clasped over her ears. "Go away. Leave me alone!"

As from a distance she heard her name.

"Angel! Angel, it's all right. It's only a dream."

She was weeping wildly, gasping for air, her heart rent with a terrible ache, when someone took hold of her arms and shook her hard. With a last, rending sob, her weeping stopped and she stared up into the grim face of *le capitaine.*

"You!" she gasped, her eyes yet wide with the lingering terror of her dream. Then, choking, she threw her arms about him. "It is no use," she groaned, shuddering in his strong clasp. "Not even you can keep them from me."

For a moment Locke held her, his eyes steely in the firelight. Then he put her from him.

"Angel, I don't understand," he said. "What can't I keep from you? *Tell* me, so that I can help you!"

His fingers about her arms were hurting her, and she could not bear the piercing look in his eyes, and yet she could only stare and shake her head.

"Angel!" She gasped as his fingers bit into her flesh.

"The dreams," she uttered like a hopeless curse. "No matter where I am, the dreams will find me. *Mon Dieu,* I cannot bear it!"

He felt her despair like a hard fist to the belly. Grimly, he gathered her to him and began stroking her hair.

"Go ahead, Angel. Cry it out. Sometimes it's the only thing that helps."

Startled, Angelique gave a watery hiccup and lifted her head to look at him.

A wry bark of laughter broke from Locke's throat as he met her eyes, round with disbelief.

"You don't think a man can cry, is that it?" he said roughly. Lines of bitterness appeared suddenly about the fine eyes and stern mouth. "Well, they do—inside, until all the hope is beaten out of them. And then, like a woman. It's when there aren't any tears left that it's the worst."

She felt the hard leap of muscle across his chest and faltered before the look in his eyes. His face appeared carved out of marble.

"I-It was like this in the war?" she queried haltingly. "I-In the prison?"

He had seemed distant, cold—his thoughts far removed from her, but now he appeared to shake himself out of the grips of whatever mood had laid fleeting hold of him.

"Yes," he said, looking at her, "in the prison. How could you possibly know that?"

"I-I told you. Angelique used to talk of you. She said you almost died at the hands of the British jailers. It is true, then, what she has said of you?"

A sardonic smile played briefly across his mouth.

"It's true enough, depending, of course, on what she told you. Sabra and Myles managed to extract me from that hell-hole, or I wouldn't be here today. As it was, I wasn't much good to anyone for a long time afterward. I was lucky to get a ship the last months of the war. It gave me something to live for."

The cold flash of his smile at the end chilled her blood, and suddenly she had little trouble imagining him as the Yankee Sea Wolf, the American captain who had bluffed an admiral into believing he had sailed into an enemy fleet. With the help of American prisoners impressed into service aboard the king's ship, Locke not only had managed to rout the admiral, but in the skirmish he had captured a British seventy-four as well. It was a story that had never failed to thrill her, but only now did she glimpse behind the legend. Captain Wesley Locke had been a man for whom the fires of hell could hold no fear. Those, he had already been made to suffer—and lived to tell of it.

"And afterwards," she said. "What did you find to live for then?"

But Locke was himself again. A wry glint of amuse-

211

ment flickered in the marvellous eyes.

"For the lure of adventure," he answered, laughing as he pulled her close. She shivered as his lips found the tender vulnerability of her neck below the ear. "For the Great South Seas and the Orient. After we've finished our business in Saint Dominique, I'll take you there. You'll be the wife of a Yankee trader and sail to all the foreign ports you've ever dreamed about. I'll never leave you behind, Angel, I promise you. You won't ever have to feel alone again."

The soft thrill she felt as he made his promise to her was quashed in the wake of the dread aroused by his mention of Saint Dominique. Angelique blanched as all the old fear and uncertainty welled up inside.

"Saint Dominique?" she exclaimed, her heart pounding. "But must we go there?"

"Mm-hmm," affirmed the captain, whose lips were exploring the delectable curve of her shoulder.

"But why?"

"Because, my love, I have a partner," he answered with extreme patience. "A partner, who expects me to arrive in Port-au-Prince with his daughter and a shipload of goods any time in the next eight weeks."

"But you do not have his daughter. And you can let some other ship carry these goods to him. Me, I do not wish to set foot in Port-au-Prince."

She felt him go suddenly still and, realizing how close she was to giving herself away, caught her lip between her teeth.

"I see," he said. His fingers played absently with a raven lock of hair. "I'm sorry, but I find that a little confusing. A couple of weeks ago you seemed anxious enough to reach the Indies. What's changed your mind?"

Angelique's chin went up at the tinge of sarcasm in his tone.

"I am a woman, m'sieu," she retorted. "Is that not enough?"

"No, it is not," he stated flatly. "It's claptrap, and you know it."

She could sense the temper in him held rigidly in check, the frustration at her refusal to let down the barrier she had erected between them. A long sigh breathed through his lips. "Don't try my patience too far, Angel. Even a woman must have a reason for changing her mind."

"Yes, and I must tell you mine, mustn't I. Because it is what you want. Always it is what you want. Bah! You are of the most *stupide*. You know only how to be the bully, the capitaine who gives the orders. But I will not go with you to Port-au-Prince. I will not go anywhere with you."

She had lashed out at him unfairly, out of anguish, because in his stubbornness he would ruin everything, and now she started to pull away, thinking only that she could no longer bear to be near him. She got no further than her knees before he yanked her back again with fingers that bruised her flesh. And all at once something snapped inside. Erupting into a cold fury, she twisted in his grasp and struck wildly at him with her fists.

A blistering oath ground out between his teeth as she connected a blow to the corner of his mouth. In the next instant she found herself flung ruthlessly to her back, her wrists pinned together to the floor above her head.

"*Goujat!*" she panted, hating him and her woman's frailty as he held her helpless beneath his strong, masculine body. He was breathing heavily, and a fire smoldered in his eyes as he raised the back of his hand to his swollen lip.

"And you, my Angel," he muttered grimly, "are an ill-tempered little hellcat."

The truth of his words was like cold water to her anger, and all at once it came to her what a fool she had been. *Tiens*, how easily she forgot the lessons of her *maman*. It was not with the fists that a woman mastered the greater strength of a man. It was with the subtlety of a woman's greater cunning.

213

"Forgive me, *bien-aimé*," she murmured, her eyes soft now, and pleading. "Now that I am to become your wife, there is nothing left for me in Saint Dominique but the bad memories. And I have dreamed so very long of seeing these distant places you have promised to show me. To go there would be for us like the honeymoon, *oui?*" He was so close to her that all she had to do was tilt her head a very little to bring her lips to within an inch of his. Letting the thick veil of her eyelashes drift slowly upwards, she gazed at him out of eyes dusky with promise. "Say we do not have to wait," she whispered huskily. "Tell me that we can sail now—this very day— for China and your beautiful South Sea Islands. You will not be sorry, *mon capitaine,* I swear it."

Her breath caught as she glimpsed the flash of steel between slitted eyelids, sensed the powerful leap of the muscles in his chest and shoulders, and then his mouth closed over hers, cruel and demanding. Almost she thought she would swoon with the violence of his desire, the arms that crushed her, the mouth that devoured, his hands that brought her swiftly to a searing heat of passion no less violent than his own.

He took her quickly, ruthlessly, his savage thrusts driving her to a frenzied height of rapture, until shuddering with blissful waves of release, they collapsed, together, in a tangled heap.

After awhile, Locke stirred and, leaning over her, brushed a stray lock of hair from her face. His hand froze as he felt her cheek, wet with tears.

"Little fool," he muttered harshly. "I suggest you think twice from now on before you try woman's wiles to get what you want—unless you're prepared to take the consequences. Dammit, Angel! I can't do what you ask. There are—reasons—other than the cargo, why I have to go to Saint Dominique."

Dazed by the violence of their joining and her heart breaking with love for him, Angelique wordlessly turned her head away. How could she tell him that to go would

214

mean the end of the passion that now was her life to her?

The captain, misconstruing her silence, stifled an exasperated sigh.

"All right, Angel. If you can't bring yourself to go with me, you can stay here, with Waincourt and Sabra. It's not what I would wish, but if that's the way you want it, I ask only that you marry me. Now—tonight. And that you'll be here, waiting, when I come back for you."

"And what if you do not come back?" she asked, despair lending a bitter edge to her voice. "What if, after you have gone to Saint Dominique, you find you no longer want me? Then will you sail away as before for the seven long years?"

"For Christ's sake, Angel!" he cursed, out of patience with her. "You have a strange notion of my character if you believe that." Then, more calmly, he added, "Trust me, Angel. Surely by now you must know nothing will keep me from coming back for you. Now tell me that you will marry me—now, this very night."

It was on her lips to beg him to stay with her, to let Fisk take the precious cargo to her papa. But he was looking at her with the eyes that melted her heart and suddenly she had no will left to fight him.

"*Oui*," she said at last, her eyes huge and haunted in the firelight. "I will marry you if that is what you want."

No sooner were the words spoken than something twisted like a knife inside. With a stifled cry, she threw her arms around his neck.

"Hold me, Capitaine," she breathed, clinging tightly. "Hold me, please."

His face grim, Locke closed his arms about her and pulled her close. Bloody hell, he thought. If he had had any doubts about fulfilling his obligation to Herman Gilbert, he had none now. Angel had just dispelled them. Whatever she was afraid of lay somewhere in her past— the "bad memories" that kept returning to haunt her in her dreams. If he could not keep the cursed nightmares at bay, then he would simply have to find a way to eliminate

215

them. To do that, he needed answers to the questions surrounding this exasperating beauty, and everything he had learned thus far would seem to point in the direction of Saint Dominique.

It was to be a long time later before Locke was finally able to persuade Angelique that they should dress and go in search of Waincourt and Sabra.

The sun dazzled in a clear sky when at last they emerged from the house and bent their footsteps along the path toward the village. New flowers littered the forest floor, and the air was rife with the scent of spring. Yet Angelique could not dispel the feeling that a shadow hung over them.

Locke, sensing her mood, was worried. He walked silently beside her, willing to give her time to work it out, whatever it was that was bothering her. Nevertheless, his glance strayed often to the delicate contours of her face beneath the straw hat trimmed in black velvet ribbons, a gift from Sabra to her young friend. He'd give a pretty penny to know what was going on in that lovely head of hers. In vain he searched for the imp that had captivated and infuriated him almost from the very first. This Angel was far too quiet to suit him. The beguiling dimple was gone from her cheeks, which were pale, and there was a droop to the sweet curve of her lips that bespoke of less than cheerful ruminations. He was conscious of a growing unease within himself, a feeling, like a prickling of nerve-endings, as if some sixth sense were trying to warn him of an unseen peril close at hand. It was something he had not felt for a very long time, and he didn't like it—the not knowing what or when it would strike.

Preoccupied with his own thoughts, Locke was caught off guard by Angelique's low, husky voice.

"Have you ever been in love before, Capitaine?" she asked, glancing up at him from beneath the brim of her hat.

"Once or twice in my youth." Inquisitively, he cocked

216

a dark eyebrow at her. "Nothing which was not of rather short duration. Why?"

"I was just wondering." Absently, she kicked at a pebble with the toe of her black kid half-boots laced in blue. "*Maman* and Papa were very much in love. He worshiped her, I think, as if she were a goddess. And when that thing happened, it must have changed him very much. I could never see in him the adventurer who won the heart of a French nobleman's daughter. He was to me of the very kind, and he has loved me in his own way. But always I think he sees in me the reminder of that night. It is sad, *non*, that there were never any other children."

Locke shrugged. "He was fortunate to have you. That should be enough for any man."

The huge eyes flew to his face, a startled expression in their blue-violet depths. Then suddenly blushing, she glanced hastily down again, but not before he caught a glimpse of the roguish dimple of old.

"It has, I think," she said, with a rueful hint of laughter in her voice, "been more than enough for you. I have been of the very great trouble to you, *non?*"

"No, how can you say so?" he retorted drily. "In retrospect, I can hardly imagine how I managed to go on without having an incorrigible young female to rescue every few days from one sort of scrape or another. I'm beginning to think you were sent by Providence to insure I'll never again know the meaning of boredom."

For once her ready tongue seemed to have failed her, as, catching her bottom lip between her teeth, she turned suddenly away. After a moment Locke took it upon himself to break the silence that had fallen between them.

"Does he live near Port-au-Prince, this papa of yours?" he queried carelessly. "Perhaps I should look him up when I reach Saint Dominique. Let him know his daughter has taken herself a husband."

He had spoken lightly, not wishing to dispel the

confiding mood that had seemed to grip his Angel. He was hardly prepared to see her go suddenly very white. Faltering in her step, she caught herself.

"*Non,*" she said in a strangled voice. "I am afraid that will not be possible." Then, before he could pursue the matter any further, she had lifted her arm and was pointing in front of them. "Oh, look, Capitaine. The village. You did not tell me there would be so many."

The village green was crowded with people, milling in and around a red-and-white-striped pavilion. There was fiddle music in the air mingled with the sounds of revelry. Stalls lined the single thoroughfare on either side, and already a number of lunging ponies with riders were being lined up at one end of the green, apparently in preparation for a race.

"Oh, *c'est merveilleux!*" cried Angelique, her cheeks flushed with excitement. "Like the carnival. Come, let us hurry."

She clasped his hand and pulled him eagerly along the path, which followed the downward slope of a hill descending into a green, fertile valley. Locke, baffled by her swiftly changing moods, gave in to her with a wry glint in his eye. Once again she had managed to put him off, but not for much longer, he vowed. Then they had reached the valley and were swallowed up by the crowd.

While it was true that Angelique, upon occasion, had been invited to the homes of various girls at the convent and had even twice been escorted to the opera by her cousin le comte du Vallenoir, never had she been to anything remotely resembling this rustic gathering. Her eyes sparkling, she drank in the festive sights. The booths boasting various and sundry foods, handmade country items, and even a puppet show, filled her with delight, as did the pony rides and the antics of a troupe of acrobats. But most intriguing of all was the band of gypsies, who were camped at the very edge of the green.

It was outside the enclosure of wagons that they came upon Sabra expostulating with the duke to allow her to have her fortune read.

"Oh, but, Myles, what possible harm can it do?" Angelique heard her say as they drew near. "You yourself admit that there's nothing to it. And it's not as if we cannot afford a few coins for what would amount to no more than a simple diversion."

"Yes, Your Grace, what harm can it do?" interjected Locke, grinning at his brother-in-law under siege. "Surely every woman should have her fortune read at least once. How else is she to know a mysterious stranger is about to enter her life and change it forever?"

"There, you see?" laughed Sabra, making a face at her brother. Then leaning her hands against her husband's firm chest, she gazed coaxingly up into his stern, handsome features. "Oh, please, my darling. It would be such an adventure. I've never even seen a gypsy before."

"Then you are undoubtedly about to be disappointed," Waincourt pronounced, his tone very dry as he relented before the pleading in a pair of irresistible sea-green eyes. "I daresay you will find the romantic appeal of gypsies has been vastly overrated."

At first sight of the less-than-prepossessing camp, Angelique was inclined to agree with him. Ragged children with unkempt hair and liquid black eyes swarmed around them, their hands outstretched for coins, while swarthy-faced men hung back, watching them from the shadows of tall wagons. Women seated before blankets spread with gypsy wares—rugs and woven baskets, or figures carved from wood—talked among themselves, the way women do the world over. Nevertheless, there was about the camp a distinct sense of otherness that made Angelique feel like an intruder. She nearly jumped when a tall, spare figure separated itself from the shadows of a tent to confront them. Her breath caught hard in her throat as still eyes, black as obsidian, singled her out from the others.

"You wish to have your fortune told, yes?"

To Angelique, it was like being caught suddenly up in a

dream, with everything fading into the background so that there were only herself and the woman with the face which seemed carved from the bark of an old tree. She was conscious of fear, which slowly faded beneath the penetrating stare of the black, discerning eyes, to be replaced by an inexplicable queasiness in the pit of her stomach. She nearly swooned with relief when the tall figure of the captain interposed itself between them.

"Who are you? What do you want?" he demanded, his arm going protectively about Angelique's shoulders.

She could feel the muscles, tensed beneath the fabric of his coat, as the gypsy's knowing gaze shifted from Angelique to the flint-eyed captain.

"I am Lucinne. I read the fortunes in the tea leaves. It is for this that you have come, yes?"

Angelique sensed Sabra come up behind them, could feel the puzzlement in the way she glanced from her brother's hard face to her, then back again.

"Wes, what is it? Angel is as white as a sheet. Are you ill, child?" queried the duchess.

"No, no. I am fine," Angelique broke in, blushing. "It is only that Madame Lucinne startled me."

Catching the look in her eyes, Sabra impulsively reached out to take Angelique's hand in sudden comprehension.

"Angel, it's all right," she murmured, startled to find the slender fingers icy cold to the touch. "You don't have to go through with this if you don't want to. No doubt it was a silly idea, and much as I hate to admit it, Myles was most probably right to try and talk me out of it."

"In which case," interjected the duke in his customarily acerbic manner, "perhaps we should take Miss DuFour someplace where she will feel more herself."

"No, that is not necessary," Angelique objected. "For a little while I was the little bit dizzy—all the excitement, you see. It is gone now. Please, you go with Madame Lucinne. *Le capitaine* and I, we will wait for you here."

On this last she remained firm despite the objections of

the others, and at last Sabra was persuaded to give in to her.

"Well, if you are really certain you'll be all right," she said, not completely convinced.

"Of course I am certain," Angelique retorted, giving the duchess a little shove. "Go. Only promise me you will tell me everything Madame Lucinne says to you."

Only then, as Sabra, accompanied by Waincourt, turned to enter the mirky entrance of the tent, did Angelique feel the gypsy's eyes on her again. Slowly she turned to face the old woman.

"I have been watching you," the gypsy said. "It is not Madame Lucinne that you fear, or the message in the tea leaves. You know already what they would tell you."

"No, you are wrong. I-I know nothing of such things."

A look of pity crossed the aged visage.

"You cannot run away from them, these shadows of things that you see. If you do not turn and embrace them, they will follow you wherever you go until you know only the darkness. Trust in what your heart would tell you. Therein lies the true path to love and happiness." Turning to follow her other visitors, the gypsy paused. "Come to me, if you find yourself in need," she murmured in a voice too low for the captain to hear. "I will do what I can to help you."

Then she was gone, leaving Angelique to stare after her.

Locke, seeing the look on her face, cursed the ill fortune that had brought them to the gypsy camp. For awhile Angel had seemed to come out of her brooding. There had been a sparkle in her eyes and a bloom on her cheeks, and she had seemed happier and more relaxed than he had ever seen her before. But the old woman with a few cryptic utterances had brought it all back again—that blasted vacant expression, the pinched look about the eyes. She looked to be a million miles away, and wherever she was was not pleasant.

Stifling a sigh, he stepped to her side and drew her

to him.

"Come now, don't tell me you believe in that guff she handed you. It's how she makes her living. Things like that are her stock-in-trade. You can bet she tells everyone pretty much the same thing."

Angelique, glancing up at him, assayed a somewhat shaky smile.

"I-I know, but she is somehow of the very convincing, *non?*"

The flash of white teeth against the tanned face made her heart lurch.

"No," he said, flicking her playfully under the chin. "She is not in the least convincing, except, perhaps, to a very green girl."

"Bah! And you think I am that very green girl," she flung back at him with a spark of the old defiance. Then immediately she sobered. "And what if she is right, this gypsy woman who tells me to follow my heart?"

"But of course she's right. That's the point, isn't it? It's advice that would easily apply to anyone. It doesn't take a fortuneteller to see it."

"No, I do not suppose that it does," she answered, an oddly stricken look in her eyes.

After that, she deliberately changed the subject, but in spite of the fact that she assumed a light and cheerful manner, Locke sensed that beneath it she was strained and nervous. Her glance strayed repeatedly to the gypsy's tent whenever she thought he was not looking.

Fortunately, they had not long to wait. No more than fifteen minutes had passed before Waincourt and Sabra emerged from the mouth of the tent and rejoined them. Sabra, somewhat pale and her lovely lips pursed in a frown, appeared anything but pleased with the outcome of her first encounter with a gypsy fortuneteller.

"You were quite right not to go in, my dear," she confided to Angelique as, slipping her arm through the girl's, she led them away from the gypsy encampment. "The woman obviously delights in trying to frighten the

222

wits out of anyone foolish enough to enter her lair. She was positively abounding with all sorts of obscure warnings of dire happenings to come—'stormclouds gathering on the horizon' and 'flames that leap out of darkness.' That sort of thing. What is one supposed to make of such nonsense?"

"A fire, it would seem," observed Waincourt, making light of it. "And the forecast of an evening storm." Something in his tone must have struck the captain oddly, for his gaze lifted speculatively to the nobleman's.

"Don't tell me that you understood a word of what that woman said," warned Sabra, who was too upset to notice anything, "for I promise I shan't believe you. I mean, all that flummery about 'demon fires' and 'vows not made.' And don't let us forget 'the angels sent to snatch one from the heart of flame.' It was all a hum, just as you said it would be."

"But undoubtedly, *ma mie*," the duke smoothly agreed. "Although I confess Madame Lucinne was perhaps rather more impressive than some, at least in her method of delivery. She is, I should judge, a consummate actress lacking only in the originality of her material."

"Well, I for one, cared not a whit either for her material or her delivery. Both made my flesh crawl."

As though to lend credence to her avowal, the duchess gave a small shudder.

At that point the captain, judging that it was time to interject a lighter note, broke into the conversation.

"Enough of Madame Lucinne and her gloomy forecasts. In fact, unless there's some objection, I suggest we turn our attention to far more important considerations—like making use of a certain official document Waincourt has gone to considerable lengths to obtain. Angel and I have decided to get married, and we've no intention of waiting longer than it takes to find a parson."

"Married!" The exclamation, coming as it did from Sabra, was accompanied by a radiant smile. "Oh, Wes, I am so happy for you both."

In spite of the captain's bold announcement that the wedding would take place as soon as a parson could be found to perform it, it was quickly made apparent that the duchess would settle for nothing less than a quiet ceremony in the great hall at Briarcroft. Charging Waincourt with the task of seeking out the rector, she and the others headed back to the manor, while, overhead, the sun dimmed behind a thickening cover of clouds.

Two hours later, Angelique stood before the ormolu looking glass in her room and stared at her slim figure dressed in a cream brocade wedding dress that had belonged to a previous duchess of Waincourt. There had not been time to do more than take a quick tuck or two in the waist of the gown, which, belonging to an earlier age, was slightly outmoded and had been designed for a somewhat larger frame. Still, it was a beautiful creation of intricate frills and lace draped over a hooped petticoat of satin embroidered in mother of pearl, and Angelique knew she had never looked more stunning.

She wore her hair in loose curls at the top, with the rest gathered at the nape of the neck in a queue. A pearl cap hugged the back of her head, and a string of pearls that had been her mother's embraced her slender neck. *Tiens*, she did not know this creature who stared back at her with the eyes that seemed too big for the face!

Heaving a sigh, she turned away from the glass and walked to the window. Outside, a storm gathered and already there was a restiveness in the air, a rustle of leaves and branches. The gray promise of dusk seemed perfectly to suit her mood. *Voyons*, she felt strangely oppressed for a woman on her wedding day. In truth, she was queasy inside, and her hands were clammy and cold, as if she were coming down with something. But she knew that was not what ailed her. It was the nagging inside her head that would not leave her alone. Or did it come from her heart, this voice that told her that what she was doing was wrong?

224

Sacriste, she did not know what to believe, for ne[...]
her life before had she wanted anything more than [...]
married to this capitaine who had taught her what it was
to be a woman. She loved him. Surely such a thing came
from the heart! And yet why should the words of the
gypsy weigh so heavily on that very same organ?

She was not to be given time to dwell on that disturbing
conundrum, as just then a knock on the door was quickly
followed by Sabra's entrance into her bedchamber.

"Angel, everyone is waiting. It's time we went down,"
said the duchess. All at once she fell silent at sight of the
vision of loveliness standing pensively before her. "Oh,
Angel," she cried, "you are breathtaking! Wes will fall
over when he sees you."

Blushing a little, Angelique dropped into a graceful
curtsey.

"*Merci beaucoup, Madame la Duchesse,*" she murmured, her heart fluttering as it came to her that the
moment of her wedding had arrived. "I-I wish to thank
you for the use of the gown, and-and for so many other
things."

Sabra laughed and gave a dismissing flutter of the
hand.

"Pray do not be absurd. I could not be more pleased
that things have worked out for you and my brother.
Especially after our little talk when you seemed so
certain nothing could ever come of it. I am glad that you
have come to realize how groundless were your fears.
Believe me, my dear, you are everything I could have
hoped for for Wes."

Angelique, feeling the tears sting her eyes at such
generosity from one whom she had learned to love and
admire, could only clasp her arms about the other woman
in a convulsive gesture of gratitude.

Touched and more than a little startled, Sabra
returned her embrace. Then patting her awkwardly on
the back, she firmly put the girl from her.

"I know you will be good for him," she said, feeling

unaccountably misty herself. "And you must promise you will not let him stay away for so long next time. Next to Myles and my sons, he means more to me than anyone alive. And now, come. The duke is waiting to give you away."

Feeling strangely heavyhearted and ill-at-ease, Angelique followed her through the door and down to Waincourt, who stood at the foot of the stairs, waiting to take her into the great hall. Bowing graciously, he held out his arm and shyly Angelique touched her fingers to the back of the strong, shapely hand.

The rest was a dream—the duke leading her into the hall gloriously ablaze with candles and the soft glow of oil lamps wreathed in garlands of spring flowers. The flutter of the drapes and the scent of rain carried on a light breeze through the casement window, left partially ajar. The smiling faces of the servants who were gathered at the back of the hall to witness the happy affair. The bewigged vicar in his robes, standing before the fireplace with Sabra and the two boys. And, finally, the tall figure of the captain, turning to look at her, his gaze seeming to drink in her beauty as she came slowly toward him.

Voyons! How handsome he was in the dark blue coat with the gold buttons, the breeches, pale blue. She felt a lump rise in her throat. Always she would remember him the way he looked at that moment—the rebellious lock of hair, falling, as ever, over his forehead, and the blue eyes, like the clear depths of the Caribbean, smiling at her.

She heard the voice of the clergyman droning over her and felt her hand placed in the warm clasp of the captain's. For a moment in which time seemed to stand still, she looked up into Locke's eyes. It was like diving into the blue depths of the sea and losing one's self, and at last, she let her gaze flutter self-consciously to the strong hand holding hers.

As if from a very great distance, she listened to the opening lines of the marriage rites being read. Perhaps she swayed or made a sound, because she felt Locke's strong fingers tighten over hers. Gratefully she looked up and through a curtain of mist saw his face turned toward hers. The drone of the clergyman's voice suddenly stopped, and Locke, gazing steadily down at her, gave his answer: "I will."

Her heart nearly failed her as the clergyman next turned to her.

"Wilt thou have this man for thy wedded husband . . ."

It seemed that she had been aware for some time of a restlessness in the back of the great hall, a movement of sound, like the rumble of wind through the eaves, and now it grew louder, more insistent, so that she had to strain to hear the words above the incessant din. It made her head hurt, this wind, and she could feel the queasiness in her stomach getting worse.

In a daze she realized the clergyman had stopped speaking, and that Locke was looking at her, waiting for her answer. She saw a frown start in the blue depths of his eyes, the sudden sharp leap of concern, like the point of a knife lancing through her. Willing the roaring in her ears to stop, she struggled to focus beyond the pain building inside her head, struggled to say the words that would bind her forever to the man she loved.

The fist of wind, when it came, slammed through the window, shattering the glass in its fury. Gasping with pain, Angelique twisted around in time to see the billowing drapes catch an oil lamp and send it flying across the room, to see oil and flames spill across the floor, reaching out toward those gathered before the fireplace. Instinctively, she shoved Sabra out of the path of the fire. Then from somewhere she heard a woman scream, and in horror she saw the hem of her dress was afire. Oblivious to everything but the fear clawing at her vitals, she beat at her burning skirt with her hands. A scream welled up inside of her as the flames leaped higher, then from out of nowhere arms like steel bands closed around her, wrestled her, kicking and screaming, to the floor. Through the blur of tears she saw Locke,

227

grim-faced and determined. And then the darkness took her, and she knew no more.

It was well after dark and the rain had settled down to a steady downpour when Locke was finally admitted into the bedchamber to which he had carried Angelique some two hours before. As he entered, Sabra rose quietly from her chair, her forefinger pressed to her lips.

"She's sleeping now," she told him. She looked weary as she came around the foot of the bed to him, but her smile was encouraging. "Dr. Enwright has given her something to help her rest."

He nodded, his eyes going to the slight figure in the bed. At sight of the bandages, his lips tightened.

"The burns . . . ?"

". . . are not as bad as we had feared. The doctor says she will be fine." Sabra touched a slim hand to his sleeve. "Don't *worry*. She's being well looked after."

Locke nodded.

"I know," he said. His hand covered hers. "You look tired. Why don't you go and lie down. I'll sit with her."

"There's no need. We've made up a bed for Phoebe in the next room. She'll stay with her tonight."

If she had expected an argument, she was to be surprised. The captain merely nodded, his glance going back to Angelique.

Sabra studied the chiseled profile, her expression troubled.

"You're worried," she stated after a moment. "Why? Is it because of what the gypsy woman said? Did Myles tell you?"

At last something like amusement flickered in his face.

"He told me. Now don't tell me you think that has the remotest connection with what happened here tonight. Not you, my hardheaded little sister."

Sabra grimaced.

"I know it's absurd, and yet everything happened just

228

as Madame Lucinne said. The storm, the fire, the thing about the vow. It's uncanny. Good lord, an 'Angel' saved me from grave harm, just as that woman foretold she would. What if the rest of it turns out to be true—all that about worse things to come if 'the one who sees continues blind'? Whatever could she have meant by it? Wes, I'm frightened."

Locke sobered, seeing the very real distress in his sister's eyes. At last he folded her in his arms. Neither one of them saw Angelique turn her head away from them, her eyes clenched tightly shut.

"It's all coincidence," Locke was assuring Sabra, "an unfortunate accident caused by a perfectly natural storm. I promise, Myles only mentioned it because he was worried about you. He doesn't like to see you upset, especially now that you're breeding. You're overwrought about what happened. Tomorrow you'll see everything in its proper perspective."

Sabra gave a reluctant laugh.

"Yes, of course I shall. Wes, I cannot tell you how sorry I am that all this has kept you from marrying your Angel. By all rights, this should have been your wedding night."

The muscle leaped along the stern line of his jaw.

"You don't need to feel sorry. What happened has prevented nothing—only postponed things for awhile. Mad'moiselle DuFour is going to marry me, you may depend on it."

He said this with such grimness that Sabra was a little taken aback.

"Yes, yes, of course she is," she murmured. Then on impulse she rose up on tiptoe to kiss his cheek. "Goodnight, Wes. I shall see you and your Angel in the morning."

That, however, was not a promise which was to be realized, as was made evident with Phoebe's flustered arrival the next morning at the breakfast table.

"Miss Sabra! Miss Sabra, you best git Mistuh Wesley down here right away. Lawsamercy, I doesn't know what he gonna say when he find out. I done looked everywhere. But that child ain't nowhere to be found. Miss Angel be gone, and the Lord only knows what be goin' to happen to her! You gots to tell the cap'n, Miss Sabra. I ain't got the heart for it."

"It's all right, Phoebe," said the duchess, looking beyond the distraught nanny to the still figure of her brother framed in the doorway. A cold chill ran down her spine at the look in his eyes. "I'm afraid Mister Wesley has already been made aware of it."

Chapter 13

Angelique lay on the cot and stared listlessly at the pots swaying on the hooks above her head. She had long since grown immune to the bone-rattling jolts, the creaks and groans, the incessant pelt of wind and rain against the gypsy wagon. She felt empty inside, so much so that she was hardly aware any longer of the pain inside, the bitter anguish which mercifully had subsided to a dull, persistent ache.

Already Briarcroft had assumed the unreality of a dream, and it seemed a very long time ago that, awakened by the sounds of voices, she had overheard Sabra and the captain talking. At first she had listened absently, hardly realizing in her drug-induced lethargy the significance of their words. And then it had become painfully clear to her, just as it must have done to Sabra, that *she*, Angelique, had been the one in the gypsy's visions. It was *she* who had been given to see and *she* who, in her own selfish ignorance, had continued blind. With what crushing certainty had it come to her then that everything that had happened was her fault!

The gypsy Lucinne had tried to warn her, and she had refused to listen. Her own heart had tried to tell her, and she had ignored it. Chantal and his cursed jumbi beads—they had been part of it, too, but she, in her own stupid pride, had not heeded even them. One could call it what

231

one would—coincidence, ill-luck, the curse of the *Rodu*, fate. What a fool she had been to think that she could escape it!

It had all been there for her to see, even in her dreams. It was never meant that she should know the joy of belonging, the happiness of walking in the light, the bliss of being wed to her beloved captain. Not she, who from early childhood had borne the hated sign of the twin-god upon her body. Not she, who was bound to a past enshrouded in darkness by deep and terrible secrets. She was *placée*, unfit to be wed. Always she had known it, had *known* her heart was not hers to give! And still she had thought to outwit the gods.

It had all seemed so clear to her. And why not? After all, she had not planned to fall in love with *le capitaine*. In truth it was the very last thing she had wanted. *Tiens*, had she not fought it with all her strength and will? Had she not even gone so far as to leap from the ship into the wretched English Channel? Yes, that is exactly what she had done, and what good had it done her? The harder she fought, the stronger grew her love, until it was the very lifeblood to her. And so it had come to her that surely God, in his mercy, had meant for her to have the happiness beyond imagining, had meant for her to be wed to this man who, in mastering her, had stolen her heart from her.

Recklessly, foolishly, *blindly*, she had dared to put fate to the touch, had dared to believe that love would prove greater than the formidable obstacles in her way. In spite of everything—her dreams, the whisperings of her heart, the incessant warnings—she had determined to snatch at the happiness offered. She would marry Wesley Locke and then perhaps Mozambe's hold on her would be broken forever. Such had been her vain hope.

A bitter laugh, which had more the sound of an anguished sob, broke from her. She had paid in full for her arrogance. In her presumption she had endangered the lives of everyone who had been kind to her, and

232

rather than expose them to the further wrath of whatever fate held in store for her, she had fled like a coward into the night.

Never would she forget the torment she had suffered when Sabra had left Locke alone with her in the room. The touch of his hand upon her brow, his lips brushing hers! She did not know how she had found the strength to go on pretending sleep when her whole heart had cried out to open her eyes to him. How she had longed to behold him one last time, to feel his arms around her, his lean body next to hers. Even now she could not believe he had not seen through her poor charade, for her heart had been pounding so violently that she thought surely he must hear it. Then Phoebe had come, and, admonishing the black woman to look after her well, he had left.

If the moments alone with him had seemed bitter torment, the agony of waiting to hear the sounds that told her Phoebe slept was endless torture. When at last she had decided it was safe to steal from her bed, she had been weary and half-sick from the suspense. It had been all she could do to dress and pack her few things, but somehow she had managed it.

The rest of it remained a terrifying blur in her mind. The fury of wind and rain, the path made treacherous by darkness and storm—all had seemed sent by a vengeful God. She had no conscious memory of reaching the village or of finding her way to the caravan camped on the edge of the green. She knew only that she had awakened from a nightmare to Madame Lucinne bending over her and to the pained lurch and sway of the gypsy wagon fighting its way through the storm.

As she had watched the old woman wrap fresh bandages about her poor hands, she had been too burdened by weariness and grief to wonder why they were helping her, these gypsies who seemed to know what was in her heart without her having to say a word. It had been enough to feel warm and dry again and to know that the passage of each mile took her farther away from

233

Briarcroft and the captain.

Feeling her eyelids growing heavy at last, Angelique heaved a weary sigh. He would come after her, she knew, but this time he would not find her. She would return to Papa and Mozambe, and by the time he gave up the search and thought to make his way to the West Indies, it would be too late. She would be dead, along with her papa, or, God willing, gone from the island, she thought, drifting inevitably toward sleep. *Plut à Dieu* when he heard of it, he would turn back before ever he set foot on Saint Dominique!

Angelique awakened the following morning to discover the caravan was camped in a hollow between two hills. Lucinne was waiting with steaming chicken broth and a potent tea for her stomach, and ointment for the burns on her hands.

"You are better," she said, nodding with satisfaction. "The wildness is gone from your eyes. Good. You have decided not to run away any more."

"No, you are wrong," Angelique uttered harshly, unreasonably put out by the gypsy's irritating knack of seeming to know everything about her. "I am running— just as hard and as fast as I can, I promise you."

"Yes, but this time you retrace your steps to the beginning. You go to put the ghosts from your past to rest. This was not an easy decision for you, yes? But you will be glad for it. Lucinne knows. She has seen it in the tea leaves."

"And what else do you see for me?" queried the girl bitterly. "A long life? Happiness? A husband who loves me? Bah, I think I will see none of these when I have returned to Saint Dominique."

The gypsy woman's knowing smile gave Angelique the shivers.

"You cannot see beyond what the evil one wishes you to see. She is filled with great hatred, this Mozambe. Beware of her. She wishes you grave harm."

In spite of herself, Angelique started.

"What do you know of these things?" she demanded, her face white. "How do you know of Mozambe?"

"You were out of your head when you came to us. In your fever you spoke her name many times. But I knew before this. It does not always happen so, that one sees or touches the hand of another, and suddenly much is revealed. But so it was with you. I saw you, and I felt the shadow of evil upon you."

But Angelique was not satisfied.

"You have not answered me," she said. "What is it that you *know* of Mozambe?"

"I know it is from her the evil comes. I know that to defeat her, you must look into the past with your eyes open, see with your heart what is real and what is only a shadow the evil one would have you to see. I know you will experience much that is painful and that you will face great peril. Beyond that I can tell you nothing."

Angelique stared into the face of the old woman and felt her mouth unbearably dry. Abruptly she turned away. A reluctant bark of laughter burst from her.

"This is a menacing picture, which you have painted for me, *non?*" she uttered in a hard voice. "It is not something to bring the joy to the heart." But the gypsy said nothing, and at last she brought her head around to look at her again.

"I must reach the coast and a ship that will take me to my home on Saint Dominique. Will you help me, Madame Lucinne? I have my mother's jewels. I can pay you."

"We will not speak of payment. Eat. Rest. Regain your strength. Tonight we will come to a place where there are many ships. There is a man, a Dutchman, who is not unknown to us. Perhaps he may be persuaded to help you find this ship you need, yes?"

For a moment Angelique felt the tears sting her eyelids. But quickly she quelled them.

"Yes," she said. "You are very kind, I think. Why do you go to so much trouble for someone you do not even know?"

Madame Lucinne gave what sounded very much like a cackle.

"Because we are gypsies." The black eyes gleamed in the lamplight. "We follow our own way. It is enough, eh? You sleep now. Maybe when you awaken, we will talk more of these things."

True to Lucinne's word, the caravan arrived at the bustling seaport of Poole late that afternoon and made camp on the outskirts of the town. Immediately Lucinne's grandson, Alejandro, was dispatched to the town to seek out the Dutchman. Before dusk he had returned with news of a ship and the Dutchman's word that passage for the West Indies would be purchased for a reasonable sum. *Voyons*, so quickly was the thing done. By midnight she would be well on her way to Saint Dominique and her papa.

Angelique, strolling beyond the circle of wagons, felt strangely numb as she stared out over the wide natural harbor, a great cove in which earlier she had counted nine islands. Shipping of every description plied a multitude of channels winding through sandy shoals, and beyond the narrow inlet to the east stretched a broad bay. Suddenly as she gazed out over the tall, stately houses of the town, she felt a bitter lump rise in her throat.

How different was this land of the English from the one to which she would sail. There was a sense of purpose and striving in the ships in the harbor and prosperity in the great homes of the merchants of the town. And yet there was stability, too, and tradition, as was evidenced in the well-kept farms and country manors that she had left behind on her journey to the coast, all of which Saint Dominique, sweltering in the heat and humidity of the tropics, markedly lacked. There, one did not build, one ravaged the thick vegetation, clearing it for the sugar cane fields, and moving on when the soil was exhausted to exploit a new area. If there was a sense of purpose, it was to reap profits at the expense of the land, and while riches accrued from such exploitation, they flowed most often out of the island into the coffers of absentee landowners. One felt, looking out over the harbor, that the English on their small island might endure forever, while Saint Dominique, a rare tropical flower, visited with the blight of slavery and ravaged by the short-sighted and greedy, trembled on the verge of destruction.

Instinctively recoiling from so bleak a prospect, her thoughts, perhaps inevitably, turned to Waincourt and Sabra and the brief, happy days at Briarcroft. How strange it all seemed now, how distant. For a short time she had known what it was to be young and carefree, to be accepted and part of a family. Always, the beautiful Sabra would loom in her memories as the sister she had never had, and she would never again think of England without calling to mind the image of Waincourt, cynical, noble, and proud, and yet a man to tame a woman like his duchesse and hold her with a love which not even the violence of war could break. She would think of young Trevor, who already showed the same strength of mind as his aristocratic father, and of the scalawag Ferdy, who one day would command his own ship in the king's navy. And yet, overshadowing them all would be the bitter-sweet remembrances of the love that could never be, of an American with the marvellous laughing blue eyes, who had mastered and made her his slave.

For a moment, she was overcome with a terrible rending grief for the beautiful dream she would give up in exchange for the nightmare of revolution and upheaval. She thought with a shudder of Etienne, who had hoped for so much and who had died for so little, of her *maman*, who, disillusioned and exiled in a land foreign to everything she had known, had wasted away living a fantasy that could never be realized. And what of her papa? she wondered suddenly. What in truth did she know of him?

Her earliest memories were disjointed and distant, hardly more than impressions blurred by time. Her most vivid recollections were of laughter that rumbled and boomed, of tall, mud-spattered boots, which had seemed to shake the house as they walked, and of big hands, callused and strong, that had been wont to scoop her up, giggling, into powerful arms. She could not remember when it had changed, when the laughter seemed to have dried all up, leaving in its wake the silence, filled only with her mama's tears. It was only later that she remembered sitting on a stool, her arms propped on his knees, as Papa told her the marvellous stories, and by then her mother had lain in the other room dying. Her last memory of him was of a man in a crumpled shirt who had sat hunched over a table littered with dirty dishes and empty bottles. He had had eyes that would not look at her and a stubbled cheek that felt cold to her kiss. Then, it had not been *au revoir* on his lips, or even godspeed, but *adieu*.

Unable to bear the painful drift of her thoughts, Angelique at last turned and made her way back to the camp.

Madam Lucinne was waiting for her.

"Come, my child," she said, drawing her into the wagon. "It is nearly time for you to go, and I wish to speak with you before Alejandro takes you to meet the Dutchman."

"Something is wrong," exclaimed Angelique, sensing something odd in the old woman's demeanor. "What is it? Is it *le capitaine*? Madame Lucinne, tell me. Has he come looking for me?"

"No, no, my child. It is nothing like that. It is only that I wish to—to prepare you for what lies ahead. Please, sit. We will share a last cup of tea together while I tell you a little about Johannes Zenger, the Dutchman."

Thoroughly puzzled, it was all Angelique could do to stem her impatience as she watched the gypsy woman go about setting out cups and preparing the tea. But at last the thing was done and Madam Lucinne joined her at the small table.

"I want you to know that I thought for a very long time before I decided to approach this man on your behalf," she began with a seriousness that did nothing to alleviate the foreboding she had already aroused in Angelique. "This Dutchman is not a man to be trusted."

"But then, why . . . ?" began Angelique, only to be peremptorily cut short.

"*Because* he was the only one who could help you. Saint Dominique is French. How many English ships do you think there are that would take you there? Not even the smugglers go so far."

"No, but they do go to France. Is there not one to be found to carry me across the channel?"

Madam Lucinne silenced her with a look.

"Enough. I have no patience for foolishness. What chance would you have, a young girl like you, alone, in that country?"

"I am not a child." Angelique bristled. "I can take care of myself."

"Not a child? Bah," the gypsy scoffed. "I have seventy-five years. Compared to me, you are a baby. It was you who came to me for help, yes?"

Angelique flushed with a mixture of chagrin and resentment.

"Yes," she answered. "But—"

"And now you say you can take care of yourself. Make up your mind. Do you want my help or not?"

A wry grin tugged at Angelique's lips.

"*Oui*, I want your help," she admitted, albeit reluctantly.

"Good. Maybe there is some hope for you yet. Now you will listen to me, and you will do as I say. The Dutchman has given his promise that a ship will be found for you. He will keep his word. But you must beware of him. He is cunning like the fox. And dangerous like the serpent. He will want to see what use he can make of you.

And so you will keep your wits about you, and you will take this, in case you find yourself in some difficulty."

Angelique's eyebrows lifted inquisitively at sight of the small vial in the old woman's hand.

"It is a powerful sleeping potion. A few drops in a glass of wine will stop even a man like the Dutchman in only a few seconds. Here. Take it," said the gypsy. "Hide it somewhere on you. This is all the help I can give you. As soon as Alejandro returns, the caravan will leave this place, and you will have no one but yourself. You understand?"

Slowly Angelique nodded and with a hand that was surprisingly steady, reached for the vial.

"I understand," she answered, her glance never wavering from the gypsy's.

Madame Lucinne nodded, apparently satisfied with what she saw in her face.

"Good. Now, you go. And remember. Keep your courage and your wits about you with this man. Johannes Zenger is a friend to no one."

Wordlessly, Angelique slipped the vial into the pocket of her petticoat. When she withdrew her hand, she held a small velvet box in her palm.

"You have been very good to me," she said. "I want you to have this. An exchange of gifts between friends, *oui?* It is an emerald brooch that belonged to my mother."

The old gypsy hesitated only the barest instant before at last she smiled. "It shall be as you wish—a gift between friends. And now may good fortune go with you."

Moments later, Angelique had bid her rescuers a grateful farewell and, accompanied by Alejandro, made her way into town. In an unprespossessing inn on Malet Street, she found herself placed in the care of the Dutchman, a gentleman past middle-age who was built on generous proportions and had shrewd blue eyes that peered out at her from above fleshy red cheeks. His voice wheezed when he spoke.

"Johannes Zenger, Miss DuFour. Your servant, ma'am."

Angelique shivered. *Voyons*, he was everything Madame Lucinne had hinted, this Dutchman, who with a look, made her feel as if she were naked. Nor was his own appearance one to inspire confidence or trust. Bewigged and unfashionably attired in heavy brocades, which gave the impression they had been recently slept in, he was made even more unprepossessing by a disfiguring scar, like a brand, on the left side of his face over the temple and eye. Even worse, he was a pig-man, she thought, hard put not to wrinkle her nose in disgust at his distinctive aroma only imperfectly camouflaged beneath the pervasive scent of musk. As soon as she decently could, she firmly pulled her hand free of the gentleman's.

"*Pardon*, m'sieu," she said, equally firmly, "but I am not DuFour. There were—reasons—why I thought it best to travel under the name that was my mother's. But as those reasons no longer exist, I prefer to use my own, please. I am Angelique Eugenie Gilbert."

The scarred eye appeared to leap at her with glittery intensity.

"Gilbert, did you say? You are not, by any chance, related to a certain gentleman of that name who, I believe, has been residing in the West Indies of recent years? In fact, on your very own Saint Dominique, if I am not mistaken?"

"But yes. I am his daughter. You are acquainted with my father, m'sieu?"

"Acquainted with Herman Gilbert? Oh, yes. I know him. As a matter of fact, he kept my ship from falling into the hands of pirates off Tortuga. A reckless rogue, your father, wholly unprincipled and a devil when it came to fighting and whoring." He guffawed, a wheezing sound, like a dry branch scraping against a windowpane. Then, apparently somewhat belatedly recalling whose presence he was in, he made a show of retrieving his error. "But then, that was a very long time ago. I remember hearing

241

something about Gilbert and a young French woman. The daughter of le comte du Vallenoir. Eloped with her, as I recall—your mother, mad'moiselle?"

Angelique hastily lowered the thick veil of her eyelashes to hide her revulsion. *Tiens,* Papa had never mentioned to her any Johannes Zenger or pirates off Tortuga. In fact, it suddenly occurred to her that her papa had told her very little about the days before he met her *maman.*

"*Oui,* my mother," she murmured, looking up at him again. "She died a long time ago. How do you know so much, m'sieu?"

The beefy shoulders lifted in a shrug.

"I make it my business to know about my competitors. In the old days your father was the craftiest of the lot. And the nerviest. Many's the time I expected to hear he had been murdered by those black-hearted devils he did business with. But then, Herman Gilbert always was slippery as an eel. Made himself wealthy where others would have lost their bloody heads. And now here I find he has as fetching a daughter as a man could ask for. It would seem that some people have all the luck."

A faint tinge of color touched Angelique's cheeks as she saw the way his eyes ran over her, lingeringly, as if she were a prime bit of blood he was considering purchasing. *Hein,* he was enough to make her flesh crawl, was this Dutchman whose tongue spoke one thing while his look said another. But, inside, she was far more disturbed by his remarks about her papa. Suddenly she wanted nothing more than to be free of M'sieu Zenger and safely aboard the ship that was to take her away from this place. But also she knew she could not afford to antagonize this pig-man—at least not until after she knew the name of the ship and where it was to be found.

For now, she would be her mama's daughter, she told herself, and from somewhere summoned a smile that would have done Eugenie DuFour credit.

"You are very kind, and, to me, the good Sarmaritan,

242

non? I was afraid I would be marooned in England for a very long time. But you have found me the ship to Saint Dominique. I am of the most grateful, m'sieu."

"Not at all, my dear. I have done very little. The arrangements were quite simple to make. We were fortunate the *Hollander* was preparing to weigh anchor with the evening tide." Angelique's heart gave a little leap. "As a matter of fact, you have a few hours before you embark. No doubt you would be pleased to dine with me, after which, I should be only too happy to see you on board your ship."

With an effort, Angelique quelled her disgust. Dining with the Dutchman did not loom as an agreeable prospect.

"Dine with you?" she replied. "It would be of the very uncivil to refuse so generous an offer. But I am afraid that I must, m'sieu. You see, it was necessary for me to leave France in the very big hurry. I have no money, only the jewels my mother left to me. Before I board this *Hollander*, I must find someone to buy the one or two pieces—enough to repay you for the passage and to cover my needs."

Instantly Zenger appeared to expand, his thick lips stretching to a smile that inexplicably made the hairs at the nape of her neck stand on end.

"But that will not be at all necessary, Miss Gilbert." His hand disappeared into a pocket and pulled out a purse. "I shall be only too happy to advance you whatever sum you require."

Angelique stiffened. *Voyons,* had not her papa warned her that no man offered a woman money unless he expected something back in return!

"You are very generous, m'sieu," she said, "but you must see that I cannot accept your offer. It would not be at all acceptable, even from one who is a friend of my father."

M'sieu Zenger, however, was obviously not a man to be overly concerned with either the proprieties or a lady's

243

tender sensibilities.

"Nonsense, my dear," he boomed. Grasping her hand, he set the purse in the palm and deliberately closed her fingers around it. For the space of a heartbeat, their eyes met and held, and suddenly Angelique felt a queasiness in the pit of her stomach. "You not only can, but you will," he said with chilling finality. Then all at once he was smiling again. "I insist. After all, I owe your father my life. I should be a poor sort if I did not take advantage of this opportunity to repay him in some small measure. Now, let us hear no more on the subject. I have ordered dinner sent up to my rooms. I suggest we repair there without further delay. After all, you would not want to risk having your ship sail without you, now would you, my dear."

Angelique's blood ran cold. Only a child or a fool could miss the implied threat in those words. She would accept the purse and accompany him upstairs, or he would see that she never set foot off English soil again. *Sacre bleue.* She was fast discovering that she did not care at all for M'sieu Zenger, the Dutchman. But maybe he would find that he did not care so much for her either, she vowed, feeling the old recklessness rising up to give her courage.

"But it is very clever of you, *non?*" she answered acerbically. "To so quickly solve another of my problems. Very well, I accept your invitation to dine. After all, what other choice do I have?"

Zenger's fleshy cheeks bulged in a hideous grin.

"But how very wise of you, mad'moiselle. I can see that you take after your father."

And you, m'sieu, thought Angelique to herself, are cold like the shark, and much less to be trusted. Her stomach clenched with fear as she started up the dimly lit stairway.

Chapter 14

Sabra rose hastily from the breakfast table as Locke wheeled and strode grimly out of sight.

"Phoebe, tell Waincourt what has happened. Tell him I need him," she said urgently, going to the door. "Hurry, Phoebe! You'll find him in his study."

"Yes, Miss Sabra," answered the nanny, following in her mistress's wake. "I be goin'. But don't you be goin' an' gettin' no crazy notions of chasin' after that girl. You gots the baby to think of now."

Sabra, however, did not hear her. She was already halfway up the stairs in pursuit of her brother, who, she doubted not, had headed for Angel's room to see for himself that she had gone.

She had not guessed wrongly, she discovered, upon entering the girl's chamber to find Locke flinging open the doors to an ominously empty wardrobe.

"The little fool!" he exploded, slamming the side of his fist against the wall. "I should have known better than to leave her alone."

"Wes, no," exclaimed the duchess, coming up behind him. "You mustn't blame yourself. How could you possibly have known?"

The look in his eyes chilled Sabra's heart.

"I know *her*," he said, his voice harsh in the quiet of the room. "That should have been enough."

Sabra bit her lip, uncertain what to say. In her heart she pitied them both.

"What are you going to do?"

Locke uttered a short laugh.

"Go after her. Find her and bring her back. We have a wedding to finish."

Sabra touched his arm.

"Wes, maybe you shouldn't. Angel must have had her reasons for—for leaving like this. Perhaps it would be better to let her go."

She had spoken on impulse, prompted, no doubt, by the bits and pieces Angel had revealed to her that afternoon when they talked. She saw at once it was a mistake as Locke turned to look at her with probing eyes.

"You know something," he stated flatly. Sabra, withdrawing her hand, turned uneasily away. "Sabra, whatever it is, you must tell me," Locke prodded, his face grim as he watched her clasp hands nervously before her.

At last her head came up, her eyes troubled as they met his.

"Wes, a long time ago you told me why you obtained permission from your captain to transfer to the *Hampden* just before it was captured. You said you owed a favor to one of the officers on board and that you left the *Warren* to take his place. Do you remember?"

"It's hardly something I'd forget," murmured Locke, suddenly wary.

"You never told me who that officer was," she continued, acutely aware that the old, familiar shutter had descended over the stern features, just as it always had whenever she broached the war with him. "It was Herman Gilbert, your partner in the West Indies, wasn't it."

"Yes, it was Gilbert. What of it?" he countered with scant patience. "Sabra, I don't have time for this now."

Sabra swallowed, determined for once to pursue the subject even if it hurt him.

246

"You never told me what that favor was. Please, Wes. It's important."

For a moment Sabra thought he would not answer, then a wry grimace twisted at his lips.

"I ran across him in the old days, when I was little more than a boy, sailing the old skipjack between islands," he said at last. "Phillip sent me out on a run to Kingston against our mother's wishes. While I was there, I made the error of falling into a game of hazard with some hard men. I nearly lost the entire cargo before I figured out the dice were weighted. And then I was foolish enough to take exception to being cheated." He shrugged. "Gilbert stepped in and bailed me out. That's all there was to it."

Sabra, however, was not fooled. It had meant everything to Wes to please his stepfather, and Phillip Tyree had placed his trust in the untried youth against Elizabeth Tyree's wishes. It must have meant a great deal to Wes not to fail in that trust.

"And later, you ran into him again," she said. "He was an officer on the *Hampden*, and the British navy was about to bottle up the American fleet in Penobscot Bay. Certain they would fall to the British, you burned the ships. Then the officers and men escaped overland to Boston. All except the *Hampden* and one other. You knew when you took Gilbert's place you would be captured, didn't you, Wes. *Didn't* you!"

The muscle leaped along the lean line of his jaw.

"I was aware there was a strong possibility of it," he admitted.

"Then why . . . ?"

Locke waved an impatient hand.

"He'd received a letter. His wife was dying, and I owed him my life. What more do you want to know? That after the bloody war he looked me up? That he offered me a partnership with terms so generous I'd been a fool to turn him down. Not that the money mattered. Tyree and Locke was sound as ever. But it gave me the excuse to do

247

what I'd always wanted." A shadow of pain flickered in the stern visage. "What Wayne and I had always talked of doing."

"Sail the Great South Sea," Sabra murmured, her eyes misty with the memories. Robert Wayne, the man who had been closer than a brother to Wes, the man who had betrayed them all and who had redeemed himself by giving his life to save Sabra and Myles from the baronet's treachery. It was a name neither of them ever mentioned, had not since Wes, awakening one morning during the weeks of slow recovery, had at last remembered his old friend and asked about him. How it had hurt to tell him the truth! Robert Wayne had sold them out to the British. Even now she could see the look of disbelief in her brother's eyes, the wound that, added to all the others, had changed him forever. And now this.

She wanted to cry out against the injustice of it all. Had not Wes suffered enough? Given enough? She had thought it would be finished when Channing's ship had gone down, lured to its death by the *Nemesis*; but instead she had seen the baronet's legacy of hatred and revenge do its bitter work. She had beheld the barriers grow between her and Wes, the wall of cynicism that he erected to shut out the rest of the world, the recklessness that had driven him away from her and everything he had once held dear. Almost, she could curse their mother for the weakness that had been the cause of it all.

"You're thinking of *him*," sighed Locke, who had been watching the swift play of emotions cross her face. "Sir Wilfred Channing, Baronet. Why, Sabra? What's the point? That was all a very long time ago. Why bring it up now?"

Jarred back to the present, Sabra looked up at him, then quickly away.

"I-I think you were not unaware that Angel and I have become very close in the short time she has been here," she began, feeling her way, searching for the right words to tell him her suspicions. "We—talked—a great deal

248

about—well, about you and her. Some of the things she said set me to thinking."

She could sense the impatience in him, the powerful muscles taut with expectancy. Restlessly she moved away.

"Wes, I used to watch her when she thought no one was looking. I could see the way she looked at you. It was obvious to anyone with eyes that she was head over ears in love with you. But she was afraid, too, or maybe *haunted* is the better word. I accused her of not intending to go through with the marriage."

The harsh bark of his laughter startled her.

"I don't suppose she bothered to deny it," he said, a peculiar glint in his eyes.

"No. How-how did you know?"

"For Christ's sake, Sabra. You must have had some inkling of the game I was playing. To insure she wouldn't run away from me, I had to bribe her. I promised her I'd take her anywhere she wanted to go if after a fortnight, she still could not bring herself to wed me. But yesterday she agreed. And I believe she was sincere. Something happened to change her mind. The fire, maybe. Or that cursed gypsy and her blasted fortunetelling. But come to the point. My time is growing more precious by the moment."

Thus goaded, Sabra steeled herself to tell him the rest of it.

"You're right," she said. "She admitted it. I-I tried to tell her that I knew you and that whatever was bothering her, she could trust you to understand. That's when she said she had come to know you, too, and that that was why she could never tell you the truth. Your sense of honor would demand that you place yourself in grave danger. Then she looked at me, and suddenly my heart was filled with fear—for her and for you. She said something about the irony of fate. That she had trapped the man she had thought to revere as the savior of her father, trapped him into a marriage he could not want.

Wes, what does it all mean?"

Locke shrugged.

"You know what it means, my dearest Sabra. Angel is Herman Gilbert's daughter."

Sabra, who had expected an entirely different reaction, stared at him in astonishment.

"You knew?" she demanded.

"Of course, I knew," he said with a tinge of impatience. "From the first moment I penetrated her disguise, I suspected it, but I told myself I was wrong. Why, after all, would she choose to play such a charade?" And why, he added cynically to himself, would she have given herself to him so sweetly if she had never any intent of marrying him? "None of it made any sense. And then something happened in the mail coach on the way here, something that suddenly made a great deal about my elusive Angel abundantly clear."

"Well?" prodded Sabra, when it seemed he meant to leave her in the air. "What was it?"

A curious smile played briefly about the stern lips as he thought back to that night on the ship. She had known then what she wanted, and it had never been to force him into marriage. "I saw the rose that I'd given her," he answered, as if that explained everything. "A woman bent on escaping from a man does not take a memento with her to remember him by—unless she is not as indifferent to him as she'd like him to believe. Don't you see?" Sabra's breath caught as Locke looked at her, his eyes like glittery pinpoints of steel. "She disguised herself because she knew I would hold Angelique Gilbert at arm's length. And she ran because she didn't want me to figure out that the girl I had dishonored was Herman Gilbert's daughter."

Sabra winced at the bitter self-condemnation in those final words.

"But if she loved you . . . ?"

"If she loved me, she was all the more certain to run." Bitterly he turned away. "Somebody has gone to a lot of trouble to make sure of that. They've bloody well convinced her that Gilbert isn't her father. She thinks she's the offspring of a bloody slave—and that because of it, she can never marry any man."

As the significance of what he had said sank in, Sabra's heart was filled with pity for the girl, and with anger at the one who was the cause of so much pain.

"But who would do such a thing?" she said, pacing a step and then coming back again. "And why, for God's sake?"

"I don't know," Locke admitted grimly, "but I intend to find out—as soon as I get her back again." Suddenly impatient, he swung around again. "There's no time to lose. I'll need a good horse. With any luck she won't have gone far."

"Then I suggest we start at once," quietly interjected a voice from the doorway. "I've some of the best cattle in England in my stable."

Locke, turning to regard his brother-in-law with gimlet eyes, nodded.

"Somehow I was sure you would." A faint smile touched the thin lips. "In fact, I was counting on it."

"Have you any idea where Miss DuFour might have gone?" queried Waincourt, cutting to the heart of the matter. "Any friends or relatives—someone she might turn to?"

A cold gleam came to the captain's eyes.

"I can think of one possibility worth looking into—an old gypsy woman with a meddlesome tongue."

"Sabra," Waincourt said, glancing from his brother-in-law to his wife, "inform William we shall be needing Corsair and Devil's Dancer saddled, if you please, while Wes and I make ready to depart. If the girl has been taken by gypsies, we've no time to lose in getting her back."

"But I'm going with you," exclaimed Sabra, girding herself to do battle.

"No, my dear, you are not," replied the duke. "Not this time. While you may thrive on adventures of a harrowing nature, I fear our future offspring may not."

Sabra grimaced, unable to deny the truth of his argument.

"Oh, very well," she conceded grudgingly. "I shall allow you to dictate to me this once, but only for the sake of the baby. I daresay even in my state I should do well enough in the carriage, and you might wish you had a woman along when you catch up to Angel. Poor child. She must have felt very desperate indeed to flee at night in the middle of a storm." Her face softened as she exchanged a meaningful glance with her brother. "I pray to God, Wes, that you find her."

Some time later, Locke, mounted on one of the duke's prime bits of blood, was to repeat that prayer more than once, even as he cursed himself for a bloody fool.

He should never have left her alone, knowing her as he did. He should have guessed that, given the circumstances, she would blame herself—the bloody curse—for what had happened. Besides, it was not as if he had not been aware of the impossible dilemma she had placed herself in with her blasted charade. He had, and realizing that, how much less could he excuse his behavior! He was no inexperienced youth, but a man of seven and thirty. He should have anticipated that she would pull a fool stunt like this. And yet somehow he hadn't.

No doubt he had been coxcomb enough to believe she loved him enough to stick it through, he thought cynically. Obviously she was not indifferent to him. No woman could have made love to him the way she had unless her heart was involved, he'd stake his life on it. Besides, she had seemed willing enough as they had discussed their plans with Waincourt and Sabra—eager even. Still, there had been something about her as she came across the room on Waincourt's arm, looking more beautiful than any woman had a right to be. There was a fey expression in the lovely eyes, a paleness about the cheek, a certain distraction in her manner—all of which he had dismissed as natural in the circumstances. After all, what bride was not nervous on her wedding day? It was not until he felt her weave slightly next to him that he became conscious of a prickling of nerve-endings, a premonition that all was not well with his unpredictable Angel. After that, it had been all he could do not to cut the verbose parson short in his blasted sermon on the sanctity of marriage and whatever else he had been rambling on about. Bloody hell, who was he trying to fool? The whole time, he had been in a sweat with the inexplicable certainty that something was about to happen.

He couldn't say how he knew, or what it was that he sensed, but the feelings had been there all the same. It was like a bloody nightmare, standing there, muscles tensed, the sweat cold against his ribs, as he waited for his hitherto reluctant bride to utter the two words that would have made her irrevocably his. He could see it in her eyes, just before the untimely fire had disrupted everything, that the answer was the one he had been waiting for. He had been so certain, in fact, that he had allowed himself to be lulled into a false sense of security. He had bloody well left her alone when she had needed him the most.

Well, that was one mistake he was not likely to make again, he told himself grimly.

Waincourt's shout above the thunder of horses' hooves brought him out of his reverie.

"There's the village, Wes, but apparently your gypsies departed sometime during the night."

Locke, pulling his mount to a plunging halt atop the hill overlooking the village green, was conscious of a measure of relief. The marked absence of the caravan seemed to hold out some promise that his troublesome love had made it at least this far without mishap. Still, he felt that unbearable pressure in his chest. Damn the chit's stubborn pride! he cursed silently to himself. She had hardly been in any condition to brave a rainstorm in the dead of night. If she did not succumb to a fatal inflammation of the lungs, he meant to strangle her for putting him through the anguish of not knowing if she was alive or dead.

"Is there more than one way out of town?" he shouted at the duke, who was watching him with expressionless gray eyes.

"The road doesn't fork for another four or five miles. Then you'll have to decide whether they are headed for Portsmouth or Christchurch, or further west. To Bournemouth, perhaps, or Poole. Either way, you had better pray she is hoping for a ship to carry her to the Indies."

Locke, not bothering to answer, clapped heels to his restive steed. He didn't need Waincourt to tell him how difficult it would be for Angel to find a ship willing to carry her to the French West Indies. No doubt she would be forced to hold up in an inn at least for the night, if not longer, while she asked about. And even then, without help, her chances of success were slim. France, however, would be another prospect altogether. Hardly a day passed that a vessel of one sort or another did not cross the Channel. She might already be on her way, and once in France, his chances of finding her would be slim indeed.

The sun shone palely through a gray cover of clouds when they came to the junction of three roads. In a few terse words, Waincourt dismissed the easterly one. Portsmouth, a bustling seaport dominated by naval vessels, seemed an unlikely choice for a fugitive in seach of a ship bound for a French possession in the Caribbean. France and England might be at peace for the moment, but Saint Dominique was closed to British shipping. Nor did Locke believe for a minute Angel would be foolish enough to show herself in the vicinity of the *Sea Wolf*, where she would run the risk of being spotted by one of his men. Christchurch and Portsmouth both having been eliminated, they headed their horses along the southwesterly course.

It was perhaps typical of his luck, thought Locke, as they came to the next junction of roads in a hollow between two hills, that his horse should suddenly turn up lame. Cursing, he dismounted to examine the affected forefoot.

"He's picked up a rock," he muttered curtly over his shoulder to Waincourt. "Maybe it's not bruised. If I can just pry it out."

Dislodging the rock, he discovered with grim satisfaction that the steed seemed sound enough. It was then he noticed the tracks leading off to a small copse of trees and the unmistakable signs of a camp. Dropping the reins, he strode with long strides to the remains of an abandoned campfire. The charred bits of wood were cold to the touch, but the tracks had been made earlier that day, after the storm that would have washed them away. Eagerly he searched the trampled ground for some sign that the camp had belonged to the gypsies.

It was Waincourt, however, who spotted the length of soiled bandages discarded beside the charred remains of a fire.

"She was here," Locke said, meeting the duke's noncommittal glance. "And the tracks head south."

"That way leads to Poole. I should say they are no more than four or five hours ahead of us."

Locke grunted assent.

"Too much of a lead for us to overtake them before they reach the coast. At least not without a change of horses."

As luck would have it, they topped the rise to discover a hamlet nestled in a fertile valley, and a posting inn from which they were able to obtain fresh mounts. An hour later, their luck took another turn for the better. Rounding a bend, they came head to head with the gypsy caravan.

Locke, in no mood to be gracious, cantered past the lead wagons until he came to one occupied by a spare figure he recognized from the previous day. Pulling his mount to a plunging halt, he swept the wizened gypsy an ironic bow.

"Madame Lucinne," he murmured, fixing her with a chill blue gaze.

The knowing gleam of a smile creased the old woman's face.

"You are too late, Captain Locke," she said. "But you will go after her, yes? To Saint Dominique. This I have seen in the tea leaves."

"Have you," murmured Locke, unmistakably dangerous despite his soft drawl. "Then you'll have no difficulty guessing what we want. Tell us what you've done with the girl, and we'll leave you to go on your way."

The old woman's cackle jarred in the sudden stillness.

"Ah, yes. You have the temper to fight. That is good. But you will need more than courage to win what your heart desires."

At last a cold glint of a smile flickered in the granite hardness of Locke's face.

"You're all generosity, madam—when it comes to handing out free advice. But it's answers I want. It occurs to me that the local magistrate would be interested to know how you came by that emerald brooch you're wearing. And what happened to its previous owner."

He was not smiling as he came to the end of his speech, and the pale gleam of his eyes left little doubt that he was through playing games. Madame Lucinne nodded in apparent satisfaction.

"Your Miss DuFour gave it to me," she admitted freely. "But you knew that. It was a gift—'between friends,' she told me. And I accepted it on those terms. If you truly love her, Captain, you, too, will accept what she has to give on her terms. It is not enough to possess such a one. She walks an uncertain path, and the dangers are great. Still, if you would not lose her, you will allow her the freedom to discover her own way."

"You may be sure of it," Locke answered coldly, "so

long as I'm along to even the odds for her. Now what the bloody hell have you done with her?"

"She wished a ship to take her home. I sent her to a man who knows about such things. He calls himself the Dutchman, and he is to be found at the Inn of the Red Lion. You will go after her, yes?"

But Locke, who had not waited to hear more, had already clapped heels to his horse.

"You will not find her," the gypsy called after him. "Not in Poole. Your destiny, Captain, lies with hers beyond the sea."

Waincourt, riding hard to catch up to the receding figure of his brother-in-law, smiled grimly to himself. If the elusive Angel had fallen into the hands of the Dutchman, whatever destiny lay before her promised to be of damned short duration.

Angelique was conscious of vague surprise and a healthy disgust at first sight of her host's less-than-inviting lodgings. And yet they were just what she might have expected of one who was *très goujat*. Neither large nor particularly lavish, they consisted of two rooms: a somewhat dingy parlor and a no doubt dingier bedroom. A large desk littered with papers and ledgers took up one corner, while a folding table laid with covers for two dominated the center of the parlor. These, along with two straight-backed chairs and a sofa, were nearly the sum total of the furnishings, all of which had seen better days. It was, she decided, just what it looked to be—the abode of a man without a family or even friends beyond business associates. Certainly, it had not the appearance of a seducer's lair. What, then, did Zenger want from her?

The meal, in contrast to the surroundings in which it was served, was both sumptuous and artfully prepared. Obviously, the Dutchman was something of an epicure, and, as if unwilling to mar the pleasure of the repast, kept the conversation away from any unpleasantries. Angelique, however, had no stomach for food. Pretending to do justice to the meal, she picked at the asparagus in cream and the beef à la royale as she waited for her host to reveal what he intended.

It was not to be until they progressed to the pistachio cream pudding, however, that the Dutchman turned the conversation from generalities to subjects of a more specific nature. Without warning, he inquired after her father's business partner.

With an effort Angelique covered the sudden leap of nerves with a low ripple of laughter.

"Is there anyone that you do not know, m'sieu?" she asked, her tone ironic.

"Not many in the business of shipping," he confessed affably. "Sailors are a gossipy lot, Miss Gilbert. And after months at sea, who can blame them if they exchange tales whenever they meet?"

"*Vraiment?* And what tales have you exchanged about Capitaine Locke?" she queried with a false lightness.

The chair creaked as the big Dutchman settled back. Planting his elbows on the armrests, he formed a pyramid with his plump fingers There was something singularly cold in the hard glitter of his eyes that made her afraid for *le capitaine.*

"Locke," he said with a contemptuous curl of the lip, "is one of those rare breeds—an honorable man. I count myself lucky to have come up against him only once. It was an encounter, however, I am not likely to forget."

"You intrigue me, m'sieu," returned Angelique, assaying a slightly bored expression. "And what makes *ce capitaine* so unforgettable?"

The Dutchman's eloquent bark of laughter brought the blood to her cheeks.

"Obviously you have never met the man, if you have to ask that. You have only to lay eyes on him to realize he is no ordinary sort. First of all, my dear, he is what heroes are made of—oh, not just brave and resourceful, a devil in a fight—all that sort of thing one popularly associates with the type. There's more to it than that. Perhaps you were not aware that Locke was incarcerated in a British prison during the war."

"Of course, I heard of it. But then, so were very many others held prisoners."

"Yes, but they were not so unfortunate as to have incurred the enmity of a man who was in a position to make their lives a bloody hell. In the norm, conditions in the prisons were—shall we say—less than pleasant. Even strong men can be broken in little more than a matter of weeks when they are given meat unfit for a dog and water contaminated with disease. But the story goes that that was not good enough for Sir Wilfred Channing, Baronet. In order to make sure of his man, he had Locke systematically tortured and beaten. Not one man in a thousand could have taken what he did and survived."

Sickened, Angelique gripped her hands tightly in her lap to still their trembling.

"And who was this Channing, who did that to him?" she asked. "He must have hated *le capitaine* to wish him the terrible suffering."

"He was one of the king's trusted agents. A vice-admiralty judge before the war. As for why he had it in for Locke?" Shrugging, Zenger leaned back in his chair. Absently he toyed with the quizzing glass, which hung on a black ribbon about his neck. "Most believe it was because Locke's half-sister spurned his advances. A good enough explanation, I suppose. I had the pleasure of seeing Sabra Tyree once in London during her come-out, and even as a young girl, the mere sight of her was enough to make fools out of most men. However, I know for a fact there was bad blood between Channing and Locke's stepfather, Phillip Tyree. It was hardly a secret that Channing used his office to try to ruin the man. Personally, however, I don't give a damn why he did it. I am only sorry he didn't get the job done."

"Why?" queried Angelique, not bothering to disguise

259

the loathing in her voice. "Why are you telling me all this?"

"Because, my dear, it suits my purposes. You see, I was on the point of making your father pay for his iniquities, when Locke—" The beefy fingers tightened on the quizzing glass. Angelique stared in horrid fascination as the ivory handle snapped in two. "—ruined everything."

The Dutchman appeared not to notice what he had done. His eye pale with malice, he continued as if nothing had happened.

"It took years to get Gilbert where I wanted him. In the normal course of events, one expects to sustain an occasional loss in our business—a ship founders in a hurricane, a cargo is lost or destroyed by some mishap. Gilbert, however, began to be cursed with one loss after another. I made sure of that. By the end of the war, he was on the verge of bankruptcy. By all rights he should have been finished."

"But instead he went to the one man who had already given more than anyone had the right to ask of him," murmured Angelique, feeling suddenly sick inside. "And *le capitaine*, he did not refuse him."

She had been merely thinking out loud, so the Dutchman's harsh bark of laughter took her off guard.

"Refuse him? Hell, it wasn't enough for him to pay off your father's notes. The bloody captain had to return from the Orient with enough silks and pearls to restore Gilbert's fortune twice over. After that, I gave up any thought of ever getting back at my old partner," he admitted, the scar hideous in the candlelight as he leaned forward. Picking up his wine glass, he lifted it to Angelique in the manner of a toast. "Until today. You have no notion with what eagernes I agreed to receive you. The moment I heard your assumed name and began to put two and two together, I started to lay my plans. Of course, I confess that I had come up with Eugenie DuFour, Gilbert's wife. But then, his daughter will do even more admirably to deliver my little message. I only wish I could be present to watch what I have sown germinate and grow. I suppose I shall have to be satisfied, however, with imagining it—and with the pleasure of giving you, in measure, what your father gave to me."

Angelique's eyes widened in mounting horror as she watched Zenger's hand rise to stroke the disfiguring scar.

"Oh, yes," murmured the Dutchman. "He is responsible for this."

"But you said you owed him your life—!"

"And so I do. Ironic, is it not?" His mirthless grin chilled her blood. With a sense of unreality she stared into pale eyes that glittered with unreasoning hatred. "Perhaps I had preferred to die than be left like this. But that's beside the point. The fact is Gilbert fired on the pirates after their vessel was already grappled to mine. When their magazine exploded, my ship went up in flames. Gilbert himself dared pull me from the burning deck. A noble act, you would agree. Except for the fact that he made sure I lost everything—my ship and my cargo—and then he left me stranded on bloody Tortuga."

"You are lying! Why should he do such a thing when he had risked his life to save you? It was an act of heroism. You yourself said as much."

"Did I? But then, you must take into account that he had decided to marry and leave his less-than-glorious past behind him. What he saw was a chance to free himself of his former business associates and appropriate for himself at the same time an extremely valuable cargo. You have to admire the man for his ingenuity, the grasping at opportunity, as it were."

"But *you* do not," suggested Angelique, trying to understand the man's convoluted logic.

"Oh, but I do. He did exactly as I should have done had I been in his place. Unfortunately, I was not in his place, else he would be the one with a face like this, and you would not be about to pay the pound of flesh for his mistakes."

Angelique stared into the gloating face with a sense of stunned disbelief. *Voyons*, this could not be happening. And yet it was. Clearly she was in the presence of a madman.

A sharp rap at the door drew his attention away so that he did not see Angelique's hand slip into the placket slit in her petticoat.

"Yes!" he rasped. "What the devil do you want?"

"It's Bruner, Mr. Zenger. The lady's barge is waiting at the pier."

Her heart pounding, Angelique reached toward Zenger's glass.

"Excellent," wheezed the Dutchman. Angelique's stomach lurched as, turning gloating eyes toward her, he just missed seeing the empty vial slip from her grasp to the floor beneath the table. "Wait downstairs. Miss Gilbert should not be more than a few moments. I shall call you when I need you."

"Yes, sir, Mr. Zenger. But don't take too long. The boatswain said the master of the *Hollander* ain't in no mood to miss the outgoing tide."

"Yes, yes, you fool! Now begone with you. Well, my dear," said the Dutchman, dabbing at his thick lips with a napkin. "You heard him. I'm afraid much as I hate to bring the evening to a close, the time grows short."

Angelique's blood ran suddenly cold as she realized he was going to forego the pleasure of finishing the wine in his glass. Already he was shoving his chair back. Heaving himself up, he came to stand behind her, his hand on her chair as he waited for her to rise.

On impulse, she reached for the glasses as she obliged him.

"Then a toast, m'sieu," she offered boldly. "To the settling of old accounts." Daring him to refuse, she drained her glass and dashed it contemptuously against the stone grate. "And my sincerest hope that you may soon rot in hell for it."

The Dutchman's face went ominously purplish, and

for a moment Angelique thought he meant to strike her dead on the spot. Then unexpectedly his head went back, and his peculiarly sinister laughter rasped through the room.

"Very well, a toast," he sneered, taking the glass from her. "May you live to deliver a message to your beloved father. You will tell him that it was Johannes Zenger who did this to you."

Without warning he struck her with his fist.

Angelique's head snapped back and she was flung backwards into the table. Gasping, she caught herself. Then in a blur of pain, she saw Zenger lift the glass and drink.

"To Herman Gilbert's daughter," he chortled and smashed the glass against the wall. In rising terror, Angelique watched him coming toward her.

"You will pay for this," she choked, backing warily before him. "If you in truth fear Capitaine Locke, you will let me go. Now, before you go too far."

"Fear Locke? You are grasping at straws, my dear. Are you truly so naive as to think he would fight for you? You were seen accepting money from me, and you came freely to my private rooms. You, Mad'moiselle Gilbert, will be branded as a whore."

Laughing, he lunged at her, but Angelique, in her desperation, ducked around the corner of the table beyond his grasp.

"You are wrong, m'sieu," she panted. "I am his promised wife. Me, I do not think he will take kindly to what you have done."

"And you, my dear, are a bloody liar!"

Savagely he thrust the table aside. In a mindless panic to escape, Angelique fled past him toward the door. Brutally he caught her. His hand clamped cruelly in her hair, he dragged her back and, with his fist, sent her sprawling nearly senseless to the floor. Weak and gagging with pain, she sensed him coming after her and began dragging herself away. A scream welled up inside of her as his hand clutched at her shoulder. Desperately she raked him with her fingernails. He cursed as Angelique, with a final burst of strength, lunged from beneath his grasp.

"Bloody bitch," he snarled and lumbered after her. But his voice sounded strangely thick, and he staggered on his feet. In a daze of pain, she watched him stumble. With something of horrified fascination, she saw him draw himself up. His thick hand ran uncertainly over his face. He stared at her with slowly dawning comprehension.

"The . . . drink," he muttered, swaying drunkenly. "Some . . . thing in . . . the bloody wine." He took a step toward her, his hand reaching out for her with murderous intent. "Curse you, you sneaking . . . little . . . devil's whore!" he gasped. In the next instant his knees appeared to buckle and with a crash that shook the room, he toppled headlong to the floor beside her.

Angelique was never sure afterwards how long she lay racked with bitter sobs before at last she dragged herself weakly to her knees. Somehow she made her way to her things in the corner where Zenger's servant had left them. With fingers that shook uncontrollably, she opened the battered valise and retrieved from her jewelry case a magnificent pair of diamond earrings.

Contemptuously, she cast them at the prone figure.

"And now, m'sieu, our accounts are settled," she uttered in accents of bitter loathing. Then struggling into her cloak, she gathered her things and made her way to the door.

Battered and weak, Angelique forced herself to stand straight as she left the stairs and entered the common room. She was grateful for the poor lighting and the concealing hood of her cloak as she met the curious gaze of a seaman.

"You are Bruner?" she queried in her haughtiest voice. At his doubtful nod, she thrust the valise at him. "M'sieu Zenger was not feeling well. He has decided to go to bed. He wishes for you to take me to the barge at once, do you understand?"

A frown darkened the man's thin visage.

"It ain't like the Dutchman to turn in early," he noted, obviously suspicious.

From somewhere Angelique found the wit to shrug.

"Maybe you would like to ask him for yourself?" she suggested with a sublime air of indifference. "Of course, I left him in a very sound sleep. Me, I do not think he would like to be disturbed, but you do whatever you want."

Angelique held her breath as the man appeared to hesitate.

"Well, m'sieu?" she demanded at last. "I do not have all night."

She almost swooned with relief as at last he grudgingly reached for her valise and bandbox.

"I expect I'll just have to take your word for it," he muttered sullenly and proceeded toward the exit without a backward glance.

It seemed an endless trek to the pier, and Angelique was close to utter collapse before at last she found herself in the sternsheets of the captain's barge. Trembling from cold and exhaustion, her brain numb to the pain of her cuts and bruises, she held herself upright through sheer willpower alone. Indeed, she stared dully at the bulge of the ship looming over her, and it was not until the ship's officer reached down to shake her gently by the shoulder that she was able to grasp the reality of her safe arrival.

Slowly she shoved herself up to stand, swaying drunkenly as the officer helped her into the sling that would lift her aboard the ship. With her last ounce of strength she clung to the ropes as she dangled precariously over the heaving sea. Then strong hands clasped her and swung her inboard, and a portly man with a not unpleasant face stepped before her.

"Miss DuFour?" she heard as from a great distance. "Welcome aboard. I am Nordquist, captain of this vessel."

265

In a daze she stared at him, unable to frame the words in answer to his greeting. Vaguely, she heard him say her name, his voice suddenly sharp with alarm. Then gently, like sinking into the depths of a welcoming sea, she slipped into unconsciousness.

Angelique did not stir as she was carried below decks to her tiny cabin and laid upon a cot. She was not aware that the ship's surgeon was summoned to tend her hurts or that the captain himself came to inquire after her once the ship was safely from harbor and on its way out to sea. And certainly she did not know that far behind her, two grim-faced and weary horsemen plunged to a halt on heaving mounts before a small, disreputable inn on Malet Street.

Nearly flinging himself from the saddle, one of them strode with long, purposeful strides through the door just as the Dutchman lurched, bellowing in rage, down the stairway.

"What's got into 'im?" queried one of the hangers-on, leering as the ungainly figure appeared precariously close to toppling down the few remaining steps.

"I expect 'e's some upset at finding 'is 'ore up and left 'im wi'out never a fare-thee-well," snickered the tavern-keeper, running a soiled cloth over the less-than-immaculate bar. "A Frenchie, she was, and a better looker, I never did see. More than likely, she dipped 'er 'ands into 'is pockets, and more's the power to 'er, I say. 'E's a bad 'un, the bloody Dutchman."

Only then did the two become aware of the tall newcomer with gimlet eyes, who stood within hearing of their brief exchange. With a single stride, he placed himself squarely in the path of the raging Dutchman.

The room went suddenly still as his voice slashed like a knife through the din.

"Zenger!"

The Dutchman froze. His eyes bulged at sight of the compelling figure waiting at the bottom of the stairway.

266

"You!" he breathed. The small eyes glittered with a venomous dislike. Then instantly he changed, hiding his malevolence behind a cunning mask.

"Captain Locke," he wheezed, coming down the last two steps. "She said you would come, but I was fool enough not to believe her."

Locke's smile was singularly cold.

"You look older, Zenger," he observed. "Dirtier. Hardly a fit companion for a lady. What have you done with her?"

Zenger's glance flickered briefly beyond the captain to two ruffians seated in the far corner, then back again. A sly look sprang to the small, piggish eyes.

"Done with her?" he echoed. "It's what the cunning little piece did to me. She's her father's daughter, all right. I expect Herman Gilbert must be extraordinarily proud of her. Slipped me a sleeping powder when I wasn't looking, then robbed me after I'd paid her top price for a whore. Maybe she was even worth it, eh, Captain?" The plump hands moved suggestively. "That supple young body. Skin, soft, and white as fine ivory. I fancy you must be intimately acquainted with every delectable inch of the little . . ."

The captain moved so swiftly that none of the onlookers was quite sure how he came suddenly to be standing with the sharp end of a knife lodged against the big man's throat.

"I suggest you hold your tongue, Zenger," he murmured softly. "And tell your men to stay out of this, unless they want to see the color of your blood."

"I think you had better do as the captain advises, gentlemen," commented a dry voice from the doorway. The ominous click of a pistol hammer sounded loud in the taut stillness. "I assure you he means just what he says."

The two "gentlemen" thus addressed cast wary glances at the elegant figure of the nobleman holding cocked pistols aimed with deadly deliberation at their chests. It took only an instant to convince them discretion was indeed the better part of valor.

"How very wise," applauded the duke as they slunk back to the obscurity of their corner.

"And now," Locke said, turning his whole attention to the Dutchman, eyeing him with undisguised malevolence. "You will tell me where she is."

"I'm afraid you've missed her, Captain," he replied. "The 'lady' is even now aboard the *Hollander* bound for the West Indies. I myself obtained her passage."

"And how do I know you're telling me the truth? For all I know you've never laid eyes on her."

Zenber's wheezing chuckle was anything but pleasant.

"Oh, but you are quite right to question my veracity. I'm hardly noted for my honesty, am I. However, this time there were witnesses who saw Miss Gilbert accept a purse from me in this very room. And if that's not enough to convince you, perhaps these will."

The Dutchman grinned as he held up a pair of diamond earrings between two plump fingers.

"Perhaps you recognize them, Captain," he gloated, dangling them before the other man's eyes. "She was wearing them when I—oh, dear, how shall I put it delicately—when she *disrobed* for my pleasure. Apparently she forgot them in her hasty departure."

A less thick-skinned man would have trembled before the cold glitter of the captain's eyes. Zenger, however, carried on the crest of his own arrogance, appeared oblivious of his danger.

"But I grow weary of the whole tedious affair," he said, no longer smiling. "I suggest that you go—now, while you still can."

"Do you," observed the captain, apparently impressed. "For a man with a knife at his throat, you appear remarkably sure of yourself."

The Dutchman sneered.

"Come now, do you take me for a fool? D'you think I don't know you have no intention of slashing my throat?

I'm unarmed, and you, Captain, are what is known as an honorable man."

"It would seem we find ourselves at something of an impasse," Locke conceded, with a faint gleam of a smile. "Much as I hate to admit it, you are right." Deliberately sheathing the knife, he made as if to turn away. But midway he stopped and in a single uninterrupted movement, he laid the Dutchman out with a hard fist to the chin. "Too bad," he murmured, rubbing his bruised knuckles in the palm of his other hand, "the same doesn't apply to a good right."

Contemptuously he bent to retrieve Angel's earrings from the other man's grasp.

"No need for you to bother with these, Zenger. I'll see they're returned to their rightful owner."

Ignoring the downed man's hate-filled glare, he turned his back on the Dutchman and sauntered carelessly toward the waiting duke.

What came next happened with bewildering swiftness. Zenger's arm came up, a pistol aimed with deadly intent at that broad receding back. Before Waincourt could utter a warning, Locke twisted around, the knife flashing from his hand. As the blade struck with a sickening thud, Zenger froze, his eyes fixed with horrified disbelief at the knife imbedded in his chest. Then slowly Locke straightened.

"My . . . compliments," wheezed the Dutchman as his intended victim came to stand over him. "Should've . . . known better than to trust a man of honor . . . when his back is turned. Unfortunately, you're too late . . . for the girl. You . . . may have won the hand, Captain . . . but . . . thanks to me, you'll never win the . . . bloody game!"

The massive body shook hideously with what was meant to be a laugh. Then choking on his own blood, Zenger fell back.

"You took something of a chance, old son," murmured Waincourt, his gaze cold as he watched the dying man's eyes set in a blank stare. "I fear my lady wife would never have forgiven me if the bastard had placed a pistol ball between your shoulder blades."

Shrugging, Locke bent to retrieve his knife.

"How much less would she have forgiven you," he drawled, "had I been strung up for murdering a defenseless man?"

"I shudder to think of it," admitted the duke as he followed his brother-in-law from the inn. "So, what will you do now?"

Locke stared out toward the sea, shimmering in the light of a crescent moon. After a moment he turned back to the duke, a pale glint in the look he bent upon him.

"When you get back to Briarcroft, I'd be obliged if you'd see Jubal rejoins the ship posthaste. I'm afraid I won't be returning with you. As for Sabra . . . tell her, if you would, that I'm sorry I couldn't give her a proper good-bye, but that . . . my wife . . . and I'll be back in the fall to make it up to her. On that, she can bloody well rely."

Chapter 15

Angelique, awakened by the bray of the conch shell summoning the field hands, slipped quickly out of bed and hurried to the window. The sun was not even a pink glow on the horizon yet, and the ruffle of breeze, scented with a mingling of wild cherry blossoms and sweet lime, was chill against her skin. She shivered a little as she gazed out over the silhouettes of the cottages behind the great house and watched the "big gang" with their torches as they gathered in the green for the day's labor in the sugar cane fields along the lower slopes and valleys. She had overslept, for she knew her father must have risen some time before and already he would be at his breakfast on the verandah.

"Pierrette!" she called, her voice impatient, as she tore herself away from the window. "Pierrette!"

"*Voici*, Mamzelle. What for you wanting Pierrette so early? It no be daylight another twenty minutes, Mamzelle."

Angelique favored her maid with a darkling glance.

"*Assez*, Pierrette. I told you to wake me before the sounding of the conch. *Faites vite!* You must help me dress. I do not wish to miss my father."

Pierrette's comely face broke into a white-toothed grin.

"*Mais oui*, mamzelle. You no worry. Monsieur not yet

271

sitting down to breakfast. You no be missing him. You see, Pierrette dress you quick."

Angelique had not been absent from La Cime du Bonheur so long that she did not remember that her maid's notions of "quick" differed a great deal from her own. Nevertheless, she did, by dint of continued urging, manage to don in something less than half an hour the one gown that she had kept carefully set aside during her nine-week voyage aboard the Dutch packet. Impatiently, she sat before the gilt-framed looking glass while Pierrette combed out her raven tresses.

How strange it was to find herself in her old room. Everything—her porcelain dolls ranged on the bureau, her pink canopy bed draped in mosquito netting, the little girl dresses hanging in the wardrobe—was just as she had left it. Almost she expected to hear the voice of her *maman* calling to her from the verandah, telling her to hurry if she did not wish to miss her breakfast. Such memories were bittersweet to her as she stared at her reflection in the mirror, for in truth, she herself felt like a stranger in this room.

No longer was she the little girl who had sat in the window seat weaving daydreams, but a woman who knew what it was to lie in the arms of the man she loved.

For a moment the reflection of the young woman with huge, shadowed eyes blurred in her vision. *Sacriste!* Would this hollow ache inside her never cease? Mercifully, she had been too ill the first two weeks of her voyage to grieve over what had almost been. Even now she did not know how she had found the strength to make her way from the inn in Poole to the pier and the barge waiting to carry her out to the ship. But somehow she had and for five days afterwards had lain in her cabin, too weak and feverish from the beating she had received at Zenger's hands to leave her bed. Had it not been for the kindness of the captain, who had looked after her and made sure she did not starve, she doubted that she would ever have survived beyond the first week of

272

her confinement.

Bitterly she cursed the tenaciousness that had kept her alive. A far more unpleasant death awaited her here. With her whole being she knew it. And yet, even to die brutally at the hands of hate-maddened slaves would be better than to pine endlessly away of the heart that was broken, she thought morbidly. With a helpless surge of self-pity, it came to her to wonder how long it would take the capitaine to forget her. One month? Two, perhaps? Already he might lie in the arms of a new lover, his "Angele" nothing but a vague, probably distasteful, memory.

Sacre bleue! She must not let her mind run away with her. Such thoughts were not good for her. In truth they would soon drive her mad if she did not cease to dwell on them.

Le Capitaine would come. This she knew. He would come to bring the shipload of goods. And he would come, too, to tell her papa how he had failed to find Angelique Eugenie Gilbert and bring her home with him. *Plut à Dieu,* he did not come before it was all over.

She had had only to step onto the pier in Port-au-Prince to sense the change in the air. In the streets there was much drunkenness, and the militia of planters had patrolled the town along with a company of French soldiers. Nowhere was there any sign of the blacks or the people of color. It was the curfew, said the farmer whom she had hired to take her the rest of the way home. But she had seen with her own eyes the buildings that had been ransacked and burned, and she had been glad to leave the city behind on the short climb to the village and from there, on the long ascent to Cime du Bonheur.

"There, Mamzelle, *c'est finis,*" said Pierrette, standing back to admire her beautiful mistress. "And now you going for to make your papa happy you home, *non?*"

"*Non,* I think only to see me boarding the ship for someplace far from here can make him happy," demurred Angelique wryly as she studied the slender

273

figure in the looking glass. *"Mais si'l plaît à Dieu,* I will find the way to change his mind."

The resonant boom, however, of her father's voice rumbling out over the clatter of dishes and silverware like the ominous herald of a rising storm was not promising, she decided a few moments later.

"Bloody hell, man! I'll not sit here and listen to such tommyrot! It's enough to spoil a man's digestion."

Angelique halted in the shadowed interior of the house and looked out on the verandah. From where she stood she could see her father at his breakfast, his broad back to her. With a fond glance she took in the thick wrists protruding from the plain cuffs of his sleeves, the bulge of muscle across the massive shoulders, and the thinning blond hair, bleached nearly white from the tropical sun and caught carelessly in a queue at the nape of the bullish neck. In his white moleskin shirt and buff unmentionables, he looked strong as an old oak and just as immovable. And, in truth, he could be of the most stubborn, she reflected, her grin awry as she thought of her arrival home only the day before.

Sacriste, he had hardly finished welcoming her with one of his powerful bear hugs before they found themselves locking horns. And such a simple thing had been the cause of it!

"How good it is to be home!" she had exclaimed, lifting her arms wide as though to embrace the whole of La Cime du Bonheur perched on the pinnacle overlooking the sea.

"Yes, well," he had retorted, "don't get too attached to it. You won't be staying long."

She had expected as much from him, and so it was no surprise. Still, coming, as it had, so close on the heels of her arrival had jarred.

"We are leaving then?" she queried artlessly, turning upon him the huge innocent eyes. "We are going to live in America—in Boston, maybe, or New York? What a good idea! When do we go?"

"Not 'we,'" Gilbert said repressively. "*You, ma petite coquine.*"

"Then I have changed my mind, and I do not think it is at all the good idea. I have been gone already for the five long years. Now, I want to be with you."

How grim he had looked then, and suddenly so very much older. In spite of herself, her heart had gone out to him.

"*Cher Papa,*" she murmured, leaning her small hands against his chest. "I have only just arrived after a very long sea voyage. I do not even have my things inside yet, and already you want to be rid of me. Can we not discuss this matter later?"

She had seen that he was sorry for his abruptness in springing it on her, but he had not hesitated to make it clear that he would not be budged an inch on this matter of her leaving.

"It is not open for discussion, Angie. You are not staying, and that's final."

Poor Papa, she thought, smiling sadly as she gazed out onto the verandah at his broad back. "You do not know yet who you are dealing with. Me, I think we have a great deal to discuss, and not just about who goes or stays on Saint Dominique!" Gilbert's sudden oath jarred her to attention.

"Hellsfire!"

The handle of a fork engulfed in a huge hand, Herman Gilbert gestured forcefully at the slender man sitting across from him fashionably attired in lace and fine satin.

"I'll have no part of murder, Vachon, and this revolution has nothing to do with me. So I'll thank you not to come to me with your bloody talk—or to my people."

"You surprise me, Gilbert," came the reply couched in the cultured accents of a gentleman—soft, unruffled, and cold, thought Angelique with a shiver. "You are an American. I should have thought that you of all people

275

must appreciate the ideals of '*Liberté, Égalité, Fraternité!*' But then, one must of course make allowances for the years. Perhaps you have no longer the courage of your convictions."

"If that is what you believe, m'sieur," Angelique coolly interjected from the doorway, "then you are the fool, I think."

As Gilbert shifted his bulk to embrace the slim figure of his daughter with frankly unamused eyes, she was acutely aware of the faint tightening of their visitor's lips. Instantly her small chin jutted in instinctive dislike of the man.

Guyon Vachon, considered handsome by not a few of the females on the island despite his indeterminate age, had not changed even a little in the five years of her absence. She remembered him of old—the unnaturally pale face, thin-lipped and aesthetically delicate with the long, pointed nose, high cheekbones, and ice-blue eyes, which were in striking contrast to hair as black as ebony. *Per Dieu!* What was he doing here? Surely her papa must know Vachon was as treacherous as the deadly fer-de-lance!

"My father," she continued, stepping out onto the shaded verandah, "was among the Fifteen Hundred who sailed from Saint Dominique in the aid of the so great General Washington."

"As was Jean-Baptiste Chavanne," muttered her father in an aside, with a certain brooding grimness.

"I think there is no man who knows better the meaning of such noble words. *Voyons!* He is the only man on Saint Dominique who has refused to employ the labor of slaves. It is proof enough, is it not, that 'Erman Gilbert remains firm in his convictions. No man, not even you, M'sieu Vachon, should have the right to own another."

If she had taken him off guard, Vachon did not show it. With practiced ease he rose to his feet and, with a peculiarly bloodless smile, gracefully inclined his head toward her.

"*Touché*, mademoiselle. Your tongue, it would seem, is as keen-edged as a cutting blade in the defense of your father."

"No doubt I should be flattered, M'sieu Vachon. For yours has the subtlety of a lawyer's thrust."

A tinge of color touched the pallid cheeks at the double-barbed meaning implied in those words. Then Vachon was smiling again, the thin lips sliding up at the corners without disturbing the cold planes of the rest of his face.

"And yet once more, you draw the blood, mad'moiselle. However, I feel moved to point out that the American Revolution was not fought for the freedom of slaves."

"No, but for the ideals of freedom, which you would deny to already free men."

"Enough, Angelique," warned her father, though the wry gleam in his eyes would seem to rob the words of their sting. "You must excuse my daughter, Vachon. She's an impertinent piece. Obviously not even the nuns of Sainte Clare could teach her to curb that unruly tongue of hers. Come here, wench, and let us have a look at what they did manage to accomplish. I suspect the Poor Sisters of Clare must have been grateful to be relieved of so thankless a task."

Angelique let her gaze slide coolly from the Frenchman as she turned to favor her father with a roguish hint of a smile.

"Do you think so?" she quizzed him. "And yet I assure you I was a most attentive pupil."

"I see," Gilbert temporized, as he took in the provocative picture of femininity draped in flowing white, the regal head crowned with a luxurious mass of blue-black hair allowed to fall freely down her back. This was not the lady of refinement who had arrived on his doorstep the night before, but a lovely, unruly sprite with a defiant sparkle in her eye.

Angelique noted the dubious quirk of a bristling blond eyebrow and girded herself to weather the coming storm.

"And I suppose next you are going to assure me that you are dressed in the height of Parisian fashion," Gilbert observed drily. "Strange, but I was not aware the ladies had abandoned panniers and hoops. Do you think, my dearest Angie, Saint Dominique is ready for such a gown?"

"Well, if it is not precisely what the ladies are wearing in Port-au-Prince, it soon will be," Angelique retorted, an impish grin bringing out the dimple in her cheek.

And in truth it was a daring gown, styled after the Classic mode which was only just beginning to be affected by the more audacious of the Parisian fashion-conscious. Short, puffy sleeves and a deep V neck left her arms and much of her shoulders bare, while the skirt of white jaconet, in contrast to the stiff brocades and satins of the day, appeared almost to cling to her soft, feminine curves. *"C'est très belle, vraiment?"* she gurgled and, holding the folds of the skirt out at her sides, pirouetted on dainty sandaled feet.

The feather-light fabric falling from a high waist floated about her bare legs, leaving little doubt that she wore next to nothing beneath it. Gilbert, watching her, was struck most forcibly with the revelation that his daughter was in truth no longer the fetching little hoyden he had sent away to Paris, but a wholly desirable and exquisitely beautiful young woman. The knowledge gave him no comfort. In fact, his first reaction was to become acutely conscious of the Frenchman's presence at the table.

"Enough!" he thundered before he had thought the matter through. "You will take yourself to your room at once, Angelique, and change that gown for something decent!"

Instantly he regretted his hasty outburst as he beheld his daughter come about with ominous deliberation. In spite of the fact that she had been away from him for nearly five years, he had not quite forgotten that not only had she inherited her mama's French temperament and

278

feminine guile, but she had acquired something of his own Yankee stubbornness as well. In a head-to-head confrontation, he was doomed to find himself at a distinct disadvantage.

"I warn you, Angie, I will have my way in this," he stated, determined for once to make it clear he would stand for none of her foolishness. But already the battle was lost, he realized as soon as she looked at him. With her lips pursed in a beguiling little pout and the devil dancing in the unfathomable depths of her eyes, she was the very image of her mother.

"*Bah!* You have the fierce manner of the bear, have you not," she retorted, making a face at him. Then laughing, she crossed lightly to his side. "But you do not frighten me. I promise you will be eating out of my hand before the day is out."

"Jade!" rumbled her father.

"*Cher barbon,*" grinned Angelique. "You must see that such a dress as this is of the most practical on Saint Dominique. You cannot wish for me to suffer the heat stroke with so many stupid clothes, *oui?*" Draping her arm about his broad shoulders, she turned her glance toward their visitor, only to find the Frenchman's gaze on her, coldly appraising. At once her head came up, her mirth changing to cool disdain.

"You are out very early this morning, M'sieu Vachon," she observed. "Is it the custom in Saint Dominique to make morning calls at the first light of dawn?"

Gilbert favored Angelique with a stern glance.

"Perhaps you have forgotten that a farmer's life is geared to the sun," he observed pointedly. "Certainly you appear to have forgotten your manners. Vachon is our neighbor."

"And so is the fer-de-lance," murmured his unrepentant daughter sweetly for his ears alone, as she bent to deliver a fond buss on the cheek, "but him we do not invite into our home, do we?"

279

"Ahem," coughed Gilbert. Egads, the girl had spirit, and a discerning eye, if she could so easily penetrate the suave mask of Guyon Vachon. "You remember my daughter, Vachon," he said, accepting defeat philosophically. If, indeed, the wench was anything like her mother, she would be more than a match for the slippery Frenchman. And if not, it didn't matter, since she wouldn't be here longer than it took to ship her out again. God willing, the one man he knew that was equal to the task was scheduled to arrive before the week was out!

Taking up his eating utensils again, he began once more to apply himself with a hearty appetite to his plate piled high with pickled eel, baked hog-fish, paper-thin slices of cold ham, ginger sweetmeats, island grapefruit, and sweetjellies. "Thought I had rid myself of the brat," he expounded between mouthfuls washed down with hock negus, "but the Assemblée Nationale took it upon themselves to confiscate the properties of the Holy Church. Closed the doors of the convent *and* the school and threw her out into the streets of Paris, so I'd no choice but to take her back again."

Pointedly ignoring her father's antic wit, Angelique extended a civil hand to the gentleman. *"M'sieu* Vachon," she murmured. "No doubt I am pleased to renew our acquaintance."

"No doubt," purred the Frenchman in such a way as to bring a slow tinge of color to her cheeks. Vachon smiled faintly. "You are to be congratulated, Gilbert. Your daughter has returned to you as charming as she is lovely." Without taking his gaze off her face, he bent his head to press cold lips lightly to her knuckles.

With an effort Angelique quelled an instinctive shudder. *Tiens!* His hand was as soft as a woman's, and his look was that of the striking adder. In truth, the so charming Vachon made her skin to crawl. Instinctively, she knew his was no friendly visit between neighbors. What, then, did he want at Cime du Bonheur?

Her expression distantly polite, Angelique gently freed

her hand.

"You are too kind, m'sieu. And how does Madame Vachon?" she pointedly inquired. "She is well, I trust?"

"Sadly, my wife did not find the climate of the West Indies at all amenable. She returned to France with our son and daughter quite some time ago for an indeterminate stay. No doubt, however, she will be pleased that you have remembered her."

"Is this true? She has left? But I am sorry. No doubt you find her absence of the most difficult to bear," she murmured with only the slightest hint of irony. "I missed Papa dreadfully when I myself was in Paris. I take the oath I shall not leave his side again."

"Then France's loss will be our gain," the Frenchman returned smoothly. "Perhaps you may be able to bring your father to see that he, too, can no longer hold himself aloof from matters which concern Saint Dominique."

"Really? And shall you tell me what matters are these which make my father bellow like the bull before the sun is hardly up?" she queried lightly, and, leaning over with a great show of indifference, plucked a plump peach from a silver bowl on the table.

"There are those of us, mademoiselle, who believed Saint Dominique should have a voice in determining the future of the French colonies," he answered, watching with a curious intensity as the small, even white teeth sank into the lush fruit. "Especially as it so closely concerns our own continued well-being."

Voyons! mused Angelique, tinglingly aware of the pale gleam that had ignited in the ice-blue depths of his eyes. Vachon was perhaps not so cold like the fish after all.

No doubt it was the French in her that made her savor the sweet juice of the peach with sublime unawareness. Or curiosity, perhaps. Where women were concerned, Vachon was as yet an unknown quantity to her.

"*Oui?*" she prompted, gazing up at him in wide-eyed innocence.

The Frenchman shrugged.

"We sent our own representatives to the Assemblée Nationale in order to be sure our views were made known. Unfortunately, the free men of color have also made their voices heard. The March decree of last year gave them what they wanted—the freedom to vote in the elections of the colonial assemblies."

"And you disapprove, M'sieu Vachon?"

"Every white man must disapprove. These are dangerous malcontents who will stop at nothing to displace the rightful supremacy of the white landowners. No man, woman, or child will be safe if they are not taught to keep their place. I have just been trying to persuade your father to listen to reason."

Angelique jumped as a fork-filled fist slammed down hard against the table.

"Reason? I'll give you reason!" uttered Herman Gilbert in a voice that struck with the force of a sledge hammer. "Vincent Ogé was a young fool pumped up with the pipe dreams of a revolution five thousand miles away. But you, Vachon, proved the bigger fool—when you and your precious 'General Assembly' condemned him to a martyr's death, along with his friend, Chavanne. However, don't listen to me. You go ahead. Refuse to honor the March Decree. Continue to murder old men, women and children on the slightest pretext because you are afraid they will finally figure out you and your friends are not all-powerful. How long do you think they will continue to submit to you once they understand that your only strength lies in the continued support of France? Support, which, I might add, has become pretty damned shaky due to your own stupidity and arrogance. Vincent Ogé was your only hope of keeping the blacks out of this. Without him it's only a matter of time before all hell breaks loose. We are about to be witness to as bloody an uprising as has never before been seen in these islands. And only a fool would deny it."

Vachon arched an arrogant eyebrow.

"You must not be swayed by your father's tendency to

exaggerate the importance of these people," he murmured in such a way as to make Angelique's blood run suddenly cold with fear for them all. "Once they, like the radical Ogé, have been silenced, that will be the end of it. The noble cause of liberty will then rest in the capable hands of our legal representatives in France."

"Oh, come now, my dear Vachon," broke in Gilbert, taking no pains to conceal either his sarcasm or his contempt of the other man's motives. "You and I have known one another for over twenty years. It's a trifle late, don't you think, to try such drivel on me?"

"But I insist, *mon cher* Gilbert, that I have not the notion of what you are talking about."

"Poppycock! You know as well as I do that any delegates the colonial assemblies have sent to France are interested only in the freedom of the white plantation owners. Which we both realize means the freedom to rule Saint Dominique as they see fit. You and your bloody friends will stop at nothing to keep the free mulattoes in their place. Just as you will do anything to prevent the abolition of slavery. You care about one thing and one thing only—the continued supremacy of *les grands blancs* on the island. And you're deluded enough to believe you can sway the National Assembly to your own way of thinking."

For an instant the careful mask of the aristocrat appeared to slip as a murderous glint leaped in the Frenchman's eyes.

"But you are making the very great mistake, Gilbert," he murmured, very gently. "It is perhaps unwise to speak with such bluntness when to do so can only alienate the other plantation owners." His glittery gaze slid suggestively to Angelique and lingered. "You should think of your daughter. In such times as these, it is better to have the loyal friends than the distrustful neighbors, is it not? And you, after all, are not even French."

"No, but I'm rich as Croesus, am I not?" countered the big American, a subtle hardness in the bluff, mocking grin that made him seem suddenly anything but amiable. "And, more importantly, the bulk of my assets resides not on this island, but in Boston and New York. That's what really rankles, isn't it, Vachon. I'm a Yankee tradesman playing at being a planter, while the rest of you either sink or swim according to the prevailing mood in France. And to make matters worse, you're beginning to fear that the innovations I've been experimenting with are starting to pay off."

"But you are mistaken. None of these things concern me in the least."

"I see. Then it doesn't bother you that I employ only freed slaves and mulattoes, or that they work not only for wages but for a share in the profits? And I suppose you don't care that we have set aside land to grow our own food or that we've begun fortifying our holdings against the inevitability of insurrection?"

"On the contrary, m'sieu. Why should I care one way or the other what you do on your own land?"

"Oh, you care all right," replied Gilbert in a steely voice. "You care because you know all of this means my people have a vested interest in the success or failure of our little enterprise. What's more, the land we've set aside to grow our own food insures our survival if the ships fail to arrive with stores from the outside. You care, Vachon, because you're smart enough to know I have the loyalty of my people, which is a hell of a lot more than you can say of yours. Perhaps now you can understand why I do not feel the least inclined to court the friendship of my neighbors, especially at the cost of my own integrity. If there is to be trouble over this business with Ogé, I'll be ready for it. And that is a deal more comforting than the uncertainty of my neighbors' friendship."

"Then it is you who are the fool!" Vachon uttered with undisguised venom. "We are white men living in the midst of a sea of black savages—slaves, who understand only the language of strength. Not even you can deny this is true."

"And what of the free men of color?" cut in Angelique, repelled in spite of the fact that she had heard it all before. "Are you not overlooking the fact that they control a sizeable portion of the wealth of this island? And that as such, they, too, have a stake in all of this? Would it not be better to make allies of them instead of enemies?"

His look left no doubt as to his utter contempt for those of mixed blood, or was it contempt for her? she wondered suddenly.

"You are young and a woman, and so may perhaps be forgiven such naïveté. But even you should know that the mulatto cannot be trusted. No matter how white his skin, underneath, he is more black than white. If he could, he would incite his black brothers to rebellion and see us all dead."

If he had not turned to look at her father with the burning eyes of the devil, he would have seen her blanch and curl her hands into tight little fists at her side. Almost convulsively she turned her back to the two men and stared blindly out over the escarpment to the sea far below.

"*Non,*" Vachon said to Gilbert. "Only so long as the white planters remain united can we hope to maintain order. For even one of us to hold himself aloof from our common cause is to increase the uncertainty for all the others. It is to commit an act of betrayal against one's own kind. And I warn you, m'sieu, for such a one there will be no mercy."

"There are forty thousand whites on this island and ten times that number of blacks," observed her father with chilling certainty. "If there is an uprising, 'mercy' will be the last thing any of us can hope for. And if you believe otherwise, my dear Vachon, then you are worse than a fool. You are a veritable madman."

"I see," murmured the Frenchman, his thoughts concealed once more behind the hard glitter of his eyes.

285

"Then obviously I have been wasting my time. Therefore, I will leave you to enjoy the more amenable company of your daughter. *Mademoiselle*. I shall pray your father's obstinacy does not cause any unpleasantness to mar your homecoming."

Bowing curtly then to each in turn, Vachon spun on his heel and left them.

"He is not of the most happy, I think," said Angelique, staring after Vachon with troubled eyes. "What is this all about, Papa? Why should our neighbors look upon us as enemies? Surely it is true that we are all in this together, *oui?*"

"Up to our bloody eyeballs," Gilbert agreed direly, "if Guyon Vachon finds it necessary to call on me." Throwing down his knife and fork in disgust, he pushed his chair back from the table. "Curse the man for interrupting my breakfast! I'm past due in the fields already."

"Oh, but must you go? I had hoped for a little time to visit."

A reluctant grin twisted at Gilbert's lips as he glanced down into his daughter's upturned face. The lovely mouth was pursed charmingly in a small pout, and the eyes were dark with disappointment. The little rogue! he mused, suffering an all-too-familiar pang in the vicinity of his heart. Except for the eyes, she might have been Eugenie standing there, Eugenie of twenty years ago.

The bittersweet realization that she was her mother all over again put him in a somber frame of mind. It had all but destroyed him when Eugenie died. He could not bear to go through it a second time, this time with her daughter. No. He must see her future settled—soon, before all hell broke loose on the island.

"I'm sorry, Angie. You know I'd like nothing better than to stay here with you and catch up on all that I've missed since you've been away. But—"

"But you cannot," she interjected with a fatalistic shrug. "It is the time of the harvest, and you are needed in the fields. You see, I have not been away so long that I have forgotten."

Gilbert frowned, thinking perhaps this *was* the time to tell her, or at least to feel her out on certain subjects. After five years a lot of things could have changed between them. For one thing, she wasn't a little girl any more. Why, she must be nineteen by now—no, by God, she was closer to one and twenty. Hell, he probably didn't know her at all any more!

"Angie . . . ," he began, intending to feel his way, when suddenly she turned and flung her hands up in the air.

"It is all the fault of Pierrette for not getting me out of bed earlier! I had it all planned. I would be waiting for you when you came to the breakfast table, just like when I was a little girl. You remember how it was? You used to let me serve the coffee—no sugar, but just a little bit of cream. It was like a game we played. I was the lady of the house and you . . ." Abruptly she stopped, a blush tingeing her cheeks. "Oh, *la vache!* I am running over at the mouth. Please, you must not think it is something I usually do. It is only that . . ." Gilbert suffered a sharp pang of remorse as the huge eyes lifted uncertainly to his. "Papa, you had such a look on your face. Suddenly I was afraid . . . You do not—despise me for coming home?"

"No—! Angie, don't be absurd. Of course, I do not despise you."

"Then what, Papa? I am not a child any more. I beg you will speak to me as a woman."

He could not bring himself to meet her eyes. Turning instead to look out over the escarpment and the blue stretch of sea beyond, he ran an impatient hand through his thinning hair. Bloody hell! Why had it to be so difficult to deal with a female? With a man it was different. You could speak straight out to a man and know your words wouldn't be twisted round to mean something you'd never intended. But with a woman, you never knew. Christ! he couldn't just blurt it out.

"You heard what passed between Vachon and myself," he ventured at last, taking the coward's way out. "Vincent Ogé came home from Paris to organize the free men of color—some say into an army—to force the colonial assemblies to accept the March Decree. They broke every bone in his body for it. Then, while he was still alive, they tied him on a wheel with his face to the sun and left him to die. His head still sits on a pole overlooking the road to Dondon. Dammit, Angelique! Saint Dominique is a blasted powder keg, and Ogé's death will undoubtedly be the match to set it off." At last he turned to face her, his jaw set in the stubborn bulge that meant he was in no mood to be trifled with. "I do not 'despise' you for being here, Angelique. I am confounded about what I am going to do with you. For the time being, I want your promise you will not leave the grounds. Under no circumstances are you to go down to the village or Port-au-Prince. Do you understand?"

"And is this, also, what happened to Etienne Joliet? Did they take him out and break him into little pieces? Why, Papa? What harm had he done? Etienne was my friend. Was it for this that he died?"

"Don't be absurd. They caught him sneaking in to see his mother. Hell, he'd been fighting with the rebel forces. He was a fool to try coming around here after that."

"'Rebels,' Papa?" queried Angelique hoarsely. Bitterly her eyes accused him. "In another war, you called such men 'patriots.'"

"Enough, Angelique!" Gilbert thundered. "I'll not be lectured on something you know nothing about."

Instantly he regretted his hasty outburst, but the damage was already done. Her eyes were huge in a face gone pearly white, and it pained him to see her draw away from him, as if he were a stranger she had never seen before.

"You should never have come back, Angelique," he

said wearily. "Dammit, can't you understand that there's not a man, woman, or child who is safe on this bloody island? Not now, not after all that's happened. It's already gone too far for anyone to stop it."

"Tell me, Papa," Angelique flung back at him. "Tell me what's happened. Then maybe I will understand."

For a moment Gilbert met the passionate blaze of her eyes. Then at last he gave in.

"All right, I'll tell you," he said bitterly. "Vachon and his bloody friends weren't satisfied with murdering Chavanne and Ogé. Somehow they won over two battalions sent from France and persuaded them to land in Port-au-Prince against the Governor-General's orders. For awhile there was absolute chaos. The rebels stormed the prison and several of the *affranchis* were set free, among them Andre Rigaud and Pinchinat, two of Ogé's staunchest lieutenants. In retaliation, the whites murdered Colonel Mauduit. His body was mutilated because the planters didn't care for his loyalty to the Colonial Assembly. Good God, they paraded his head through town on a bloody damn pole! They run things around here now. Call themselves the Western Provincial Assembly. And they won't stop until they've set the whole goddamn island on fire. Which is why I've made arrangements for you to get out while you still can."

"I see," murmured Angelique warily. "And what are these 'arrangements' you have made?"

"Some months ago, when news reached us of what was going on in France, I made a hurried jaunt to Boston to set all my personal affairs in order. You, of course, will get everything, should anything happen to me."

"Should anything happen—!" Suddenly she went as white as death as the full significance of his words sank home. "*Mais non!* I will not hear of this!" she cried, her small frame taut with defiance. "Me, I do not want your money. I will not go without you."

"Yes, you will. You have no choice. Shortly after my return, Locke arrived from the Orient with a shipload of goods. He was to sail for France on business. At my request, he agreed to fetch you home with him. Since he has obviously failed in his commission, I expect him here any day now to report that failure. When he does, he will be obliged to keep his word to see you safely settled in the states."

"But that is very generous of him," choked Angelique. "And to what else has your business partner agreed?" She laughed a trifle hysterically. "Will he be my guardian? Perhaps introduce me to eligible bachelors and see that I am at last safely married? What, Papa? What does the so noble Capitaine Locke intend to do with me?"

The grim look in her father's eyes made her stomach clench with foreboding.

"Papa?" she queried uncertainly.

Deliberately Gilbert steeled himself for the unavoidable storm.

"Captain Locke, my girl, has agreed to marry you," he answered shortly.

"Marry me!" An incredulous laugh seemed wrenched from her. "*Mon Dieu!* So this is the 'other matter' which brings *le capitaine* to Saint Dominique. Oh, it is of the very clear to me now. He is pledged to marry Angelique Gilbert, when he finds himself trapped by Angele DuFour. Trapped between the devil and the deep blue sea! How very funny!"

"Really, Angelique, I fail to see what you find so blasted funny. What in hell are you ranting about?"

With an effort she got hold of herself.

"Nothing, Papa," she answered cynically. "You would not understand."

"I see. Then perhaps you will pardon me. I've work to attend to."

"Yes, Papa," she retorted frostily, her back to him. "You go to your fields, which mean so much to you. But me, I will never marry this capitaine who comes for me. Do you understand? Never will I be the wife of your

Wesley Locke. You cannot make me. You have not the right!''

"That's enough, Angelique!'' Gilbert thundered. "I have every right to do as I see fit to insure your welfare. Christ, Angie, I'm your father!''

"Are you?'' she flung back, turning on him in sudden bitterness. "Does a father send his only child from him as soon as *la mère* is dead? And again when she has only just come home to him? Does he give her to a man she has never even seen before? Is it the sight of me you cannot bear, Papa? Or the fear that I am *not* your daughter. *Damn* you! Is it that you believe what they say—that I, no less than Etienne Joliet, am the bastard of an African slave!''

Without thought, Gilbert struck her hard across the face. Gasping, she staggered back, a hand clasped to her stinging cheek.

It was all he could do to meet her eyes then. Inwardly he groaned. In her whole life he had never raised a hand to her, and now, white-faced, she was staring at him as if he were a bloody monster.

"Angie,'' he muttered hoarsely. "What—happened— to your mother before you were born has nothing to do with you. Eugenie was already carrying you inside her, you must believe me.''

"And if I do not, how shall you convince me otherwise? Even the Sisters of Ste. Clare used to make the sign of the cross when they thought I was not looking. I have the sight, Papa. Shall I tell you the vision that came to me as I lay in bed in the convent one night?''

Held spellbound by something in her face, Gilbert could only stare at her.

"I saw the Goat Girl dancing to the beat of the *Rada* drum,'' she said, her eyes huge as they stared into the distance. "And the Pethro that summons the god who lusts for the blood of the sacrifice—Damballa, the Serpent-god. I saw you lying dead in the ruins of La Cime du Bonheur. And I saw myself, half-naked, and dancing the bridal dance of the god. And I knew, Papa. I knew all my life I had been living the great lie. I am not your daughter, am I? I am *his!*"

Unable to bear the look of fear and anguish in those haunted eyes, Gilbert grabbed her roughly by the arm.

"Do you think that is proof you are not my daughter? I'll show you all the proof you shall ever need!"

Mercilessly he dragged her to the screened door that led into the bedroom he had shared with Angelique's mother, the same room in which a half-crazed maroon had savagely raped his Eugenie over twenty years before.

"Look!" he uttered fiercely, yanking her in front of her mother's looking glass. "Where is the African in you? Is it in your eyes, the color of violets? Your skin like palest ivory? Where is it, Angelique? You must show me if I am to believe your mother lied to me. Perhaps it is your hair, as black as a raven's wing, and fine as new-spun silk. There, look at your mother's likeness, and then see if you can tell me I am not your father. Look at it, Angelique! Look into her eyes and tell me what you see!"

Forcing her head up, he made her look at the painting of her mother, which hung on the wall near the dressing table. Slowly she stilled, her gaze fixed on the huge orbs staring back at her. A long, shuddering breath escaped her lips, and suddenly her gaze sought his, wonderingly.

"I-I never realized before how much like her I am," she whispered hoarsely. "It is no wonder you look at me sometimes as if it is a ghost you see before you."

He winced, unable to deny the truth.

"Do you think, Angelique, that an African could have had any part in creating you? Think, girl—your skin, your eyes, everything about you cries out a denial."

"And if he was not African, Papa?" she murmured, driven to it in spite of the hurt it must inevitably cause him. "What if he was mulatto or quadroon or even mustee? Is that not why the people of color are forbidden to dress in the same fashion as the whites—because with many, it is the only way to tell they are of mixed blood? Forgive me, Papa, but before I can believe Mozambe's whispers were nothing but lies, I must have something more than a picture of *Maman*. I must speak with Mozambe and see with my heart what is the truth."

For a long moment he held her with eyes that made her draw away from him in sudden uncertainty that twisted at his insides. Bitterly he cursed the toothless old hag who had made her doubt him and herself. He remembered now—Mozambe on the pier the day Angelique sailed for France. It must have been then the cursed *mamaloi* had whispered her poison into Angelique's ear. At the time he had thought the child's unnatural pallor was due to fear at the prospect of going so far from the only home she had ever known. What a blasted fool he had been! And now that Angelique was back in Mozambe's reach again, how long could it be before the girl discovered the bloody truth about herself—about her father and the lies upon which La Cime du Bonheur had been built over twenty years ago? God help him, instead of making a bargain with the old devil's hag, he should have killed her along with all her cursed seed. Christ, he should have let them burn, Mozambe and Zenger, and all the pathetic creatures trapped in the holds below. Better that than to have sold his soul to Satan.

At last he tore himself away.

"You will do as you must," he stated coldly. "As will I to protect you from Mozambe and her poisoned tongue, you may be sure of it." Abruptly he turned away from her. "It's time I was going," he grunted and strode quickly to the door. He had already stepped off the flagstones of the terrace into the grass, still damp from the morning dew, when her low-voiced cry came after him, hoarse with hurt and anger.

"Papa! Please, we must talk."

Gilbert hesitated, half-turned back to her.

"It's all been said, Angelique. You will wed Locke, and that's final. I will see you when the work is done. Until then, do not leave the grounds!"

Having given her his ultimatum, he left her, making his way with long, impatient strides around the corner of the house and out of sight.

Angelique stared after him, the blood seeming to roar in her ears. Thus she did not hear the light step at her back.

"Papa!" she shouted after him. "Papa, this changes nothing. I will not leave you. Do you hear? I will not marry your capitaine. I will not marry anyone. I swear it!"

"I'd be careful what I swore, if I were you," drawled a low, thrilling voice behind her. "Especially in light of past experiences. Not too long ago you swore something quite different."

Angelique froze, her heart pounding wildly. Nor did she turn around as, "Capitaine Locke," she pronounced with utter certainty.

Chapter 16

Angelique's gaze went out over the escarpment to the sea, to the schooner, which, moored in the cove far below, appeared no larger than a toy. For a moment she felt weak as the memories came flooding over her at sight of it. Then she forgot everything, but Locke standing behind her. *Voyons*, she could sense him, his eyes on her, piercing, like a flame, between her shoulder blades, and the air seemed filled with the waiting, with all the things left unsaid and unresolved between them—with the feelings! The blood was racing in her veins, and she thought she must be shaking all over, but that was as nothing to what she sensed in him—the keen edge of his temper, held rigidly in check.

"Your ship must have wings, Capitaine," she said, not trusting herself yet to turn and face him. "I did not expect you so soon."

Her whole body seemed to vibrate to the sound of his voice, cool and acerbic, but with the hint of steel beneath the velvet-edged softness.

"Did you expect me to linger in England after you decided to disappear?" he queried mockingly. "You left too many unanswered questions behind you for that, I'm afraid. The one posed by the parson, for instance. Somehow I had the distinct impression you were about to answer in the affirmative."

Oui, she thought, her heart bitter. But then the fire had leaped out of the darkness, the bad luck that would not leave her. Oh, *why* had he to follow her here where the luck had *all* turned bad?

"I am sorry, m'sieu," she answered in a cold voice she hardly recognized as her own. "But that was someone else."

Deliberately she turned to look at him. Her resolve nearly failed her as she beheld him, lean and powerful, his shirt open at the collar. *Voyons,* with the pistol thrust carelessly into the waistband of his pants and the long blade of his knife slung in a scabbard at his side, he had the look of a man prepared for trouble. She steeled herself to meet the piercing points of his eyes. They were as blue as she had remembered them, but unreadable, dangerous somehow. Strangely, they gave her the courage she needed to go on.

"Angele DuFour is no more," she declared. "And Angelique Gilbert has sworn never to marry anyone. I am afraid, Capitaine, you have come for nothing."

"Maybe." Hooking a thumb in his belt, he propped a broad shoulder against the door frame and studied her with cool deliberation. "But then, I keep asking myself: Why should the daughter of my old friend Gilbert find it necessary to fabricate the mysterious Angel? And why did she suddenly decide to vanish? You must admit these are intriguing questions. Questions, in fact, that I mean to have answers to."

"I see," she murmured. Then in a sudden fit of nervousness, she crossed to the table still littered with the remains of her father's breakfast.

"You do not seem surprised," she noted, absently running her fingertips over the linen tablecloth. "Perhaps Fisk warned you what you would find?"

"As it turned out, he didn't have to. I'd already figured it out for myself," came the answering drawl, infuriating in its seeming imperturbability. Angelique gritted her teeth to keep from giving herself away. *Sacriste,* how easily he worked on her. With only a look he battered her defenses, made her vulnerable like the rabbit before the wolf.

She lifted her eyebrows in disbelief.

"Really? What was it that gave me away? Something I said?"

Locke shrugged, watching the play of emotions in the lovely face. "The pieces were all there. It just needed me to fit them together. Something to occupy my mind while I followed the trail you left when you fled Briarcroft. That, and *why* you lit out the way you did. In a storm, without a word to anyone."

His coldness pierced her like a chill wind, and suddenly she turned on him with flashing eyes.

"You should not have bothered, Capitaine. Why did you? I ran away from you, just as you said, without a word. It must have been plain even to you that whatever we had was *finis*."

The faint curl of his lip mocked her.

"Curious," he murmured. "I never figured you for a coward, Angel."

"Do not call me that! To you, I am Mademoiselle Gilbert." Her voice cut like a whiplash, but beneath the sharpness had been a note of panic. Chagrined, she turned away, so she did not see the way he looked at her, the blue blaze of his eyes between slitted eyelids. "I-I told you," she said, struggling to recover her equanimity. "Angele DuFour does not exist. She was a foolish girl's fantasy, nothing more. And now it is over, do you understand?"

His sigh seemed to punctuate the stillness.

"So you did," he agreed drily. "But you see, I'm not too clear on what happened to bring about her—demise. Or why you dreamed her up in the first place. Maybe you'd like to enlighten me."

Angelique swallowed. *Hein,* how could she tell him the truth—that always she had been waiting for the day to come when she would make him love her? And then

297

Mozambe had changed everything so that only Angele could have what Angelique had always dreamed of. No. These things she could never tell him. Far better to play the role of the adventuress.

"All my life I have heard Papa speak of you, Capitaine," she answered, surprised that she could sound so cool when, inside, her heart was pounding. "I was— curious—to know if the stories were true. You have the reputation of a rogue; thus, I wanted you to make love to me. This you would not have done with the daughter of your old friend. And so I came to you as Angele DuFour, the Nobody." At last she turned her head to look at him. "But alas, Angelique woke up, m'sieu," she said, shrugging. "What more can I say?"

"What, indeed?" he murmured, his expression unreadable. Her breath caught hard in her throat as he straightened and sauntered toward her. "And did you find the stories about me were exaggerated?" he queried, coming to a halt a breathless few inches away.

She could not suppress the faint tinge of color that came to her cheeks, nor the helpless flutter of her heart as the tantalizing scent of shaving soap mingled with tobacco assailed her nostrils at close range.

"No," she admitted, forcing herself to remain where she was. Then, with a hint of defiance, "I'm afraid in one respect you did prove something of a disappointment. I mean, a rake with your reputation insisting on marriage. This was not at all what I expected from you, Capitaine."

At last a hint of ironic humor shone briefly in the stern visage.

"Yes, I can see where that might have been something of a nuisance," he agreed, "especially when you finally decided to accept my proposal. Did you plan to tell me the truth on our wedding night, I wonder. Or had you truly believed you might keep your identity a secret in-definitely?"

"Of course," she retorted, "and why not? Angele DuFour was free to do whatever she pleased. While

Angelique Gilbert . . ." Here, her voice trailed off as a haunted expression unwittingly invaded her eyes. "She, m'sieu, was from birth bound to a different destiny. One which she cannot wish to share with anyone."

"Somehow," he reflected cynically, "I've always found the concept of 'destiny' a damned troublesome notion. Just when you think you're holding a pat hand, 'destiny' has a nasty habit of turning up a trump card. Oh, it's a devil of a good excuse when you're left holding the bag, but for myself, I'd rather make my own luck—good or bad. I kind of figured that's the way it was with you, too, Angel."

Angelique glanced hastily away.

"Maybe it was so for Angele," she said in a low voice. "But me, I already told you Angelique woke up to the truth. For some, there can be no escaping what is meant to be."

With an effort Locke quelled the swift surge of impatience that swept him at those words. A keenly perceptive man, he had not missed the expression on her face before she turned away. Further, thanks to his confrontation with Chantal over the fever-stricken Angel, he had a fairly good notion what lay behind it. A shame the maroon had vanished from the ship less than twenty-four hours after his captain disembarked for Briarcroft, he reflected grimly. There were still some matters that the former topman might have cleared up. For the present, however, it seemed he had no choice but to play along with his obstinately elusive love, at least until he knew for sure who the other players were—and what game it was they were playing.

"I don't suppose this 'awakening,'" he drawled, determined to push her as far as he dared to get the truth from her, "had anything to do with a meddling gypsy or the unfortunate coincidence of the fire at Briarcroft, would it?"

"Gypsy?" she echoed, finding it difficult to think with him so near. She could feel the tension in him, the

299

muscles in the lean frame strung like whipcord. "I do not know what you are talking about, Capitaine."

"No, naturally you wouldn't." His voice cut like the sharp edge of a knife, and she could not stop herself from flinching. A sardonic smile touched his lips. "You weren't awake either when I came to see you that night. You didn't overhear what passed between Sabra and me, did you."

"N-No, how could I? *Le docteur* gave me the medicine to make me sleep."

"Yes, that's right, he did," he agreed. "And so you couldn't possibly have jumped to the conclusion that somehow what happened was all your fault. That wasn't the reason you snuck out in the middle of a storm and made your way to the gypsy caravan."

At her sharply indrawn breath, he smiled grimly.

"Did you think I wouldn't remember the old hag or the marked attention she paid you, my love? Only a fool would have failed to realize the gypsies were the only ones who could have taken you in. It took some time to find her, and no little persuasion, but Madame Lucinne finally decided to be cooperative. Oh, don't worry. I didn't harm her. Though maybe I should have—for leaving you in the hands of a man like Johannes Zenger."

Angelique felt the blood drain from her cheeks.

"Zenger," she gasped. "So, you know even about that."

"I know you were reckless enough to take money from him in front of witnesses and that you went upstairs with him to his private rooms. You cannot be so naive as to believe Zenger would not make sure I learned all the sordid details." At last he suffered a crack in his composure. "You insane little fool," he growled. "What in hell did you think you were doing?"

"What I had to do to get away from you!" cried Angelique, her temper flaring at last. "I had no money, no hope of finding a ship to bring me home. So, me, I think why not take his gold? After all, it is a small price to pay for passage to the West Indies. Much less than what you demanded of me. Him I did not have to marry."

It took all her courage not to quail before the terrible leap of his eyes.

"No," he drawled icily. "Only with Zenger, you ran the risk of losing a lot more than your virginity." The faint curl of his lip mocked her. "A man like the Dutchman doesn't play by the rules. But maybe you enjoyed that."

Stung by his contempt, Angelique brought her head up, her eyes flashing.

"Of course. It was an evening to remember always. He is a man who beats women for his entertainment, this pig-man who meant to put the scars on my face so I might carry them like a message to Papa. But he was not laughing when I left him. I took care of him myself."

Something about the silence with which he accepted her heated avowal brought her up short, her heart sinking. The look in his eyes chilled her blood.

"You-you did not know . . ." She faltered, her voice trailing off.

"Zenger never got past bragging about how he'd made a whore out of Herman Gilbert's only daughter. It was the last brag he'll ever make." A cold smile flickered briefly about his lips. "I believe," he said, holding up a magnificent pair of diamond earrings, "these belong to you."

Angelique stared at the brilliant display of light flashing from the heart of the stones.

"Y-You killed him?" she whispered, her mouth suddenly dry.

Locke's silence was answer enough, and in spite of herself she shuddered. Zenger had been a brute, crafty and dangerous. She was not sorry he was dead, only that Locke had been the one to do it. And for her. *Tiens*, what if it had turned out differently, and Locke had been the one to die because of her?

"*Why?*" she asked bitterly. "Did you think to redeem

301

my honor? For this you risked your life? And now you think maybe I will fall into your arms and thank you for it, *non?* But me, I did not ask you to make yourself my guardian. Go away, Capitaine. Angelique Gilbert was born without honor. And your protection she does not want.''

Angelique winced at the harsh bark of his laughter. His face looked carved from granite, and she could sense the bafflement in him, the anger.

"No, you've made that patently clear, haven't you, my love. But you aren't the only reason Zenger is dead. The last months of the war, I happened on one of his stinking slavers off Barbados. I'm afraid he took exception to being relieved of his bloody ship and his cargo. When I looked him up in Poole, it was pretty much a forgone conclusion only one of us would walk away. I preferred it to be me.''

Angelique reeled, her face pale as death.

"He—was a slaver?'' she uttered hoarsely, sickened at the implications of all that Zenger had told her about himself, had hinted about her papa. The echo of his voice whispered through her brain: *I make it my business to know everything about my competitors, and Gilbert was the craftiest of the lot.* No, she thought. It was not true. It was a lie. La Cime du Bonheur, everything he had worked for on Saint Dominique, was proof of that. Herman Gilbert was not like Zenger. She would not believe it. And yet . . .

Suddenly steely fingers clamped hard on her arms. Over the roaring in her ears she heard Locke call her name.

"Angel! What is it?''

In a daze she lifted her head to look at him. The blue glint of his gaze pierced the fog that momentarily had clouded her mind. Biting her lip, she pulled away.

"N-Nothing,'' she faltered. "Forgive me. For a moment I felt dizzy, but it is gone now.''

Locke's mouth thinned to a grim line as he watched her move fitfully away. Now what the bloody hell? When at last she came around to face him again, she appeared pale

302

but composed.

"You should not have come, Capitaine. You owe me nothing. If anything, the debt is mine, and my father's. And so I tell you for the last time—go away from here. Forget that you ever knew me. Forget that you ever knew Herman Gilbert!"

Her voice broke at the end, and stifling a sob, she started for the house.

His hand on her wrist stopped her, dragged her hard around. She trembled before the look in his eyes.

"And will *you* forget so easily, my little Creole tart?" he demanded harshly. Before she could summon the breath to answer, he yanked her brutally against his chest. "Or is it that you already have?" For a seeming eternity, Angelique stood frozen in his arms, her mind paralyzed by the ice-cold fury of his eyes boring into hers. Then something like bewilderment flickered behind the probing intensity of his gaze. "Damn you!" he muttered strangely. "Damn your cursed, lovely face!"

"No!" cried Angelique, trying at last to pull away. Too late. His mouth closed savagely over hers.

Never had she felt such hunger in his embrace. Her senses reeled before the violence of his kiss. His lips bruised her, even as they ignited the searing flames of passion only he could arouse in her. He usurped her will and melted her resistance, until, with a groan, she clung to him.

She felt battered and defenseless when at last he pulled away to gaze into her face, his own breath harsh in his throat. Deliberately he studied the pallor of her cheeks, the eyes huge in the perfect oval of her face.

"No," he murmured, his smile triumphant. "You haven't forgotten, have you, my love."

Returned to her senses by the mocking gleam in his eyes, Angelique jerked furiously out of his clasp.

"Demon!" she choked, nearly incoherent with rage. "You take advantage of me. And—and then you have the arrogance to laugh. But I swear I will never marry you.

303

Never, *M'sieu le Capitaine*. Me, I will die first!"

Tears stinging her eyelids, she turned and ran into the house, the image of Locke's mocking eyes burned into her brain.

She heard her name shouted after her, but as if pursued, Angelique fled blindly down the hall. She must escape, she told herself, ignoring Pierrette as the maid called to her from one of the rooms. She could not bear to be near him, the capitaine, who robbed her of her will and made her forget who and what she was. For his sake, and for the sake of those whom he loved, she had fled halfway around the world. And now he would ruin everything with his stupid arrogance. For pride and duty, he would pay the price of his life if ever she gave in to him—nay, gave in to her heart.

Feeling only that she must get away from her father's house, she let herself out a side door and headed more by instinct than anything else toward a long-familiar path. *Mais oui,* she thought, realizing at once what she had done. *C'est bien.* She would go to the one place in which she might be alone to find herself.

After the shaded interior of the house, she was nearly blinded by the sunlight, and so she did not see the tall figure come around the corner of the house and, hesitating only briefly, go after her as she vanished into the thick press of trees. She wended the tortuous path up the mountainside with long, eager strides, her singlemost thought to escape the uncertainties, the bitter doubts, *voyons,* the longing that Locke had aroused in her.

It was late August, the season of the hurricanes, but today the sky was clear, the sun warm against her face. Already it must be sweltering in the lowlands and on the vast beaches of sand beyond the encroaching jungle. Logwood, mahogany, and mango trees formed a solid wall all around her, at times even obscuring the little-used trail, but to Angelique, climbing with eager, unfaltering steps, it seemed like yesterday since last she had fled to her secret haven high above La Cime du Bonheur.

The cavern mouth embraced by pink shower and the clinging jumbi-bead vine with its brilliant red flowers appeared unchanged, save to have grown denser, perhaps. Her heart pounding, she slipped through the opening and paused to catch her breath and let her eyes adjust to the darkness.

The stone at her back felt cool against her skin, and all around her the shadows resonated with the secret life of the grotto. As if drawn, she pushed herself away from the rock and felt her way among the boulders, toward the unmistakable rush of water. An eager gasp broke from her as, without warning, a pale wash of sunlight penetrated the gloom. Then, knowing what she would find, she emerged from the murky recesses of the tunnel onto the smooth hump of a great boulder.

"*En fin,*" she breathed, as she gazed out over the high-vaulted basin, the breathtaking rise of rock walls, the slash of sky through a narrow fissure, the sheer plunge of crystalline falls into a pool of shimmering blue water.

A sudden burble of laughter rose past the lump in her throat. "*Voilà,* in truth I am home," she cried. The echo of her voice coming back to her sounded high-pitched and wild.

Suddenly impatient, she cast off her gown and slipped out of her silk underthings. Free at last of the constricting clothes, she stood poised, slim and straight, on the lip of the stone shelf high above the rippling pool.

How glorious to be naked and free! she thought, shivering a little in the mist cast by the falls. It was as if she had, for the moment, shed her troubles along with her clothing. She laughed, feeling reckless and more than a little rebellious. For a brief time she would be a little girl again, safe in this womb of the mountain from the world outside, safe from the bitter uncertainties—*alors!*—safe from *le capitaine* and the terrible yearnings of her own unruly heart. Giving a small toss of her raven curls, she raised her arms high above her head and leaped outward over the water. Then arching her body, she plunged into

305

the pool.

She dove deeply, delighting in the sensuous fluidity of the water against her bare skin, rejoicing with animal-like pleasure in the suppleness of her own body as she pulled herself along with sure strokes. At last, feeling her lungs ready to burst, she was forced to come up again. She drank in deep draughts of air. Then again she dove, and again, slipping through the water with the same supple ease, exploring the transparent depths with an eagerness she had not felt since her childhood. Then, she had spent hours delving the watery recesses of the grotto.

Finally exhausted, she pulled herself from the water onto a low, sandy shelf and stretched languourously out in a pale swath of sunlight. Only then did the bitter doubts that had driven her to her secret place return to haunt her.

Zenger's words floated through her head like evil murmurings from the grave. He had wanted her to find out the truth about her papa's past. This had been the true vengeance he had been after. To scar that which was most precious to the man who had disfigured him—the trust between father and daughter. These were the "seeds" he had planted—seeds of doubt, which would bear the fruits of a secret so dark and terrible that it might destroy everything Herman Gilbert had sought to achieve.

"Oh, Papa," she groaned, flinging her arm over her eyes against the dazzle of sunlight. "The whole world turns upside down, and suddenly I am certain of nothing. God in heaven, tell me it is not true."

But in her heart she was very much afraid that it was. For in truth would it not explain many things—how a man who had started with nothing, an adventurer, should find the means of amassing a great fortune? And why he should choose never to talk about the years before he had met her *maman*. The slave-trade had made many men rich, but it was not a thing in which one would take pride. She shuddered, remembering the stories

Mozambe had told of the black men who came to take captives from her tribe. Soulless dogs who plundered the villages of their enemies and sold their captives into slavery. But far worse had been the white men who chained the helpless victims by the hundreds in the airless holds of ships and carried them far from their homelands to work in the fields or the mines of the New World. They were demons without hearts. Men made calloused and hard by the suffering they caused. Surely Herman Gilbert had not been one of these!

Mother of God, was there no end to the evil that was the legacy of dealing in human misery? Had not her own mother been raped by the son of a slave? And was not she, Angelique Eugenie Gilbert, cursed to bear the burden of not knowing who or what she was because of it? Was this the Providence of God visited upon her papa for his greed—that the only child of his beloved Eugenie might instead be the seed of the African whom he had wronged? Indeed, were not the sins of the father visited upon the child? She, who bore the mark of the *Rodu* upon her body—was she to be doomed to bear the burden of uncertainty to the grave and beyond?

Bitterly she cursed the magic of the *Rodu* that sought to enslave her soul. Mozambe had made certain she would come back—Mozambe and that other. Why? What did they want from her? Were the dreams visions of things to come? Did the wicked priestess truly think to make her one of them—a bride of the god whose brand she bore upon her shoulder? Mawu-Lisa, the twin-god of earth and sky, ruler of daylight and darkness, the mother and father of all—was it her destiny to be priestess to a heathen god?

It sounded so bizarre, a nightmare to frighten children. And yet once before she had dared to defy the power of the *Rodu*, and out of darkness had come the fire. And if it had all been only coincidence—the warnings of Chantal, the forebodings of the gypsy, the reality of the fire—what did it really matter? The truth was that unless she could

307

persuade her papa to leave, they would all still be made to suffer the final act of Providence.

Then did she know the real meaning of despair, for she saw clearly the bitterest reality of it all. She, who bore the burden of her papa's sins, was cursed to bring doom upon the only man she had ever loved.

Mother of God, had not *le capitaine* been made to endure enough in the name of her father? For Herman Gilbert, he had suffered the torment of hell in the British prison. And now, because of her he would die in this land cursed by God. In truth, she could not bear it!

In the throes of anguish, Angelique writhed upon the bench. The gypsy had told her she must confront the shadows of her past if she would not be claimed by the powers of darkness. This she had done, and now all she could see before her was a blackness so terrible it robbed her of all hope. For *le capitaine* had come for her in spite of everything she had done to discourage him. And her heart dared to whisper that he could not have done it out of a mere sense of duty. *Hein*, how bitter was the fate that demanded she drive him from her, now, when in truth he might be falling in love with her!

God grant that she would find the courage to do what must be done before it was too late, she thought fiercely. *Le capitaine* must not die because of her! Because of her papa!

How long she lay in the torment of her thoughts, Angelique did not know. She knew only that at length, her tears were exhausted, leaving her in the arms of a deep despondency, until at last she fell asleep.

The dream, when it came, began no differently from the others. She was with Mozambe in the thatched-roof hut, and beyond the thin walls, the drums throbbed to the terrifying beat of her heart. A scream was torn from her throat as flames leaped out at her, the god-fire summoned by a sorcerer's command to torment without consuming flesh.

"Stop it!" Angelique cried, turning and twisting to

308

escape the flames. "Stop it!"

Strong hands clasped her in a grip of steel and dragged her from the torment of her hellish nightmare.

Still in the throes of bitter despair, Angelique erupted in a violent struggle.

"Let me go!" she sobbed, hurting herself in her reckless fight to free herself. "Let . . . me . . . go!"

A blistering oath rent the air. Then a strength greater than hers pinned her mercilessly to the sandy floor.

"Bloody hell, Angel. *Look* at me! It's a dream. There's nothing to be afraid of."

At the sound of that beloved voice, Angelique's eyes flew open. A shuddering gasp broke from her lips as she met the blue blaze of Locke's penetrating glance. Instantly she saw he must have stripped on the rock above and then dived into the pool to reach her, for water streamed from his hair and clung in beads to his naked body. And suddenly she was swept with a terrible, burning need to feel his arms around her. She countered the unsettling emotion with a blaze of anger.

"You-you followed me!" she gasped. "How dare you! For this, I will have you flogged. I have only to tell Papa how you have intruded on my-my privacy!"

Her heart lurched as the piercing eyes narrowed sharply on her face. Then a flame leaped between the slitted eyelids.

"Then tell him and be damned!" he muttered thickly and forced his mouth down over hers.

Chapter 17

"No!" muttered Angelique, struggling to twist her head away. Locke pinioned her wrists in one hand, and, grasping her hair with the other, held her. A muffled cry of rage sounded deep in her throat. She was not a whore to be taken at the whim of *le capitaine!*

All at once Locke uttered a blistering oath and jerked his head up, blood trickling from his lip where Angelique had bitten him.

"*Goujat!*" she spat at him. Tears of fury stung her eyelids.

The captain's eyes flashed steely sparks. Then at sight of her defiant beauty, a dangerous glint of laughter sprang into their depths. "And you, my love, are still an ill-tempered little hellcat," he returned the compliment, grinning.

Angelique stared at him, her heart pounding. For just so had he looked as he faced the fury of the mob in L'Arbalète, she thought. The next instant found her pinned beneath a muscular thigh. The blue fire of his gaze held her paralyzed, and her breath froze in her throat as she waited for what she knew must come next.

"And now, my love," Locke murmured huskily. "I think it's time we came to an understanding."

Angelique blinked back her tears of loathing. "Me, I understand only that I despise you for this," she flung up at him. Then a gasp burst from her lips as his fingers trailed lightly over the heaving mound of her breast.

"Now why, I wonder," he mused out loud, "don't I believe you."

Helpless to do more than glare her defiance, Angelique held herself rigid as he stroked her, gently, and with a strange tenderness she had never known in him before. Willing him to stop, she turned her head away, but all the while the flow of his touch wove its spell over her, until in spite of her resolve, she felt the resistance inexorably melting from her body. Her muscles went lax and she moaned softly, lost in the velvet sensuality of his hands upon her.

A faint smile touched the captain's lips as he felt her move to his caress. So, he thought, he had not utterly lost her—his sweet, fiery Angel, who long ago had bewitched and captivated his soul. Then forgetting everything but the exquisite creature held prisoner in his embrace, he lowered his head, his mouth shaping itself to the soft vulnerability of her flesh. Bitterly Angelique cursed as shudders of pleasure rippled upwards through her belly, igniting the smoldering fires of the passion that had ever been his to command.

"Damn you," she groaned, when at last he lifted his head to look into her eyes. They were dusky with desire. His own breath was harsh in his throat as, drinking in her sultry beauty, he lowered his mouth to hers.

She thought she must die as he kissed her mercilessly, his mouth rubbing sensuously over hers until she groaned from the sheer ecstasy of the feelings he aroused. With a moan she parted her lips to the hard thrust of his tongue. It was pointless to resist him. She had neither the strength nor the will, and her hunger was like a living thing inside her, a ravening beast of desire. Forgetting everything but the need to possess and be possessed, she clung to him, returning his kiss with a feverish abandon.

In the throes of a raging fire, she writhed beneath him,

312

his name a frantic plea upon her lips. But he was pitiless. His mouth punished and bruised her tender flesh, sending ripples of flame pulsating upwards from the molten depths of her. Her breath came in ragged gasps and in anguish she sank her teeth into the sinewy hardness of his shoulder, and still he held back, his lips, his hands, the lean masculine length of him driving her to an ever-greater frenzy. Willing him to end their bittersweet torment, she pressed upwards against his swollen manhood.

"Angelique," he groaned at last, arching over her. The muscles stood out in ridges along his neck and shoulders as he tantalized and teased the swollen orifice of her desire. Then without warning, he drew up and back. A cry burst from her as he plunged deeply, savagely—again and again, until she knew only the white heat of mounting ecstasy.

No longer the master, but a man possessed by her supple beauty and youthful fire, Locke drove them both ruthlessly toward the culmination of their desire. With a groan wrenched from him, he gave a final savage thrust. A keening sigh broke from Angelique as she felt his seed burst forth inside her and experienced the exquisite explosion of her own release. Shuddering, she clung to him, her flesh constricting about his in molten waves of pleasure so fierce she thought she could not bear it.

Nestled at last in the cradle of the captain's shoulder, she felt shaken and dazed by the violence of their joining and the intensity of the passion it had unleashed. A tremulous smile curved her lips as she listened to the strong beat of his heart beneath her cheek. When she was secure in his arms like this, how insignificant everything else suddenly seemed—her fears and foreboding, the danger, *voyons*, her dreams. Never before had she felt such tenderness for anyone as she did then for this man who had mastered and tamed her heart.

In the wake of that thought she found herself in the grips of sudden bitter realization. Her love had grown during the weeks of separation, until it knew no bounds. The discovery gave her no comfort. Rather was she filled with a terrible, rending grief, for in not finding the strength to deny him, she had failed him, had perhaps condemned him to the death from which she had vowed to save him. She was despicable and weak, when love should have made her strong.

"Damn you," she whispered despairingly. "Why could you not have stayed away?"

"Now you are being absurd," murmured Locke, tightening his arm around her. "After all we've been through together, you didn't really think I'd let you steal out of my life, did you?"

"*Oui!*" she declared. "I prayed that you would. But you are hardheaded like the bull. You think you can make everything the way you want it. But you cannot. How can I make you understand? I will not be your wife. I can never marry anyone!"

She felt Locke go still beside her, heard his sigh, heavy in the quiet.

"Why?" he said. "Because you have some fool notion that Gilbert's not your real father? If you want to convince me I don't stand a chance with you, you're going to have to come up with something better than that, my love. Frankly, I don't give a damn whose blood runs in your veins. You belong to me—body and soul. And I've no intention of ever letting you go."

As if a bucket of ice water had been flung without warning over her, Angelique went suddenly rigid. *La vache!* What a fool she had been to think something other than pride had brought him to her. He was no better than the others, she thought, swept by anger and bitter resentment at all those who wished to own her or use her for their own ends. She was nothing to them but a pawn in a game, which, having had its beginnings long before her birth, she did not fully comprehend. And now *le capitaine,* too, was trying to pull her this way and that as if she were only the puppet on the string. Alas, she could not bear it!

Sensing the resistance in the silken body, which only moments before had been so delectably pliant, Locke lifted himself on one elbow to look into eyes smoldering with resentment. A dark eyebrow rose inquisitively in the handsome brow.

"What could I possibly have done now," he said wryly, "to bring the sparks to your eyes?"

"Is that all I am to you?" Angelique bitterly demanded. "Something to be owned—a slave, is that it?" In sudden, unspeakable loathing, she shoved against him with all her strength. Locke, caught off-guard, was thrust neatly to his back. "Well, me," declared Angelique, scrambling to her feet, "I do not choose to belong to the so great capitaine. Not you, not Papa, not Mozambe— not anyone 'owns' Angelique Eugenie Gilbert. Do you hear me? Not anyone!"

Without warning, Locke's hand shot out, the fingers curling about a slender ankle. A startled cry burst from Angelique as she felt her feet swept out from under her. The next instant she plunged full-length on her back into the pool.

She came up sputtering and choking. At the sound of Locke's laughter, her eyes flashed glorious sparks of anger.

"You-you devil," she gasped, the slash of her fist sending a spray of water at her grinning tormentor.

"A devil? Perhaps," he magnanimously agreed. "But I'm damned if I'm going to humor your ill temper. *Or* your unfortunate habit of jumping to conclusions. It's bad manners, Angel, to be forever unloosing your temper at people for little or no reason at all."

"*Oh!* And you think *you* are one to teach me how to behave better?" she demanded furiously.

The flash of white teeth against his tanned face made her heart suddenly lurch. *Voyons*, how young he looked, and how beautiful with the filtered sunlight golden on his magnificent body.

315

"I think we're not leaving here until we've set a lot of things straight," he answered, infuriatingly sure of himself. "Like ridding you once and for all of the absurd notion that I'm remotely interested in acquiring a slave for myself. Not that I don't want you. I think I've already made it abundantly clear that not only *do* I want you, but I mean to have you, whether you like it or not—as my wife. And that, my love, is an offer I've never made to any other woman."

"Bah," she retorted, eyeing him with disdain. "And this is supposed to make a difference to me? What woman would be stupid enough to accept an arrogant, conceited man like you?"

An appreciative gleam of humor flickered in the handsome face.

"I may be arrogant," he assented without rancor as he reached out to pull her from the water. "And maybe even conceited, but at least I've been honest in my intentions, which is more than can be said for you." Suddenly he looked at her, the amusement gone from his eyes. "Don't you think, my love, it's time you leveled with me? I'm willing to cry paix if you are."

Angelique stared warily at the strong, supple hand he offered her. Her heart cried out to her to tell him everything, to let him share the burden of her fear, her uncertainty, but her mind told her that there was nothing he could do to stop the tides of fate.

"Non!" she cried, shaking her head as if to convince herself. "Once before I listened to you, and *la duchesse* was nearly made to pay the price for it."

"Bloody hell. Is that all that's bothering you—the cursed fire?" Reaching out, he clasped her shoulders between strong hands. "You saved my sister from harm, at the risk of your own life. It was a blasted accident. Only a fool or an ignorant savage would believe it was anything else."

"Then maybe me, I am the fool," she retorted, her magnificent eyes huge in her face, gone pearly white.

"But I will not be persuaded again. Go away, Capitaine. There is nothing here for you but the very great danger."

"There is nothing here for anyone but a bloody certain death," growled the captain. "Christ, do you think I don't know the whole blasted island is ready to blow up? I came to take you away from here."

"*Mais oui,* it is the promise you made to Papa. But I release you from it."

She winced at the terrible flash of his eyes.

"The hell with what I promised your father," he uttered in chilling accents. "It has nothing to do with this. You're coming away with me because of the bargain we made. Or had you forgot you pledged yourself to me at Briarcroft?"

"N-No, I forget nothing," she answered, wishing he would stop hounding her with what could never be. "Angele DuFour made that pledge."

"And Angelique Gilbert will honor it. You might as well accept the fact that I'm not leaving Saint Dominique without you."

Angelique stared at him, her heart bitter with the realization of what he offered her. Freedom, home, the security of his arms. But alas, he did not know the power of the *Rodu.* Merciful God, what was she to do?

"Angel," he murmured, seeing the emotions at war in her troubled face. "There's no obstacle we can't surmount if we trust one another, I promise you. Tell me what you're really afraid of."

At last she pulled away from him, unable to meet his eyes.

"I-I do not know," she faltered. "All my life I have worshipped my father. Believed in him. A-And now I am filled with doubts."

"Because you've just found out he's a man, no different from anyone else?"

Suddenly she turned to face him.

"*Non.* Because I have found out he was a slaver. A man to sell other men for the profit."

317

She did not know what she had expected—surprise, outrage, disgust—his contempt, surely. But in his face she could read nothing.

"You already knew," she stated with sudden certainty. "He told you? When? When he asked you to become his partner to save his fortune?"

"Don't be absurd. Who told you that bit of nonsense? Zenger?" he demanded.

"*Oui*, Zenger," she said. "It is the truth, *non*? Do not lie to me. I will know if you are lying."

"I've never lied to you, Angel. Why should I? The truth is Gilbert told me about his slaving days long before the war. I was a boy in a tight spot, and he pulled me out of it. For some reason he must have taken a liking to me, because he told me a lot of things he wouldn't have to anyone else. Sometimes it happens that way when people face danger together, especially if they don't expect ever to meet up again."

"But you did—in the war," murmured Angelique, beginning to glimpse how it must have been between these two men. "And this is why you took his place on the ship, *vraiment*? Because of the thing that happened before."

"Your father did more than save my life," Locke confessed with a thin smile. "Maybe you had to know my stepfather to understand how it was. For all his soft-spoken manner, he was a man others looked up to. And maybe me, most of all. I could never have faced Phillip Tyree if I'd lost my vessel and my cargo in a game of chance. Especially one that was rigged. I owed Herman plenty."

"But you almost died." Angelique gave an involuntary shudder. "It is true what Zenger said? There was a man of great influence who ordered you to be tortured and beaten while you were in the prison?"

She was not prepared for the pale flash of his eyes.

"So Zenger told you about that, too, did he. Yes, I suppose it's true enough."

318

"This man, the baronet, who was he?" she asked, compelled to it in spite of the marble hardness of his face. "Why did he hate you so?"

The cynical bark of his laughter made her wince. In awe she stared at him as he turned to look at her with the eyes that had seen the fires of hell.

"He was my father," he said.

Angelique lay with her cheek resting on Locke's chest, her attention riveted on his low-voiced narrative. In truth, she was almost afraid to move lest she interrupt the story as it unfolded, a tale of seduction and betrayal, of revenge that had nearly destroyed her beloved and his beautiful half-sister Sabra. Her heart was wrung with pity for Wes's mother, Elizabeth, a young girl, who, having placed her trust in one twisted by greed and made heartless by envy, had sought to drown herself and her unborn child rather than bring disgrace on her family. Silently she thanked God for sparing her and blessed Josiah Locke for having given his brother's bastard son an honorable name.

"I never guessed the truth," said the captain grimly. "Not even when, years later, I heard the rumors that Phillip Tyree had taken a horsewhip to a man in London, a man who was to wed his sister. When the truth finally came out, a lot of things suddenly made sense. My mother had learned from one of Josiah's agents in London that her former lover was betrothed to Lady Caroline. It was she who wrote Phillip and told him."

"Then it was your real father, this man to whom Phillip Tyree took the whip. And that is why he followed your stepfather to America—to get his revenge."

"Yes, only Tyree wasn't my stepfather then. It wasn't until Josiah drowned at sea a few years later that my mother and Phillip were married. By then Josiah's brother had changed his name to Channing, and he'd managed to obtain the office of Vice-Admiralty Judge.

Before Parliament finally put an end to his little game, he made himself wealthy while he nearly ruined Tyree and Locke."

"And afterwards?" queried Angelique. "How was he able to do so much that was evil?"

A singularly grim smile curved his lips.

"Parliament may have broken the power of the customs agents, but the king granted Channing a baronetcy nevertheless for his loyal service. After all, my 'father' had amassed a sizeable fortune, which he was not unwilling to use in the purchase of favors. It was a small matter for him to see that a certain captured American naval officer was confined wherever he desired. He meant to make sure I never survived that bloody hell-hole. His intent was to expose my half-sister as a rebel spy and confiscate her properties in the name of the crown. Then, as sole survivor of the Locke family, he would come into his brother's fortune as well. A neat little plot of revenge, don't you think? He nearly succeeded in it, too. Only he not only underestimated Sabra Tyree, but he failed to make allowances for the appearance of a wild card. Channing sealed his own fate when he set the French on the British frigate *Black Swan*. He should have known Trevor Myles would never rest until he'd found out the man who betrayed his ship."

Angelique's blood ran cold at the captain's mirthless laugh.

"It was damned lucky for me that he did. I'd had about all I wanted of the *Jersey* when Myles got me out of there. In exchange for certain papers Sabra had stolen from Channing, he said, but I knew better. He did it because he had fallen head over heels in love with my beautiful sister."

"*Oui*," murmured Angelique, thinking of all the duchess had told her about these same events. Involuntarily, she shivered. "*Voyons*, he was an evil man, this baronet. But he was your father. How could he do such things to you, his only son?"

Locke shrugged a broad shoulder.

"He was not the first man to entertain a total lack of feelings for his offspring. I doubt that he'll be the last. At least the same cannot be said of your own father. In spite of whatever sins he may have committed in his past, I don't think Gilbert is guilty of not loving his only daughter."

Angelique's brow creased in a troubled frown.

"No," she said at last. "If, in truth, he is my father. In his own way he has loved me. Even if he could not bear to have me near after he lost *Maman*. I think in some small way he has blamed me for her loss." She swallowed hard. "Just as you have blamed your *maman* for what came of her moment of weakness. It is the real reason you have never married, *non?* Because in your heart you have never forgiven her for loving a man like this Channing?"

Her heart leaped in her throat as she felt the powerful muscles tense. Perhaps she had gone too far, but she had to know the truth—she had to know if *en fin* he could let go of the hurt. How else could she ever be sure the passion between them would not one day turn to ashes!

Taking the bull by the horns, she lifted her head to look at him.

"It is why you have never let a woman get close to you. No woman, except for your sister."

The breath caught in her throat as she met the blue blaze of his eyes.

"And what makes you so sure she is the only one?" he queried. The faint curve of his lips made her heart flutter strangely.

"Because I overheard what you said to Fisk," she answered, giving a little toss of the head. "'One place is as good as another. And one woman the same as every other,'" she imitated in a fair approximation of his otherwise inimitable drawl. "It is plain you have the very low opinion of my sex, and now I have learned the reason why."

"You think so, do you," he remarked, his hand

321

reaching up to curl a raven lock about a slender finger. "And what if I told you you were far off the mark, my wise little Angel? That there was at least one other than the incomparable Sabra who had wormed her way into my heart?"

"Then, m'sieu," she said, the roguish dimple peeping irresistibly out at the corner of her mouth, "I would say you are telling to me a story."

Before he knew what she was about, she leaned forward and kissed him on the mouth with a sweet, passionate longing that took his breath away. A long sigh breathed through her lips when at last she lifted her head to gaze at him with eyes, huge and vulnerable, like a child's.

"But it is very pleasant to hear—such words from a man like you," she murmured whimsically. Folding her hands on top of his chest, she rested her chin on them. "For a while I will pretend that you mean them. Here, in my secret place where the world seems very far away."

"Angelique . . ."

"*Non.*" She stopped him with the fingertips of one hand placed lightly to his lips. "When I was a young girl, I used to lie here on this rock and spin dreams of the brave Capitaine Locke. Today is only another of those dreams. Let us make it last as long as we can, I beg you."

For a long moment Locke stared into the soft pleading of her eyes and knew a bitter sense of helplessness. Never had he known such a female before, a woman so utterly elusive he was nearly driven mad thinking about her, wondering what the hell she would pull next. Quelling the urge to shake some sense into her, he forced himself to bide his time. After all, she was very young, hardly more than a green girl. And someone had done a thorough job of convincing her she dared not marry him—or anyone, for that matter. He'd give a pretty penny to know how they had managed it, planted her head full of bogus superstitions. And the cursed nightmares that wouldn't leave her be. What the bloody hell were they all about?

A singularly hard look came to his eyes. The unlucky incident of the fire may have driven her from him at Briarcroft, but it was something deeper, more sinister, that had given the event such frightening significance for her. A single name echoed in his mind—Mozambe—the name she had repeated over and over in her delirium, and then again a few moments ago in her anger. Mozambe. And Chantal. Somehow they were both mixed up in this. Silently he cursed as it came to him to wish that she would trust him.

"In your fantasies about me," he drawled at last, curling a lock of hair behind her ear, "did you always end up wishing me to the devil?"

"Not at all, *M'sieu le Capitaine*," murmured Angelique, twin imps of laughter springing to her lovely eyes. "Always you worshiped at my feet and swore your undying love for me. Alas, they were only the foolish daydreams of an innocent girl."

"I see, and now that you are a woman of experience, you find that I don't live up to your expectations, is that it?" he countered wryly.

"Let us say instead that you proved somewhat— different—from what I expected," she answered, tinglingly aware of the danger in this game they played. "More pig-headed," she added sweetly. "More set in your ways than the gallant young officer of the stories Papa told."

An appreciative gleam of amusement flickered in the chiseled face.

"Jade," he uttered feelingly.

"More of the gentleman, too, I think," Angelique reflected with a guileless pucker of enticing lips.

"Baggage," growled the captain. Clasping her in his arms, he rolled without warning onto his side so that his tormentress lay partially beneath him.

Laughing, Angelique lifted her arms about his neck.

323

"There, you see?" she gurgled. "You use me shamelessly."

The captain gazed ruefully down into the beguiling face. She was a bewildering minx, was his Angel, the one woman he had ever met who could never pall on him. Suddenly he was filled with a burning impatience to have her away from here, in the safety of his ship.

"Not as shamelessly as you deserved," he growled at last and, disgusted at his inability to win her trust, shoved himself away from her.

Startled, Angelique stared at the long, lean back. She saw the muscles tense and ripple beneath the smooth skin and felt her stomach clench in apprehension.

"You are angry with me," she said, hurt by the abrupt change in him.

"Angry?" he drawled cynically. "Now why should I be angry? Bloody hell, Angel. I'm too old for children's games."

"I see. And that is what you think this is, a game for children?"

"No, it's what you think it is." She felt the blood rush to her cheeks as he turned to look at her with the hard points of his eyes. "I've never liked being played for a fool."

"If you have been the fool, it is your fault, not mine," retorted Angelique. "I have told you from the beginning how it must be."

"Have you? Then tell me this," uttered the captain, turning to grasp her by the arm. "Where did you get this scar?"

Locke had the dubious satisfaction of seeing her draw away from him, her expression shuttered, where before it had been open to him, unguarded.

"I do not remember," she answered in a voice utterly devoid of emotion. "I have had it since I was a very small child."

"You're lying. For once in your life, Angel, tell me the truth."

324

She winced as his fingers tightened their hold on her.

"I have told you. I do not remember." Twisting in his grasp, she turned on him eyes blurred with tears of pain and anger. "Stop it. You are hurting me."

Uttering a low curse, Locke loosened his grip, but did not release her.

"I won't stop," he said, in deadly earnest. "Not until you tell me. How did you get this scar?"

"I do not know! Why are you doing this to me?"

"Who is Mozambe?" he came back at her. "What is the hold Mozambe has over you?"

"She-she is an old woman, the *houngan*, a priestess of the *Rodu*. She used to take me with her to the villages when she was called to care for the sick. There. Are you satisfied?" she demanded, the hurt plain in her eyes. But Locke was merciless and hard. His glance bored holes through her.

"Why are you afraid of her, Angel?" he prodded. "Think. Try to remember. It was Mozambe who put that mark on you, wasn't it. *Wasn't* it!"

"*Oui!*" she cried, driven to it. Then all at once she stilled, her eyes huge in her face gone white as death. "*Oui*," she repeated in a hoarse whisper. "*Mon Dieu*, I remember. There was a ball for the governor. In Cap Français. *Maman et* Papa, they left me in the care of Sanchon, the old woman who looked after me since I was a baby. Mozambe came for me. She took me deep into the forest—to the temple of the *Rodu*. I remember it was a mud house with the whitewash. The roof thatched, like all the other houses of the blacks. But inside it seemed like a thousand candles burning. And—"

Suddenly she swallowed.

"She gave me something—a powder made from the bark of the mahoe tree, I think. I slept, and still I was awake. Strange dreams came to me, visions. Only later, when it was over, and I woke up in my own bed, I bore this mark on my shoulder. And I-I knew they were not dreams."

325

She lifted her head to look at him with eyes cold-flecked with the memories.

"Mozambe branded me with the sign of the twin-god, while I lay in the spell of the mahoe. Mawu-Lisa owned my soul. This, Mozambe told me. I was made *placée*. Never could I marry, never have children. I was very young, no more than four or five. In time I forgot."

"She frightened and hurt you," murmured Locke, his aspect exceedingly grim. "It's more likely you buried the memories. Until something happened to bring them to the surface again. Something that triggered the dreams."

"Yes, but of course." Angelique let out a long breath. "It-it was Mozambe who told me about *Maman*. The day Papa sent me away. She told me I was the daughter of a slave. She said I would come back. No matter how far away I went, one day she would call me, and I would come. I told myself it was a lie, and again I almost forgot. Until the night I saw Etienne Joliet at the opera."

Locke pulled her into his arms as she gave a helpless shudder.

"He was my playmate when I was a little girl. But when he looked at me, it was with the eyes of a stranger. Then I knew I had been living the lie. In truth, I was a person of color, and the time had come when I must return to Saint Dominique, even as Mozambe had said I would. That night the dreams came back to haunt me."

"And why not, when the seeds of fear, the guilt and shame, had been carefully planted there long before you were prepared to deal with them. Mozambe made sure of that." He took her by the shoulders and made her look up at him. "But that's all there was to it. Everything that came after was pure happenstance. You must believe that."

"If only I could," she whispered, lifting her hand to touch his face. "Oh, if only I could!"

Chapter 18

The grotto was stepped in deepening shadows when Angelique and the captain at last decided it was time to return to La Cime du Bonheur. Angelique made her way in silence up the back side of the boulder to her clothes, left in scattered disarray. She could feel Locke, studying her as they dressed—gauging her mood. But she herself did not know how she felt. Neither could she have told him what she meant to do.

In the wake of the confrontation, which had brought the memories flooding back to her, she had been ready to believe that in truth the only hold Mozambe had over her lay in the realm of her own mind. For a time, she had even been able to lose herself in the spell of the moment. As if by tacit agreement, no more had been said between them of what waited beyond the safe haven of her secret place. Instead, they had divided their time between love-making on the sandy bench beside the pool and bathing in the clear waters.

Strange, how they had felt neither hunger nor the swift passing of the time. Only the inevitability of soon being plunged into impenetrable gloom as the sun passed its zenith overhead had at last driven them to leave this place of dreams for the world outside. Yet how easily the spell had been broken! No sooner had they left the pool to ascend the precarious path to the bouldertop, than she

327

had been overtaken once more by bitter uncertainties.

What if Locke was wrong?

The captain's quiet drawl startled her from her reverie. "I think, if you're ready, we should be going. It must be nearly dusk. Your father'll be worried if I don't have you home before dark."

"*Oui.*" Still, she did not leave, but turned to look back on the grotto—the waterfall, silvery in the fading light, the blue shimmer of the pool. Suddenly her heart was heavy with the thought that she might be seeing them for the very last time. In truth, she had the feeling that when she emerged from this womb of the mountain, it would mean the end of everything—the childhood fantasies that were the link to her *maman*, the memories and illusions she had woven around the man she called "Papa," *voyons*—her girlhood. She tingled as she felt the captain come up behind her. Her blood quickened as he spoke her name. "Angel?" And suddenly her mind was made up for, she thought with a slowly dawning wonder, it was to be a beginning as well, was it not?

Abruptly, she faced Locke with pleading eyes.

"You will make him agree to come with us? Promise me," she said. "I will not leave him behind."

Locke's strong hands lifted deliberately to grip her shoulders.

"He'll come," he said. "If I have to bind and gag him."

A smile trembled on her lips at such a thought. Her papa, bound and gagged, would indeed be a sight to see.

"Very well," she murmured, "then let us go now."

"Wait. There's just one thing more." With a hand on her arm, he stopped her as she started to turn away. "This time be sure, Angel. When we board the *Sea Wolf*, we'll be putting all of this behind us once and for all. You know that, don't you."

Angelique returned his look gravely.

"Yes, I know," she answered.

For a moment Locke studied her face. Then abruptly he pulled her close.

"No matter what happens," he said, holding her with his eyes, "I want your word you won't go off half-cocked on your own again. No more running away, Angel. From now on, whatever comes, we face it together. Promise me."

All at once, she could not keep the dimple from peeping impishly out at the corner of her mouth.

"My poor capitaine," she grinned, reaching up to cup the side of his face in her hand. "I fear I have been a very great trial to you."

As if in answer, his strong, slender fingers captured her wrist and held it firmly.

"Yes, well," he drawled in very dry tones, "strange as it may seem, I find that somehow I cannot do without you. And so, your word, my love. Promise me—now, before we go another step further. No more running away."

Angelique, however, was grown suddenly, ominously pale.

"*Chut!*" she hissed. "Listen! Do you hear it?"

Locke went still. The rush of the waterfall sounded loud in the sudden silence, and for a moment he could detect nothing to cause alarm. Then it came again—the keening wail of a conch shell, faint, as if issuing from a long way off; and then, afterwards, another, answering wail.

"*Voyons*, what does it mean?" whispered Angelique, clutching at the captain's sleeve.

"Probably nothing. Just the laborers returning from the fields more than likely," Locke answered, but with a sudden piercing glint in his eye.

Slowly Angelique shook her head in the negative.

"*Non.* I do not think so. If it came from the fields, we would not be able to hear it." All at once she looked at him. "Capitaine—Wes, I am afraid."

A dark eyebrow arched in his forehead at her use of his given name. He'd waited a long time to hear it from her lips. What was more, he was finding that he did not

329

dislike in the least that she had turned to him in her uncertainty. In fact, he was experiencing the uncommonly strong urge to gather her in his arms and whisper assurances in her ear.

Instead, he took her hand and started for the entrance to the cave.

"My guess is it's your father sending a search party out after his missing daughter," he said over his shoulder. "But suppose we go and see for ourselves."

Angelique did not answer. The fear like a cold hand clutched at her vitals. In her heart she knew it was not her papa coming for her.

The onset of dusk cloaked the mountain in soft shades of lavender fading rapidly to indigo as the two stepped free of the cavern mouth. From their vantage point they could catch glimpses through the trees of the sea far below them and of the silvery descent of the river where it emerged from its underground passage. But the tranquil wash of the breeze from off the sea brought a shiver to Angelique. Something was wrong. She could sense it all around her.

Locke's low-muttered oath brought her head up, her eyes searching on the stern features.

"What is it?" she asked, her heart suddenly pounding.

"Look there. Do you see it?"

Angelique felt the breath hard in her throat as she looked where the captain pointed. Even as her glance found the ominous roil of black cloud billowing upward from the land, the distant crack of gunshots reached her ears.

"*Mon Dieu*, it's Cime Bonheur! They have set the house on fire!"

"No, not the house," Locke uttered grimly. "Not yet. They've fired the fields and probably some of the outbuildings. Look. Further west. There's another one."

Swallowing hard, Angelique slowly nodded.

"Chateau Vachon," she said. "And there, the house of

Fernand Justin. *En fin*, it has begun. And when they are through, there will be nothing left, I think. Wes—Papa and Pierrette, and-and the others. We cannot let them die like this. There must be something we can do."

Locke, however, was not listening. Silently he swore to himself. He had known as soon as he landed on the cursed island that things were ready to explode. If he had followed his first instincts and packed the girl off, by force if need be, they would not be in this bloody fix. Well, their one chance now lay in the *Sea Wolf*. From what he had seen on his way to the great house, he judged Gilbert had men and arms enough to hold off the first wave of attack. After that, it would only be a matter of time before they were overwhelmed by sheer force of numbers. Somehow he had to signal the ship. With twenty or thirty of his men, he could rout the black devils long enough to get Angel and her father safely down off the mountain.

Grimly he turned to the girl, who was watching him with doubtful eyes.

"Angelique, think. Is there another way down from this side of the mountain? A way around the cliffs. We have to get word to the ship somehow."

"No, that's impossible. The only way down to the bay is the way you came up. We cannot reach your ship, Capitaine. Not without going through La Cime du Bonheur."

For a moment their glances met and held. Angelique could sense the tension in him, the fear he felt for her. Deliberately she lifted her head, determined to show him she was not afraid. At last the captain's lips curved in a mirthless grin.

"Then I guess that's what we'll have to do, my love. Just as soon as it's dark."

They had not long to wait. Already the jungle was closing in on them, the trees blurring into each other as the last light of dusk faded before the onset of night.

Angelique nearly jumped as Locke leaned suddenly near.

"How are you," he drawled, framing her face between the palms of his hands, "at finding your way in the dark?"

"Etienne used to say I was like the cat," she answered with a tinge of sadness. "When we were children, we used to sneak out sometimes at night to watch the Africans dance. I was never afraid of the night. Maybe it is true I am a daughter of Mawu-Lisa, do you think?"

Her breath caught as Locke wordlessly lowered his head to hers. His kiss filled her with a strange sort of warmth, which was not passion, but something more profound, tender somehow.

"No," he said, lifting his head. "But if you were, it wouldn't matter. Not to me. Just keep your eyes open and don't stumble into any discontented slaves. I intend to get us out of here all in one piece."

"Of course, *M'sieu le Capitaine*," she grinned somewhat crookedly back at him. "It is how I would like best to get out of here."

"Then on your way, wench. Remember, I'll be right behind you all the way."

As the flat of his hand smacked her smartly on the rump to urge her along, Angelique gave a small yelp of mock-indignation.

"When I am your wife," she tossed over her shoulder at him, "I will make sure you treat me with more of the respect."

Locke's only answer was a grin, which slowly faded as he watched her begin to pick her way through the thick growth. She was a marvel, he thought as he started after her. How many women of his acquaintance would have the courage to laugh in the face of the kind of peril that lay before them? Not many, he decided. Except for the irrepressible Sabra, he couldn't think of a single one.

As for Angelique, she was discovering that there was a

332

strange sort of exhilaration in feeling one's way down a mountainside in the thick of night with the nerve-shattering crack of gunshots splitting the quiet somewhere in the distance. She was conscious of both fear and a heady sense of recklessness, somewhat reminiscent of the feeling she had known when she stole out of the convent and made her way alone through the streets of Paris. Only then, she reflected soberly, she had not had her father's safety to worry about. Or the well-being of the others at La Cime du Bonheur.

That thought, along with the smell of smoke, which was growing stronger, more pervasive, effectively brought home the seriousness of their undertaking. If they were somehow lucky enough to reach those under attack at the great house, they would hardly be any better off than before. They would only be trapped with the others. And yet what else could they have done? It had been completely out of the question to flee to safety over the mountain when her papa was fighting for his life. Rather would she be dead than to live knowing she had taken the coward's way out! Firmly putting such thoughts from her mind, she concentrated on the business at hand.

In spite of her earlier boast to the capitaine, it was not an easy matter to find her way in the dark. Invisible snags reached out of the night to trip her and tear at her limbs, so that more than once she had to stifle the urge to cry out in pain and bitter frustration. There were times, too, when she lost the way and had to rely on instinct to find it again. But worst of all, her imagination invested the forest with vengeful slaves behind every tree. At the least rustle of a branch, her heart leaped wildly to her throat.

Luckily the trail did not wander far from the river till it reached a craggy point above the great house, which meant that so long as they stayed within hearing of the swift rush of water, they could not be far astray. From the knoll they would be less than a few hundred feet from the outer fringes of the plantation. Then what? she thought,

333

wondering what they would find upon reaching the wall Gilbert had had constructed long ago as a first line of defense. They might be discovered and made captive or worse. But more than anything else she worried about what they would find when they reached La Cime du Bonheur itself—whether they would find her papa alive.

She could not forget that terrible moment when she had seen the smoke rising from the jungle and had thought her father's house was on fire. Never had she felt such fear as had struck her then. In that single instant it had seemed that the worst of her dreams was coming to pass with a vengeance, and she could not bear it. If it had not been for the capitaine—for Wes—she did not know what she would have done. His calm strength had given her the courage to believe they might somehow reach Cime du Bonheur alive, but it had not kept at bay the small voice that said all of it was going to come true— everything that she had envisioned time and again in each tormenting nightmare. She was Angelique Eugenie Gilbert, and from early childhood she had been given to see such things.

In the dark she almost blundered into the river where it diverged from the path. One moment she was groping her way through a tangle of liana vines, and the next she was poised on the edge of a precipice. Locke snatched her back.

"Bloody hell, Angel," he growled, catching her roughly to his chest.

With a low sob, she clung to him.

"I-I could not see where the-the path turned. I knew it m-must be near, b-but I . . ."

"Hush," Locke murmured, his face grim as he felt her tremble against him. "It's all right now. We'll take a moment to catch our breath and reconnoiter. It can't be much farther now."

"No, not far."

Impossible to miss the somber tone in her voice, Locke

334

looked in the direction she was staring.

"It is the sugar cane field in the valley," she said, her gaze fixed on the long line of orange flame visible in the distance. "And also the mill, I think. Those others, just below. They will be the campfires of the slaves, *oui?*"

"More than likely," uttered the captain, acutely aware of the girl beside him. There were at least half a dozen smaller fires ranged in a half-circle between them and the great house. It would be a close thing, managing to slip past them without falling victim either to the marauding savages or a rifle shot from the defenders. One way or the other, they had to make their attempt soon. Even in the dark he could sense the strain in the girl, the fatigue. She was hardly in any state for a lengthy game of cat and mouse with bloodthirsty slaves on the rampage. At least, he mused wryly to himself, the gunfire had ceased. More than likely the devils had given up the attack until the dark hour before dawn. Then, he doubted not, all hell would break loose.

"Papa and the others," Angelique murmured, still staring at the orange glow of the fire. "Do you think they are still alive?"

"You can bet on it. Otherwise, it'd be Cime du Bonheur on fire."

Slowly she nodded. Yes, it must be so, she thought, and was suddenly aware of a weight lifted from her.

"In my dream," she said, leaning her head against Locke's shoulder, "I saw Papa lying wounded among the charred ruins of the house. Perhaps it is not too late to change what is meant to be."

Her pulse gave a little leap as Locke's long arm tightened about her.

"I told you, I don't go for the idea that things are meant to be. From now on, Angel, we fashion our own dreams. And Mozambe's not going to have any part of them, *savez-vous?*"

His low drawl, edged with steel, sent a soft thrill

335

through her.

"Bah, you are of the very sure of yourself, I think," she retorted, assaying a small moue of comic displeasure, "to give the orders to Eugenie Gilbert. Me, I am not so easily tamed."

"If you were, my love," he instantly returned, "you wouldn't be Herman Gilbert's daughter."

The utter certainty of his remark left her speechless. *Voyons,* if only she could be as sure of it herself, she thought, staring blindly into the distance.

Locke, however, did not give her time to dwell on the matter. Deliberately he drew the long knife from the scabbard at his side.

"It's time, Angel," he said quietly. "From here on I'll lead. Stick close to me, and no matter what happens, keep moving unless I tell you differently."

Without waiting for an answer, Locke took her hand firmly in his and started back the way they had come. Almost too weary to care what lay ahead, Angelique followed.

They had gone only a few yards before the scream, terrifying in its awful agony, shattered the stillness.

A cry welled up in her throat. Then a hard hand clamped ruthlessly over her mouth and dragged her, resisting, into the brush.

Locke's low whisper sounded next to her ear.

"Softly, Angel. We almost crashed their little party."

As comprehension slowly dawned, Angelique forced herself to go lax in his arms. Satisfied, Locke removed his hand from her mouth. Then, leaning near, he whispered softly, "We've stumbled on the main camp. There must be twenty or thirty of them down there."

Angelique clutched at his shirt.

"That scream . . . ?"

"They have prisoners. Two white men as far as I could tell . . . No. Don't look. They just dispatched one of them. It's nothing you wouldn't do better without seeing."

"But I must know who . . ."

"It's no one I've ever seen before," Locke sternly interrupted. "Certainly no one closely associated with your father."

"Then who?" she insisted, straining to see past him to the unmistakable glow of firelight flickering through the trees.

"Plantation owners. One of them, a stout gentleman with white hair, has met his Maker. The one that's still alive is a small, slender fellow with the bearing of a French aristocrat. Has the air of a man who'd never believe anyone'd dare lay a hand on him, not even now when he's staring death in the eye."

"Vachon!"

Locke's glance narrowed at the utter certainty of her tone. Then it hit him when he'd heard her say that name before. Chateau Vachon had been one of the plantations she had seen burning.

Her fingers clamped tightly on his arm brought him swiftly back to the present.

"They mean to kill him?"

"They mean to kill anyone with white skin," he muttered grimly. "But at least M'sieu Vachon may make it possible for us to slip by without being spotted. And there's no time like the present."

Her lips parted on a protest left unvoiced as Locke pulled her along, leaving her no choice but to follow.

They did not progress very far, however, when the sound of voices forced them to seek cover once again. No sooner had they melted into the thick underbrush than a small party approached.

"What for you keeping this man alive?" carried clearly to the two crouching in the shadows. "Maybe you no have the heart to kill him. That it? Maybe you more Vachon than you know."

The footsteps stopped, and the sudden tension in the air was tangible even to Angelique, straining to hear

337

above the rush of the stream.

"You accuse me, *mon ami?*" murmured a voice, all the more dangerous for its softness.

Angelique went stiff with recognition. Chantal! she thought, her heart suddenly pounding. And yet the other man called him Vachon. What did it mean?

"Did you ever stop to think, Jean-Louis," continued that soft and deadly voice, "that Salvador Chantal has, within, the very great hunger. To devour in haste what he has waited the many long years to have served before him would only leave him hungry. The day of atonement has finally come, and the feast he would savor."

Apparently not mollified, the other man growled a warning.

"Many black fella dead because of that man. They hunger, too. You no be careful, they gonna swallow Salvador Chantal alonga Vachon, his papa."

Angelique bit her lip to keep from uttering a sound. Guyon Vachon was the father of Chantal? Why had she never heard it mentioned before? In truth there were many things she would like to know about this man Chantal, such as why he should pretend to be an untutored savage, when obviously he could speak in the cultured accents of a gentleman. Peering through the foliage, she caught sight of the proud, slender figure at the forefront of three men. *Voyons*, she would have known it had she ever seen him clearly before. How very like his papa was the arrogant Salvador Chantal! she thought, just before Locke dragged her head down.

Her heart nearly failed her as a low hiss sounded in the sudden quiet.

"*Qu-est-ce*, Jambeau?" came the sharp query.

"It is something in the brush." A wooden spear thrust through the leaves missed Angelique by inches. "It no be nothing. The iguana maybe. He be gone now."

"Then let us be gone as well," said Chantal. "There is much to be done before morning."

338

"You insane little fool," murmured Locke in her ear as soon as the others had passed out of earshot. "Another trick like that, and you'll have us tethered to a tree beside your friend Guyon Vachon. And I don't think either of us would care for whatever Chantal might have planned for us."

"He means to steal my soul," Angelique answered in a strange voice. "When I lay in the fever on your ship, he came to me in a dream. I was surrounded by the flames of the Pethro *loa,* and he told me to go into the water of death. It is the rite of *hounsi canzo,* when the woman is made the spouse of the god." She shuddered, remembering it. "It was a true dream. In my heart I sensed it to be so."

"Well, this time you're way off the mark. Chantal came to you in my cabin, all right, but not in any bloody dream. I caught him chanting his gibberish over you and sent him packing. And now that's what we're going to do."

"No, wait." Angelique stopped him with a hand on his sleeve. "I cannot explain what I feel. But I know I cannot leave without at least trying to save Guyon Vachon from them. Wes, please, I beg of you. Help me to get close enough to see and hear what is going on." At the look in his eyes, she lifted her head in stubborn defiance. "If you will not go with me, I will do this thing alone."

Grim-faced, Locke stared at her with a feeling of exasperation. If he had any sense at all, he'd knock her alongside the head and carry her out. Obviously she hadn't the glimmering of a notion what she was asking him to do. But then, she hadn't seen what the bloody savages had done to their earlier victim. For anyone else the sound of his voice just before they put him out of his misery would have been enough, but not Angel. He'd be the worst kind of fool if he went along with her harebrained idea.

"And just how do you propose we get close enough to

pull this off?" he queried acidly. "The place must be crawling with lookouts."

"Then we will have to be of the most careful to see them before they see us, *non?*" she came back, looking at him with those huge, innocent eyes of hers.

Silently he cursed.

"Only tell me one thing, Angel. Just what do you think you're going to find down there—other than a most damned unpleasant end."

"I-I told you. I am not sure." Even in the gloom she could see his jaw harden formidably, and hurriedly she rushed on, "Look, when I woke up this morning, Guyon Vachon was at breakfast with my father. He said he had come to win Papa over to his cause, but I think he came for something else. I think he came to look at me."

"Look at you?" Locke echoed incredulously.

"*Oui.* He has known my papa for many years. He must have realized Herman Gilbert would never change his mind about such things. So why else should he have come?"

Obviously Locke was far from convinced.

"How should I know? Maybe he was out for a free breakfast. But so far you've given me damned little reason to go traipsing down into a bloody hornets' nest."

"Oh, why cannot you understand?" she demanded passionately. "Do you not see? Chantal is Guyon Vachon's son, but no one ever mentions him. It is like the big secret someone has been of the very careful to keep from me. And does it not strike you as strange that this very same Chantal should show up suddenly on your boat? He is *tonton macoute.* He must have known you were going to France to fetch home the daughter of Herman Gilbert. And then, when he suddenly appears bending over my bed, he pretends to be the maroon, who has escaped his master. Is it not odd that just now he speaks the language of an educated man? *La vache!* How can I make you see? There are very many things I would know about this man Chantal. But me, I think he

340

is my father!"

For a moment he stared at her as if he thought she had lost what few wits she possessed. Unconsciously, Angelique's head lifted in resentment.

Then at last Locke's jaw set in a grim line.

"And me," he growled, "I think you're barking up the wrong tree. But obviously there's only one way to convince you."

Grabbing her hand, he headed grimly down the mountain.

Chapter 19

Angelique knelt down beside the captain and peered through the thick cover of leafy branches at the slave camp little more than twenty yards away. It had taken them nearly an hour to work their way around the outer perimeter to this point, which was nearly halfway between the camp and the earth wall that formed the first defenses of La Cime du Bonheur. From where she was, she could see the slaves, perhaps twenty men and half as many women, most of them stretched out on the ground asleep. A handful, Chantal among them, sat about a fire seemingly deep in an argument. The prisoner stood with his back to a mango tree, so that all she could see of him were his hands tied behind him around the trunk. Of the slain captive's body, there was no sign. Possibly they had flung him into the river to be carried out to sea, she thought, with a shiver.

She almost jumped at the touch of Locke's hand on her shoulder.

At her grimace of disgust, the sudden gleam of a smile shown whitely against his face.

"Easy. This was *your* idea," he reminded her. The next instant saw a small pocket pistol placed in the palm of her hand with the instructions. "Use it if you have to. Just be sure what you're shooting at. I'd hate like the devil to be shot with my own gun."

"Pooh. It would only serve you right for scaring me half to death," she said, hiding her dismay from *le capitaine*'s too-discerning gaze. How could she tell him she had never even held a gun in her hand before, much less fired one! *Voyons*, if it came to having to fire it *at* someone, she was not at all sure she could do it, especially at someone she knew. And in truth, in spite of her five-year absence, she was quite certain that she had recognized more than one of those in the slave encampment. Some of them were hardly more than children.

At that moment she almost envied Guyon Vachon his singleminded dislike of all who were not white or French or gently born. *Hein*, if only she felt *something*—hatred, rage, some sort of conviction one way or the other— anything except this terrible ache for all those who would be made to suffer.

Locke's low-voiced murmur brought home to her the bitter realization that whatever her feelings, she was about to be swept up in events over which she had no control.

"Don't wait, Angel," he was telling her. "Once Vachon is free, you start running and don't stop until you're over the wall. Is that understood?"

"*Mais oui*," she whispered nervously back. "And now what do we wait for? Let us go *en fin*."

His hand on her arm stopped her as she started to her feet.

"Hold it. Nobody said anything about you coming along."

"But of course I am going. From now on we face together whatever comes. It is what you have said, *non?*"

"Taking on a score or more bloodthirsty, rebellious slaves in their own camp wasn't exactly what I had in mind," he observed dryly.

"Then you will just have to promise not to do anything so stupid," Angelique countered resentfully. "It was my belief we would sneak in and free Vachon, not start a

344

senseless fight."

"Don't think I haven't repeatedly questioned both my sanity and my intelligence since I first allowed myself to become infatuated with a female who is obviously suicidal, headstrong, and impossibly mulish," murmured Locke in a voice peculiarly lacking in humor, "because I have. However, no matter how irrational it may be, the fact remains that if you fall into their hands, I'll have no choice but to take on the whole bloody gang to get you out again. And those, my love, are not particularly attractive odds."

Angelique's chin came up, her eyes flashing dangerously.

"Me, I am not afraid. And-and if they did catch me, I do not think Chantal would let them harm me. Even if I am wrong and he is not my-my father, he believes I am pledged to the god."

"Unfortunately, the same cannot be said for me," Locke sardonically pointed out. "I'm afraid my former topman and I didn't part on the best of terms, which means Monsieur Chantal would like nothing better than to get his hands on me. Now try and get this through your head: If both of us attempt to sneak up on them, we only double the odds of being spotted. Only one of us has a real chance of pulling this thing off, and in spite of your fearless disregard for your own well-being, I happen to be the better man in a fight. This is as far as you go, Angel. And no more arguments, or I sling you over my shoulder and we get out of here right now. You got that?"

The protest that sprang to her lips died unuttered as she met the hard glint of his eyes scant inches from her own. There could be no doubt that he had meant every word. Reluctantly she acknowledged to herself that she had no choice but to swallow her pride and remain behind, nor did it help in the least to realize that he was undoubtedly right in not wishing her along. In the one and only other brawl in which she had ever found herself embroiled, she had only managed to get herself shot.

345

"Oh, very well," she grudgingly acceded, "but you, I think, are not very much of the gentleman. I, m'sieu, for your information, am neither suicidal nor mulish."

"Then prove it," he said unequivocally. "Promise for once in your life to do exactly as you're told."

Angelique felt her cheeks grow hot at his heavily acerbic tone.

"Beware, m'sieu," she uttered in measured accents, "that you do not go too far. I have already agreed to remain behind. I suggest you do not push your luck."

In spite of the fact that he suppressed the grin that threatened, to a mere twitch of the lips, she could not but glimpse the gleam of laughter in his eyes. A circumstance which not only exacerbated her already uncertain temper, but which also served to make her realize the moon had risen and was shedding its light over the jungle. With a sinking heart, she saw that Locke's chances of surprise were dwindling with every moment.

"Very well," she exclaimed impatiently. "Hurry and go! I give you my word I will not follow you."

Apparently satisfied, Locke flashed her a grin of approval. The next moment he was on his feet, running noiselessly toward a cover of trees a little behind and to one side of Vachon. With her heart in her mouth, Angelique watched him disappear in the shadows. Her hand tightened unconsciously on the grip of the gun when he did not emerge for what seemed a very long time. Anxiously she shifted her gaze to the men in the camp.

She experienced a measure of relief when she saw that the others had turned in, leaving their apparent leader to his lonely vigil by the fire. Watching him stare into the flames, she found herself wondering about him.

She was conscious of feeling a vague surprise at his appearance. Somehow in her dreams he had loomed as a sinister, imposing figure, the scars rendering him hideous of aspect and indescribably evil. In reality he was slight of build and not above average height. Furthermore, in spite of the muscled, well-knit body, he was obviously long past the first blush of youth. She could see the glint of gray in his hair, and there was a weariness in the slight droop of the shoulders. In truth he wore the aspect of a man greatly burdened, and his thoughts would seem to be of a deeply troubling nature.

Something about the lonely figure affected her strangely. Somehow she felt drawn to him and yet repelled at the same time. *Voyons*, he might be the man who had savagely raped her *maman!* she reminded herself with a shudder.

What kind of a man was he to lay waste to the house of his own father and make of him the prisoner? Her blood ran cold as she remembered his words and the sound of his voice as he spoke of the feast he would savor. The feast of his father's cold-blooded murder! And yet, was not Vachon just as unfathomable? What was it he had said that very morning? A mulatto was more black than white and not to be trusted. *Hein*, was this the root of the hatred that lay between them? Could he despise a son because in his veins ran the blood of the African? Or was it that he hated the African because in them he saw the son who betrayed him? All at once she shuddered. Was Vachon responsible for the terrible scars that marred the shoulders of Chantal?

She did not know. Obviously there was a mystery here that she did not understand, and somehow she was a part of it.

Her thoughts were interrupted by a furtive movement off to the right. Unconsciously she caught her breath and held it at sight of Locke, bent low at the waist and running across a wide swath of moonlight. As he melted once more into the shadows, this time less than ten feet from Vachon, it suddenly came to her that he stood not a chance of releasing the prisoner undetected by the only man left on guard in the camp. All at once her blood went cold in her veins as it came to her that Locke must have realized it as well.

"*La vache,*" she whispered hoarsely to herself. "He

347

means to kill him! From the very first it must have been what he intended."

Thinking only that somehow she must stop him, she slipped from her hiding place and stole through the trees at an angle away from the captain. If she could get far enough to one side, maybe she could distract Chantal long enough for Locke to release Vachon without being seen. Her heart was racing, and her breath came in short little gasps as she drew near the clearing, and all the time her ears strained to hear the sound of alarm—a shout, a gunshot, a muffled cry from the rebel slave struck dead by the captain's long-bladed knife. But nothing happened to disturb the eerie quiet of the night, and at last she dropped to her knees behind a clump of bitterbush.

Drawing in a long, shuddering breath, she willed her heart to cease its terrible pounding as she sought frantically for some way to draw the maroon's attention to herself without bringing the whole camp down on her or *le capitaine*.

Vachon's arrogant tones cut across the silence like a velvet-edged blade.

"Well, Chantal," he said, "have you and your friends reached a decision at last? Am I to be broken on the wheel? Or perhaps you prefer to have me buried alive. You have, after all, the distinction of being *un tonton macoute*, and the method has merit. Perhaps in the end you shall even hear my cries echo through your mind as I slowly suffocate."

Angelique's stomach clenched as she watched Chantal rise and deliberately cross toward the Frenchman.

Barefoot and clad only in loose-fiting white trousers cut off at the calf, he yet had a certain dignity about him, a presence totally out of keeping with his primitive garb.

"Perhaps, Vachon, we should follow your own example," he said, pausing a few paces away from the Frenchman. "How you must have enjoyed the spectacle of Etienne Joliet's death, and in truth, you were inspired. Who but Guyon Vachon would have thought to place his

348

victim alive in the freshly slain carcass of his prize stallion and then inter them both in the ground. And all because Joliet had the bad luck to lame the beast in his ill-fated attempt to escape you. No doubt Etienne was grateful to have had his eyes blinded by hot pokers before the final event. But I confess I am curious why you chose to have both his hands cut off."

Sickened, Angelique clasped her arms over her stomach. "Etienne," she moaned, rocking to and fro with the anguish she could hardly contain. "Etienne."

As if in a nightmare she heard Vachon's cold-blooded answer.

"Joliet determined his own fate when he put his filthy hands on a white woman. Babette Vachon is my daughter. Did you think I would let him go unpunished after his eyes had gazed upon her nakedness? For that, he had to die. I feel certain you understand my reasoning. Once, you were my son."

Chantal's answer was no less chilling for its total lack of emotion.

"No, you are wrong. Jean-Claude is your son. I am the son of your black whore. It is a distinction which you and your legitimate white heir never let me forget."

"The years have not changed you, I see. As ever, you weep over what is only the way of the world. You always did listen too much to the poisoned tongue of Mozambe."

Chantal's ironic laughter rang softly in the glade.

"And who was I supposed to listen to?" he demanded. "You, Vachon? She is the mother of my mother. She, at least, was never ashamed of who I am."

"She is a cunning witch with the soul of a viper. She knew I entertained great hopes for you."

At last Chantal's facade of indifference appeared to suffer a fissure.

"Hopes, m'sieu? What 'hopes'?"

"Why do you suppose I sent you to be educated in Paris? Do you think I am not aware my heir is a weakling and a fool? Bah, he is like his *maman*. I was preparing you to oversee my estates. In time you would have been a very rich man; on Saint Dominique, a man of power."

"Do you expect me to believe that? *Me*, Papa. I am of the people of color. You have done more than anyone to demonstrate that power is the last thing *les affranchis* can expect under the white man's rule. You did not lift a finger when *he* sold me to the English slavers."

"And did you think I would? You brought the shame on your own head. You and your precious Mozambe. In time you could have had the woman, but you and the black witch could not wait. Was it worth it, Chantal? Look at you. There is nothing of Vachon left in you. Your soul belongs to them. Mozambe made sure of that."

The maroon's face twisted with some terrible, rending emotion.

"You know nothing of that night. And nothing of me. Mozambe taught me the ways of my people. You taught me that I had no one."

"She taught you to betray your father—almost from birth. For that I should have put her to death long ago. That error in judgment I owe to the beautiful Laila. It was the only thing your *maman* ever asked of me. For that, I should have killed them both."

Angelique saw Chantal's hands clench into fists as he turned eyes full of loathing on the man who had spawned him.

"As it turned out, you did not have to. Your wife took care of it for you. That *is* why you sent Madame Vachon away to Paris—because she had your mistress poisoned."

"That and because I had no more use for her. She had borne me the heir I required, and it was obvious there would be no others from her body. *En fin*, I saw no further purpose in suffering her fatiguing presence. But none of this is to the point. *C'est passé.* We were discussing how you mean to assassinate me."

Something in Chantal's demeanor brought a chill to Angelique's spine.

"No, none of it is to the point. For once we agree on

something. As for the manner of your death, that is not up to me. It is for Mozambe to decide."

"Ah, but of course. I should have known. And where is she? You know how I detest being kept waiting."

Something like admiration, mingled with contempt, passed fleetingly across the face of Chantal.

"For that I most humbly apologize, m'sieu," he said, bowing ironically at the waist. "Mozambe is occupied elsewhere for the time being. I fear you have no choice but to accept our—hospitality—for a few hours longer."

"I see. She lays her plans for the *coup de grâce*. But, Gilbert, it seems, has proven more troublesome than either of you had anticipated. Beware, my son. The witch will not be pleased to discover you have not accomplished the task she set down for you. Cime du Bonheur still stands, and the exquisite Angelique has yet to be taken. Tell me, when you have wreaked your vengeance on Gilbert, do you think his daughter will thank you? She is no fool, that one. Mozambe will not find her easy to rule."

"You have seen her? When?" demanded Chantal, taking an eager step toward Vachon.

"This morning. I came to enlist Gilbert's aid in eradicating the vermin that threatened to overrun the island. Obviously I was already too late. Gilbert laughed in my face. He and his beautiful daughter. I wonder if they are laughing now."

The hatred that burned in Chantal's eyes made Angelique's blood turn to ice.

"He will not laugh when his precious Cime du Bonheur lies in ruins about him. Soon, Papa. Soon it will all be over."

In his excitement, he had moved even nearer to the prisoner, and all at once Angelique was reminded of the captain concealed somewhere nearby.

Per Dieu, she had waited too long. In another moment it would in truth be over—for Chantal. The one man with the answers to all of her questions would lie dead on the ground. Frantically she searched the brush for some sign of Locke. He must be there somewhere, waiting for Chantal to come close enough for that single, swift blow. In her mind's eye she saw him, crouched in the darkness, the knife clasped, ready, in his hand.

The next moment she was on her feet. Hardly knowing what she intended, she stood up in plain sight of the rebel slave, no more than a dozen feet from her. Either she made some noise, or the sudden flash of her gown, silvery white in the moonlight, caught his eye. He stopped and turned toward her, his hand going to the haft of a machete thrust through a sash about the slim waist.

Angelique could almost hear her heart pounding beneath her breast as their eyes met across the distance. She saw the recognition in his face, the unexpected flash of eagerness, quickly fading to puzzlement. And, finally, dawning realization. His head moved with a small jerk as if to look at the prisoner, then stopped.

Angelique could not have moved if she wanted to. Her limbs were paralyzed with the awful uncertainty. In seconds one or more of them might lie dead. She felt her muscles, taut with the strain, as she willed herself not to let her glance flicker toward the brush where the captain must surely lie in wait. And yet she could sense somehow that Chantal knew. In truth, it was as if he could read her mind. Then the sorcerer moved.

"I fear I must ask you to excuse me, Papa. *En fin*, I grow weary and would retire. No doubt you will find your own accommodations worthy of you. They at least will assure that you live until morning."

Vachon did not deign to answer, and Angelique could not believe her eyes as she beheld Chantal turn leisurely and saunter back to the fire. How coolly he stretched out on the grass, his head pillowed in the curve of his arm! In the red glow of the flames, she fancied she could still see his eyes on her, could sense the faint curve of his lips. Neither of them moved as Locke slashed through the ropes that bound Vachon.

Locke caught the Frenchman as he sagged. Acutely aware of the slim figure of the girl, silvery in the moonlight and vulnerable, he heartily wished Vachon to the devil. The planter, as if sensing his rescuer's impatience, thrust Locke's hands away.

For an instant their glances locked. The captain experienced a *frisson* of dislike tinged with grudging respect as the Frenchman, chafing his wrists, forced himself erect. He was an arrogant bastard all right, flashed fleetingly through his mind. A cynically amused smile brushed his lips as he watched Vachon turn without a word and, ramrod-straight, vanish into the shadows in the direction of Cime du Bonheur.

Then he forgot everything but the girl, standing like a bloody statue, her eyes glued to the slight figure lying near the fire. Cursing softly to himself, he flung caution to the wind and darted across the edge of the clearing in plain sight of the camp. The sound of his footsteps must have awakened the guard. A shout rang out and suddenly all hell broke loose as he flung Angelique unceremoniously over his shoulder. Without waiting to hear more, he bolted for the wall.

"Put me . . . down!" gasped Angelique, jarred precipitously out of her trance. In horror she lifted her head to behold a burly, half-naked slave less than ten feet behind them.

"Capitaine, I beg you!"

"Hang on!" shouted the captain.

A shot rang out. Angelique heard the bullet whistle past her ear. In disbelief she saw the black man fling wide his arms and hurtle backward to the ground. Two others raced past him, their faces distorted with hatred. The crack of a rifle shot nearly deafened her. A savage cry curdled her blood. Clutching at his chest, one of the slaves spun halfway around and went down. The other man veered off. The next moment found her being thrust over the wall into strong eager arms.

"Angie! Thank God!" boomed a glad, familiar voice,

353

loud in her stunned ears.

"Papa!" she cried, clutching her arms hard about Gilbert's bullish neck. But almost instantly she remembered. "Wes!" she gasped, lifting her head to search the shadows for the beloved face.

"It's all right, child. He's safe," Gilbert assured her as he lowered her feet to the ground. "He's right over there."

But Angelique's gaze was fixed on a point beyond the wall. It was as if all the world had receded, leaving only herself and the man standing at the edge of the clearing staring back at her.

"Chantal!" she exclaimed softly, hardly aware that she had spoken his name out loud. Nor did she see the look on her father's face, the hard gleam of bitter loathing.

A rifle shot shattered the stillness, and in horror she saw the maroon stagger and drop to one knee, a hand clutched at his arm.

"No!" The cry seemed ripped from her heart. And then she saw him—Guyon Vachon, poised with deadly intent only a few feet away. A rifle propped on top of the wall, he took careful aim.

Her blood went suddenly cold in her veins, and then, as if in a dream, she raised her arm and pointed Locke's pistol at the Frenchman's back.

"Put down the gun, Vachon," she said in clear, menacing tones. "Or I swear I will kill you."

She could see the slim figure go ominously still, and some instinct prompted her to thumb the hammer back. The soft click sounded loud in the unnatural silence.

"Now, m'sieu. At this range I promise I will not miss."

"After all the trouble you went through to gain my release, Mlle. Gilbert?" queried the Frenchman coolly. "I think you are bluffing."

Angelique's grip tightened on the gun.

"There is one sure way to find out, m'sieu. But me, I do not think you should try it."

With a dreadful sense of inevitability, she saw the Frenchman's finger curl around the trigger and knew with awful certainty that he meant to pull it. But, *aussi*, she knew that if he fired, she would kill him.

"Don't be a fool, Vachon," warned her father. "Believe me, she means it."

A sigh seemed to breathe through the night as carefully Vachon let the hammer down with his thumb. The next instant, a tall figure loomed out of the shadows.

"Congratulations, Vachon," murmured Locke, snatching the rifle from the Frenchman's hands. "You made the right choice. Another second, and I'd have killed you myself."

The Frenchman's eyes glittered coldly in the moonlight.

"You surprise me, Capitaine. I would not expect you to let sentiment take the place of logic. You know as well as I that to kill a snake, one must cut off the head."

"That was the reasoning you used when you and your friends made a martyr out of Vincent Ogé, wasn't it, Vachon?" queried the captain coldly. "Unfortunately, you can see for yourself what has come of it. Watch yourself, *mon ami*. I begin to believe our mistake was in not letting the blacks keep you."

Without waiting for a rebuttal, Locke contemptuously turned his back on the Frenchman. Only then, as he came to her, did Angelique begin to grasp that in truth it was over. Dragging her eyes from Vachon's unnaturally pale face, she looked to the place where Chantal had fallen. A long, shuddering sigh breathed through her lips as she saw that he was gone, vanished with the others into the jungle.

"Don't worry," muttered a singularly dry voice. "Vachon only winged him. He'll be back before sunup, and you can bet he won't be alone. It might turn out we'll be sorry we didn't let the Frenchman finish what he started."

Strong fingers pried the pistol gently from her hand. Jarred from her stupor, Angelique glanced up into Locke's face and felt her heart turn over.

355

"*Hein,* until I saw Vachon preparing to shoot Chantal down," she admitted with a wry grimace of distaste, "I had forgot I had it, this gun of yours."

"That wasn't all you forgot," he noted grimly. "There was the small matter of your promise to stay put. What the hell did you think you were doing when you sashayed out into the open like that? You damn near got us both killed."

Angelique drew back as if she had been struck.

"Oh, how very like you! It is just what I would expect from someone as stupid as you."

"You set yourself up like a bloody target, and *I'm* the one who's stupid?"

"*Oui! Goujat!*" she flung at him. "You must have seen what happened. Chantal let us go."

"Maybe. Or maybe he figured it was his own worthless hide he was saving. If you hadn't stood up when you did, he'd be feeding the vultures right now."

Angelique's head came up, her eyes flashing in triumph.

"I *knew* it! That is *why* I did it. Somehow I had to stop you."

"Then, mademoiselle, you are twice the fool," observed a soft voice with chilling finality.

Angelique turned on Vachon, her revulsion plain in the look she bent upon him.

"He is your son," she accused passionately. "Can you in truth be so bloodless?"

"He was my son. Now he is one of them. I would have as little compunction in killing him as I would a mad dog."

Angelique felt sick inside.

"Just as you killed your daughter's lover?"

"But of course, mad'moiselle," Vachon admitted coldly.

"And just so did your daughter Babette try to murder me. You did not know? She blamed me for Etienne's death, because he came to me before he left and told me

356

everything he meant to do. She thought I betrayed him. She must have learned from his friends that Papa had sent Capitaine Locke to bring me home from the convent. She discovered his lodgings in the inn in Paris and waited for me to come. She would have killed us both if she could. Bah, you are all alike, you Vachons. Me, I would rather be dead than know your blood ran in my veins."

"Angelique! Enough!" cut in Gilbert before Vachon could say anything more. "This is neither the time nor the place. Come away from the wall, all of you. You must be hungry and thirsty. I've ordered a hot meal prepared for everyone." His gruff laughter rang out. "By this time tomorrow we may all be feeding the vultures, but till then, welcome to Cime du Bonheur and whatever hospitality we can provide."

"But, Papa," Angelique began, determined, after all she had gone through, to have the truth out once and for all.

A firm hand took her by the arm.

"Not now, my love," murmured Locke, propelling her away from the others. "Gilbert's right. You've waited twenty years to hear the truth. Another hour or two won't make any difference."

Instinctively Angelique started to protest. How dared he think he could boss her around! But she found herself pinned suddenly against a broad chest, a pair of muscular arms wrapped securely about her, and all at once she could not remember what it was she had been about to say.

"I ought to beat you senseless for pulling a stunt like that one tonight," he muttered, his eyes searching on her upturned face. "When I saw you standing in the moonlight, like some blasted fearless angel, I nearly lost my mind. Did you have any idea of the risk you were taking?"

He said it so savagely that she nearly winced, but then she saw the look on his face, and suddenly her heart began to beat erratically.

"No," she admitted truthfully, her voice little more than a husky whisper. "I did not stop to think. I knew only that somehow I must make the diversion without waking the others from their sleep." The roguish dimple flashed at the corner of her mouth. "I cannot understand why you should be so very angry with me," she added, all childish innocence. "It worked, did it not?"

A low growl sounded deep in his throat.

"Oh, it worked all right. Like a damn charm." Her breath caught as he yanked her hard against him. "Witch!" he uttered fiercely and crushed her lips beneath his.

Angelique was like a reed before a storm as he vented the pent-up fury of his passion on her. He had never before known such paralyzing fear as had gripped him in that moment he saw her appear out of nowhere before the rebel chieftain. At any second he had expected to see her cut down or taken captive, and he had been in no position to stop it. He meant to make her pay in full for the anguish her harebrained gesture had cost him.

Sensing his need, Angelique returned his impassioned embrace, until her strength was spent and she could do no more than cling to him, her senses reeling.

When at last he had punished her thoroughly for having placed herself in deadly peril, he released her, shaken and somewhat bruised, but filled with a delirious warmth. Wishing that time would stand still, she laid her cheek against his hard chest and listened to the strong beat of his heart.

"Did you hear?" she queried softly after a moment. Her eyes were huge in the moonlight. In spite of the blood pulsing warmly in her veins, she could not quite stifle a shudder. "*Mon Dieu*, did you hear what they said?"

"I heard," he murmured, running his hand over the tangled mane of her hair. "You mustn't let it work on you. There's enough hate stored up on both sides to fuel the bloody war. It's got nothing to do with us. Do you

358

understand? What we've got to do is hold out until Fisk gets here with the men. And then we're out of here for good."

"*Oui*, out of here," she echoed, her voice muffled against his shirt. But she could not quite keep the tinge of uncertainty from her tone, for it seemed that it had a very great deal to do with her—this hatred on both sides, like a festering sore that has at last broken open.

When Angelique was a child, the *houngan* Mozambe had put the mark of the god on her. It was a curse, and the only weapon she had against it was the truth. As long as there were secrets left untold, mysteries from her past to shadow her future, she would never be free of it. In her heart she knew it.

Suddenly afraid, she clasped her arms tightly about the captain's lean waist.

"Hold me," she whispered fiercely.

Locke frowned. Now what the devil?

"Angel," he said, trying to see into her face, "what is it? What's the matter?"

Angelique shook her head.

"*Non*, do not say anything, I beg you. Please, just hold me for a little while."

Frowning, Locke pulled her close.

"It's going to be all right. We're going to get out of this. All we have to do is hang on until Fisk makes it here with the men," he assured her, stroking her hair. But not even he could completely shake the feeling that time was swiftly running out.

Angelique made no answer, nor did she resist when Locke at last led her firmly into the house.

"Eat something and then rest awhile," he ordered as he drew her near for a final kiss on the drooping lips. "I'll see you in a few hours."

Angelique gave him a somewhat wan smile and obediently went with Pierrette, who was waiting to help her out of her soiled clothes and into a warm bath.

Locke watched her go, then, turning with the intent of

discovering someplace where he might grab himself a bite of food, he found himself face to face with Gilbert.

"That was well done," his host observed gruffly. "The girl looks ready to drop."

"She's been through a lot," agreed Locke, thinking of the courage she had already shown that night.

"Yes, well, and so have you. I know you must be looking forward to a well-deserved rest yourself, my boy. However, I'm afraid I'm going to have to ask you to postpone it for awhile longer. I'd be grateful if you'd join me for a drink in my study, Wes. There are a few things we should go over—matters of defense and what not, you know."

Locke, sensing something more behind Gilbert's request than he was letting on, reluctantly abandoned all thoughts of food and a soft bed as he turned to follow Gilbert into his study.

Chapter 20

"The conch was the signal that set them off," said Gilbert as he poured Locke a brandy. "They turned on their own plantation-owners first--Vachon and Justin on this side of the mountain and God only knows who else to the north. They burned the big house, killed any loyal servants and all the whites they could find. Tonight they'll have *un grand bum bosh,* get plenty drunk on clairin, the local rum brew. After that, they'll take to burning the other plantations, any of them that haven't already been pillaged. So far, the loyalty of my people is the only thing that's saved us."

"Maybe," Locke murmured, staring moodily into his drink. "Or maybe that's the way Chantal and this Mozambe planned it. At first I figured you had to be damned lucky to drive off the first wave of attack. But now I'm not so sure. I get the feeling the cunning bastards have us just where they want us. Everything has been just a little too easy."

Gilbert gave a short bark of laughter.

"Yes, well, I have the feeling it's going to get a lot worse. Think, boy. Have you ever seen an uprising before? It's not like a war with soldiers squaring off on a field of battle. It's total lawlessness. Men, women, and children hacked to death. Yet, there couldn't have been more than a hundred in the band that hit us. If they were going to take us on, by all rights I'd expect to see four times that many coming at us right this minute. So, where in hell are the others?"

Locke gave his partner a long look.

"Maybe the real question is, where's Mozambe? I'd give a whole lot to know what she's up to right now."

"Hell, yes. My guess is she's out gathering recruitments. My plantation is isolated. They'd be coming out of their way to take us on, and everyone on the island has heard we're prepared to fight off a small army. You can bet she's working her magic on the nearest big band of blacks, convincing them they're invincible, or whatever it takes to get them here. The one thing I'm counting on is that she doesn't know yet that you're here with the *Sea Wolf*. Everything, my boy, depends on your Mr. Fisk getting here before she does."

Locke's expression was grim.

"I was a fool to let Angel get away from me in England. It's my fault she's in the middle of this."

"Nonsense," Gilbert rumbled. "I'm bloody grateful you were with her when it counted. When Pierrette told me Angelique had run out of the house right after I left for the fields this morning . . . well, I think you know all that went through my mind."

"Nothing which hasn't gone through mine on numerous occasions since Angel dropped unexpectedly into my life. This evening's misadventures being but one case in point. It has occured to me to wonder more than once how your daughter's managed to survive to womanhood."

Gilbert's booming laughter momentarily filled the spacious room, which had been furnished with a discerning eye for comfort in the tropics. Well-wrought chairs and a settee, all of rattan and designed to accommodate Gilbert's large frame, were arranged to take full advantage of the sea breeze. Venetian blinds, ubiquitous on the island, covered two large windows on either side of French doors overlooking the verandah. A mahogany desk, littered with papers and ledgers, was set within easy reach of glassed shelves filled with leather-bound tomes. It was a room made to suit a man, which somehow led Locke to believe a woman had designed it with that very object in mind.

"Now you know why I sent Angie to the convent in Paris," Gilbert remarked, a wry gleam in his eye. "She always was a spirited lass—like her mama, full of the devil, but fine and good. I wanted her to grow up a lady, but I'm glad they didn't take that out of her."

Locke smiled reminiscently to himself.

"Angel might be enough to drive a grown man to drink," he observed in exceedingly dry tones, "but rest assured, she is everything you could have hoped for, and more."

"I'm glad you feel that way, Wes," Gilbert replied soberly. "In fact, you might say I was counting on it. I'm well aware that I was taking undue advantage of our friendship when I pressured you into agreeing to wed my daughter. At the time I believed that I was doing neither of you a disservice, and I still believe it. May I safely assume from what I have observed of the two of you together that this will not be a marriage of convenience only?"

"I doubt there is a man alive who could live with Angelique Gilbert on such terms. Our life together promises to be many things, but one of 'convenience only' is hardly among them."

"Then at least my conscience is clear in that one respect," declared Gilbert with an odd, rather distracted air. After a moment, he appeared to shake himself out of whatever mood had momentarily gripped him. "I'd like you to know that there's no one I'd rather entrust her to than you, lad. Angie is the one blossom in an otherwise barren existence. I shall rest easier knowing that she is in your capable hands. Once again I'm in your debt, Wes, and with damned little prospect of being able to make it up to you."

Locke, observing his partner from beneath hooded eyelids, carelessly shrugged a broad shoulder.

"I wasn't aware we were keeping track," he commented dismissingly. "If I didn't know you better, old man, I'd say you were about putting your affairs in order."

A brandy in hand, Gilbert turned and walked thoughtfully to the French windows overlooking the verandah.

"As a matter of fact, I am," he said, slowly swirling the brandy around in the glass. "The truth is, I deliberately waylaid you. I asked you to join me, here, in the study because I wanted a chance to speak to you, without any interruptions. And not just to discuss defenses. I have considerably more on my mind that that."

"You want to talk about Angel and my intentions."

"Among other things, yes," the older man admitted. "After all, the only thing that really matters to me is the safety and happiness of my daughter. And I mean to make sure of them both before this night is over. Let's face it, it might be the only chance I'll ever have to square things with her." And to make things right with the memory of his beloved Eugenie, he added to himself.

Turning, he looked Locke straight in the eye.

"Now, tell me," he said. "Why the devil didn't you corral Angelique in Paris and take her to Boston as I asked you to?"

If he had meant to catch his partner and future son-in-law off on the wrong foot, he was to be immediately disappointed.

"Oh, but I did," answered the captain without hesitation. "'Corral her in Paris,' as you so aptly put it. Unfortunately, I didn't know it."

"What do you mean you didn't know it?" demanded Gilbert. "How could you not know?"

"Because, old friend, she wasn't exactly made up to look what one might expect of a young girl who had spent the last five years of her life in a convent. It wasn't until after she had managed to embroil herself in a brawl and get herself injured that I began to suspect she was not what she had represented herself to be. By then, I had her on the *Sea Wolf* with every intent of settling her in a boarding house somewhere in the south of England. Before we ever reached English shores, however, I knew that would be imposible. Obviously she was a female of refinement, and by simply having her unchaperoned on board my ship, I had irrevocably compromised her reputation. Naturally, I wasted little time in informing her we would be married as soon as we arrived at my brother-in-law's, the duke.''

"Good God, and Angelique, I suppose, was receptive to this arrangement?" queried Gilbert with the air of a man profoundly stricken at such a notion.

"Hardly. Rather than agree to it, she chose instead to fling herself from the ship into the Channel.''

Gilbert, who was in the process of sipping his wine, suddenly choked and went into a paroxysm of coughing.

"I . . . see,'' he wheezed, when he had gotten his breath back. "Well, obviously, the experience did not prove fatal, since she is here. But if you didn't realize the female you had gotten yourself involved with was my daughter, what the hell were you doing in England? You should have been in France leaving no stone unturned in your search for the woman you were already promised to.''

"You may be sure that I had already exhausted every possible source of information before I gave it up as a lost cause. For all I knew, Angelique Gilbert was on her way to Brussels to become a nun. Or so Angel informed me on one particularly memorable occasion. She is an accomplished actress as well as being an unconscionable liar when she chooses to be. When I did manage to put it all together, it was already too late. I had discovered I could not be satisfied to have her on the terms you and I had agreed on. I played along with her charade because I wanted her to accept me on her own. I succeeded, too. As a matter of fact, she was on the point of saying 'I do' when an act of Providence intervened. A fire broke out, interrupting the ceremony. And, here, we come to the really interesting part."

Something in his tone must have warned Gilbert. Locke could almost see the big man brace himself.

"Yes?" he prodded. "Well, go on with it. What happened?"

"Angelique ran away. Waincourt and I tracked her to Poole, straight to an old acquaintance of yours. A Dutchman with a particularly unsavory reputation. She knows, Herman. Maybe not all of it, but enough to put two and two together and come up with five. Johannes Zenger made sure of that."

Gilbert's fingers tightened on the glass until the nails shone white.

"Zenger! My God, if he put his hands on her . . . !"

"You're too late. I've already taken care of Zenger. Right before I put a period to his existence, the lout bragged about having entertained Herman Gilbert's daughter in his private rooms. Rest easy. He knocked her around a bit, but that's all he did. Angel managed to slip him a sleeping draught. He hit the floor before he could do any permanent damage."

"Thank God," groaned Gilbert, sinking heavily into a chair.

"Yes, thank God," Locke echoed grimly. "And now it's time *you* did a little plain speaking, my friend. You see, Angel has the absurd notion that she is cursed, and in spite of the fact that she's beginning to believe she's in love with me—or perhaps because of it—I get the distinct impresion that she has no intention of coming away with me. She won't leave Saint Dominique—not until she has some answers. And certainly not without you."

"Yes, well, that's why I'm depending on you to convince her otherwise. I'm not leaving Saint Dominique, Wes. Not ever."

For a moment Locke studied the brandy in his glass, lifted up to reflect the candlelight.

"Mind telling me why?" he murmured at last.

"It's fairly simple, really," answered Gilbert. "Look around you. The settee, the chairs, even the books and the shelves they're on. She did it all for me while I was away, playing the bloody soldier. Everything in this house has known the touch of her hand. I've kept it exactly as she left it, all those long years ago. You see, it's all I have left of her."

"Eugenie, your wife," murmured Locke.

Gilbert got up from his chair and crossed once more to the doors to stand looking out.

"She was never really happy here," he said reflectively. "I knew that. The Caribbean is no place for a white woman. Even up here away from the sultry heat of the lowlands, it saps the spirit of a woman. It's the isolation, I suppose. Or the callousness, the eventual degradation of the soul, to which none of us are immune. It's the curse of slavery. It touches us all, one way or the other. Sooner or later. Like a disease. Like the bloody fever. It's Gods retribution for the way we have ravaged paradise out of greed and arrogance. And I brought her here to this, in a ship whose hold was full of slaves."

Locke's head came up in startled surprise.

"But I thought . . ."

"You thought I had finished with the vile business years before I eloped with Eugenie. And so I had. This was a fluke, an accident of fate. I had the bloody misfortune to come on one of Zenger's slavers about to be boarded by pirates, and I was fool enough to try to save my former partner's bacon for him. The hell of it was that one of those in chains was the black witch, Mozambe."

In a single, abrupt gesture, he threw back his head and downed his drink. Then, lowering the glass, he stared down at it as if it held the answer to some dark and terrible secret.

"I wish to God I had left them all to burn in hell," he

367

uttered with a chilling lack of emotion.

Locke, frowning, watched him turn and walk to the grog tray to refill the empty glass.

"No doubt," he murmured, trying to fit these new pieces into the puzzle that was Herman Gilbert. "But I'm afraid there's something I don't understand. I overheard Chantal say this Mozambe was his mother's mother. And yet you say she was on a slave ship bound for the Caribbean only a little over twenty years ago?"

"You always were a clever lad," remarked Gilbert, seemingly irrelevantly. "Yes, it would seem an ironic twist of fate indeed that Mozambe should appear so belatedly in the scheme of things. She's an old woman now, but she couldn't have been more than five and forty when I made the fatal error of bringing her aboard my ship. She knew me at once, though she meant nothing to me. It was only much later that I made the connection, and by then it was too late."

Gilbert paused in his narrative to stare bitterly into space. He could see it all as clearly now as if it had happened only yesterday—Eugenie, frightened but refusing to go below as the blacks were carried on board more dead than alive. All of them, except for the woman who had stared at him with those eyes full of hate, at the scar she had given him long years before on the Ivory Coast. *She* had been very much alive.

Locke's voice brought him back to the present.

"You were saying you made a connection?" prodded the captain.

Gilbert expelled a heavy breath. God, he had hoped never to have to dredge it all up again. But he owed the lad that much at least, and, yes, maybe it was better to get it all out in the open one last time before the day of judgement. He smiled cynically to himself.

"A young girl of the Fon," he answered, " a rare beauty of twelve or thirteen. It was over forty years ago. I was only a boy myself, and it was my first time to sign on with a ship. I didn't know until we had already put out to sea that it was a stinking slaver. Just more of my rotten luck." He laughed and drank some of his brandy. "Anyway, we eventually rendezvoused with a tribe who made it a practice to raid the other villages for captives. I myself tore the girl from her mother's arms and carried her on board the ship, just moments before the Fon fell on us. Mozambe escaped, but she never forgot. The bloody witch left her mark on me—you've seen it," he said, yanking his sleeve up to bare the scar. "Laid my arm open from elbow to wrist with a knife when I took her daughter from her."

"And the girl?"

"She was sold to a wealthy plantation owner, here, on Saint Dominique."

"Vachon," Locke stated with utter certainty.

"Yes, you begin to understand. What you don't know is that my young bride for some reason took pity on Mozambe; talked me into bringing her here to Cime du Bonheur, as a matter of fact. Maybe because the woman was already past her prime. Or maybe because Eugenie sensed what lay between us. My wife had a way about her. I used to accuse her of having a sixth sense about things. Angelique must have inherited it from her. She sure as hell didn't get it from me."

Locke looked at him.

"The dreams, you mean," he said.

Gilbert nodded darkly.

"Yes, the bloody dreams. She's been plagued with them for as long as I can remember. But maybe now they'll stop. When it's all gone—this house, the plantation, the secrets I'll carry with me to the grave— maybe then."

Giving an ironic bark of laughter, he rose to his feet and stood with his back to Locke, while his eyes wandered over the room his Eugenie had created for him.

"You know," he said, without turning around, "sometimes I fancy I see her, moving about the rooms at night. If I remain perfectly still, I swear I can actually

369

feel her presence." A wry chuckle shuddered through the massive frame of the man. "I know. You think I'm either drunk or crazy. And maybe you're right. In either case, it doesn't matter. I won't leave her."

The muscle leaped along the lean line of Locke's jaw. Christ, he might have known. And he supposed he even understood Gilbert's obsession with the memory of his dead wife—at least up to a point. The point of dying for a memory when Gilbert had his flesh and blood daughter to live for.

"I see," he drawled. "You'd rather hang on to a ghost and see your daughter ripped apart by savages. Christ, Gilbert, you turn my stomach."

Gilbert jerked like a man struck a physical blow.

"Funny," he said in a voice hard as granite, "I thought you, of all people, would understand."

Disgusted with the part that had been thrust on him, Locke heaved himself to his feet.

"Yes, well, you aren't the first to mistake his man. It seems I've been equally wrong about you. All the years we've known one another, I never figured you for a coward. But as it turns out, Angel was the one who had you pegged right. She said you couldn't stand the sight of her because she reminded you of what happened to her mother. She thinks it's her fault, did you know that? She thinks she's carrying a blasted *Rodu* curse because of it."

Gilbert's eyes glinted coldly.

"I don't know what the hell you're talking about. Why should Angelique think she was to blame?"

"No doubt the brand Mozambe put on her when she was a little girl has something to do with it," Locke said, his patience wearing thin. "The mark of the *Rodu*. And don't tell me you didn't know anything about that."

Gilbert's face assumed an oddly ashen hue.

"No," he said; then just as suddenly he was himself again. "But no matter. You gave me your word, Locke. You swore to see her safely to the states, and I hold you to it."

"Oh, I mean to get her safely out. The trouble is, she's convinced the curse will follow her. And I've seen how it works on her. If you die here because you refuse to save yourself, it'll haunt her the rest of her life. But what do you care? You won't be around any more to see it. You'll have what you've always wanted. You'll have made it up to a dead woman for what you think you did to her, and to hell with her daughter."

Gilbert took a step toward the captain, like a bull on the prod.

"What the hell gives you the right to preach to me, boy?" he demanded.

"Maybe the six months I rotted in a British prison give me the right." He shrugged. "You said it yourself. You owe me, old friend, and now I'm calling in the marker."

Locke silently cursed as he saw Gilbert rock back on his heels. At that instant he looked old, older than Locke had ever seen him before. Still, the massive shoulders straightened.

"Then call it in and be damned," growled Gilbert. "It doesn't change a thing. I'm not leaving. As for Angelique, you can still back out if you want to. After all, when it comes right down to it, you don't owe either one of us a thing."

Locke's answer was cold-flecked with steel.

"I want her, and not because I owe either of you anything. The truth is, you don't deserve her, Gilbert. If you really loved her, you wouldn't be set on dying a martyr's death. You'd leave the bloody island and end this thing, once and for all. But maybe you haven't the guts, is that it?"

Gilbert's face flushed an angry purple. The big hands clenched into fists. Then just as suddenly he retreated once more into a flinty shell.

"I expect Fisk will have spotted the fires and worked things out for himself by now," he commented in the manner of one thinking out loud. The eyes he lifted to Locke's were hard as slate and just as expressionless. "If he's half the man you say he is, he should be able to fight his way here by midmorning. My people and I'll hold them off as long as we can. After that, you're on your own. With any luck, you and Angelique will be out of here before noon."

At last Locke's temper flared.

"You think you can just leave it there?" Taking hold of the other man's arm, he swung him halfway around to face him. "Send her on her way as if she meant nothing to you? Good God, doesn't she deserve to have the truth from you once and for all?"

Anger, mingled with anguish, twisted across the older man's face.

"Just what is it you would have me tell her, boy?" he demanded, wrenching his arm free. "That twenty years ago I destroyed her mother?"

Locke's glance narrowed sharply. He had been counting on the man's love for his only child, the daughter that was the spitting image of her mother.

"No," he murmured half to himself. "There's got to be something else—something you're not telling me." He stopped, feeling as if he'd just received a hard fist in the gut. "Maybe you don't think she's your daughter. Is that it? You think she's *his.*"

"Don't be a bloody fool! She's mine. I've never doubted that for a moment."

"What then, Gilbert? Tell me, or by God I'll beat it out of you."

Other than an almost imperceptible shudder, Gilbert acted as if he had not even heard. Turning away, he ran a hand savagely through his hair. Then suddenly he stopped and uttered a harsh laugh, like a curse.

"You want the bloody truth?" he said, coming around again. "All right, I'll give it to you."

At last it all came out, the truth that he had kept to himself for so long, the dreadful secret that he had meant to carry with him to his grave. Nor did he spare himself or make excuses for his part in it. He had left her, his young bride, left her alone in the isolation of La Cime du Bonheur, with only the servants to keep her company—the servants and Mozambe.

Locke listened grimly as his friend unburdened his soul to him. With what repugnance he spoke that name—Mozambe! The old witch, who had poisoned Eugenie's mind against him, filled her head with lies, caused her to doubt in his love for her—and then, when she judged the moment was ripe, had fostered her grandson on his unsuspecting bride.

"Chantal," he said with a chilling lack of emotion. "Vachon's misbegotten bastard." For a moment he seemed to forget Locke as he stood, stone-faced, his eyes fixed on something only he could see. Then suddenly he appeared to shake himself. "He was hardly more than a boy then—fresh from the university in Paris. Young, idealistic, his head full of books. It was hardly any wonder that she was drawn to him, or he to her, for that matter. And when you come right down to it, he was just as much a pawn as Eugenie."

At the bitterness like gall in those final words, Locke hardly needed to hear more to picture it as it must have been—Gilbert, hurrying home, all eagerness to be reunited with his young wife. Bloody hell, it was no rape that he had stumbled on.

"I had been drinking," Gilbert said. "My brain was on fire with the picture of the two of them, naked, her body like purest ivory beneath his, his hands—his cursed hands touching her. I dragged the bloody whoreson off her and beat him till he lay senseless on the floor, and then—I turned to her."

He had spoken in the flat tones of a man distantly removed from the events he had recited, but now the terrible blankness gave way before a tormented rending of his features.

"She swore she loved me, had never meant for it to happen. Said it was all her fault. Said she couldn't stand being alone. She begged me to let him go. I wouldn't listen. All the time she was pleading with me, I kept seeing the two of them together. It made me crazy. Afterwards, I couldn't even remember hitting her."

He drew in a ragged breath. His face, contorted with grief, was terrible to behold.

"I made her watch while I took the cane to her lover. I cut him to ribbons before her eyes, and then I told her I would make certain she never laid eyes on him again. And I kept that promise. That very night I had him taken to my ship. On my orders, he was transported to Jamaica where he was sold on the auction block into the lowest kind of slave labor. By all rights he should have died. By God, I hoped he would."

Angelique's agonized gasp behind them sounded loud in the unnatural silence.

"It was you," she uttered hoarsely. "You beat her. She was the way she was afterwards because of what *you* did to her that night."

Gilbert turned to see her framed in the doorway, the enormous eyes filled with disbelief and dawning horror. Angelique stared at him, her face white as death.

"*Mon Dieu,*" she breathed, her heart sick within her, "it is true, *vraiment?* I am the daughter of Chantal. No wonder you cannot bear the sight of me!"

Gilbert flinched at the bitter accusation in her tone. He took a stumbling step toward her.

"Angelique, no! I never meant to punish you for what I did. You must believe that. What I did was unforgivable, but you were the one good that came out of it. You are my daughter, no matter what anyone says. And I've always loved you. You must know that. I've spent my life trying to make amends for my past mistakes."

Angelique turned away as if she could no longer bear to look at him.

"Me, I know nothing," she said, feeling as if she had been plunged into a world of darkness and pain. "And your love I do not want." Her eyes shimmery with bitter

374

tears, she bolted toward the verandah. "I want nothing that is yours!"

"You always were a hardheaded bastard, my friend," Locke murmured coldly behind the stricken Gilbert. "Now don't be a bloody fool. Go after her. Whatever happened twenty years ago, you can bring Angelique to forgive you."

Gilbert stood stock-still, his ravaged face hard as granite.

"I suggest you've said and done enough, Captain," he said. "No doubt it's better this way."

"And I suggest you think long and hard before you make up your mind to die for something that doesn't make any sense," Locke came back at him. "Bloody hell, man! Give it up. It's time to let go of the past. For Angel's sake, if for nothing else. Don't throw it all away for nothing!"

Ignoring him, Gilbert lifted the glass and drained it. Then wordlessly he crossed to the grog tray.

His mouth bitter with the taste of defeat, Locke left him to go after Angel. He knew all the signs. Gilbert would drink until he numbed his brain. But it would make him no easier to deal with. If it weren't for Angel, he might even pity the old man. Gilbert had been dead for a long time. Maybe nothing could bring him back now, not even his daughter.

Chapter 21

The verandah was silvered with moonlight, the air perfumed with logwood and hibiscus. Overhead, the stars glittered palely through ragged drifts of cloud. The sound of laughter, muffled in the distance, carried to Locke. Gilbert's people, he thought, guarding the outer rim of defenses. It was hard to believe death stalked the jungles only a few yards beyond the earthwork walls.

A flash of movement off to the side caught his eye, and he half-turned to glimpse a woman's slim figure running heedlessly across the lawn.

"Angel!" he shouted. He saw the shimmer of a white face as she flung a glance over her shoulder at him, the luxurious mane of hair, loose, and flying wildly about her shoulders. "Dammit, Angel, come back!"

As he broke into a run after her, he could feel the fear clamp like a vise on his innards. She was making for the cliffs, and there was a recklessness about her flight that filled him with an unreasoning dread.

The moon vanished behind a cloud, and he lost sight of her as he came to the edge of the lawn, to the escarpment of exposed granite overlooking a steep ravine and, nearly three hundred feet below, the restless wash of the sea. He could feel the sweat break out in beads on his forehead with the fear that he was too late. But almost immediately he saw her again, a pale, wild figure limned against the transparent brilliance of the moonlit sky.

Silently, Locke cursed.

Herman Gilbert had lived his life on sailing ships, and his house he had built on a bulge of the mountain overlooking the sea that he loved. It was to be the summit of happiness, his *cime du bonheur,* and now the one living reminder of the happiness that had been denied him stood poised on the precipice, ready to fling herself off.

"Angelique, no!" The cry seemed ripped from his throat. He saw her draw back from the edge, a hand reaching up to brush the hair from her face as she turned her head toward him.

"Go away!" she shouted. "Do not come any closer!"

The desperation in her voice brought him up short, his heart pounded madly. He was no more than three or four yards from her, close enough to read the resolve in her face, but too far to reach her if she threw herself forward. Spreading his hands wide at his sides, he took another step toward her.

"I was just coming to look for you," he said, playing for time. "What are you doing out here? If you wanted to go for a moonlight stroll, you might have waited for me."

"*Don't!*" Her voice filled with anguish lashed out at him. "You do not have to play the games with me. *He* sent you after me. But it is of no use. He does not want me. He says I am his daughter, but I do not believe him. How can I when I am less than nothing to him? When he has *lied* to me about everything. Lies, all lies." She laughed, a short, bitter laugh. "It's very funny, isn't it? When I ran away from the convent, I said I would be 'Angelique the Nobody,' and now that is in truth what I am."

"Enough, Angel," uttered Locke, assaying the old arrogant tone that had never before failed to rouse her fighting spirit. "You're very close to behaving like a tediously spoiled child. Do you expect me to feel sorry for you because you've just discovered things aren't exactly the way you want them to be? Well, I've got news for

378

you. They seldom are."

The look of longing in the beautiful eyes, luminous in the moonlight, went through him like a knife.

"Do you think I do not know what you are trying to do?" she flung wildly back at him. "But it is no good, Wes. You must see that. *En fin*, Mozambe, she will win, for it is true, everything she has told me. I *am* cursed, like my father and mother before me. My soul belongs to the *Rodu*, and there is nothing you can do."

"Do you think I give a bloody damn what she's told you?" He took another step forward. "She's got no hold over you, except what you give her."

"*Non!*" Locke stopped, his heart in his throat as he saw her teeter on the edge of the cliff. "You do not know the power of the *Rodu*. I watched the curse kill my mother. Before my eyes, she wasted away, until there was nothing left, but the weeping and the madness. And now it takes Herman Gilbert, too. Go away, Capitaine. I am no good for you. I am no good for anyone!"

With the sense of being caught up in a nightmare, he watched her turn away, watched her fling up her arms as though to embrace a reality only she could envision.

"I will not dance for Damballa," she cried, her head high in defiance. "Do you hear me, Mozambe? Me, I will never belong to the god!"

Locke did not wait to hear more. In a single, swift stride, he reached her and yanked her into his arms.

"You're damned right, you'll never belong to the god," he muttered grimly as he lifted her high off her feet and carried her to safety. "You belong to me. And to yourself, and nobody else. And it's about time you got that through your head."

Weeping, Angelique struck at him with the sides of her fists.

"*Non.* Let me go. It is because of me that you will all die. I'm the one they want. The priestess of the *Rodu*. The sacrifice to the god. When I am dead *en fin*, it will be over!"

"*Nothing* will be over. You'll be dead, but the killing will go on," Clasping her arms, he shook her. "Angel, *listen* to me!"

Angelique gave a choking sob and went suddenly still, her tormented eyes huge on his face.

"You do this because of the promise you made to Papa. But now there is no need. There is no Angelique Gilbert. Go *away*, Capitaine. You are free."

Piercing flames leaped between his slitted eyelids.

"I'll never be free," he growled, bruising her flesh with his fingers. "Do you understand? *Never!* Whatever happens to you happens to me. You stubborn, little fool, can't you see it's too late to turn back now? You've already made me fall in love with you."

With a choking sob Angelique stared up at him, her face white in the moonlight.

"What did you say?" she uttered haltingly.

"I said I love you," repeated Locke, framing her face between his hands, but still she only stared at him, until, at last, with a rueful bark of laughter, he pulled her close.

"Did you truly think I'd follow you halfway around the world if I hadn't hopelessly lost my heart to you long ago?" he queried huskily against the raven mass of her hair.

Angelique drew in a shuddering breath.

"I-I thought you did it out of honor," she answered, her voice muffled in the folds of his shirt. "Because I tricked you into lying with me. It is what you told me, *non?*"

"It was what I told myself," he admitted wryly. "But even then it wasn't the truth. The first time I laid eyes on you in that ridiculous gown, with the dirt on your face, and your magnificent eyes blazing with anger, I wanted you." She felt the hard leap of muscle through the lean frame. "The trouble was," he said, his voice wry, "you were so young and blasted innocent. I should have stopped you that night on the ship. I meant to, but I didn't. The truth is I couldn't have, even if I'd wanted to.

You were too delectably wild and sweet. You drove me mad with wanting you. And then it was too late."

Angelique clung to him, afraid to believe, afraid to accept the vision of happiness that he offered. *Le Capitiane* had said he loved her. It must be a dream from which she soon would awaken, said the voice in her head. And yet her heart told her to trust in it, for had not the gypsy said that out of darkness would come great joy?

She swallowed hard. Then she lifted her head to dazzle him with eyes like deep pools of moonlight.

"I—I did not want you to stop," she whispered throatily. "All my life I have dreamed of such a night, when you would hold me and make love to me. It never occurred to me that you would think it was your duty to marry me because I was the virgin. I thought only of what Mozambe had told me, that I was not meant to be the wife of any man. Then, too, I was ashamed. Already we owed you the debt of my papa's life, and this was how I would repay you. I could think only to get away, to save you from a marriage you could not truly want. But afterwards, at Briarcroft, when I discovered I had fallen in love with you, I could not bear it—the thought of ever losing you. Oh, Wes, I have tried so very hard not to, but I cannot stop myself. I do love you. Always and from the first, my heart has been yours. And that is why I wish you had let me jump, because it changes nothing. Mozambe will come for me."

His arms closed around her in an embrace so fierce it took her breath away.

"To hell with Mozambe. If she comes, she'll have me to deal with. And if you ever try anything like that again, I swear I'll beat you to within an inch of your life. Do you hear me?"

"Yes, *bien-aimé*, I hear you," said Angelique, smiling uncertainly through the tears that shimmered in her eyes. Then overcome all at once with a sense of desperation no less than that which had driven her to this place, she pressed her body against his. "Hold me, Wes. Make love to me," she whispered. "Now, before the dawn comes to banish the dream."

For a moment he held back, troubled at his inability to break the spell Mozambe had woven about her, the certainty that nothing, no one, was greater than the cursed power of the *Rodu.* Then he forgot everything but the girl, whose arms had entwined themselves about his neck and pulled his head down to hers.

"Angel," he muttered, giving in to the pleading in those spellbinding orbs. Pressing his lips to hers, he lowered her slowly to the thick carpet of grass and knelt down beside her.

Never had Angelique known love could be so bittersweet. She felt that her heart must surely break as Locke whispered words of endearment in her ear and roused her with the hands of great gentleness to a passion that was like the swelling tides.

He took his time with her as if death did not stalk the night, as if, in truth, they had all the time in the world to explore the depths of their feelings for one another. His hands stole tenderly over her body, disrobing her as if for the very first time, discovering her as if for the very first time. With his lips he caressed her, and with his words wooed her from the dark spell that had gripped her heart, until at last she shuddered and gave into the rippling tide of arousal.

Her blood coursing through her veins, warm with awakening desire, she tugged at the fastenings of his shirt until she had bared the hard chest to her touch. Feverishly she wove her fingers through the golden mat of hair, and still it was not enough. Wanting to see him in the pale light of the moon, she pulled free of his arms and rose to her knees before him. His eyes smoldered blue flames as she bent near him to draw the shirt down over the musclar shoulders.

All the awe she had experienced when first she had seen him, naked in the moonlight, came back to her as deliberately she undressed him, first his boots and then the breeches, molded to powerful thighs. Running her hands over the hard chest, she gazed at him in wonder. In truth, her breath caught at his masculine beauty, the muscles well-defined and powerful without being bulky, the torso lean and tapering to the firm, narrow waist. Her heart aching with love for him, she bent to caress the hard thrust of his manhood.

She experienced a heady sense of power as she felt a shudder course through the lean masculine frame. Then she lost herself in the wonder of his arousal, the leashed strength of his body which she would unloose with her woman's touch. This would be her gift to him and his to her, the consummation of their oh, so brief love.

No sooner had that thought drifted feverishly through her mind than a groan seemed torn from him. Merciless hands pulled her astraddle his thighs, then lifted and guided her to the turgid pinnacle of his desire.

"Angel. Tormentress," he murmured thickly, his eyes glinting pale flames in the moonlight. Thrusting upward, he pulled her down on top of him.

A gasp burst from her lips as she felt him plunge deep. Then lifting her again with arms of steel, he drew her down upon him once more, this time with aching slowness. "Angel, love," he groaned, the sweat beaded on his chest and forehead as she engulfed his flesh with the moist warmth of her loins. Then again he lifted her and again lowered her, controlling her descent, filling her with himself, tantalizing and driving her mad with the swelling ache his probing member aroused in her. Never had she known such exquisite arousal. And yet she sensed his anguish, his need, no less than her own. At last, carried on a molten swell, she arched, her fingers clutching at the powerful shoulders.

"Capitaine," she moaned. "Wes."

Locke, engulfed in the rising tidal wave of passion, rolled over on top of her to thrust with mounting savagery. Again and again, until at last his seed burst forth within her and she shuddered with her own release. With a groan, she collapsed beneath him and pulled him down to her. His face pressed into the curve of her neck, he nibbled deliciously at her tender flesh.

For a long while they lay together, their hearts beating as one, when at last Angelique shivered in the cool mountain air.

Immediately Locke stirred.

"You're cold," he exclaimed softly, running his hands over the silken smoothness of her back. "We should be heading back. The others will wonder what's happened to us."

Angelique shook her head, not wanting the moment to end. In just a few hours, the night would be gone and, along with it, the fleeting dream of happiness. *Per Dieu*, she could not bear it! And yet she must, she told herself firmly. For Wes, she must be strong. When Mozambe came for her on the morrow, she must be ready.

"No," she murmured. "They will not care, I think. Maybe they will not even miss us. Me, I would stay out here forever."

"Well, I hate to be the one to disappoint you, Angel," Locke retorted dryly, "but while you may be able to exist entirely on fresh air and love, I find that I require a meal now and then. I was just about to remedy that situation when your father waylaid me."

At once she was all contrition.

"But you must be famished," she cried, ashamed that she had been thinking only of herself when he could not have had as much as a bite to eat since he left the ship. "We will go at once."

Making as if to rise, she shoved herself up, only to have his arms tighten delectably about her slender waist.

"Hold on, not so fast," he scolded, grinning up at her. Angelique felt a small pang in the region of her heart as she saw the warm light of amusement in his eyes. *Hein*, when he looked at her like that, she was helpless to do anything.

Pulling her down to him, he kissed her on the tip of her nose.

"I hate to interject a sobering note, my love," he said, the laughter fading from his eyes to be replaced by a gravity that made her suddenly wary. "But I think we have to talk. It's time you faced up to the truth. Whatever he is guilty of, Gilbert has been punished enough for it. It's time you forgave him. He loves you, Angel, and in spite of what you may think, I believe him. You are his daughter. Surely you can no longer doubt it."

Angelique's brow knit in a frown.

"And still he so little can bear the sight of me that he would rather die here than go with us to safety." She glanced away from him, her bottom lip trembling ever so slightly. "It is because of *Maman, non?* He will not go from this house he built for her—the memories. Very well," she said a trifle gruffly and, leaving him, climbed to her feet. "I understand. In truth nothing has changed since I went to Paris. Nothing, except that this time he sends me away without any illusions that I will ever see him again."

"Angelique—"

"*Non!* It is of no use. Perhaps if I could only face Mozambe—now that I am no longer a child—maybe then I could know for certain what is the truth. But there are still so many things I do not understand. If Chantal is not my real father, why has he risked so much to keep me safe? If Papa is what he says, then why do I feel the barrier between us? *Why* will he not come away with me—with us—to begin his life over?"

At last she looked at Locke, and even though her head was high, he could not fool himself that she was not hurting inside.

"I cannot stop the doubts, and I do not know how to forgive him. Not when he would die rather than go with me—with us—to safety. If he would stay for *Maman*, then somehow I must make him want to leave for the sake of her daughter."

Locke frowned, made suddenly uneasy. Somehow he did not like the sound of that. He knew all too well to what lengths his Angel would go once her mind was set on a thing. The possibilities in this case were not pleasant to contemplate, and the consequences even less so. Bloody hell, he swore, rising and putting on his clothes.

Preoccupied with their separate thoughts, they made the walk back in silence. The air was perfumed with flowers, the grass wet with dew, and above them the moon was slowly sinking toward the western horizon. But they noticed none of it. Locke was the first to stop, his hand reaching out to grasp Angelique by the arm.

"Listen!" he uttered sharply.

Angelique halted in midstride, her nerves tingling at the nape of her neck.

The throb of drums leaped out of the darkness, reverberating through the jungle like a primitive heartbeat. Angelique blanched. These drums she had heard before, when she was a child, and, again, in her nightmares. The drums of the *Rodu*.

"Mozambe," she breathed. "The *houngan* has come, and now the dance of Damballa begins."

Locke flung a glance at her, his face grim. It was hardly likely the old witch had come alone, which

386

meant Fisk's chances of making it through to them in the morning had just diminished drastically.

"Come on," he said, pulling Angelique after him. "I think it's time we found your father."

Gilbert was on the verandah with the Frenchman, who, having put his time to good use, showed little sign that he had been a captive only a couple of hours earlier. His brocade suit had been neatly brushed and the stains removed, so that he appeared the same arrogant aristocrat who had breakfasted with Gilbert the morning before.

As for Angelique's papa, he looked hard-faced and worn, and it was obvious he had been hitting the bottle heavily. Though he appeared in control of his faculties, his color was high, and his hair bore the marks of his having run his fingers through it more than once. With a pang Angelique realized he must have been worried nearly to distraction by her lengthy absence. Nevertheless, in spite of the fact that he did in truth seem to care for her a little, she still could not find it in her heart to forgive him. If anything, she was seeing him with new eyes, and suddenly she did not know what to think of him at all.

"Angie," he uttered hoarsely, striding quickly forward to grasp her hard by the shoulders. "Where the devil have you been? Pierrette's raving something about your having been stolen away by the *tonton macoute*. She's been in hysterics ever since we discovered you were not on the grounds. And by God I was beginning to believe she was right."

With an effort Angelique masked her anguish at thus finding herself in the embrace of this man who was like a stranger to her. Pride decreed that, before the discerning eyes of the Frenchman, it must appear nothing had changed between them.

"I'm sorry, Papa," she said, summoning from somewhere the strength to meet his probing gaze with unflinching eyes. "I—I could not bear the waiting. *Le*

387

Capitaine—Wes and I, we went for a walk along the escarpment. We hurried back as soon as we heard the drums."

Though her face might reveal nothing of the turmoil within, Gilbert could not but sense the resistance in her taut form.

"Yes, well, you should have told someone where you were going," he grumbled, releasing her with an abruptness that tore at her heart. "You at least should have known better," he added, glowering at the captain, who had remained standing a little distance away, his face and form partially obscured in the shadows cast by the light from the house.

"I'm afraid we weren't thinking clearly at the time," he drawled, a certain dryness in his tone that brought a faint blush to Angelique's cheeks.

It seemed to Angelique, observing the look that passed between them, that some message was exchanged.

Suddenly Gilbert coughed and noticeably appeared to relax.

"I suppose there's no harm done," he conceded gruffly. "It's the cursed drums. They're enough to set anyone's nerves on edge."

"But of course," murmured the Frenchman with a bloodless smile. "That is what they are supposed to do, *vraiment?*"

Angelique, feeling the pale eyes on her, quelled the urge to shiver. *Voyons,* it was the very great irony that this man who had butchered Etienne and who had the soul of a viper might in truth be her grandfather! She did not know which was worse—that she might have Vachon's tainted blood or Mozambe's in her veins. Revolted at the thought that she should have either, she turned with unconscious longing to the man who would ever be Papa to her.

He, too, was watching her, but with a hooded expression. Almost she cried out in hurt as abruptly he turned away from her.

"I suggest that everyone get what rest they can. They'll beat those damn drums until they're convinced they're impervious to our bullets, and then they'll come like a swarm of locusts." He cast a somber glance at the waning moon. "It'll be in the darkest hour just before dawn. You're welcome to arm yourselves from the guns in my study. We'll need every man on the wall when they make their move."

"And what about me, Papa?" demanded Angelique, acutely conscious that not once had he looked at her as he gave his orders.

For a moment he paused, his back to them, as he stood at the edge of the verandah. She could almost feel the rigidity in him, the muscles flexed in his powerful frame. He did not so much as turn to look at her as his deep voice cut through the stillness.

"You're to keep out of sight," he rumbled. "Wes, you stay with her. And don't take your eyes off her. Make sure she doesn't pull one of her harebrained stunts."

Angelique's eyes flashed angry sparks.

"That is not what I meant, and you know it, Papa," she said accusingly. "We need to talk. Me, I think we will not have many more chances than right now."

"I'm afraid we don't have even that," he answered, his voice sounding strangely weary. "When you reach Boston, you will find a letter instructing you to go to my solicitor. John Maxwell's his name. He'll give you a strongbox. Inside you'll find everything you want to know. And now, if you don't mind, I have our defenses to see to."

Angelique stared after his broad, retreating back as he strode quickly away, presumably to check the men posted along the wall. *Sacriste*, he was *impossible!* she fumed, wanting to scream at him, but constrained by the presence of the Frenchman. He at least must not see the rift that had come between Gilbert and herself.

Stifling a sigh, she started into the house when Vachon's coldly amused voice brought her up short.

389

"He is not so much the raging bull now, I think. Perhaps he begins to see what price he will pay for his arrogance."

Angelique's back straightened. Deliberately she turned toward Vachon.

"He is a man with very much on his mind," she answered, coldly. "He has on his shoulders the responsibility of saving us all."

"I fear not even Gilbert can do that, mad'moiselle," Vachon shrugged. "I tried to warn him it would avail him nothing to set himself off from those of his own kind. But he would not listen. We should have crushed this rebellion long before it came to this. Now it would take an army from France, and even then such help would come far too late for us. The House of Vachon already has been burned to the ground. And my son, whose life you so foolishly preserved, will not rest until La Cime du Bonheur, too, lies in ruins."

"And whose fault will that be, m'sieu? My father's for treating his people with generosity and decency? Or yours for the cruelty with which you and your kind have used not only the slaves, but the free men of color as well."

The pale gleam of his smile should have warned her.

"Me, I think it will be because of you, Mad'moiselle Angelique. And those like you—like Chantal. Our error was in ever spawning a mongrel race, which would in the end inevitably rise up to betray us."

Angelique had only time to draw a sharp breath before a tall figure stepped menacingly between them.

"I believe you've said enough, Vachon," drawled the captain, his voice dangerously soft. "Perhaps you should do as Gilbert has suggested."

"*Non*, wait!" Angelique broke in. "I am interested in what M'sieu Vachon has to say. I want to know why you hate him so. You must have felt something for his *maman*, and her son is very like you. Can it hurt so much that he is like her too?"

390

She felt a cold shudder at the leap of malice in his face.

"He destroyed Chateau Vachon. In the end it was her blood that won out." His lip curled in a sneer. "I should have smothered the life from him at birth."

Angelique stared, mesmerized, into the soulless eyes like those of the viper. She did not hear Gilbert's hurried step, coming toward them.

"*Mais non,* M'sieu Vachon," she said at length, her voice filled with loathing. "It was not *their* betrayal, but that of people like you who see only white and shades of black. I pray God one day this hatred will stop."

Her voice broke at the end. Pressing the back of her hand to her mouth, she fled into the house.

"Angel!" Gilbert shouted, starting after her. "Angel, wait!"

Locke's tall form stepped in front of him.

"Let her go," he said, blocking the other man's way. "She needs time to think things out for herself. I suggest you give it to her."

For a moment it looked as if Gilbert would shove past him. But then something appeared to change his mind.

"Yes, time," he muttered. He seemed to look right through Locke. "Something, it would seem, we've just run out of."

Vachon's cynical laugh rang in the preternatural silence.

"The drums," he said. "They have stopped, Capitaine."

391

Chapter 22

When Angelique reached her room, Pierrette was pacing outside the door.

"Mamzelle! *Dieu Merci!* Pierrette for you was so frightened. She think never to see you again," she cried, flinging herself on her knees before her mistress. In her agitation, she grasped Angelique's hands in hers and babbled hysterically something about blood of the sacrifice and goats slain by the light of the moon.

It was only by dint of great effort that Angelique was able to make any sense at all out of it. But when she managed to glean that the girl, coming to check on Angelique, had found blood smeared on the walls and the inside of the door, she felt her own blood run cold with horror. But more horrifying still had been the discovery of a goat carcass in Angelique's bed, which Pierrette erroneously assumed had been left by the *tonton macoute* in exchange for the stolen body of her mistress.

"Hush, girl," commanded Angelique, squeezing Pierrette's hands tightly to break through her hysteria. "Take a deep breath. *C'est bien.* And another. Good. Now look at me and tell me what you see."

The frightened maid servant swallowed convulsively.

"You, mamzelle," she answered, her eyes huge on Angelique's face. The girl shuddered violently and clung to her mistress. "*Le Malin,* the Evil One, he be come for you, but you fool him. You run away, *non?*"

"*Oui*, Peirrette. I ran away," Angelique answered in lieu of a lengthier, more fatiguing, explanation. "And now that you see everything is all right, I want you to do something for me," she added, grateful for an excuse to send the girl from her. "I want you to prepare a tray and take it to Capitaine Locke. He has not eaten since yesterday and has the very great hunger. I want you to see to it at once, do you understand?"

"*Mais oui*, mamzelle," nodded Pierrette, frowning. Obviously she was torn between relief and guilt. The warning left behind by *Le Malin* was nothing to be taken lightly, and while Pierrette was very much afraid for her mistress, she did not think she would be much help against the sorcerer. At last, rising to her feet, she hurried gratefully away in the direction of the kitchen.

Behind her, Angelique stood for a moment, undecided, before her bedroom door. At last, compelled by a morbid sense of curiosity, she grasped the knob and flung it open.

A shuddering gasp burst from her lips as she stared at the grotesque leavings of the intruders' visit. Words, scrawled in blood on the walls, leaped out at her, hideous reminders of the fate that still awaited her, the doom of anyone who sought to escape the curse of the *Rodu*. Mercifully, someone had seen to the removal of the carcass, but her bed was soaked in the crimson stains. Gagging at the stench, she slammed the door shut and fled wildly.

Instinct, perhaps, guided her to the room which had been her mother's. Gasping for breath, she flung herself across the bed and waited for the tears to come. But instead, she lay dry-eyed and restless, her heart bleeding inside.

Sacriste, she moaned, feeling sick with what she had just seen and all that she had learned. Was there no end to it? Bitterly she cursed. She had turned to face the darkness, just as Madame Lucinne had told her she must do, and now she did not see how she could ever be free of this torment that filled her. *Voyons*, how she wished she had never listened to the gypsy!

She groaned and rolled over on the bed, clutching the pillow to her. *Mon Dieu*, it was so much worse than she had ever dreamed it could be. When she had run away from the convent to begin her great adventure, what a child she had been. In truth, until this day, she had understood nothing. And now she would never be the same again.

Tearlessly, she wept for that lost innocence. Her papa was false, his soul blackened with the sins of the past, and she—she no longer knew who or what she was.

Perhaps inevitably her thoughts turned from the horror of her discoveries to the one ray of light in all the darkness—to Wes, who had said that he loved her.

Then did she in truth curse herself for a fool and the gypsy for having persuaded her to such an ill-advised course, and yet she had no one to blame but herself. For had it not been her decision to flee Braircroft when she might have remained and wed her *capitaine*? Of course it had, and how bitterly she regretted it. Now they would all die, and for what? For so much that had happened a very long time ago?

She no longer cared who her real father was or why Mozambe had laid the curse upon them. In her disillusionment, none of it mattered. There was only Wes and the love that belonged just to them, the life that should have been theirs—*voyons*, the dreams they, two, would have fashioned together. It was for these that she grieved, not for her papa or even her *maman*, both of whom had destroyed their own chances for happiness and love before she was even born. Already she had wasted too much time living for what she thought they had expected of her, and now it was too late to live her own life. Oh, why had it taken so long for her to realize it?

In the wake of that anguished thought, she suddenly

sat up, her heart pounding violently. Or maybe it was not too late. Was she in truth a coward to give up before the fight had even begun? While there was yet breath in her, was there not hope?

The shot that crackled and reverberated through the silence seemed an answer sent from the gods to mock her. For a moment she froze in awful certainty as a shout rent the air.

"They coming, M'sieu Gilbert! Hundreds of 'em. Nothing gonna stop them black devils."

The next instant she was off the bed and heading for the door. She nearly collided with a tall figure, striding purposefully into the room.

"Wes! Oh, Wes!" she exclaimed, flinging her arms around his lean waist. "Thank God, I was afraid I would not find you."

"Did you think I'd wander off with a fight in the offing? I've been right here, outside the door, ever since Pierrette showed me where you were. Come now, pull yourself together. It's time I took you to the other women and children."

Only then did Angelique notice the long gun balanced in his hand and the pistols, two of them, lodged in his belt.

"*Non,*" she cried, bitter realization sweeping over her at last. "I will not be parted from you. Not now. Not ever again." Clinging tightly to him, she gazed up at him out of eyes shimmering with tears. "I love you, *bien-aimé.* Without you, my life would be worth nothing to me."

Locke stared into the beautiful face turned pleadingly up to his and could not find the strength to deny her.

"All right," he said huskily, his desire to keep her safe at all odds at war with the bitter sense that she was right. In a short time it might be all over anyway, and if they must die, it might as well be together.

Taking her hand, he headed with long strides

around the back of the house toward the wall, which formed their main line of defense.

The outcropping of rock on which Gilbert had built his house was defended on three sides by the sheer escarpment. Along the fourth, he had erected the wall of earth and coral rock hauled up the mountain from the sea below. It was a formidable fortification, nearly a quarter-mile long and perhaps four feet in height, with loopholes left at regular intervals for the defenders to aim and fire without being exposed to the enemy. Angelique knew there must be close to sevety-five men and boys crouched behind the barricade watching and waiting in the half-light of dawn.

"Locke, what the hell?" carried with ominous clarity to her ears as the captain pulled her down beside him next to a bullish figure. "What's Angie doing up here?"

"I would not be separated from him, Papa," she said and was surprised at the calm strength in her voice. "Besides, I think I am not the only woman here. I can help load the guns as well as those others."

For a moment fraught with bitter uncertainty, she met his eyes, her own glittering defiance.

"I mean it, Papa," she stated flatly. "I will not go."

Pity touched her heart as she saw the powerful shoulders sag ever so slightly as though with a great weariness. Then deliberately he squared them again.

"If that's the way you want it," he answered gruffly at last and turned deliberately away, "then far be it from me to stand in your way. Anyhow, I expect it's too late to send you back now."

As he moved away, further down the line, something in his voice made her blood run suddenly cold, and then it began—the full-throated cries of the slaves sweeping down the mountainside in a frenzy to kill. Angelique felt her limbs suddenly paralyzed as she stared out over the wall at the human tidal wave bearing down on them.

The next instant she was flat on the ground, Locke leaning over her. His eyes like blue flames bored holes through her.

"Stay *down!* Do you hear?"

A hot tinge of color flooded her cheeks at his fierceness. Biting her lip to keep from delivering a stinging retort, she glared back at him. But Locke was already turning away. Seconds later a steady stream of gunfire cannonaded up and down the wall, and in moments the air was suffocating with smoke. Then Locke was kneeling beside her once more, showing her how to prime and load the long gun and pistol.

Clumsy at first and fearful lest she do something wrong, she was yet grateful to have something to keep her mind occupied through the seeming eternity of the first wave of attack. The din of exploding firearms and the bloodcurdling cries of those cut down in the deadly barrage evoked visions of hell, but at last she was too numbed to everything but the never-ending process of sponging out the barrel and reloading to realize when at last the shooting had ceased.

She started dully as Locke's hand bracingly gripped her shoulder. Wearily she glanced up.

"It's all right. They've pulled back for the moment," he said, the white flash of his teeth startling against his smoke-blackened face. "You did just fine. Now rest while you can. I'm going to check on our casualties. No." His hand shoved her firmly, but gently, down again as she made as if to rise. "You stay here. I won't be gone long, I promise."

For once too tired to protest, she sank down with her back against the wall.

"Be careful," she murmured, her smile wan in spite of her best efforts to put up a cheerful front.

Feeling drained, she watched him turn and run,

bent over at the waist, along the line of defenders. Then leaning her head back, she shaded her eyes against the sun, which was riding low on the horizon. Conscious of dull surprise, she realized the entire battle could not have lasted more than twenty or thirty minutes from start to finish. In truth, it could not have been much past six in the morning, which, under different circumstances, would have been serenely beautiful. She sighed, wishing vaguely for a cool drink of water, and closed her eyes as if by that she might shut out the memories.

She must have fallen into a doze, because the next thing she knew, Locke was kneeling beside her. A spyglass to his eyes, he was scanning the jungle beyond the wall. For a moment she contented herself with studying the hard planes of his face, trying to read what was going through his mind. He looked so exceedingly forbidding that she suffered a sudden sharp pang. What if he were regretting having followed her here, she thought, and was immediately inundated with all the old, tormenting doubts, colored with the inevitable feelings of guilt that always accompanied them.

"Were there many casualties?" she queried at last, needing to hear the sound of his voice, if only to silence the ones in her head.

Her stomach gave a little lurch as he glanced down at her. The warmth springing to his eyes eased the sternness from his face, so that in spite of the grime he appeared less the forbidding captain and more the man who had wooed her and won her at Briarcroft.

"You're awake," he said, stating the obvious. Then he grinned, the old reckless curve of the lip that never failed to quicken her pulse. "For a hardened soldier, able to snatch a catnap between battles, you look remarkably pretty."

In spite of his banter, Angelique sensed a strangeness in him, a hardness like steel, which filled her heart with an odd sort of ache. Somehow she knew that if she touched him, he would draw away, and yet instinctively she sensed that he needed her near. Hurt by what she felt, but did not understand, she yet tried valiantly to rise to the occasion.

"Bah, if I look anything like you, I must be enough to frighten children," she flung back at him. "Now answer my question, please. Papa and the others, are they all right?"

Locke shrugged, the coldness creeping back into his eyes.

"Gilbert's fine, and we were lucky. Four dead and half a dozen wounded, only two of them seriously. The blacks fared a lot worse," he added grimly, and, turning away, lifted the glass once more to his eye.

Curious to know what he found so interesting on the bluff above them, she stretched the kinks out of her limbs and climbed cautiously to her feet. Then she beheld the field of battle for the first time, and all at once she understood what it was in him that she had sensed. A hand flew to her mouth, and she gagged at the grisly scene before her.

The slaves, armed, for the most part, with primitive weapons—scythes, hoes, shovels, whatever they could put their hands to—had fared badly against Gilbert's small, but well-equipped force. Even during the worst of it, Angelique had been aware of the terrible carnage, the pointless loss of human life, but never had she dreamed it was as bad as this.

The tract of land Gilbert had kept cleared of trees, a swath perhaps fifty yards wide and paralleling the wall, was strewn with the dead. They lay at grotesque angles, their faces frozen in the final moment of agony—scores of them, so many that she could not begin to count them.

"*Mon Dieu!*" Feeling her legs rubbery beneath her, she turned her back on the dead. Too late. Already the sight of them had been permanently burned into her brain.

"Angel!"

The sound of her name uttered sharply held no meaning for her. She knew only that she was endlessly falling, sinking to the ground, and that she could not stop herself. From out of nowhere a pair of strong arms caught and held her. Gently they eased her down to the grass, her back against the wall. At length a metal cup was pressed to her lips and she swallowed and choked as someone trickled the tepid liquid into her mouth.

Her eyelids fluttered open as strong, sensitive fingers brushed the hair from her forehead. A smile trembled uncertainly on her lips at sight of Locke's anxious face, hovering over hers.

"*Bien-aimé*," she murmured, surprised at how weak her voice sounded. "What happened?"

"Nothing much," he answered, the worry only gradually beginning to fade from his eyes. "You, my love, fainted."

"But I have never before . . .," she started to protest, before the memories came swooping over her. Blanching, she closed her eyes and swallowed painfully. "*Mon Dieu*, I remember now."

Locke, kicking himself for not having kept a closer watch on her, silently cursed. He should have been able to find a way to get her to safety before she had to witness what had happened that day. And the worst was yet to come. Not for the first time he toyed with the idea of tackling the sheer slopes of the ravine, using ropes, if need be. But immediately he discarded the notion. It would have been tough enough if Angel were agreeable; impossible if she weren't. It didn't take much to figure how she would view the proposition of abandoning her father and the others to save her own neck.

Besides, he tried to tell himself, they hadn't fared

too badly. Chantal had come at them with everything he had, hadn't he? And they had still managed to hold on with only minimal losses. So long as the ammunition didn't run out, they could hang on practically indefinitely. And that was precisely what bothered Locke the most.

Chantal was anything but a fool. He must have known even a horde of blacks armed with pitchforks and knives was no match against men with firearms. Then why the seeming futility of an all-out attack? It was a question that had been nagging at him ever since he had seen the undisciplined charge down the mountainside.

Angelique stirred and uttered a shuddering sigh.

"You were right," she murmured, opening her eyes to him. "I was the fool to think my death could change anything. The dead goat in my room, the blood, they were only to frighten me—all of us. But this, this has nothing to do with me."

She had been merely voicing her thoughts out loud as she tried to make sense of the terrible things that were happening. Consequently, she was taken off guard when Locke leaned suddenly over her, an odd sort of intensity in the look he bent upon her.

"What did you say?" he queried sharply.

Angelique stared blankly back at him.

"I-I said that this has nothing to do with . . ."

"No. No, you said something about blood and a dead goat."

Remembering, Angelique shuddered.

"Last night, when we were on the cliffs. Someone stole into my room and put a goat in my bed. Its throat had been cut. They wrote things all over the walls with the blood. It was horrible!"

But Locke was after something else. Grasping her wrists, he forced her to look at him.

"*Who*, Angel?" he demanded. "Think carefully. Who would have had access to your room—to the house? Who could have done it?"

"This is Saint Dominique. There are no locks on the doors. The windows are always kept wide open to let in the breeze. *Anyone* could have done this thing."

"No," Locke rejoined grimly. "Not anyone. There were guards on the wall all night. Only someone inside, someone you trusted could have done it."

Suddenly he straightened as a shout rang out.

"They coming, Capitaine, just like before!"

Locke uttered a blistering oath and glanced up and down the line.

"No," he muttered. "Not like before. Something's wrong. Where the bloody hell is Gilbert?"

"Him gone to the storehouse, Capitaine." It was one of the houseboys. Vaguely Angelique recalled his name was Louis.

Locke stared at him out of gimlet eyes.

"Why, what's in the storehouse?" he demanded in steely accents that caused the boy to back a step. "Hurry, boy. Why the storehouse?"

"The-the gunpowder, m'sieu," stammered the frightened boy. "Him gone to fetch some." The arm he raised pointed in the direction of a solid log structure, no fewer than fifty feet from the great house.

Locke cursed.

"That's it. Bloody hell, why didn't I think of it before!" Then he seared Angelique with the flames of his eyes. "*Stay here!* No matter what happens, don't come anywhere near the house. Do you understand?"

"But where are you going? What is wrong? Tell me!"

Locke lifted a silencing hand.

"I said, Angel," he grimly repeated, "'Do you under*stand?*'"

"*Non!* I understand none of this," she flung back at him. Then, at the look on his face, she grudgingly relented. "Very well, I will stay if that is what you want."

Without waiting to hear more, Locke yelled at the
403

men nearest to follow him and set off at a run in the direction of the small outbuilding. Behind them, the firing started once more. Angelique hardly noticed. Gripped by some nameless dread, she watched the captain draw near the house. Beyond him, she glimpsed Gilbert's large frame emerge from the storehouse and come toward Locke, a keg of gunpowder hugged to his chest. She saw the captain yell something, but could not distinguish the words above the gunfire on either side of her.

What came next happened so quickly that she was left stunned and bewildered. From around the far end of the great house she saw Chantal appear in the company of a score or more armed men, beheld Locke gesture wildly and bring the rifle to his shoulder. Gilbert half-turned as Chantal brought a pistol to bear. A scream tore at her throat. Even as Locke fired, bringing down the man who stood next to Chantal, a puff of smoke went up from the rebel leader's gun. Gilbert, still clutching the keg, dropped heavily to one knee, blood spurting from a wound in his thigh.

Paralyzed by the startling swiftness of events, Angelique watched, helpless, as Locke threw down the long gun and reached for the pistols at his belt. Two more slaves went down and one of the men with Locke. Then, jarred out of her lethargy, Angelique turned to grab Louis by the shoulder.

"Run. Warn the others!" she yelled in his ear and, snatching his gun from him, started toward Locke and her father. Too late. In horror she saw Gilbert stagger to his feet. Saw him jerk as another bullet found its mark. The powerful muscles bulged as he heaved the keg of gunpowder toward the rebels, crouched in the lee of the great house. Drawing the pistol from his belt, he deliberately aimed and fired it.

The force of the explosion threw Angelique to the ground. For a moment she lay, stunned, the breath knocked from her lungs. Then fear for Locke and her father drove her to her knees.

It seemed the whole world was in flames as the great house ignited like tinder. The explosion had left a huge, gaping hole in the side from which smoke billowed and poured. Blinded and nearly suffocated by the roiling cloud, Angelique struggled to her feet and stumbled in the direction she had last seen the two men.

She did not have far to go. Locke, half-carrying her father, emerged out of the smoke right before her.

Angelique's exclamation of joy died on her lips at sight of Gilbert, his face and upper torso blackened and covered with burns.

"Papa, no!" she cried. "Why, Papa? Why!"

Locke's voice, lashing out at her, at last broke through her grief.

"Angel. Get a grip on yourself. Dammit, we've got to get out of here. The storehouse might go up any second!"

Stifling a sob, Angelique nodded and, stumbling, turned to lead the way. They did not stop until they had reached the shelter of the wall. Staggering beneath the other man's weight, Locke lowered Gilbert to the ground.

For a moment he hesitated.

Locke didn't like the thought of leaving Angelique, but Gilbert was past saving. The most he could do for him now was try to save his daughter. And that meant making sure the munitions did not fall into the hands of the rebels. Making up his mind, he ordered Angelique to stay put and darted back in the direction of the storeroom.

A few moments later found him crouched in the lee of a stone hutch used for storing farm implements. Cautiously he peered around the corner at the storehouse only a few feet away. Upwind from the burning house, it had apparently escaped the threat

405

of flying embers and debris from the explosion. So far there was no sign of fire. The door, however, was ajar, and a party of blacks was occupied in transporting Gilbert's store of munitions on to mule-drawn carts.

The captain's lip curled sardonically at sight of the man giving the orders. Salvador Chantal, it seemed, was blessed with a charmed life, he noted grimly. But then, the scene being enacted before him was really no less than he had expected to find.

He had to hand it to the rebel leader. Either Chantal or the elusive Mozambe was one hell of a tactician. Gilbert had been trying to figure out what would lure a sizeable force to take on a relatively small and insignificant holding, one, moreover, which wasn't worked by slaves and might be depended upon to be loyal—and all the time he had been sitting practically on top of the answer. Rebellious slaves armed with farm implements remained just that, an undisciplined mob, but guns and ammunition would transform them into a force to be reckoned with. Having supplied the horde with sophisticated weapons, Salvador Chantal would be elevated from a chieftain to a general. It would place him in a bargaining position with men like Rigaud, Pinchinat, and Beauvais, Ogé's former lieutenants. It might even mean that in the event of a takeover, he would assure himself a voice in the new governing body, headed, no doubt, by the French-educated free men of color. It was a far-reaching plan suited to a man of ambition. And it all made sense. The one thing he couldn't figure was how Angelique fitted in.

That was a question, however, that would have to wait till later. Right now there were more pressing matters, like how to keep the rebel leader from getting away with his scheme.

Obviously, he had someone on the inside helping him. Everything pointed that way. The four casualties, for example, who had all fallen where the fighting had been at its lightest. It seemed obvious now that they'd been murdered by Chantal's spies, and that the first wave of attack had been meant as a diversion. While the main body attacked at one end, the small party of armed men had been allowed to slip through the other with the intent of reaching the storehouse. Only, Gilbert had nearly spoiled everything for them.

As soon as he saw Chantal's band approaching the storehouse, Gilbert must have put it all together, too. His desperate gesture had cost him his life, but it had left only a handful of slaves to empty the storehouse—Chantal, loading crates on the cart, his back to Locke, and four others. Drawing the long knife from his belt, Locke slipped from behind the hutch and stole across the open.

At the cold touch of steel in his back, Chantal stiffened and went still.

"That's right, Chantal," murmured Locke. "Don't move. Tell the others to go inside. *Do* it, Chantal, or I'll shove this blade through your yellow spine."

"Vachel! You and the others go inside for the powder kegs. Go! I will come in a moment."

As soon as the other four had vanished into the interior, Locke dropped Chantal with a punishing blow to the back of the skull. Leaping over the body, he slammed the door shut and slid the bar in place.

"*M'sieu le Capitaine!* Behind you!"

At the shout of warning, Locke flung himself instinctively to one side. There was the hollow crack of a rifle shot, and pain, like a white-hot iron lanced aross his ribs. He twisted with the blow, caught himself against the wall to keep from falling. Then, through a red mist, he saw Chantal break and run as Louis sent a shot winging after him. Clenching his jaw against the pain, he thrust himself upright.

"Capitaine," shouted the boy, seeing him start after Chantal. "Wait! You come quick. We no can hold them."

Locke hesitated, seeing it all in a single glance.

Without Gilbert's solid figure at the forefront to give them heart, his people were falling back in a panic. In moments it might all be over unless someone could rally them.

Realizing he had no choice but to leave the rebel leader for later, Locke turned and followed after the boy.

Tears streamed down her face as Angelique fell to her knees beside her father. She did not hear Locke tell her to stay put or even know when he left her. Thus she did not see him vanish once more into the thick pall of smoke or realize he was making a reckless dash for the storehouse. She knew only that Gilbert was slipping away from her and that their last words together had been bitter, filled with misunderstanding.

"Papa! Papa, you cannot die now. I will not let you," cried Angelique, wanting to touch him, but afraid to because of the burns.

Her voice must have reached through to his stunned brain, because suddenly he groaned and his eyelids fluttered open. Angelique bit her lip as she saw him stare at her as if he did not even know her.

"Oh, Papa," she groaned, "forgive me. Forgive me. I did not mean those words that I said."

Slowly, painfully, Gilbert shook his head.

"Not . . . you," he whispered faintly. "Me. All my fault. Should have told you . . . long time ago. Made a pact with the she-devil . . . I wouldn't."

Angelique drew in a shuddering breath and brushed impatiently at the tears that were blinding her.

"A pact, Papa?" she repeated, leaning close as she tried to make out his labored speech. "With-with Mozambe? I don't understand. What sort of pact?"

"The silent tongue for a magic spell," answered a new voice, one that Angelique had not heard in a very long time.

"Mozambe," she uttered in accents of bitter loathing.

"You've been here all along—how?"

Even on the threshold of death, Gilbert's eyes burned with hatred. She thought she could not bear it as she saw him try to lift himself.

The woman's cackle rattled like the dry pods of the shake-shake tree.

"Mozambe priestess of Damballa. Like the smoke, she come and go."

At last Angelique lifted her head to look at the old woman.

She was tall and spare, just as she had been for as long as Angelique could remember. And proud. The fleshless points of her shoulders remained stubbornly unbowed by the years. She was all sinew and bones, and weathered brown skin beneath the flimsy red kanga, draped loosely over one shoulder and wrapped around the wasted body like a skirt. Even her breasts had dried up long years since, so that they hung to her waist, flat, shapeless, empty reminders of the infants that had suckled at them—seven of them, all dead in infancy, save one. Laila, the first-born, now gone like the others.

She was Mozambe—old, withered, and proud, and filled with an unspeakable malice.

"No, not like smoke," said Angelique. "Like a thief in the night. Like the serpent, slithering unseen through the grass. You put the goat in my bed. You did this to *him*. Look at him, old woman. Are you satisfied at last? You took everything, and for what?"

A gap-toothed grin ruffled the leathery wrinkles of the old-woman face.

"*Oui*, like the serpent. That fitting Mozambe, the *houngan* of Damballa, him who be serpent-god. Almost Mozambe revenge complete. First, this man Gilbert. Soon that one, Vachon. Then you, Daughter. Daughter of Gilbert for daughter of Mozambe. It be fitting, all. The *loa*—him smile on Mozambe."

As the full meaning of those words swept over her, Angelique stared at the old woman as if seeing her for the

409

first time. And in truth the scales had been lifted from her eyes.

"You made a pact with my father," she said. "What did you give him for his silence?"

Angelique winced as Gilbert's hand closed about her wrist with inhuman strength.

"Eugenie," he said, straining to get the words out. "She gave her . . . back to me. Used her bloody spells . . . to erase the memories." Gilbert's tortured eyes compelled her to understand. "Must believe me. Didn't know she was . . . poisoning your mind, too. Didn't know about the scar until Locke . . ."

He could not finish it. Taxed beyond his strength, he fell back with a shudder.

"Papa!" cried Angelique as she felt his hand go limp. Desperately she willed him to hear her. "Papa, I know the truth. Do you understand? Mozambe lied. Salvador Chantal is not my father. *You* are. I know that now. Do you hear me, Papa? Your daughter for hers. It is what she said. You must listen to me, Papa!"

Angelique caught her bottom lip between her teeth as through her tears she saw his eyes had opened and he was looking at her strangely. In wonder, she saw a beautiful light flicker in their depths.

"Papa?" she whispered, her voice harsh in her throat.

"Eugenie? Is it you?" His hand lifted to touch her cheek. "Have you come back to me then?"

Angelique could feel Mozambe watching them, could sense her triumph. Gilbert lay before her, his mind and body broken and his life oozing from him with every heartbeat. *En fin*, he did not even know his own daughter. But the old witch had won nothing, Angelique told herself. In death Herman Gilbert would be the victor.

Swallowing her tears, Angelique cradled his hand in both of hers.

"Yes, *bien-aimé*," she said clearly, "I have come back to you."

"Knew you would. Knew if I waited long enough." He

410

faltered as troubling memories impinged on his consciousness. A frown etched itself in his forehead. "No," he muttered fretfully. "Not safe—slaves! You must . . . go. Take Angie . . . with you."

Angelique felt her heart breaking within her as he struggled to sit up.

"No, *bien-aimé*" she cried, trying to hold him. "Angelique is well. But you are hurt. You must not try to get up. You must rest, *mon chou*."

The pet name her *maman* had always used for him reached through his terrible urgency. With a groan, he sank back, and Angelique could sense that his sight was growing dim. Seeing his lips move in a whisper, she bent near.

"Always . . . loved you, Eugenie. Never meant to hurt . . ."

Her grief bottled up somewhere deep inside, Angelique felt him slip away. It was better this way, she tried to tell herself. He would rest now that he was with his beloved Eugenie. And in his last moments he had remembered Angelique, his daughter.

Tenderly she folded the lifeless hands over her father's breast and, feeling strangely old and detached from the world around her, rose stiffly to her feet. Only then did she become aware that Chantal stood beside his grandmother, his face expressionless as he watched her.

Straightening her back, she deliberately turned her eyes from him to the house, collapsing beneath its own weight. It was all just as she had seen it in her dreams, Cime du Bonheur in ruins, and her father dead at her feet. And still it was not over.

With a sense of unreality she saw the slaves rush the wall and break through the line of defense, beheld her father's people fall back and then rally around *le capitaine*. Inside, her heart cried out as she realized it was no use. Wes would be slain along with all the others, and there was nothing she could do to stop it.

Wanting to die with him, she broke without warning

into a run. A shout rang out. Then ruthless hands caught
her and dragged her back. In her struggle to break free,
she came up hard against the wall. A dazzling light
seemed to explode in her brain just before the ground
came up to embrace her.

Mozambe's voice came to her from beyond a thickening curtain of darkness.

"You no belonga them, *Omo Mi* Angelique. You be
hounsi canzo, god-bride. You belonga me."

Angelique, slipping deeper into the waiting arms of
oblivion, did not hear the sudden renewed barrage of
gunfire. She did not see the slaves break and flee in panic
as the determined band of sailors attacked them from the
rear, nor did she know that Fisk and Jubal Henry led
them, clearing a swath through the melee, to their
captain. She knew only paralyzing grief, and weariness so
great the she could no longer find the strength to fight it.
With a moan she gave in to it and knew no more.

Chapter 23

Angelique felt adrift in a sea of unreality. Sometimes she thought she was on the ship again, rocking gently with the swell. At others she knew she was lying on a litter, being borne deep into the jungle. Faces came to peer down at her—Mozambe's and Chantal's and those of strangers—dark, curious, some of them hostile. Somehow she did not care.

She did not seem to care about anything that was happening to her, not even that she was a prisoner, her hands and ankles bound with strong vines. It was as if she were merely a spectator, separate from herself, uninvolved save for a vague fascination with what passed before her. She stared at the tree branches passing overhead or at the slow drift of clouds against the azure sky, or at the faces that came to look down at her. She was distantly aware of the chatter of birds above the constant rush of water and of the sounds of voices, talking, sometimes even singing, but all without meaning. And somewhere down deep inside, locked away with all the rest of her emotions, she sensed a hard kernel of loss, a knot of darkness in which terrible things lurked.

She was aware of it, but without being particularly concerned. She was imbued with the feeling that it could not touch her, that, in truth, nothing could touch her. Vaguely she thought it was because of the bitter draught

413

that Mozambe gave her to drink. She had tasted it before, had felt its soporific tentacles steal over her. The thought came to her that it was rather like being awake in a dream—until they came at last to the hut, tucked away in a clearing. Then she knew she was living the nightmare that had haunted her night after night in her sleep.

Odd, how everything was so exactly the same as she had dreamed it—the candles, dazzling in the windowless confines, the hard-packed earthen floor, the center post down which the *Loa* Legba descended when summoned. But then, of course she had been there before. Long ago, when the *houngan* had brought her and taught her the chants. When Mozambe had put the mark on her.

Suddenly she was that little girl again, dressed in the white gown that Mozambe had brought for her. She had been frightened until Mozambe gave her the drink, and then she had seemed to sleep, without being asleep. She had not moved when the old woman came toward her, not even when she saw the poker in her hand, the end red-hot and glowing.

A light step sounded near her, and she could feel the presence of another in the hut. Then Mozambe's face leered down at her.

"You remembering. In your eyes Mozambe see it. You wanting know what for you been chosen."

Angelique stared up into the fleshless mask of the witch's face and felt nothing. Mozambe laughed, the dry cackle of the shake-shake tree.

"You wondering. Mozambe know. Mozambe tell you story of the long ago. Many turnings of the seasons there be two powerful clans of the Fon. One belonga Damballa. Other belonga twin-god Mawu-Lisa."

Through the drug-filled mists that clouded her mind, Angelique saw the old woman's eyes grow distant with the memories as she told the story of two rival clans of the Fon, one dedicated to the *Loa* Damballa, and the other to the twin-god Mawu-Lisa. Both clans were strong and many wars were fought between them. Many on both

414

sides died, until Mozambe's father, the priest of Damballa, was granted a vision. Mozambe would wed Samu, and there would be peace between the two clans.

At first Mozambe had been unwilling. Samu was the eldest son of the tribal chieftain, but he was an enemy to her own clan, a priest of the rival god, Mawu-Lisa, while she was pledged to the *Loa* Damballa.

"*A se toluwa,*" murmured the *houngan.* "We do God's will. Together Mozambe and Samu joined. Bring peace between our peoples, bring many seasons good crops, good hunt. That marriage bring beautiful child Laila from out of Mozambe."

All at once the old woman's face hardened, and Angelique could feel her bitterness like some palpable thing.

"But White Man's God, him jealous god. Him send white men steal away Laila. Make Damballa angry with Mozambe. Make Mawu-Lisa angry. Six babies come outa Mozambe belly. All die. When slaver him come again, Samu to him sell Mozambe. Say Mozambe gone, *loa* no more unhappy with Fon. Make all good again."

The fierce old eyes glittered coldly.

"It no be good for Mozambe. Nothing no be good till white man daughter, she die. The gods bring Mozambe to Gilbert. Now you die. End curse on Mozambe." Angelique struggled to turn her head away as the witch wove spidery fingers through her hair. "You, daughter of Gilbert. You die! Then *loa,* him happy."

"Enough, old woman!"

Mozambe stiffened at the sound of Chantal's voice, harsh in the stillness. Angelique held her breath as he stepped closer. In the candlelight he resembled very much his father, she thought, staring at the slim figure, straight-backed and proud.

"Mozambe *houngan* here," rasped the witch. The sinewy fingers tightened their hold till Angelique nearly gasped with the pain.

"You are old and a woman. I am *tonton macoute*—I,

Chantal. Our people follow me. Now I say again: leave her be."

For a moment their eyes met, the old woman's black as night and the man's pale blue, like his father's. Angelique could feel the struggle between them, the clash of two powerful wills, but in the end it was Mozambe who broke.

"That one belonga me," she hissed, moving past him toward the slash of sunlight splayed through the opening. "She no die, the curse of Mawu-Lisa be on your head."

Chantal's hand shot out, and the old woman winced as the man's strong fingers bit into the fleshless arm.

"Her death will mean nothing to Mawu-Lisa," he said softly. "But me, it would anger very much. *Comprends-tu*, old woman?"

She understood. Angelique could see in her eyes that she did. In truth, perhaps it was the first time Mozambe had ever seen her grandson for what he really was—a man who would no longer be ruled by another. Chantal, like Samu before him, had turned on her, and once again she would be shut out as if she were less than nothing.

Inevitably it was the white woman she blamed, the daughter of the one who had first brought the curse of the gods down upon her. With a last venomous look at Angelique, Mozambe turned and vanished from the hut.

"She will not let it end there, I think," murmured Chantal, his gaze inscrutable as it came to rest on Angelique. "So long as the others believe you are of my blood, I can keep them from killing you. But even I cannot let you go. Mozambe knows that as well as I do."

"Does she?" Angelique looked at him curiously. "And will she not tell them the truth if it means she will have what she wants—my death?"

"Perhaps. But I do not think she will go so far." The cynical flash of his smile was self-deriding. "It would mean losing the one thing she values most—the power I give her."

Angelique frowned as she tried to make sense of that.

Chantal, seeing it, laughed.

"Woman have their own power, but only the man rules. A long time ago Mozambe had a vision. She saw me as a leader of my people. From that moment my grandmother began to groom me for the part. It was the one way she could rule—through me. Thanks to the revolution, she has succeeded beyond her wildest imaginings. We will drive all the whites off this island. There is nothing that can stop us now. And then it will be men of strength who decide between them who will rule. I already command an army, and am thus not a man to be taken lightly. If she chooses to cross me, I will cast her off. And without me, she is only an old woman who sells magic charms and healing potions."

Angelique took a moment to digest what he had said and, more, what he had revealed about himself. He was a complex man, this Salvador Chantal, a man of thought and intelligence. Somehow she was not really surprised. After all, had she not already learned the ignorant savage was only a charade?

"You let me go once before," she said suddenly. "Why is it different now?"

"Perhaps then I did not need you," he answered, his face unreadable.

"And you do now? Why?"

"You are very beautiful, like your *maman*," he answered, seemingly irrelevantly. "To look at you is like seeing her again. As if time had not passed. And still, there is a difference in you. In you, I think, is a strength Eugenie never had."

A strength, she thought. *Oui*, her *maman* had ever seemed delicate—fragile, even, like the dreams into which she had retreated. Suddenly it came to her to wonder if somewhere in that clouded dreamworld the memory of Chantal had occupied some secret place.

"Did she love you—my mother?"

A fleeting shadow, like pain, flickered across the still, handsome features. The scars on his bare shoulders appeared to writhe in the candlelight as he shrugged and moved a little away.

"I loved her. Enough to believe she might care for me a little. Enough to believe that when she looked at me, she saw Chantal and not the colored bastard of Guyon Vachon. In truth, I think she never knew her own heart. To Eugenie, love was a game. I never understood that until it was too late."

Angelique looked at him and wondered.

"Too late?" she prodded, compelled to it.

"Vachon warned me, and I would not listen. Mozambe filled my ears with her lies. That night she gave me one of her potions to drink. To give me courage, she said." His laughter was bitter. "It made me blind to everything but Eugenie's beauty and what I wanted. I could not see that she was a child, living a child's fantasy. And so, like the rutting beast, I took her."

In spite of herself, Angelique winced at his bitter self-mockery.

"I do not understand. Papa himself said it was not rape."

"Rape? No, it was not a rape, not in the sense that you mean. I did not force her. I could never have hurt her. Not Eugenie."

"Then what . . ."

He swung on her with eyes that mirrored the torment of his soul.

"Eugenie DuFour was the only daughter of a French nobleman. Always she was pampered and adored. That was her life before she eloped with Herman Gilbert. And he brought her here to this. To his precious Cime du Bonheur. And then he left her alone. *Mon Dieu!* It is hardly any wonder, is it, that she should succumb to the advances of a lovesick youth: But I, I should have known better. I did know better. I was a person of color. All my life it was made plain to me that I was not fit to even look upon a white woman."

His voice had risen to a savage pitch, but now he

seemed to recollect himself.

"She did not know the price she would pay for her single moment of weakness," he said with brittle calm. "Therein lay the rape—a rape of innocence. Even had Gilbert not found us together, in the end it would still have destroyed her. I knew it, and still I could not stop myself. It had perhaps been better had Gilbert killed us both that night, and then himself. Except then, of course, there would never have been you."

He said it so strangely, almost as if it really mattered that the child born in the wake of so much anguish should have lived. Confused, she turned her eyes from his.

"But instead he beat you till you were nearly dead and then he sold you into slavery." She swallowed, her gaze lifting once more to him. "You must have hated him a great deal to have survived so much."

His smile was cynically amused.

"In a way he did me a favor. Because I was damaged goods, I went for a pittance to an elderly trader in need of a servant to help sail his small coaster. His tastes ran to smooth-skinned young boys. My scars he found repugnant. They were enough to keep him at a distance. At least until I had regained my strength."

Angelique felt the bile rise to her throat. Had her father known? she wondered, sickened by the tale.

"I have shocked you," observed Chantal, watching her.

"It is what you meant to do, *vraiment?*" she flung back at him.

"Perhaps. Perhaps I was only curious to see what you would do. At any rate, I was not long with the Englishman. His peculiar excesses led to his death while we were at sea. There was no living family, and no one ever questioned the will, bequeathing me my freedom and his boat and strongbox. After all, who would ever have suspected that his trusted servant was lettered, let alone that he had been educated in Paris? Would it surprise you to know that I am possessed of a reasonable competence? I am, you see. I have prospered, smuggling contraband between the British and the French Islands. I even have my own house above Port-au-Prince, where I reside when I am not traveling."

"You have been here?" exclaimed Angelique, taken off guard. "All the time, you have been within a few miles of Cime du Bonheur?"

"But of course," he admitted. "It was the only way I could keep informed of you."

"And were you here, too, when Etienne returned from Paris?" she demanded, beginning at last to understand a lot of things that had happened. "You saw him, spoke with him, *c'est vrai*? From him you learned I was coming home. You said you kept informed of me. You must have had spies in Cime du Bonheur as well. You knew when Papa sent for *le capitaine*, he meant to ask him to bring me back with him. That is why you were on the ship in France."

"*Oui*, I knew, but I was gone when your capitaine came here. I was in Jamaica on business when I heard an American trader had been driven into harbor by a hurricane. It was, *naturellement*, the *Sea Wolf*. When I learned they were in need of a topman, it seemed the gods had truly smiled on me."

Angelique stared at him.

"Why?" she said. "On the ship you said you were looking after me. Why would you go to much trouble? What is it that you want from me? Unless . . ." She stopped, sudden realization sweeping over her.

Chantal's lips curled mirthlessly.

"My grandmother is a cunning woman," he observed with a chilling lack of emotion. "She used me, just as she used Gilbert."

Angelique could see it all too plainly.

"All those years she plotted her revenge against my father, she kept you near, letting you believe you were protecting your daughter. You even went to France, knowing Etienne believed I had betrayed him, knowing his friends might make some attempt against me. How ironic that it should be your half-sister who nearly succeeded."

The effects of the drug were wearing off, and things were coming back to her. Suddenly she frowned.

"All that talk about spells, the potion you forced me to drink—"

Chantal's harsh bark of laughter sounded shortly.

"Your capitaine's distrust of me almost killed you then. I guessed as soon as I saw you that the pistol ball had been tainted with the poison from the manchineel tree. It was a thing Babette learned from her mother, who used it to poison mine. Another hour without the healing potion, and you would not be here today."

Bitterly the thought came to Angelique that it would have been better had he let the poison do its work. Her papa and Wes were dead. What had she to live for?

"And now that you know the truth?" she said. "Are you sorry you risked so much for nothing?"

"Is your life nothing to you?" he countered, watching her with the eyes that hid his inner thoughts.

"You tell me what my life is worth *en fin*. You have your revenge. Herman Gilbert is dead and you have his daughter."

How strangely he looked at her then, as if he had never truly seen her before.

"*Mais oui*," he said. "I have his daughter."

She stared at him, her face suddenly white with bitter realization. *Mon Dieu*, in truth he meant to make her pay for what her father had done to him. He did not mean to kill her. *Mais non*. He meant to keep her alive, a slave to his vengeance!

Then at last did she know the real meaning of despair. And yet what did it truly matter? She would not live long. She had not the will for it. In truth it was as if her heart lay dead already somewhere in the charred ruins of Cime du Bonheur, slain along with her beloved capitaine.

He must have seen it in her eyes.

"And now you understand," he murmured. "*En fin*, you have put all the pieces together, and you have guessed why I have brought you here."

"Yes," she answered contemptuously. "To be your slave. But me, I will die by my own hand before I let you or any other man touch me. This I swear to you."

Something flickered behind the controlled mask of his face. Cynical amusement? Vague disappointment? She did not know what it was. And then he shrugged.

"But of course," he said. "It is what I swore to myself when I woke up to find myself in chains. A slave to be sold like an animal on the auction block. It is what we all swear to ourselves. But the strong survive in spite of themselves. I did, as did my mother and grandmother before me."

In dread fascination she watched him come toward her, a vial in his hand.

"Soon Mozambe will return to prepare you for the rite of *hounsi canzo*. When it is done and you are the bride of the god, the others will not be so easily persuaded to kill you. You will drink this," he told her as he poured the contents of the vial into a vessel of water. "It will not harm you, but it will protect you from Mozambe and her spells. For awhile you will sleep, and when you awaken, you will not be afraid."

Angelique stiffened, her heart pounding, as he put a hand behind her head to lift it. In his other, he brought the cup to her lips. Feeling the resistance in her, the fear, he stopped.

"I said you have a strength in you. You will be stronger than Mozambe, stronger than your fear. You, too, will survive. Believe me." His lip curled cynically. "After all, you are no use to me dead, now are you."

His answer gave her cold comfort. Nor was it that which convinced her to swallow the pungent drink, but something in his eyes that held her spellbound.

A long sigh breathed through her lips as Chantal

lowered her head once more to the pallet on which she lay. Already she could feel the paralyzing effects of the drug stealing over her. More than anything she wanted to give in to it, and yet something would not let her—a question that kept nagging at the back of her mind.

Fighting to hold on to consciousness, she struggled to force her eyelids open one last time.

"Why?" she whispered, as the darkness closed in around her. "If I am not . . . your daughter."

Angelique did not resist when Mozambe and the other women came to rouse her from her sleep. Obediently she allowed them to disrobe and dress her in the feathery light fabric of purest white. Nor did she find it strange or discomfiting that her shoulders and arms were left bare, the soft swell of her bosom covered by the beaded collar of liana vines draped around her neck to the waist. She sat quietly as one of the women brushed the tangles from her hair.

She was filled with a strange contentment, imbued with the feeling that none of this had anything to do with her. And yet, in some peculiar way, her senses seemed heightened, so that she might find herself one moment staring with awed fascination into the golden dazzle of a candleflame or, the next, lost in the rhythmic flow of the brush through her hair. She felt dreamy, detached, absorbed in sensory awareness.

At last the women placed the woven cap on her head and stood her with her back to the center post. It never occurred to her to try to escape as they left her. The earthen floor felt cool to her bare feet, and she amused herself with curling her toes into the smooth black dirt until a shadow fell over her. Curiously she lifted her head.

"Mozambe," she murmured, gazing into the witch's eyes, like bottomless black holes of malice.

"Yes, Mozambe." Yellowed teeth gleamed in a smile

oozing venom.

The old woman spun on her heel and, sending the others away, began to douse the candles. Angelique watched, fascinated by the lank shadow moving spider-like about the circular confines of the hut. Then all was plunged into darkness, leaving Angelique alone and cut off from the world.

She could feel the darkness like a living thing, velvety and thick, and throbbing with the unseen. Strangely lightheaded and giddy, she listened as the priestess began the chants to summon the spirits of the dead from the water. It was just as she had lived it over and over in her dreams. Mozambe was weaving her spells, preparing the way for the coming of the god who would possess her, but this time she knew she would not wake up to find it was only a nightmare.

Unbidden, images of the past flashed through her mind—her *maman*, doing needlework as she listened to Angelique's lessons; Sister Thérèse, making the sign of the cross against evil; Etienne, his dark eyes eloquent as he extolled the ideals of the revolution. She thought of the wild ponies, running free in New Forest and the happiness which had eluded her. And finally of laughing eyes as blue as the Caribbean.

Alone in the darkness she remembered. Wesley Locke was dead, and nothing could ever bring him back again.

Then at last did she writhe in bitter agony. Never again would she melt with tenderness at his touch or feel her pulse race at his nearness. Never again would she know the ecstasy of his embrace, never burn with the raging fire that had made of her his willing slave. Their dream of love was finished as if it had never been, and she was left with an aching emptiness which could never be filled. All along the nightmare had been the one true reality.

Then let it be done, she thought, giving in to the euphoria of the drug, giving in to the inevitability of fate. God in heaven, let there be an end to it.

She did not know when the chanting stopped. She

424

knew only that the darkness was filled suddenly with the flapping of many wings. There was the touch of a cold wind like the breath of evil against her neck, and she cried out.

"Why am I here? *Mon Dieu*, what is it that you want from me?"

A blinding burst of light dazzled and made her dizzy. Shading her eyes with her arm, she beheld Mozambe limned against the light of the ritual fire.

Slowly the old woman came toward her, a gourd rattle filled with pebbles in her hand. It was the asson, a thing of power with which a priest commands the dead and masters the living. Deliberately Mozambe began to shake it. As if in answer the drums began beyond the windowless confines of the temple, louder and louder until the hut was filled with the throb and Angelique felt swallowed up in it.

And all the time there was Mozambe, leering at her through a curtain of mist. Mozambe exuding an unspeakable malice.

"You feeling the god. Him know there be darkness in you. The capitaine, him dead, slain by the hand of Chantal. Hear what the god say, woman. Him say you no want live. Him say you want drink the water of death. Then you no feel nothing."

Angelique could only stare at her, her mind reeling, as she struggled to make sense of the words through the mesmerizing throb of the drums.

"No," she mumbled, shaking her head. "Mozambe lies. Mozambe lies."

"Mozambe speak with the tongue of the god. You already dead inside. You filled with darkness. You die, white man's daughter."

It was not true, a voice cried out somewhere inside. Had not Chantal said she could not trust Mozambe? Or had he? She could not be sure. It all seemed a very long time ago. And the drums, the incessant rattle of the asson, the sing-song voice of the witch—they would not let her think.

"You dance the dance of the god," whispered Mozambe's voice. "You do the will of the god. You drink of the god's potion. Then you die. Be with your capitaine."

The words reverberated through her brain.

"You want die. You want be with your capitaine. *A se toluwa*. We do God's will."

She felt the vial thrust in her hand and closed her fist around it.

"*Oui*. The will of the god," muttered Angelique.

Chapter 24

Locke sat, clench-jawed and impatient, as Fisk finished binding his ribs in a bandage.

"You're lucky the bastard only grazed you," muttered the first mate with a grimness that was not lost on his superior. "Even so, you've already lost more blood than's good for you. I'm telling you straight, Captain. I don't care for your chances if you break this thing open again."

Wordlessly Locke tested the bandage. Then, steeling himself, he stood up. The sweat broke out in rivulets over his body as a fresh wave of pain washed over him. Ignoring it, he stuck his arms through the sleeves of the shirt Jubal Henry held out for him.

Fisk glanced uneasily at Henry, who remained stolidly impassive.

"Dammit, Wes!" he exclaimed, provoked by his captain's silence. "What the hell are we doing out here? Man, you can't even be sure she's alive."

Locke's gaze went out over the jungle to the smoke still rising from the ruins of Cime du Bonheur far below them. The small company of men, numbering ten in all, had been on the trail of Angel's abductors for two hours or better, and only the necessity of a fresh bandage had induced him to stop now.

"She's alive," he stated flatly and finished shrugging

on his shirt. "Depend on it."

It was on the first mate's lips to ask how the hell he could be so sure, but a single glance at his captain's face decided him against it. He had seen that look before. A man might as well try reasoning with a brick wall as argue with him now.

"Aye, aye, Captain. Whatever you say, Captain. Go ahead and kill yourself. Jubal and me, we'll see that you get a real nice funeral, won't we, Jubal. Providing, of course, that we're still around."

Apparently unmoved, Locke favored him with a stony aspect.

"If you've finished, Mr. Fisk?" he murmured coldly.

Flushing an angry red, Fisk subsided into silence.

"Then perhaps we can prepare to get under way. Jubal, the Frenchman is yours. I don't trust him, but since he insisted on coming along, I'll feel easier knowing you're keeping an eye on him. Now if there's nothing else, gentlemen, it looks as if the bastards that took Angel can't be more than an hour ahead of us. I don't mean to lose them in the dark. Fisk, tell the men we're ready to move out."

"Sure, why not," retorted Fisk, half-turning to leave. "A man ought to know when to save his breath."

"Mr Fisk," said Locke, wearily. Impatiently he ran his fingers through his hair, then turning his back on the others, he stared out over the blue expanse of sea.

Fisk shifted his weight sullenly from one foot to the other.

"You and Jubal and the others have already done more than a man has a right to ask of his friends," Locke said, his back still to them. "I just want you to know I won't think less of any man who decides he'd rather turn back now."

"Bloody hell, Wes, you know I didn't mean that!"

Locke swung sharply around, his face granite-hard.

"Be sure the men understand that. And that I won't forget them. In the strongbox I sent aboard ship with the other things, there's a letter. If I should fall, one way or the other the cargo's yours to split up among the ship's company.''

For a moment Fisk stared into the uncompromising glint of ice-cold eyes.

"Sure. I'll tell them.'' Turning, he stalked ill-humoredly away. "But that's not why they'll be doing it,'' he grumbled, half under his breath. "Not for any bloody damned cargo. But then, you always were too thick-skulled to see it. I reckon we're all fools.''

Locke, however, had already turned his attention elsewhere—to Angel and the task of getting her back again.

He was not fool enough to believe it would be easy. For whatever his reasons, Chantal had let her go once. It was not likely he would do so again. Especially if Mozambe were running the show now, and Locke had every reason to believe that she was. Both Gilbert and Vachon were convinced that Mozambe was the controlling force behind her grandson, and, perhaps more importantly, more than one of Gilbert's people had reported seeing her in the compound. No doubt it had been her idea to take Angelique with them when they fled—a smart move, considering the fact that Chantal had been forced to retreat before he got what he came for. That meant that his position among the rebelling slaves would be shaky at best. *If* he could regroup, he no doubt would be back, but the blacks had already paid heavily for his failure. He would need an ace in the hole to win them over again, and right now the only card left in his hand was Angel.

Locke smiled coldly to himself. It was the one thing that might keep her alive long enough for him to get to her in time. After that, it would be a question of whether or not he had gauged the man correctly. The plan he had worked out depended on it.

Realizing that Jubal Henry still hovered at his back, the captain swung irritably around.

"What is it, man?'' he demanded, pain and weariness

429

lending an edge to his voice. "You have your orders. What in hell are you waiting for?"

The big man's gaze was expressionless.

"Your sword, Cap'n. We was in too big a hurry for me to give it to you before we left Mr. Gilbert's. I jest thought you might be missin' it."

For a moment Locke stared at him, a wry glint in his eyes. Trust Henry to think of the sword, left hanging in his captain's cabin. It was Henry who'd strapped it on him that first time, the day he left Marblehead to take his commission on the frigate *Warren*. He'd gone easier knowing Jubal was staying behind to look after his spirited young half-sister Sabra. And he hadn't let him down. Locke experienced an uncomfortable twinge of conscience for having vented his ill-humor on his two subordinates. Neither one of them, Jubal or Fisk, ever *had* let him down in all the years he'd known them.

With a sigh, Locke relented.

"All right, out with it," he said, not bothering to mask the tiredness that was dragging at him. "We've known each other a long time—too long to pussyfoot around. Why don't you tell me what's really on your mind. I suppose you think I'm going on a fool's errand, too, is that it?"

The massive shoulders lifted in a shrug.

"It don't matter none what I think, Cap'n. I reckon you got to find out for yourself if Miss Angel be alive. If you doesn't, you won't never be no good—to yourself or nobody else. I expect Mr. Fisk done know that, too."

"Yes, I expect he does," agreed the captain wryly as he spread his arms to let the other man buckle the sword around his waist.

The thing is, Cap'n. What good you gonna be to Miss Angel if you kills yourself tryin' to get her back?"

Locke did not have the answer to that. He thought of Angel, the feel of her in his arms, the fear that had twisted at his gut when he came back to the wall to discover Gilbert dead and Angelique gone. Maybe it was already too late. Maybe she was dead. The one thing Henry had failed to guess with all of his insight was that without Angel, his life wouldn't mean a bloody damned thing.

Suddenly unable to curb either his impatience or his temper, he glared at his subordinate.

"So what's your point, Mr. Henry? Maybe you think I should camp out here or return to the ship while you and Fisk go after her, is that it?"

"The thought had crossed my mind, Cap'n," admitted Jubal. "I reckon Miss Sabra wouldn't never forgive me if I didn't at least try to make you see sense."

"Yes, well, I'll be sure to inform Miss Sabra that you made the attempt. But in spite of what you may think, I'm a long ways from being on my last legs, I assure you. And now I'm through talking. Get Fisk. We're pulling out."

Wordlessly, Jubal watched him stalk away. The captain was a stubborn man. But then, if he hadn't been, he wouldn't be here today, he reflected, thinking of how it had been after the *Jersey*. His refusal to give in had been all that'd kept him alive in prison and afterwards. Maybe it would be enough to get him through this time, too, and maybe it wasn't. But one thing was for sure. There wasn't nobody going to stop him trying.

For a moment he wondered about the girl, wondered if she were better off dead. On the way to Cime du Bonheur, they'd passed through the burned-out farm on the other side of the valley. He'd seen what was left of the white woman after the slaves got through with her. Slowly he shook his head. It hadn't been a pretty sight.

At last, shrugging broad shoulders, he went to carry out the captain's orders.

From that point on Locke drove himself and his men with a relentlessness that had them all shaking their heads. Fisk thought he had seen him in all of his moods, but he had never seen him like this before. He was like a man possessed by demons. But then, he could not have

431

known that Locke was tormented with the thought that in leaving her, he had allowed Angel to be taken or that had he killed Chantal when he had the chance, she would not now be in the hands of the rebels.

It was dusk when at last Locke called a halt to reconnoiter. A full moon was already hanging palely in the darkening sky. Night was closing in on them, and they had yet to come upon the slave camp. Bitterly he cursed the jungle, which had seemed to swallow up Chantal and his band without leaving a trace. Time was running out.

He looked up to find Vachon watching him. Probably like the others, he was gauging how much longer he could go before he dropped. The thought brought a grimly amused smile to his lips. They had reason to wonder. For some time now he had been sweating profusely just with the effort of staying on his feet, and his side burned with a white-hot fire, a constant reminder of the wound that was steadily draining his strength. Bloody hell! he swore silently to himself. Where were Jubal and the boy? They should have been back by now.

When Henry had brought the boy to him, it had seemed their luck might be changing for the better at last.

"You're Louis," he had said, studying the sensitive features of the boy. He was a well-knit youth of about fourteen, shy, without being timid.

"Oui, M'sieu le Capitaine." The boy ducked his head, pleased that the man had remembered his name. "Me, I was the houseboy for M'sieu Gilbert."

"Yes, I remember Mlle. Gilbert said you were. You saved my life back there at the storehouse, and I'm grateful. But you shouldn't be here. You know that, don't you?"

Locke was not prepared for the passionate flash of stubborn brown eyes.

"That Chantal. Him kill M'sieu Gilbert. Burn Cime du Bonheur. Louis shoot that colored man. Louis know where they take Mamzelle Angelique."

432

With an effort Locke had concealed the hard leap of excitement he felt as the boy described the temple in the mountains where the *Rodu* practiced their secret rites.

"It is a place forbidden to nonbelievers. But Louis take you there."

"What do you think?" queried Locke, drawing Fisk and Henry a little to one side.

"Me, I think you are a fool if you believe him."

It was Vachon, standing in the shadows only a few feet away. Leisurely, he walked toward them.

"Why should the boy come to you with this tale only now, when we have lost the trail? He is probably one of them. I know these people. It is a trap, Capitaine." The Frenchman's arrogant glance rested with seeming casualness on Jubal Henry. "One cannot trust any of them."

Jubal stared at Vachon, his eyes expressionless.

"The boy's mama died of the measles, Cap'n," he said evenly. "She was a freed woman without no man. I reckons as how Louis be beholdin' to Mr. Gilbert for takin' him in." At last he turned his gaze on the captain. "He didn't know where we was till he seen that rock up there." The second mate's arm lifted to point out a barren cliff shimmering in the last rays of the sun. "He say he recognize it from things his mama tol' him."

It had been enough to persuade Locke to let Jubal and the youth scout out the terrain ahead. They had been gone for better than half an hour now, time enough for Locke to wish he had been the one to go. Unable to rest, he was wearing himself down with the waiting.

Suddenly he froze, his head canted to one side, listening.

It had begun as a low rumble of sound that grew louder, until the darkness throbbed with it—the beat of drums, coming from the direction in which stood the pinnacle of rock.

"Christ, it sounds like one hell of a party," muttered Fisk, looming out of the shadows to stand beside Locke.

"What do you think they're doing up there?"

"Cap'n! Cap'n, we found 'em. Jest where Louis said they'd be. Here, boy. You tells 'em. I gots to get my breath."

Jubal, emerging from the brush, pushed the boy forward.

"*C' est vrai,* Capitaine. They maybe half a mile that way. We go now, *oui?*"

"Soon, lad," said Locke; then to the black man, "How many, Jubal?"

"Don't know for sure, Cap'n. Twenty men and a dozen women maybe. Maybe more. Looked like a Saturday night social, them all painted up and dancin'."

"Did you see Angel or Chantal?" Locke's voice rang with a steely edge.

"Sorry Cap'n. We didn't see nothin' of Miss Angel. The boy here, though. He seen a man he claim was Chantal. He was sittin' there, bigger than you please. Like one of them kings on a throne."

Locke smiled grimly.

"Well, we'll just have to see if we can bring him down a peg or two, won't we, lads."

A rumble of agreement greeted that sally.

"We'll teach them buggers a lesson they won't never forget, Captain," called out one of the sailors.

"All right now, lads. Remember what I told you Chantal is the key to everything. If anything happens to him, it's all over for us. Now, let's go."

When Locke and his men arrived on the outskirts of the slave camp, they found everything just as Jubal had described it. The slaves were half-naked, their faces and upper bodies streaked in white paint. Like demons out of hell, thought Locke, seeing the frenzied dance of the *Rodu* for the first time.

"That be the dance of the Goat Girl," whispered Louis. "Them be possessed by the Unseeable Ones. You see that one in the great chair. Him Chantal, *tonton macoute,*

434

the sorcerer."

Locke nodded grimly. It would have been hard to miss the arrogant figure garbed in white coat and breeches. Seated in an oversized wicker chair, he presided over the dancers.

Deliberately Locke turned his gaze from the rebel leader to scrutinize the surrounding terrain.

The camp was situated in a clearing, hacked out of the jungle at the base of the cliff. Locke judged it was the site of an old mine that had played out, the side of the mountain left barren in its wake by erosion. Any structures that had existed had fallen long since into decay, save for one, a large circular hut, which was of rather more recent construction.

It was here that his gaze became riveted as the melee of slaves parted before the entrance and ceased their gyrations.

His breath caught hard in his throat as he beheld the pale figure limned in the doorway. For a moment she stood, her body swaying to the pulsating rhythm of the drums. As if lost in their sensual throb, she started to dance. Only then did he glimpse her face.

Something was wrong. He could feel it in the sudden prickle of nerve-endings. In the next instant, he was on his feet.

"Cover me," he flung over his shoulder at Fisk. "I'm going in."

"Don't be a bloody fool, Wes!" whispered Fisk savagely after him.

Locke, ignoring him, stole through the shadows skirting the camp until he came to a point behind Chantal. From there he worked his way toward the rebel leader. Drawing the pistol from his belt, he knelt behind the wicker chair.

"Good evening, Chantal," he drawled. "So kind of you to invite me to your little shindig. Easy! I wouldn't make any sudden moves, if I were you."

Chantal stiffened at the press of cold steel against his

435

ribs. But then slowly he relaxed.

"Ah, Capitaine. It took you longer than I expected. I was beginning to think you would be too late for the featured performance."

Locke smiled coldly.

"The featured performance is you and me, Chantal. I'm here to work a deal. The munitions for Angel."

"You are hardly in a position to bargain, Capitaine. You are, it would seem, rather badly outnumbered. With you out of the way, the munitions will fall to me easily enough. You yourself must have seen how Gilbert's defenders panicked with no one to lead them."

"And your people, Chantal," remarked Locke in a steely voice. "How will they do with you gone?" Deliberately he thumbed the hammer back. "We can end it now, if that's the way you want it."

Chantal laughed.

"No, you are right. I am afraid that would not suit me at all. You see, I am enjoying the performance of the beautiful Angelique. It would be a shame to end it so unpleasantly."

The bastard was too sure of himself, thought Locke, feeling again the cold prickle of warning at the nape of his neck. As if drawn, his gaze went to Angel.

Angelique danced as one possessed. With sensuous fluidity, she moved, the drums pulsating over and through her. It was as if they had awakened some primitive thing inside her, which had long lain dormant, a thing of the soul more powerful than reason. She appeared one with it, one with the god for whom she danced. He could not know her mind was filled with the darkness, at the center of which was a hard knot of grief, or that soon the ache would be ended.

"If anything happens to her, Chantal," Locke murmured, "it'll be more than you that dies. I have men itching for an excuse to open fire on you. All it'll take is one wrong move."

"Perhaps you have wondered why there are so few of

436

my people here with me," remarked Chantal conversationally. "The others are at what is left of Cime du Bonheur, taking the firearms needed to drive the whites from this island."

He stopped and turned to look at the captain.

"You do not seem surprised," he suggested, one eyebrow cocked curiously at the other man.

"It was the only explanation that made any sense. Why else should you take Angel with you, unless you meant to draw me and my men from the plantation? I'm afraid, Chantal, that your army is in for a disappointment. They have probably already discovered that Cime du Bonheur is abandoned."

Chantal studied him out of expressionless blue eyes.

"*Vraiment?*" he said carefully. "And the munitions, m'sieu?"

"I told you: Angel for the munitions. It's my one and only offer. Surely you did not expect me to leave them there for you to take at your whim? By now they are in the holds of my ship. The minute Angel's safely aboard, I'll have them put on shore."

The rebel's smile was strangely mocking.

"It would seem, Capitaine, that you have the advantage after all." Ignoring the gun in his side, Chantal rose smoothly to his feet. "Very well, I accept your offer."

As one, the drums ceased.

Angelique dropped heavily to one knee, her breath harsh in her throat. The drums had stopped, leaving her dazed and disoriented. For a moment she remained where she was as she tried to think what it was that she was supposed to do.

Fragments of memories drifted through her head— Chantal telling her about her *maman,* the women dressing her and combing out her hair, Mozambe and the asson, the beating of the drums—and a voice reminding her that Locke was dead. *Mon Dieu,* she remembered all of it. Cime du Bonheur, her papa, and Wes—all gone, everything she had ever loved or held dear. And she was the slave of the man who had believed he was her father, a slave to his vengeance!

"Angelique." It was the voice of Chantal. He had come for her.

All at once her hand tightened on the vial that would bring her release from a life of degradation and slavery. With her teeth she pulled out the cork stoper. She knew now what it was that she was meant to do.

"Arise, child. It is over, *en fin.*"

Bitterly Angelique took his hand and allowed him to lift her to her feet.

"I am not your child," she reminded him, her head held proudly. "I am your slave. It is what you have said, *vraiment?* But me, I would be a slave to no man!"

Throwing back her head, she raised the vial to her lips.

Merciless fingers clasped her wrist and dragged down her hand before she could drink. The next instant found her clamped in a grip of steel.

"Not *his* slave," murmured a soft, thrilling voice. "But mine, whether you would be or not."

She had time only to grasp that it was Wes and that he was alive before his mouth closed over hers in a kiss that left no doubt that she was in the arms of her beloved.

"Wes! Oh, Wes, thank God!" she choked when at last he released her. Clinging to him, she gazed up into the beloved face. "When I thought you were dead, I did not want to live any more. Mozambe gave me the vial to drink. She tricked me. She wanted me to die."

Suddenly she shuddered, stricken with the knowledge of how close the old woman had come to seeing her vengeance complete. Thus she did not see Chantal nod to one of the men standing near nor realize when with a gesture he sent him to the temple-hut. Her only thought was that Wes was alive!

"Fisk must have arrived with the men in time to rout

the rebels," she exclaimed softly. Upon which, a frown darkened her brow. "But then, that must be why I was brought here, why *you* abducted me?" she exclaimed, her face suddenly white as she stared at Chantal. "You used me to draw *le capitaine* and the others into an ambush. *Mon Dieu*, Wes. Please do not tell me I have found you only to lose you again!"

"Easy, Angel," Locke said, a curious glint in the look he gave Chantal. "It's your father's munitions he wants, not us."

"The munitions?" queried Angelique, bewildered. "But why?"

"You saw my 'army,'" Chantal answered, his tone ironic. "I needed the guns and ammunition in your father's storehouse." The slim shoulders lifted in a shrug. "Unfortunately, Gilbert and your capitaine interrupted us before we could get them out."

"All along it was the guns you were after?" she said, feeling the laughter like bile in her throat. "And now I am to be traded for them? My life for hundreds of others you and your men will murder?"

"It is war. Many will die in the cause of freedom. Many, like Etienne and Ogé, have already died. But it was not only for the guns that I brought you here."

"No, not only for the guns. There was Mozambe's revenge as well," she said bitterly. "You left me to her while you waited for *le capitaine* to come. You let me believe I was to be your slave. How you must have enjoyed seeing the daughter of your old enemy dance to the glory of Damballa! Was it you who told Mozambe to give me the poison? Or was that her idea?"

"That was the one thing I did not foresee," Chantal murmured in a voice that brought a chill to Angelique's spine. His glance narrowed at the approach of one of his men. Inexplicably, Angelique experienced a *frisson* of foreboding as she watched the two men engage in a whispered exchange. Then he looked at her, and suddenly she knew.

439

"Come," he said. "You will see the punishment for disobedience."

Taking her by the arm, he led her toward the temple-hut with long, impatient strides. She felt his fingers tighten as they came to the entrance, could sense the fist of emotion in him. She gagged at sight of the spindly creature lying asprawl in a pool of blood.

"*Mon Dieu,*" she gasped, turning her face into Locke's chest. "You had her put to death for what she would have done to me? What kind of an animal are you?"

Chantal stared at the poor remains, his face set in granite.

"For her disobedience, I would have pronounced her dead to me. But this, this was not of my doing," he said. Kneeling, he pulled the blade from the body. "Perhaps your capitaine can tell us who this belongs to."

Deliberately Locke put Angelique from him, his hand resting apparently casually on the butt of the pistol thrust through his belt.

"I'm afraid not, Chantal," he drawled, his gaze never leaving the other man's "I've never seen it before."

"But I have." Both men turned to stare at Angelique. "It was my father's. He used to wear it on his belt always. *Mais*, he did not have it on him when he . . ."

She could not finish it. For a moment she stared back at them. Then unable to bear the stifling confines of the hut, she turned and fled.

Chantal started after her. Locke stepped in front of him.

"This doesn't change anything," he murmured dangerously. "I'm not in the habit of stabbing old women in the back. And neither are my men. The way I see it, that leaves only two other possibilities: either one of yours did it, or Vachon managed to sneak away from the man I set to guard him."

"Vachon!" breathed the rebel. "I should have known."

"Yes, well, that's pretty much the way I figure it, too."

Locke's hand went meaningfully to the bandage beneath his shirt. "Back-shooting seems to run in the family."

Chantal looked at him, the pale eyes expressionless.

"Perhaps, Capitaine. But it was not I who shot at you. My gun was empty.

The minute he said it, Locke knew Chantal was telling the truth. It had been a rifle that fired the shot, and Chantal had been carrying a pistol. But if he hadn't been the one, then who? Vachon? There had been murder in the Frenchman's eyes when Locke stopped him from shooting Chantal the night before. But then, why try to kill himself and not Chantal when he had the chance? Then it came to him that Chantal had been on the ground. If Vachon had fired from the hutch, he probably hadn't seen Chantal until after he had already taken his shot at Locke.

He didn't have any of the answers, but somehow he knew it was indeed Vachon who had tried to shoot him in the back and Vachon, too, who had killed Mozambe. And now he was out there somewhere, waiting—to do what?

Suddenly he swore out loud.

"Angel!" In a single swift stride he was out the door, Chantal close on his heels.

They found her outside the entrance, standing as if carved from stone.

"Wes, no!" she cried as Locke started toward her. "Vachon!"

Without waiting to hear more, Locke launched himself at her. His arms went around her, and he dragged her down, his body covering hers, as the shots rang out, one nearly on top of the other.

A fist of pain shot through him as the fall wrenched his wound. Then he was rolling to his uninjured side, his hand reaching for the pistol at his belt.

It was all over. Vachon lay face down on the ground, a gun still clutched in an outflung hand. And behind him, his face set and pale, stood the boy, Louis. Slowly he lowered the still-smoking rifle.

"He was going to shoot Mamzelle," said the boy, his voice gruff with defiance. "It was for M'sieu Gilbert that I kill him first."

Clenching his teeth against the fire in his side, Locke shoved himself up, then reached a hand down to help Angel.

She stared at the body of the Frenchman, her eyes haunted with shadows.

"He was insane," she uttered in a stunned voice. "He said he was sorry his bullet only grazed you. Oh, Wes! Why did you not tell me you had been wounded: *Mon Dieu!* You are bleeding!"

"Never mind that now,"he said, clasping the hands that fluttered to his shirt, to the dark stain spreading down his side. "Are you all right? Did the bastard hurt you?"

"N—No." She shuddered, as if suddenly recalled to the Frenchman, lying ominously still. "He—he meant to kill me. I saw it in his eyes. Just as he murdered Mozambe. He meant to see us all dead. You, because you stood in the way of his vengeance. Me, because I, like my father, was a traitor to my own kind. And you," she said, looking to Chantal, stern-faced and silent. "You, because you were the son he loved and who betrayed him. *En fin,* you stood for everything he hated most."

"And he for everything that made being the colored son of the white *patron* intolerable," said Chantal. "There is no more room for his kind here. Or for any white man or woman. Saint Dominique and the tyranny of France are coming to a close. Haiti shall belong to the black man and the colored. And on her soil no man will be slave to another."

At last he turned to look at her.

"You and your capitaine must go—now, while you still can. There are those who have vowed that no one of white blood will leave the island alive, and I can no longer guarantee your safety."

Angelique looked up at him quizzically. How odd that

442

she should suddenly feel a reluctance to bid him the final farewell.

"But am I not *hounsi canzo,* the god-bride?" she queried, her smile tremulous. "And did you not say it would protect me from those who would wish me dead?" All at once she was grave again, the smile gone from her lips. "A short while ago you said it was not only for the guns that you abducted me, and I foolishly jumped to conclusions. Now I am asking you. Always, from the very first, you have tried to keep me safe. What was the real reason you brought me here?"

For the first time she thought she glimpsed a crack in his facade of aloofness, a faint smile playing about his lips.

"There are some things that cannot be explained," he answered, "the things of the *Rodu.* But know this: even I could not break the curse of Mawu-Lisa. I could only protect you from the potions and spells of Mozambe."

"I see. And now I, too, am free—like you and the others." Without warning, she lifted herself on tiptoes, and bringing his head down to hers, brushed her lips lightly against his cheek. *"Merci,"* she whispered, smiling through her tears. "You have given me a new life, a life with the man I love. You are my father, no less than was he whose blood runs in my veins. In my heart it will ever be so."

Epilogue

Angelique stood at the ship's stern, staring through mist-filled eyes at the island, receding in the distance. So much had happened. She felt dazed by it, saddened and grief-stricken, and suddenly, now that the nightmare was over, a little afraid. Locke's voice rang out behind her, ordering more canvas to be laid on.

"In two and a half days, we'll anchor off Jamaica," he said, coming to lean over the taffrail beside her, "or I'll know the reason why."

"You are in the very big hurry, *m'sieu le capitaine*," she observed, noting with an odd little pang how young he looked with the wind ruffling his hair. Young and virile and handsome. Just so must her papa have looked to her *maman* as they came long ago to this island and the new life, which had seemed to promise so much.

All at once she swallowed and turned her head so that he might not see the shadow of fear in her eyes. What if her newfound joy turned out to be just as hollow as had that of her *maman?* Everyone, even her dearest Sister Thérèse, had said they were very alike. Perhaps, she, too, like Eugenie, would fail the test of love. *Sacriste,* she could not bear such a thought!

"I am," he said. "In a very great hurry. The sooner we're rid of the cargo, the sooner we can set our course for Boston. Or had you forgotten we have unfinished business waiting for us there?"

She tried to think, and then it came back to her.

"Of course, the lawyer. I forget his name. He has the strongbox with the papers Papa left for me." Because it was something that brought back only painful memories, she shied away from any thought of what awaited her in Boston. "How is it," she said instead, assaying to change the subject, "that you can land in the British port of Jamaica? You are American, *M'sieu le Capitaine.*"

"It pays to have connections in high places. And they don't come much higher than Waincourt," he answered. She started at the touch of his hand beneath her chin, gently forcing her to look up at him. "It wasn't the lawyer I had in mind. It was the wedding. What's wrong, Angel?"

The look in his eyes sent little shivers down her spine.

"N-Nothing," she retorted, little understanding why she should suddenly be compelled to pull away from him, when what she really wanted was for him to take her in his arms. She gave a small toss of her regal head. "Why should anything be wrong?"

Ignoring the obvious answer to that question, Locke studied her for a long moment. She had lost everything in the fire, and, dressed in borrowed sailor's pants and blouse, she appeared absurdly young and vulnerable.

She had been through a lot, he reminded himself, but she had borne up under it with more courage than many men he had known. That wasn't what the problem was.

Still, he could not but be aware that something was bothering her, something other than grief and the loss of home and family. Grief would eventually pass, and he would have been willing to give her all the time she needed for that. But this, whatever it was, was erecting a barrier between them, and that was something he could not tolerate.

Suddenly a dangerous gleam ignited between the slitted eyelids. In his book, enough was enough.

446

Angelique let out a startled gasp as two arms swept her off her feet.

"Mr. Fisk, the helm's yours," called the captain, heading purposefully for the companionway.

"Aye, aye, sir!" grinned Fisk, but his voice was nearly drowned out by the gleeful cheers of the men.

"That's right, Cap'n. You got yer course set. See the gale through!"

"Let's hear it for the captain and his lady."

"Capitaine, your wound," protested Angelique, the blood rushing to her cheeks as the decks erupted in loud, enthusiastic huzzahs. "Put me down at once!"

"I'm afraid not, my love," he rejoined, ducking through the cabin door. "You heard the men. The course is set, and I do fully intend to ride out the gale."

Her heart nearly skipped a beat as she gazed up into laughing eyes the clear blue of the Caribbean.

"Me, I think you forget, m'sieu, that I am no longer the slave to be ordered about," she reminded him.

He stopped before the stern windows and, holding her with one arm, deliberately let her legs slide down the length of him till her feet rested on the canting deck.

"Are you not?" he queried, feeling her heart beating wildly next to his. She thought she must swoon as his heavy-lidded gaze traveled over her face till at last it came to her lips and lingered. "Are you not indeed?" he murmured thickly and lowered his head to hers.

Like sparks to tinder, the fire ignited within her, and for a time everything was forgotten but the wild flames of desire that coursed through her veins. Slowly they sank to the windowseat.

"Angel," he groaned, burying his face in the enticing curve of her neck.

Fleetingly the memory came to her of that first time, an eternity ago, when, on this very same windowseat, she had learned what it was to be a woman with a man. She had loved him without knowing it. And yet how much

447

greater was her love now!

Then at last did she realize that in this she was nothing like Eugenie. For her there could only be one man, ever in her life. Then, now, and always she would be his, for in truth she was a willing slave to love's sweet passion.

Bien-aimé!" she gasped on a shuddering sigh and arched her body against his.